Brush with Death

Brophy asked the tech about the blood pressure.

"Two-twenty over one-sixty. Is that possible?"

Not only was it possible, it was Lars' blood pressure. Fortunately for him, he wasn't conscious to hear it.

Brophy looked around for Wendel. "Wendel? Where's the Regitine?"

Wendel recovered just enough to point to the stretcher and say, "By his head. . . ."

In one sweeping motion, Brophy ripped the syringe from the underside of the stretcher, stripped it from the adhesive-tape anchor, and plunged the needle end into the rubber valve on the IV line. He squeezed the plunger, sending a bolus of 5 milligrams of Regitine rushing into Lars' bloodstream, and Lars' blood pressure plummeted to more civilized levels.

Two minutes later, Lars had a blood pressure compatible with life. There was a swirling, whirling very fast, and he could see nothing and know nothing. Not where he was, not even who he was, just that he was alive. He was able to hear and that was all there was. . .

Books by Neil Ravin

M.D.
INFORMED CONSENT

INFORMED CONSENT

NEIL RAVIN

PINNACLE BOOKS NEW YORK

ATTENTION: SCHOOLS AND CORPORATIONS

PINNACLE Books are available at quantity discounts with bulk purchases for educational, business or special promotional use. For further details, please write to: SPECIAL SALES MANAGER, Pinnacle Books, Inc., 1430 Broadway, New York, NY 10018.

Acknowledgments

Phyllis Grann, editor, who sifted the novel out of the textbook; Professor Sam Alberstadt, who read the early manuscript and urged me on; Kenneth Kelleher, MD, who tempered my medical perception with his surgical views.

This book is fiction. It's about medicine and medical research, which is a good work of man. The characters, incidents and hospitals are products of my imagination and are not to be construed as real. I have spent ten years in five different university hospitals, and if people or events seem "real" it is only because experience has clarified certain personality types and patterns of behavior. But this is a novel, not a portrait, of actual individuals, nor is it a memoir.

INFORMED CONSENT

Copyright © 1983 by Neil Ravin

All rights reserved, including the right to reproduce this book or portions thereof in any form.

A Pinnacle Books edition, published by special arrangement with The Putnam Publishing Group.

First printing/June 1984

ISBN: 0-523-42179-6

Can. ISBN: 0-523-43165-1

Cover art by Joe DeVito

Printed in the United States of America

PINNACLE BOOKS, INC.
1430 Broadway
New York, New York 10018

9   8   7   6   5   4   3   2   1

For
Claudia Reid, Nurse-Midwife
and
Andrew Stewart, MD

Doctors did things to you and then it was not your body any more.

—Ernest Hemingway,
A Farewell to Arms

The trouble with life is that the stupid are cocksure, and the intelligent full of doubts.

—Bertrand Russell

BOOK ONE

THE UNIVERSITY HOSPITAL

1

His older brother dropped dead one July, without warning and for no apparent reason. This unfathomable behavior fascinated the doctors, who put their patient on a respirator in the Intensive Care Unit of the Manhattan Hospital. By the time Lars Magnussen arrived from Boston, his brother had been dead and on a respirator for twenty-four hours.

The Manhattan Hospital is a university hospital, and doctors at university hospitals require explanations. In the case of Olaf Magnussen, none suggested itself. There wasn't even a satisfying hypothesis. For people who show up dead at the emergency room, history is often the key, and the hysterical secretary who summoned the ambulance and came with it was incapable of providing anything useful. "He just got white as a ghost," was all she could say.

When Lars arrived from Boston, the intern and residents interrogated him intensely in a conference room down the hall from the respirator, but got nothing. Lars told them his brother had been made a partner at his New York law firm on his thirty-first birthday, six weeks prior. The skinny-necked intern did not write that down. He had written every "don't know" Lars had regretfully admitted, but not that. Making partner was no reason to suddenly drop dead.

Nobody was providing the doctors any useful information—not Lars, not the secretary, who in fact could have mentioned that she had her legs wrapped around Olaf as he thumped into her, before he rolled over, clutching his head. His pants were zipped back up by the time the ambulance arrived. He had died in his office with, ostensibly, propriety.

3

Olaf Magnussen, partner at a law firm with fifteen highly recognizable names on its letterhead, was now a brain stem prep being breathed twenty-four times a minute, blowing off carbon dioxide to raise his blood pH to constrict the blood vessels in his brain, to keep the swelling down. Olaf had very little living brain to worry about. He was in truth, very dead—a nuance that did not escape his brother. Nor did it deter his physicians, who had quite enough to worry about trying to figure out what had happened. And Olaf wasn't talking.

So they worked on Lars, trying to make him feel uninformed. No, Lars did not know if his brother had hypertension, diabetes, shot dope, did coke, amphetamines, had a history of heart attacks. His brother lived in New York; Lars in Boston.

After the long list of "Did he ever have . . . ?" and the inevitable "I don't think so—I'm not sure," the intern asked, "Were you close?" It took considerable restraint for Lars to refrain from punching out that intern. They were close.

"Hey buddy—" Olaf always opened the same way on the phone. They were buddies. They went fishing in Minnesota, jogging in Central Park and along the Charles. Olaf would never have called had he developed any of the things the intern mentioned. He would never have worried his little brother.

They were saying they didn't know enough about Olaf, trying to ignite in Lars the same burning will to know. Lars lifted Olaf's dead arm and let it drop. Like a rag doll. There was a tube down Olaf's throat. And there was a tube in his discolored penis. And one in his heart. (Lars didn't know about the one in the heart. That one looked like an ordinary IV in the left arm.) There was an IV in his right arm and lights and alarms over his bed. The alarms sent Lars flying for the nurses. The nurses had taped Olaf's eyes closed with sheer-white adhesive tape, right over the lashes.

The intern, a medical student, and two residents each asked about Olaf's heart. The electrocardiogram showed "giant T-wave inversions." Lars didn't like the sound of that: "giant" sounded so catastrophic. The intern told Lars that giant T-wave inversions could mean heart attack or stroke, or stroke following heart attack, or vice versa.

"What difference would it make?" Lars asked.

"We like to know which organ has been damaged," the intern replied.

Who was he trying to kid? Lars had heard the doctors talking in the hallway; he had heard the nurses, too. *All* Olaf's organs were damaged. He was dead, virtually. The nurses knew it but couldn't say it. Lars knew it. Maybe Olaf did too. Their parents didn't know. They were on holiday, back in Norway, unaware. And Lars was with Olaf. And Olaf was dead on a respirator.

Then came the chief of Neurology. The thundering herd brought him. Lots of white coats and bowing and scraping. The chief wasn't there to talk with Lars. The Master had come to teach—over Olaf's dead body. Lars wasn't allowed in the room during the discussion. The intern would come out later to translate, to transmit the Word. Later, after rounds.

"I want to hear it from the chief, myself," Lars said. "Today."

They took Lars to the chief's office at ten-thirty.

"Sorry to rush by you this morning," said the chief. The chief looked Lars right in the eye, something the intern and residents did only rarely. Rounds ran on a tight schedule, he explained. Besides, no one had told the chief Lars was waiting.

The chief agreed: Olaf was indeed dead.

The awesome Manhattan Hospital: three days on a respirator, three electroencephalograms, neuro exams beyond counting, and they needed the chief of Neurology for that.

The respirator would be stopped, gradually. "Weaning," they called it.

Olaf was officially dead that afternoon. The skinny-necked intern pronounced him at three-fifteen. He pulled the curtain around Olaf's bed and pulled out the tube from Olaf's throat. He slapped an intubation blade in the palm of a third-year medical student, Donald Brophy. Brophy tried three times to place the tube back in Olaf's dead trachea. He got in two out of three.

"Not bad," the intern said, and he went to talk to Lars, satisfied he had done his good deed for that day—helping a medical student learn intubation. Lars didn't know about Olaf's posthumous contribution to medical education.

The nurses cleaned up Olaf while the intern talked to Lars. They pulled out the IVs. They pulled the tube from that once happy penis and threw the tube into a plastic trash bag.

"I have the news you've been expecting," said the intern. Then he asked for permission for an autopsy, coming perilously and unknowingly close to sudden death at the hands of Lars

Magnussen. The intern said they wanted to know what had killed Olaf. Lars wanted to know why they had strung his brother's body up like a marionette with their tubes. Now the final insult. Cutting up what's left of Olaf—and their parents didn't even know.

"Someday you may want to know," the intern said. "Your parents may want to know."

"No," Lars replied. His parents would know enough knowing Olaf was dead.

"I know this has all come at you pretty fast," the intern went on, doing his best to sound like a human being and failing miserably. "But sometimes getting the autopsy done now, even though it seems unnecessary at the moment, you're glad you did later. For the family's sake. Questions come up."

"For the family's sake?"

"Questions come up sometimes. Later."

"What questions?"

"The family wants to know—later. What it was."

"You trying to win the prize for autopsies or what?" Lars said with a vehemence which even the intern couldn't miss. Lars stood up and the intern backed quickly out the door.

Providence, Rhode Island

Five years later, Lars drove past the University Hospital at Providence, daily, coming and going to work. He never looked at it. And it was difficult to avoid. All those red-brick towers and turrets, at the bend in Route 95.

In the five years since Olaf had not been saved at the Manhattan Hospital, Don Brophy had become quite good at tracheal intubation, and had saved at least a dozen patients with a timely and neatly placed tube. Saved them for death in the ICU mostly, where other medical students learned on them.

In those same years, Lars had graduated from law school, packed up his wife and kids, and taken a job with a firm in Providence, where he was about to make partner after only five years with them. Don Brophy had graduated from medical school, become an intern, then resident at the Manhattan Hospital. Then he had to leave. He got a Fellowship at University Hospital, Providence. It was July, and Brophy had been in Providence a week.

Lars drove by Brophy's hospital on his way home. Lars had a house on the water in Barrington. He had an accountant for his taxes, a stockbroker for his stocks, a Volvo station wagon for his wife, a silver BMW for himself, a sailboat for weekends, high blood pressure, a German shorthair dog, season tickets to the college football games, and a sliding inguinal hernia. The hernia was the spoiler. The sailboat ran aground occasionally; the BMW burned oil; the football team lost to Yale every year—but it was a fine life except for the hernia. The hernia had absolutely no redeeming value. The least strain could send it on its treacherous way toward the right testicle, stretching peritoneum and compromising blood flow to all kinds of delicate and vital structures, and setting off thunderclaps of pain.

Whenever Lars strayed from the path of intraabdominal relaxation and increased the pressure on his bowels by tensing his stomach muscles—lifting the barbecue or pushing his boat off a muddy shoal—his hernia rumbled along its track headlong for testicle, urogenital plumbing, whatever got in its path, and doubled Lars over with pain. If it happened at home, he could hobble off to a warm bath and uncrumple. But if he was at work, or worse, on the boat, he just had to suffer.

His wife believed in doctors for hernias. She had a friend, a nurse-midwife, who knew every doctor at the University Hospital. That nurse-midwife could point the way to hernia deliverance.

"No way," Lars said. He'd suffer his hernia. The University Hospital could get by another day without stamping his Blue Cross card on their triplicate forms.

"Go in for a hernia, come out a guinea pig—no way those clowns will get this boy. No way."

2

Brophy was in the Fellows' Office at three-thirty Monday when Duncan Gordon, one of the second-year Fellows, sailed in. Duncan always looked like he was on roller skates. He had been very nice to Brophy and had given him a selection of papers to read that were written by various faculty members in the Section so Brophy could decide to whom he wanted to apprentice himself.

"Don't let some asshole hustle you into working with him," Duncan had said. "Look around."

Unlike all the other Fellows, who seemed thrilled to have won Fellowships at University Hospital, Duncan sounded unimpressed by research in general and by the University Hospital in particular.

He had given Brophy and the other new Fellows the orientation tour. They had passed fat women on treadmills and young men lying on phlebotomy tables hooked up to IVs. "What you just saw was research," Duncan had said, conveying exactly what he thought of the importance of those studies. Brophy started to run to help at a cardiac arrest when the code call came across the overhead page, Duncan caught his arm. "You're not here to save lives now," he said. "They've got people for that. You're one of the select now."

"Everyone has his cross," Brophy replied. Duncan smiled and picked Brophy out from the group of new Fellows as his own special charge.

Now he stood in front of Brophy.

"Want to see a real clinical investigator in action?"

Brophy followed him up five flights of stairs to Chemistry. "Why do they always put the chem lab up six flights of stairs?" Brophy asked, breathless.

"To keep guys like us in shape," said Duncan, who wasn't at all breathless although he had turned quite red in the face. "I check calciums every day."

That's how Duncan ferreted out the hypercalcemic patients for his studies. The calciums were printed out on the computer terminal next to the atomic spectrophotometer machine. They weren't ready until four P.M. That meant if there were patients with high blood-calciums, you had to start calling their wards late in the afternoon, when everyone was trying to go home and didn't want to talk to you.

Checking the calciums consisted of going down the list of a hundred-odd names and picking out those with the high numbers, then finding out the diagnosis on each one, if anyone would tell you.

They were leaning against the wall outside the lab; Brophy was catching his breath, and Duncan's face was returning to a more normal color.

"Someday I'll have my assay going, and I can stop all this running around," Duncan said.

"Your assay?"

"You gotta have an assay. Clinical investigators are a dime a dozen. Anyone can hump upstairs every day and find patients. But get your assay and you've got a salable commodity."

"Oh."

"Sure. Look around. Lionel's got all these assistant profs, and everyone's got his assay," Duncan continued, referring to Lionel Addison, chief of Endocrinology. "Whenever we decide to study something, they just draw one blood sample for each guy."

"The team approach," Brophy added.

"Can't beat it," said Duncan, happily.

Duncan pushed through the door to the chem lab, followed by Brophy.

"It's the calcium maven," said the calcium technician. She was finishing her run for the day.

"What've you got for us?"

"There's one or two. Hey—congratulate me."

"What for?"

"I'm off calciums starting tomorrow. Six weeks on electrolytes."

Calciums by atomic spectro were tedious and the technicians hated doing them. But atomic spectro was the gold standard, and the chief of Endocrinology would settle for nothing less.

"You don't run a first-class program with second-class lab work," Lionel maintained.

There were two high calciums—one on a ward patient, the other on a private patient. Duncan was not happy about the one on the private service.

"A royal pain."

Private docs had to be called for permission to see their patients.

"You just can't walk through the door and tell some private patient his calcium is high without telling the Attending first."

But getting the private doc at four or five in the afternoon, when the calciums were ready, was problematic.

"They're all at their clubs, talking about mutual funds and what Mercedes to buy, and how to write it off," Duncan said. "They don't give a shit about learning anything new." He snorted. "Oh, they like their university titles, their university gym privileges, their discounted football tickets"—he was stoking his own flame now—"but ask them to cooperate with a little university research and all you get's a shitload of hemming and hawing and not this times, not my patient, sucker. Or they just don't answer their phones and won't call back."

So they went to see the ward patient. Duncan felt better, having had his say on LMDs (Local Medical Doctors), but still felt guilty about not trying for the private patient.

The ward patient had a calcium of 14.0.

"Fourteen-oh is for real," Duncan said. "There are twenty-three known entities that cause hypercalcemia, but a calcium above twelve's usually hyperpara, renal failure, or crab."

Duncan was hoping for crab. He hadn't recruited a malignancy patient for ten days.

There was a black housekeeping aide in the hallway, talking to the head nurse.

"I'm not going back in there," she was saying. "Smell's so bad could kill you. Looking at him like to make your blood run cold."

"His bed has to be made," the head nurse said, trying to sound implacable but not looking very convincing.

"Make it yourself," said the aide. "Sheets is all covered with blood and pus. They's stiff with it!"

The head nurse opened her mouth to speak, but the aide had the last word.

"I don't do no bloody sheets." And she turned and stomped off.

The head nurse walked the other way, back to the nurses' station, Duncan and Brophy following. They asked where Mr. Heimler's room was. She looked up angrily. Then her face became impassive, controlled.

"Ten twenty-three," she said. They took Heimler's chart from the metal rack and followed the numbers down the hall to 1023. It was the room before which the aide and nurse had had their row.

She could have said, "Follow your nose." The door was open and they got a whiff of it in the hallway.

Duncan held his breath and poked his head in the room.

"Let's read the chart in the nurses' station," he said.

Mr. Heimler had been picked up on Westminster Street. The police brought him to the ER. He couldn't tell anyone anything more than his name and he said he had a brother. Heimler's neck and left arm were socked in with tumor from chin to chest. Areas had ulcerated and wept a purulent yellow pus.

"Must have been some kind of derelict," said Duncan. "If he had a family, they'd have never let it get that far. Malignant melanoma. Big tumor burden. You don't see calciums of fourteen unless there's a whole lot of tumor somewhere. With him it isn't hard to see where."

"Big calcium, big tumor," echoed Brophy.

"Seems obvious enough," said Duncan. "But it's not sometimes. Blades had me see a guy last month they swore they had cured. Cut out every last crab cell, they said. But his calcium was still twelve. Came to autopsy a week ago. Tumor all over his diaphragm. Loaded with it."

They went to see Heimler, moving down the hall into the stench. With each step, Brophy took another step back toward his first days of internship at Manhattan Hospital's Whipple Cancer Ward. Two rotations, both during the summer. Brophy had been buried alive. By the end, he had numbed to the smells, the dying, the heat. It took months to get some feeling back. And here it was, all over again.

Heimler sat on the bed, facing the door. They had put him, mercifully, in a single room.

His neck was enlarged to twice its normal size.

"I'm Joe Heimler," he said as Duncan and Brophy stepped in.

Brophy was amazed that he could be sitting there, oblivious to the odor, yet alert enough to introduce himself.

Duncan introduced himself and Brophy.

"Joe Heimler," said Joe Heimler.

"I've come to see you about your calcium," said Duncan.

"Joe Heimler," said Joe Heimler, with what once would have been a smile, but which now was distorted by his inability to lower the jaw enough to really grin.

Duncan looked at Brophy, who stared at the equanimous Heimler. A few more questions made it quite clear that Mr. Heimler hadn't a chance of understanding where he was, much less the lengthy explanation Duncan had sailed into. The explanation was required by the Human Investigation Committee.

Duncan was engaged in the sacred process of obtaining "Informed Consent."

The HIC wanted every patient informed of the reasons and risks behind every study, and Duncan was informing. He talked about the protocol. He explained very carefully about the phenomenon of hypercalcemia of malignancy, the biopsy, high calciums. Duncan was very pleased with his own clarity. So was Mr. Heimler, who obviously had no idea what Duncan was talking about, but interjected "Hi, I'm Joe Heimler" every time Duncan paused for a breath.

It was very edifying. Mr. Heimler was one of the best patients Duncan had talked to in weeks. Also one of the most cooperative. He took the pen Duncan offered and managed a scrawl on the appropriate signature line that could fool even the HIC, it looked so much like "Joe Heimler." It could have been a signature, had Mr. Heimler sufficient neurons to sign his name and know what he was doing.

Mr. Heimler signed not only for the fasting blood and urine samples, but for the bone biopsy. Duncan would have had him sign for the autopsy, too, since it was obviously going to be a problem, Heimler having no readily contactable family. But the HIC forbade pre-death autopsy consents.

"See you tomorrow, Mr. Heimler," said Duncan, who was now so elated he had completely forgotten about the smell, and shook Heimler's hand.

Then Duncan pushed Brophy out of the room. Joe Heimler raised his hand in a little wave.

"Hi, I'm Joe Heimler . . ."

3

Lars Magnussen was up at six o'clock Monday morning, an hour earlier than usual. He ran water for the bath. The tub was down the hall from his sleeping wife, but the noise carried at that quiet time, even through the bathroom door, and it woke Beth.

Lars was in the tub, looking very pale, when she came in.

"Any time," she said. "You can suffer or I can call Clarissa. Any time."

Lars looked up to meet her eyes.

"You look like a six-year-old," Beth said, moving to the tub and taking his head in her arms, rubbing his shoulders and his neck. She stroked his chest and his eyelids and kissed his lips, which were dead white.

"It's different this time," he said. "Hurts like a cocksucker. Woke me up . . ."

"Will you let me call Clarissa?"

"What's she going to do?"

"She knows all the doctors."

Lars looked at the ceiling.

"Sometimes it gets better if I just soak."

Beth went back down the hall, pausing to look at the boys. "Little buggers," she said. It was what Lars always said when they stood watching them sleep. She went on to the bedroom and showered in the bathroom off their room, the one Lars hadn't used, not wanting to wake her. She dried and put on her Laura Ashley sundress.

Then she went back to Lars. He was sitting with his head in his arms. He didn't look up when he heard the door open. "Uncle," he said without lifting his head.

13

"Give up?"

"My heart says 'No,' but my groin says 'Go ahead.' Call her, for Chrissake!"

"Hallelujah."

It was seven-fifteen.

Beth caught Clarissa Leonard as she was gathering her lab coat and briefcase, trying to get out the door. Clarissa had spent the last fifteen minutes searching for her keys, becoming more and more frantic. Now she had them and was trying to get to U.H. for breakfast with Sol Zigelman before seven-thirty rounds. She always ate breakfast with Sol from seven-ten to seven-thirty, before they did rounds. But this morning she had wasted a quarter of an hour searching for her keys.

"Oh, you're still home," Beth said. "I was so afraid I'd miss you."

"You could always page me at U.H.," Clarissa told her. Beth fell silent. Clarissa sat down, chagrined. "You're upset," she said.

"Are you trying to get to the hospital?"

"Seven-thirty rounds. Not to worry. What's the story?"

"Nothing that urgent. You can call back. It's Lars."

"He know you're calling?"

"Yes."

"He must be close to death."

"I feel so ridiculous calling. Like it's a major emergency."

Clarissa listened and looked at her watch.

"But he's in agony. This is my big chance."

Beth got the story out and Clarissa laughed. "I'll call around after rounds and get back to you. We'll get him seen today."

"You're a doll."

"Don't let him squirm out of it."

Clarissa didn't get to the cafeteria until seven-forty. Sol was gone. She had to page him. He was not happy she had missed breakfast.

"Three bagels, two doughnuts, I ate, waiting all that time," said Sol. "How'm I suppose to lose weight with you keeping me in the cafeteria all morning? You're not there—I eat."

Clarissa explained about the keys, the hernia.

"Nancy Barnah's a good hernia man," said Sol. "Sounds like he might be strangulating one."

"Sol," said Clarissa, "this guy's refused to see anyone for years. He doesn't like docs. How's he going to like a woman surgeon?"

"That's his problem. He's a meathead, he'll suffer."

"Sol . . ."

"If he's got a hernia, especially an incarcerated hernia, he's got to be seen. She can do it in ambulatory surg. In-out. No big deal. But he has to walk through the front door."

"Who else? A man. Bill Waters?" Clarissa asked.

"Sure. Waters is fine. What's with this guy?"

"Waters?"

"No, the patient."

"Doesn't like docs."

Clarissa called Waters' office from the nursing station on postpartum. He was operating all morning but his secretary made Lars a squeeze-in for one P.M.

Then Clarissa called Beth, who answered on the first ring.

Beth thanked Clarissa, the U.H., the surgeon's secretary, and every painful nerve ending in Lar's groin—he was finally going to get his hernia fixed. She went to see him.

He was walking around the bedroom, getting dressed, feeling more comfortable. He didn't want to go.

"Lars!" Beth stormed. "Clarissa had to *beg* this guy to see you today. Don't embarrass her—he was all booked up."

"He's so fucking busy, he'll be happy if I cancel."

Beth started to cry.

"She said you might be strangulating the hernia."

"What's that suppose to mean?"

"It gets caught. Like in a noose."

"What's Clarissa know about hernias? She's a midwife."

"What are you so fucking afraid of?"

"What are you so eager to get me under the knife for?"

"Clarissa said it could be done as an outpatient. You wouldn't even have to stay overnight. No big deal."

Lars didn't say anything, but his face softened and he sat down on the bed.

"What do I need this aggravation for? My own wife twists my arm."

"You're in pain."

"True."

"Most normal human beings get help if they're hurting so bad they're waking up at six A.M. and can't even get out of the bath." She had his head in her arms again, stroking his fine long hair.

"Most normal human beings don't know any better than to see doctors."

Lars pulled on his jacket and grabbed his attaché case, which was heavy, loaded with briefs. His abdominal muscles tensed and tripped off a truly magnificent, lacerating pain from groin to mid-belly and down to testicle. It was a ten-on-a-scale-of-ten pain, a throbbing, ominous pain, impossible to ignore, a shot to the solar plexus.

He dropped the attaché case. "What time's the appointment?"

Lars was walking back and forth in Waters' waiting room when Waters did not show at one P.M. Lars couldn't sit down. Lars couldn't calm down. Waters wasn't there at ten past one. Lars seethed. A cholecystectomy had run over, and Waters didn't arrive until one-twenty, by which time two other patients with appointments ahead of Lars were also in the waiting room. Beth had large wet rings in the armpits of her Laura Ashley sundress and a burning in her stomach.

Waters finally saw Lars at two, by which time Lars had begun looking at his watch so frequently, he looked as if he had a wrist tic. Waters' nurse had Lars strip down, put on a paper gown, and wait on the table in the examining room.

"Isn't he going to talk to me first?"

"He'll be in when you're ready," the nurse said. Her hair was white and tinted blue. She pronounced her words very carefully, as if she were speaking to a small child or someone who didn't understand English very well.

She took Lars' blood pressure and took it again. She looked at him through her big glasses with the turquoise rims and smiled in an attempt to be reassuring. The smile wasn't right and had the opposite effect.

"Anything wrong?" asked Beth. She was sitting on a stool next to the examining table.

"It's just a little high."

It was in fact more than just a little high. It was so high the nurse couldn't believe it. She got 240/140 the first time and with each repeat.

"I'm a little overwrought just now," Lars said.

The nurse smiled unconvincingly.

Waters popped into the room. He had shiny black hair, slicked back, and one of his eyelids seemed to hang lower than the other. As he talked, he read the form Lars had filled out in the waiting room, never glancing up to meet Lars' eyes.

"Lawyer, huh? Malpractice lawyer?" he said, looking over

to his nurse, who laughed dutifully. He didn't wait for Lars to answer. He was in a hurry. Lars was his second squeeze-in and was supposed to be a straightforward problem. Waters asked Beth to step out of the room and knelt before Lars, inserting his finger into Lars' right scrotum, invaginating the skin.

"Which side is it?"

Lars told him.

"Cough."

Waters bounced up.

"We better do it tomorrow. Get over to the hospital this afternoon. Don't forget to bring your Blue Cross card." He laughed and winked. "Don't be caught without it. Better than American Express over there."

"You mean, get admitted?"

"That's what I had in mind," Waters said, opening the door and looking back into the room. "Can't do it on the kitchen table."

Beth came back into the examining room through the door Waters held open.

"I thought this could be done as an outpatient," said Lars.

"Who told you that?"

"Clarissa told my wife."

"I'd have to put you in," said Waters. "Your blood pressure's up. Have to have you seen for that. Cleared for anesthesia." He was almost out the door.

"How high is it?"

"High enough."

"Look," said Lars, "this is getting to be a big deal."

"I'm giving you my opinion." Waters was hoping that word would trigger the phrase "second opinion." Waters was becoming less and less willing to have anything to do with this hostile lawyer and his sliding inguinal hernia.

To Waters' great relief he heard Lars say, "Why don't I just go home and soak on it a while?"

"Fine," said Waters, hoping he'd never come back.

Beth was trying hard not to cry.

Lars got dressed and hobbled out of the office.

"Did you hear that? 'High enough.' Only the great Dr. Waters can know the actual number."

Beth said nothing. She drove Lars out of the parking lot and home to his tub.

4

Tuesday morning, Brophy was sitting in Endocrine Clinic with a thirty-year-old woman who had somehow managed to slip past the normal screening for subspecialty clinics and got herself an appointment without benefit of referral. Her chief complaint, printed firmly on her clinic sheet, was "Hypoglycemia." Brophy surreptitiously looked at his watch as she detailed each of her last twenty-five episodes, using the seven pages of printed notes she had brought with her to clinic.

"Around noon I got all sweaty and my heart began to pound. I felt totally wiped out."

Brophy sneaked another look at his watch. He had conference at noon, and Lionel expected conferences to start on time. Every week one Fellow had to present his clinic patient, and this week Brophy was the lucky Fellow. He was doubly lucky to have Mrs. Kroc for his patient.

Mrs. Kroc did not have an insulinoma, which was the only explanation for hypoglycemia which could possibly have interested Brophy. She had gone to a doctor and he had done a glucose-tolerance test, during which her blood sugar fell to 49, which impressed her doctor, who announced gravely he had made the diagnosis and charged her one hundred and fifty dollars.

"Mrs. Kroc," said Brophy, "it's not abnormal for blood sugars to go that low after you swallow highly concentrated sugar for a GTT. What would be abnormal is if it did not drop."

Mrs. Kroc's face went tight and impassive: she had run afoul of doctors like Brophy before.

Brophy fell into the tell-'em-everything's-all-right-honey category who didn't believe Mrs. Kroc had anything wrong with her, or that it was ruining her marriage, rendering her unable to continue at her job as an accountant, and slowly destroying her brain from repeated episodes of low blood sugar which killed two hundred brain cells each time. She had seen Brophy's type before.

Brophy knew Mrs. Kroc did not have an insulinoma because one of the eleven doctors she had previously sought out to find her hypoglycemia had actually known how to work her up for it. He had put her in the hospital and fasted her for three days, during which time her blood sugar had fallen to 48. The doctor eliminated all doubt about insulinoma for Mrs. Kroc by running a serum insulin on that blood sample: No measurable insulin. No insulinoma.

Brophy was most impressed by the doctor who did the three-day fast. Mrs. Kroc loathed that one. He had robbed her of her tumor. She liked the one who had done the glucose-tolerance test she didn't need and charged her a hundred and fifty dollars. She liked him, but she didn't trust him, because he had nothing to offer but diet changes, and she got better diets from *Redbook* and *Cosmo* and still felt tired and listless and was about to wind up divorced, unemployed, and in an insane asylum with very few functioning brain cells, so many had been killed off by her hypoglycemia.

One thing was clear: Mrs. Kroc would never believe, no matter how many tests Brophy did, in anything but hypoglycemia. It was a religion more than a diagnosis.

Brophy managed to get her out of his examining room by four minutes to twelve, which gave him time to dictate a note.

He finished dictating and made it to conference at twelve-ten. The Fellows were drifting in from clinic, along with some late-arriving private Attendings. The full-time faculty was already there.

Brophy presented Mrs. Kroc's case, and Lionel the Chief called for comments. Dick Cecil, head of research for insulin and carbohydrates in the Section, began expounding on the theory and practice of hypoglycemia. Cecil told a story about a forty-five-year-old "girl" who was convinced she had hypo-glycemia and was so determined that her doctors, her boy-friend, and employer believe it that she began injecting herself with insulin on the sly. Dick caught her with a neat trick: he tested her serum for antibodies to insulin, which she had in great quantity.

A person only makes antibodies to the insulin that comes from a bottle, not to the insulin produced by her own pancreas. Dick had her cold.

He laughed a shrill laugh, which Duncan later described as a cackle, and which sent a cold chill through Brophy. Then he said that about 12 percent of normal women drop below 40 when they fast. Hypoglycemia was significant only if symptoms matched the nadir of the blood sugar measured—45 in some women, as low as 35 in others. Mrs. Kroc felt fine when her sugar was 48.

One of the older private Attendings, John McCullough, cleared his throat at the far end of the conference table and said that he didn't know about the numbers, but he considered a blood sugar below 50 to be abnormal. This statement, made in a rich baritone, had the ring of authority and irrationality: "normal" being defined by numbers, averages, and large studies like the one Cecil had cited. Here was a man who faced ineluctable truth and said "Nay." There had to be a certain genius there, Brophy thought, as Lionel tactfully adjourned the meeting. Brophy's head began to spin, pondering what McCullough had meant.

"He meant he thinks Cecil is an asshole, no matter how smart he is," explained Duncan.

Brophy started to make a break for the stairwell to dash to the cafeteria when he felt someone catch his elbow. It was Dick Cecil. "Why don't we get together this afternoon? Say, five-thirty?" said Cecil. "I've got some stuff you might be interested in." He was grinning broadly.

Brophy walked down the hall with him.

"I hear you're looking around for a project," Cecil said.

"I'm still trying to figure out what research is all about," Brophy told him, starting to sweat.

"No problem. I'm just the guy to show you. Meet me in my office at five. Be expecting you." He squeezed Brophy's arm and hurried down the hall, disappearing into a stairwell.

5

Lynn Ann Montano was sitting on her editor's desk looking very good, swinging her crossed legs and talking about the three phone calls she had from patients and employees at University Hospital.

"I told you it was a can of worms," she said. "Now I get a call from a nurse works in a clinic. She says, 'You think the emergency room's got problems—you ought to see the clinic!' She says half the doctors never even show up. Patients wait three hours."

"Did Jack tell you how many letters we got about the ER story?" the editor asked. "Sixty-three."

"People are hungry for this stuff, Wally."

"What about this business with the pregnant women?"

"I told you who that came from."

"That obstetrician? He got an angle?"

"It's that same old Zigelman thing."

"What's your friend say about it?"

"Clarissa? Haven't talked to her yet. But I doubt there's anything there. They're still trying to get Zigelman."

"But if he's giving radioactive isotopes to pregnant women . . ."

"I'll call her. But I think this clinic thing might be better."

"What? Some menopausal nurse trying to sock it to the old farts?" The editor leaned back in his swivel chair and clasped his hands behind his head, looking at Lynn Ann's legs. He had piled his deskside chair full of papers before calling her in, and she sat on his desk, as he hoped she would.

"It's not just her. Clarissa mentioned it once and I nosed

around." Lynn Ann recrossed her legs, providing the editor with a breathtaking but fleeting view which made him consider how sad it was that he had not yet managed to get Lynn Ann into bed, which he had heard was not too much to hope for.

"I talked to one of the young docs who works in the clinic. He won't go on the record, but he says the director of the clinic moonlights across town during clinic hours, so gets paid double, and the clinic is way understaffed."

"So what? Lynn Ann, who's going to get worked up over a little free enterprise? The emergency room stuff had pizzazz— life and death. Someday maybe *your* life or death because they don't do things right. Who cares about the charity clinic waiting time?"

"Wally," said Lynn Ann, leaning forward, bouncing her leg, "the more time I spend over there, the more I hear. The place is full of stories. I've got to meet people over there."

"If you can come up with something like that emergency room story, you're on."

Lynn smiled.

"I was thinking we might do a series on the place— 'University Hospital: Patients into Guinea Pigs.' That kind of thing," the editor said. "We could work on it together."

Lynn Ann smiled again and slid off the desk.

"That sounds interesting," she said, turning to go.

The editor followed her out of his office with his eyes. She walked with a lot of movement.

6

Brophy was leaving the Fellows' Office when Duncan blew in at five to five.

"Want to come check the calciums?"

"Got to see Dick Cecil at five."

"What for?"

"He wants to show me how research is done."

"What?"

"He cornered me after conference today."

"Tell Dick to stuff it. You've only been here a week. You're still reading."

"I don't have any projects. I've got to at least listen to some offers."

"Tell Dick to stuff it."

"Sure."

"You're going to work with that maniac?"

"What can I do? Everyone keeps asking me about my research. I'm reading like mad, but my day isn't exactly crampacked."

"Tell Dick to stick it in his ear. You'll be on Clinical Service August and September anyway. You can't start a project now."

"I'll tell him," said Brophy, looking at his watch.

"He's a maniac," Duncan said, throwing some journals into his brown knapsack. "He's got no class." He flew out the door.

Brophy listened to Duncan's footsteps receding down the hall, then started for Dick's office, feeling more and more guilty and inadequate with each step, thinking about all the minutes of the day he wasn't doing research. He knew he was lucky to get a high-powered Fellowship among these research-

23

ers, with all their laboratories, and this depressed and panicked him. He knew he was lucky because the endocrinologist back at Manhattan Hospital who got him the Fellowship told him so. They did all the best research at University Hospital.

"But I hate research," Brophy had told him.

"You've never done any," said the endocrinologist. "How can you know?"

So Brophy had taken the Fellowship, which, after all, was a magnificent program. He was supposed to be the envy of hundreds of young physicians all over America who wanted nothing more than to cap off their final years of medical training pummeling calculators and publishing papers at Lionel Addison's program. Lionel Addison, world-renowned laboratory maven, molecular geneticist and cell biologist, had assembled a large and talented group of rising stars who did their research and taught the Fellows how to do assays, how to write papers that never got rejected, and how to play with hormones.

Brophy got more and more depressed thinking about how Dick was going to put him in a lab somewhere. Duncan had shown him Dick's lab on the tour. Dick had some intimidating machines. Brophy had looked at all those knobs and dials and blinking lights, at the analyzers, scintillation counters, and test tubes, and at the scales that could measure things in micro-, nanno-, and picograms, and he was seized by the same panicky feeling he used to get in his college organic chemistry lab, where he once broke two hundred dollars' worth of glassware during a single three-hour lab session, thereby establishing a record for pre-medical undergraduates.

"It's all set up for you," Dick said the moment Brophy appeared in his doorway. "All you have to do is plug in." He flashed a toothy grin. His facial skin had big pores and needed sun, but he was blond and pale as an albino.

"I'm starting Clinical Service week after next," Brophy said.

Dick seemed not to hear. He went on, telling Brophy about catecholamine infusions. Dick had about seven projects going, and hopped around his desk, scanning the piles of papers, moving one pile onto another, shifting charts and boxes of slides around.

He wanted Brophy to work on a project that involved infusing lipids, adrenalin and other catecholamines into well-trained athletes. Watching Dick shift around behind his desk, Brophy imagined him trying to keep all seven projects aloft like a juggler.

Dick handed Brophy some articles he had written about the infusion technique.

"Don't worry if you don't understand everything in those," he said, pointing at the papers. "If you knew everything the first day, you wouldn't have to do the Fellowship—we'd have to make you an associate professor and move you into this office and kick my ass out in the hall."

Dick laughed a high-pitched laugh, called out, "See you tomorrow morning," and disappeared out the door, leaving Brophy waiting by his desk with a sinking feeling. He tried to think of how to tell Dick he couldn't possibly begin sending people into adrenalin fits the next morning. He sat there clutching the articles in sweaty, cold hands, until he realized Dick wasn't coming back: he had left for the day.

7

Lars went to work Tuesday, but the day was punctuated by disconcerting spasms and twinges. By the time he arrived home, the discomfort was constant. He paced around his room, from bed to chair and back to bed, trying to find a comfortable position. He soaked right through dinner, past midnight, past one A.M. At one-thirty Beth pushed open the bathroom door and sat across from him on the floor.

"Staying all night?"

Lars looked up, eyelids red-rimmed.

"Feels better."

"You'll fall asleep and drown."

"No."

"Going to work?"

"I'll see how I feel."

Beth sighed. "You're pissed at Waters so you're just going to show him and sit here in agony."

"Go to hell."

She got up and went back to bed.

Lars came into the bedroom with a towel wrapped around his waist. He walked stiffly.

"Didn't mean that."

"You must be real fun at the office."

"So what do you want me to do? Go back to the turkey?"

"See someone else. He's not the only surgeon in Providence. You're turning this into a major production."

"Let's see how I do tomorrow."

Lars felt better in the morning and drove to work. But, swinging his leg out of the car, he felt a twinge. He was in the

26

lot in the basement of the building and he leaned up against the car, feeling the pain build.

When he set down his leather attaché case in his office, the soft handle was wet and deeply imprinted—he had been gripping hard in pain. There was a seminar that morning, but Lars wasn't listening. He was too busy shifting in his seat, trying to find a comfortable position. When the seminar ended at ten, he went back to his office.

John Collier, one of the senior partners, called at ten-twenty. They were supposed to go over a brief. By this time Lars discovered the only comfortable position was standing.

"Hope you don't mind my looking over your shoulder, John. My back. Standing's okay, but sitting just kills it."

Lars was not about to get into hernia explanations. Everyone knew about backs. It was an executive disease.

The session went well enough under the circumstances.

Collier wanted him to find an expert witness to testify that it is not reasonable to expect a wristwatch to remain intact and accurate once it was dropped thirty feet to a dock and been run over by a four-wheeled derrick, despite the fact that the watch manufacturer uses a gorilla in its ads demonstrating the durability of the timepiece.

"Call the gorilla's agent," said Collier. "Maybe the gorilla will give a deposition."

Lars didn't laugh. He was too busy breaking out in a drenching, cold sweat. The pain had started in earnest and was searing and sweeping up from below.

Collier looked up. Lars was trying to smile appreciatively, but it came out a grimace.

"That was a little joke," Collier said, noticing the beads of perspiration popping out all over Lars' ashen forehead.

The pain was abdominal, but the response was generalized: his heart was racing at a prodigious rate, pounding; his fingers and toes were tingling; and he was breathless.

"You look like you've seen a ghost. The back's really bad?"

"Comes and goes," Lars said, feeling lightheaded.

"You better see someone," Collier said, getting up to catch Lars, who didn't fall.

"Yeah."

"And go home and lie down, for Chrissake."

"Yeah. Thanks."

Lars made it down the hall. His heart felt as though it might leap out through his mouth, and he was developing a throbbing headache.

Back in his office, he leaned against the wall. A secretary came in.

"Mr. Collier asked me to see if you were all right."

"Much better now."

"Will you be going home?"

"I'm better now. I'll tell Judy if I do."

Lars did feel things subsiding. He made some calls but started getting chills in the air-conditioned office. He was dripping wet.

At lunch he took the elevator down to the lobby and bought two shirts and two undershirts in the haberdasher. He was ravenously hungry and went outside into the stultifying Providence heat to buy hot dogs across the street at the diner next to City Hall. He bought three and finished them by the time he got back to his building. Walking along in the heat, with his shirt bag under his arm, he felt better.

But when he stepped through the revolving glass door to meet the cold shock of the air-conditioned lobby, it squeezed down on him all over again.

Back at his desk, he tried to collect himself. His secretary buzzed him with a call.

It was Beth. "How's it going?"

"Not real well."

There was a silence. Beth was determined not to tell him what he ought to do.

"It hurts all the time," Lars said finally.

Beth still said nothing.

"Do you think Clarissa's pissed at me about Waters?"

"I'll call her."

"No. She tried to help. I blew it."

"Waters was a prick. Let me call her."

"Okay."

"Okay?"

"I said okay."

Beth got Clarissa by page at U.H. She was making rounds with Sol Zigelman.

"Didn't hit it off with Waters, I hear," Clarissa said.

Beth told her Lars was contrite now.

"Let's try Nancy Barnah this time. She's very low-key. Think Lars would accept a woman surgeon?"

"Let me get back to you," Beth told her. Beth knew there was no way Lars would accept a woman surgeon.

"What the hell do I care if she's a woman?" said Lars when Beth called back. "Is she any good?"

"Clarissa says she's the best."

"Then why didn't she send us to her in the first place? Can you find out more about her? I know Clarissa's doing us a favor. But where'd she go to school, and all that?"

It took only three more phone calls for Beth to get the book on Nancy Barnah—who had lots of academic merit badges—and to tell Clarissa to go ahead.

Clarissa had to go over to the Operating Room Suite to catch Nancy Barnah between cases, explain, and set things up for that afternoon.

"She can't see him this morning?" Beth said, disappointed.

"She's doing a colon this morning," said Clarissa, getting annoyed. Clarissa had other things to do besides running around arranging Lars' appointment—like doing clinic and finishing rounds with Sol, who was being very nice about letting her run off to make all these arrangements. "She's got a full schedule in her office this afternoon. She's squeezing Lars in And tell Lars that, so he'll know. She'll see her scheduled patients first. He may have to wait a while."

"He was upset with Waters because he was in so much pain," Beth said. "And Waters wasn't even in the office."

"Well, if Nancy's case runs over, she might be late getting to her office, too. She's not going to rush through a colon to get to Lars in the office. And her scheduled patients can't be kept waiting for a squeeze-in."

"Jesus, Clarissa. I can't make him behave."

"Sorry—this must not be a pleasure for you either."

"You're a doll for doing all this."

Clarissa felt bad she had snapped, once Beth had thanked her. "Hang in there," she said.

She caught up with Sol Zigelman on the postpartum floor.

"Get it straightened out?"

"That remains to be seen," Clarissa said, pouring herself coffee from the coffee maker at the nurses' station.

"How can you drink that stuff black?" Sol winced.

"Sol, I drink it black every morning—and every morning you say that."

"It's just as amazing this morning as it ever is."

"Well, I made them an appointment with Nancy."

"Nancy could fit them in?"

"That's where I just was—over at the OR. Nancy'll see him. He'll get taken care of today," said Clarissa. "If he behaves."

8

Wednesday morning, Brophy arrived at the hospital at five minutes before seven. Donna, one of the clinical research nurses, was already there, and not at all impressed that Brophy was early.

The subject was a smiling undergraduate who ran the mile for the college track team and was spending the summer in Providence, working as a lifeguard at a lake near Woonsocket and subletting an apartment he couldn't really afford. His name was Stanley. He had seen one of Dick Cecil's notices advertising for subjects for a medical study at a coffee shop on Thayer Street. Dick's grant paid fifty dollars for three hours of adrenalin infusion.

"Sounded like easy money," said Stanley.

Stanley was a superb athlete and had wonderful veins, but Donna missed on her first try with the big angiocath. Stanley turned a little pale, and Brophy offered to start the IV, but Donna's look cut him off. New Fellows didn't come around at seven A.M. suggesting they might be better at IVs than Donna. She told Brophy to mix up the solutions of various concentrations of adrenalin, lipids, propanolol, and radioactive tracer.

The instructions were printed on the wall. Brophy followed them, fumbling around for the required graduated cylinders, splashing radioactive tracer over his trembling fingers, damaging untold generations of brophy chromosomes and raising his own adrenalin level.

Finally he had what he thought were the solutions required. It was seven-thirty, and Donna was making noises about all the other studies she had to get moving. She took the solutions

31

from the syringes Brophy held and hooked them up to two Harvard infusion pumps.

Dick came in at seven thirty-five.

"Now, all you have to do is press this button here. That starts the pump. This dial regulates the rate. If his heart rate gets up above here, you turn it back like that. But at the lower concentrations, that shouldn't happen. Keep taking his blood pressure. Donna'll check his blood sugars about every twenty minutes."

And he was gone.

Brophy started the pumps, and waited for things to happen. Donna finally came huffing in and went over to Stanley. "How are you, Stanley?"

Stanley looked startled, as if he had suddenly just awakened. Donna looked over to Brophy. "His eyes been this dilated long?"

Brophy nodded. She took Stanley's blood pressure. "It's too high," she said.

Donna went to the wall phone and dialed a number.

"Well, where is he?" Brophy heard her say. "Terrific!" She slammed the receiver down.

"The secretaries don't know where Cecil is. He just runs off and you can't find his blond butt. I've got too much to do this morning without this grief."

Dick came in at eleven-ten. He looked at the graph Brophy had been constructing. He turned down one infusion rate, turned up another, said, "He'll be okay now," and disappeared. Brophy's mouth was open, about to form the words "Don't leave me." But Dick was gone.

Dick was right, though. The blood pressure came down and so did the heart rate, with Brophy adjusting the dials just as he did prior to Cecil's diddling. Whatever magic Dick had done had worked. Trouble was, Brophy had no idea what he had done. He was relieved to see Stanley looking comfortable, and overjoyed to see his blood pressure and pulse inscribing a happy little plateau right down the middle of the predicted range. But what if Donna couldn't get Dick on the phone the next time Stanley's pressure took off? Or what if it rose faster and higher the next time?

Brophy could see day after day of the next two years stretching out ahead of him in that windowless room, plugged into a track star or a swimmer, whomever, fastened to the infusion pumps.

Around one P.M. Duncan buzzed into Brophy's peripheral field of vision. Brophy was waiting for Donna to finish running Stanley's most recent sugar in the glucose analyzer. Brophy's own blood sugar was dipping lower and lower. He hadn't eaten breakfast, and lunch was fast becoming less and less likely. The cafeteria closed at one-fifteen.

"Eaten yet?" Duncan asked.

"Eighty-four!" Donna barked out.

Brophy fed 84 into the computer panel, got an infusion rate from the instrument, adjusted the dial to that new rate, and marked the values on his graph.

"No," he told Duncan, "I'm beyond eating. I just turn dials."

Ten minutes later Duncan returned with a peanut butter and jelly sandwich and a Coke. Brophy gulped down both.

"You really *were* hungry," Duncan said.

"Ninety-two," Donna called, scowling at Duncan for distracting Brophy.

Brophy moved a dial with a reflexive little response.

"Call me Univac."

Brophy wasn't finished until six P.M., when Dick flew in and decided the study could end.

He went over Brophy's chart.

"Nice study. We've got another guy tomorrow."

Brophy could see Steve Reynolds, one of the other new Fellows working for Cecil, looking over from his stall, but he couldn't see Reynolds' subject, who was behind the partition.

"Donna was real pissed today."

"Oh, forget Donna. She doesn't know her ass from her elbow. She wants everyone to think the place couldn't run without her."

"Dick," said Brophy, "we'd better talk about today, and where this might all go, before I sign on."

"What'd ya mean?" Dick asked. "Now, don't go lazy on me. You said you were interested. You don't want to get a rep as a goof-off."

"I don't think I'm getting a lot out of this."

"What'd ya mean, 'getting?'" he demanded with an incredulous expression. "We're just collecting data. We got to go over it before anybody gets anything out of it." Then he grinned, punching Brophy on the arm. "All we've got to do is about six patients. Then we'll write it up. Ought to take about two weeks. You'll have your first paper inside of a month. How'd you like that?"

Stanley was getting up to go, still a little wobbly. Donna was helping him to the door, listening to Brophy and Dick.

"Can I talk to you," Brophy asked Dick, "in your office?"

"Sure. Clean this place up. I'll see you downstairs. Just don't give me a hard time. I've been taking shit all day."

Dick Cecil was in his office, on the phone. Shouting. He had his feet up on the desk. He put his hand over the receiver when Brophy came in and said, "Have a seat." Brophy sat down and Dick continued yelling into the phone.

"So they wanted to know how many Fellows I had working with me for six grants," screeched Dick, looking at the Bo Derek poster next to his University of Chicago diploma. "And I said, 'Three and a half if you count Al. He should really count as a half a Fellow.'"

He laughed his high-pitched, too urgent laugh, then went on to talk about a conference in France to which he had evidently been invited.

"They're gonna fly me over. Sure . . . all expenses. Think I'd go if I had to pay my way? I don't like the Eiffel Tower that much!" He laughed. He liked his joke about the Eiffel Tower. "Then I gotta go to Vienna or Cologne or one of those places. Same talk, yeah."

Brophy had the feeling some of this was being said for his benefit, so that he could appreciate what a world figure in catecholamine metabolism Dick Cecil was.

By this time Brophy was aimlessly looking at Bo Derek, too. Dick caught this and winked, hanging up the phone. "Some boobs, huh?" he said. "See her tits right through that wet suit."

Brophy started to say something.

"Be right with you," Dick told him, stacking papers and pushing the piles around his desk. His knee was bouncing up and down and he seemed to be going in six directions at once.

"Did you bring the graph?"

Brophy had brought the graph. They went over it, then Brophy told him.

"What'd ya mean?" Dick said, looking surprised, hurt, and ironic all at once.

"I mean, I don't think this is my area of interest," said Brophy. "I'm going to devote my time to the cancer project." Finally, getting it out straight: "Today was my last infusion."

Dick leaned back in his chair and put his hands behind his head. It was a swivel desk chair, so he could tilt way back and look at Brophy from under his eyelids. "You know . . . I know all about you."

Brophy said nothing.

"You didn't even have a Fellowship until a few months ago. Lionel only took you 'cause he was doing some old buddy of his down at Manhattan Hospital a favor."

Brophy said even less.

"You got a couple of strikes against you already. You don't want to screw up here, too. You'll be doing life insurance physicals the rest of your life."

"I appreciate your concern."

"What?"

"I agree with you about one thing," said Brophy. "I want to make the most of this place." Then, smiling: "That's why I'm not working with you."

"You think you're gonna just keep outta sight for two years, hang out at the library, cut out at four o'clock? We'll get someone in here wants to work, someone—"

He was still talking when the door closed behind Brophy.

9

Nancy Barnah finished her colon case at four o'clock Wednesday and walked into her office at four-thirty. She had left word to put Lars in the examining room and to draw blood.

Under Beth's glare, Lars went along reluctantly with the blood-drawing. Beth was not going to tolerate any more fights or flights.

Nancy's nurse checked Lars' blood pressure twice. Lars asked her what she found. "One-eighty over one-ten," she said. "That's high. We'll have to check it again when you settle down. People are usually a little high when they first walk in."

Lars smiled and looked at Beth. "No secrets among friends," he said.

Nancy stepped into the examining room, smiling. "I'm Nancy Barnah," she said, extending her hand to clasp Lars' clammy palm. She looked him straight in the eye. Beth was sitting on the stool next to the examining table. Nancy shook her hand too.

Beth looked apprehensively at Lars. Nancy didn't look old enough to be a medical student, much less a surgeon. She was blond and freckled and reminded Beth of the adolescent cheerleader who lived next door.

Lars, on the other hand, looked pleased with her. "You don't look old enough to've been to all those impressive places we heard about," he said happily.

"What places?"

"Yale, Cornell, Duke . . ."

Nancy laughed, looking even younger. "You know my whole academic pedigree."

36

"We don't just take pot luck," Lars told her, "when it comes to doctors."

"I'm not sure the pedigree's any great assurance."

"It's a start."

Nancy smiled with her eyes and let it go. "Clarissa tells me you've been in a lot of pain," she said.

"To put it mildly," Beth said, as Lars opened his mouth to speak.

Nancy smiled. "Now, he wasn't going to deny it, was he?"

"It's tough to get it out of him," said Beth.

Lars shook his head and looked at the floor. Nancy turned back to him. "I understand you've had this a while," she said. "When did it really flare up?"

"Really got bad three or four days ago when I bent down to open the garage door."

Nancy asked a series of questions, waiting for Lars to finish each time, then turned to Beth and said, "I'd like to examine him." Beth stood up and walked to the door. "We'll just be a minute." Nancy asked Lars to strip below the waist and wait on the table, then she stepped into the hall with Beth.

"To listen to him, you'd think I made this all up," Beth told her.

"He tends to minimize his pain, I gather."

"He's been in agony. He spends every night in the bath."

"The bath?"

"Only thing that seems to help."

"Well, let me take a look. But I don't think we're going to get anywhere if we push hard. He has to make the decision."

Nancy stepped back into the exam room and invaginated the right scrotum, then the left, asking Lars to cough. The exam took less than two minutes.

"You've got trouble, all right. The hernia slides back into place now. But from what you tell me, I suspect it doesn't always make it back so easily."

"What do you think?"

"Let's get Beth in here so I only have to say it once."

Nancy told them she thought surgery could wait, but that it would have to be done eventually, and that Lars would run the risk of strangulating the hernia until it was fixed. But there was no emergency. She wouldn't do him in ambulatory surgery because of his blood pressure. He'd need medical clearance for anesthesia because she wasn't sure she could do this type repair under local, which she ordinarily preferred. She recommended he take care of it as soon as possible, but she left it up to him.

"I appreciate your not hustling me," said Lars. "Some surgeons are pretty quick to unsheathe the knife."

Beth shifted unhappily on her stool.

"Don't get me wrong," Nancy said, looking for the first time old enough to be a surgeon. "The safest thing, surest thing to do is to repair that thing. Actually you've got trouble on both sides, and it won't be as simple as these things usually are. But," she said, smiling just enough for Lars to pick it up, "it'll be Friday before I can get you a bed, and I never like doing things when the hospital's emptying out and there's nobody around to help me or to watch you."

Lars smiled back. Here was a woman who was willing to acknowledge the fallibility of the system. They said good-bye, and as soon as Beth and Lars were out the door, Nancy called down to Admitting and scheduled Lars for admission for Monday or Tuesday.

"I thought they didn't want surgery," Nancy's secretary said.

"He doesn't. But those hernias aren't going to fix themselves. He'll be back. And when he does show up, I don't want any hassles from Admitting when I need the bed."

10

Duncan was in the Fellows' Office reading *Metabolism* when Brophy staggered in, back from the day in the library, vision blurred.

"You look terrible!" Duncan announced cheerfully. "You'll make a lovely endocrinologist. Your skin's already a perfect shade of gray."

"It's a nice library, really."

"Did you see all those Xerox machines in front?"

"They're hard to miss."

"My first day here last year I see there's no electrocardioram machine on the Clinical Research unit. Money's tight, they tell me. Someone's having chest pain and you've got to wait for the nurses to bring one up from Browning-Four on the elevator. Then I go down to the library and see where all the money's gone. Ten Xerox machines."

"I was told the place is research oriented," Brophy said. "Guess that's called Setting Priorities."

"New Knowledge," Duncan said, winking, "is the business of the University Hospital."

"It *is* a splendid library."

"It's a wonderful library. Every time you get a spare minute, you'd be well advised to get your ass over there and see what the competition's up to. Keep up with the journals. Somebody's always trying to beat you to press with some piece-of-shit article. So you read. Don't go running off to cardiac arrests, taking care of patients."

"Hard breaking old habits."

"I know," Duncan said. "I was the same way when I got

here last year." He sighed, leaning back in his chair. "But then I got into this malignancy thing with Jethro, and patients began looking like a pain in the ass to me, too." Duncan smiled at himself, shaking his head. "I mean, some of 'em are nice people, and you need 'em if you're going to do clinical studies. But they're always getting sick or scared and calling you up when you've got an assay cooking." Duncan shook his head, thinking of all those sick and frightened phone calls. "Look at Chuck Mersault: started getting wrapped up with his patients, had him on the phone all day long. Couldn't get any work done. When time came for his review, he'd published about four papers. Took care of a shitload of patients, but got passed over for associate professor. Shipped him out to the VA. . . ."

Duncan slammed *Metabolism* shut and leaned back in his swivel chair, hands clasped behind his head, considering the Xerox machines in the library and the absence of electrocardiogram machines on the CRU.

"I'm going sailing," he announced suddenly. "Want to come?"

"What? Right now?"

"It's four-thirty. What's wrong with now?"

"Where do you go?"

"Brophy, this is Rhode Island. Come over here. Look out my window."

Duncan had an office with a window. He felt very fortunate having one and loved looking out it. "I won this window from Dick Cecil. Remind me to tell you. . . . Look out there. What do you see?"

"Route Ninety-five."

"Beyond that."

"Oil refineries. Oil tanks."

"Next to the oil tanks."

"Oil tankers."

"That's it! You're getting closer. What are the ships floating in?"

"Water."

"That's it! Water. More specifically, the Narragansett Bay. No place in Rhode Island is far from it."

"You sail in that?"

"Brophy, there are two things you do not do in Providence:

you do not speak ill of Italians and you do not disparage the Narragansett Bay."

"When do we sail?"

"Soon as I check the calciums."

Duncan flew out of the room, leaving Brophy to wonder why he hadn't been invited. Suddenly checking calciums sounded like a wonderful thing to be doing. It had such a nice sound, so purposeful. It was like having a real job. Thinking that his fling with Cecil might have spoiled things with Duncan, Brophy felt acid forming in his gut.

Ten minutes later Duncan was back, looking refreshed and exhilarated from his calcium checking. He stuffed *Metabolism* and a few other journals into his little blue knapsack and said, "Just one to see before we go."

They headed for the surgical ward to see Dianne Tamborlotti, who was twenty weeks pregnant and had a calcium of 11.9. "She's one of Jethro's Stone Clinic patients," Duncan told Brophy. "Had three kidney stones before anyone realized she had hyperpara."

"Hyperparathyroidism?"

That's what Dianne had, but she didn't like thinking about it. She had married at seventeen, divorced at eighteen, two kids—seven and four. She was twenty-four, worked in a luggage factory, and got no child support. Dianne had enough problems to worry about without her hyperparathyroidism. Then she became dehydrated, her urine flow slowed to a trickle, and she precipitated out calcium kidney stones.

"When she got pregnant, her OB doc told her to drink four glasses of milk every day," Duncan said. "She got two stones the first week she did that. She's had one a week ever since. This last one obstructed her ureter, put her in renal failure for a couple of days."

Dianne thought she had troubles enough from the pregnancy and the stones. Then they cut out her parathyroid adenoma and cured her hyperparathyroidism, only to leave her with something Duncan called "hungry bone syndrome." When her hormone level fell back to normal after surgery, her bones started to reabsorb calcium with a vengeance. Her blood-calcium level fell so low, so quickly, that she got monumental muscle cramps, twitched all over, and the surgeons were afraid she might have a grand-mal seizure, as patients with rapidly falling blood-calciums sometimes do.

She was Jethro Brown's patient until the surgeons took over. Jethro was the head of calcium research in the Section, and Duncan was his Fellow, so Duncan had to go by every day and make sure the surgeons were giving Dianne the right amount of calcium.

Dianne was unperturbed about her hungry bones, which were giving the surgeons fits. She was worried about her baby, who had absorbed every milligram of anesthesia she got during surgery.

"I should've listened to Dr. Brown," she said. "He told me to have the operation a year ago." She shook her head with a rueful look. "Dr. Brown says it didn't hurt the baby. The operation didn't hurt the baby." She was dark-eyed and had very pretty skin. "My mother says the ether will make the kid a retard. It kills brain cells."

"They didn't use ether for your surgery," Duncan assured her. "Sure wouldn't help the baby if you kept making stones and got dehydrated and couldn't eat or drink and went into renal failure and went ketotic. We were between a rock and a hard place with you."

"That's just what Dr. Brown said." She started to cry.

Brophy was amazed that anyone receiving a dose of morphine the size of Dianne's could become as agitated.

"There's been a fair number of women who've had this operation in pregnancy," Duncan said. "The babies do just fine."

"They do okay? Really?"

"Would I kid you?"

Dianne cheered up momentarily, then her face pinked and a tear brimmed over and rolled down her cheek.

"If this kid's a retard, I'll slit my wrists. I really will."

"It all might've happened anyway," Duncan told her.

"Not if I'd had this fixed when Dr. Brown told me to."

"You didn't know you were going to get pregnant."

"That's the truth." Dianne shook her head. Now she was going to be an unmarried mother of three instead of two, still without child support and currently with hungry bones to boot. And a retard. "Dr. Laxalt told me it was the milk that gave me the stones."

"Nobody can really know," said Duncan. "We're just starting some research to find out about what happens in pregnancy."

"I brought it on myself," Dianne continued.

Duncan gave up trying to reassure her and took Brophy out to the nurses' station.

"Who's Laxalt?"

"Her surgeon. Stupid son-of-a-bitch. Tells her her calcium problems all come from drinking her milk. Her OB doc told her her baby needed milk. Now she talks like she poisoned the runt drinking the stuff."

"Well." Brophy smiled. "What do surgeons know?"

Duncan looked at Brophy and smiled, then said suddenly, "My father's a surgeon."

Brophy tried to read his expression, but couldn't.

"At your alma mater," Duncan added.

Brophy stared blankly at him.

"Manhattan Hospital."

Brophy still looked uncomprehending.

"Lyle Gordon."

"Of course!"

Lyle Gordon Brophy knew, but would never have connected him with Duncan. Lyle Gordon was a prototypical Manhattan Hospital surgeon: big, stately, white hair, Mercedes in the hospital lot. He cut a lot of gallbladders out of moneyed bellies. Real Park Avenue practice. Hard to connect him with quick, revved-up, frayed-collared, scaled-down Duncan.

Brophy waited for Duncan to say more about his father, but Duncan became immersed writing a note in Dianne's chart, telling the surgeon to collect a twenty-four-hour urine for calcium and to keep her well hydrated.

Brophy went to the window in the nurses' station and looked out at the Bay. Duncan looked up from his chart and said, "I ever tell you about the time Dick Cecil tried to take away my window?"

He put away Dianne's chart, picked up his knapsack full of journals, and they walked off the ward toward the parking lot. Dick Cecil had discovered that Duncan had an office with a window—and was only a Fellow, whereas Cecil was an associate professor and shared a windowless office with an Ethiopian PhD who was very inoffensive and was thrilled to be at University Hospital, even if it meant sharing an office with Dick. Dick tried to shift Duncan into the windowless office with the Ethiopian, but Duncan went to Lionel. The chief kept

Dick windowless but made him the sole occupant of his very own office.

"I consider it an act of kindness to the Ethiopian," Lionel had said.

Duncan hated the Ethiopian for being shoved into his office, but he liked the window too much to move out. Duncan told this story as they walked along, enjoying reliving his ultimate semitriumph over Dick Cecil and the forces of tastelessness.

"Dick's a blot," he said. "There's all kinds of guys doing research. It all depends who you work with."

"You work with just one guy?"

"Pretty much. You get apprenticed," Duncan said, smiling at Brophy's sad face. "You just have to work with the right guy."

"Who's the right guy?"

"That depends on who the Fellow is."

11

They arrived at the parking lot in front of the hospital. Duncan owned a beat-up VW. He threw his knapsack on the back seat.

"I always bring home at least three journals. Never read 'em. By the time I sail, bring the boat in, have dinner with the kids, talk to my wife, it's bedtime. But if I don't bring 'em home I feel guilty as hell."

He tugged at his tie, unbuttoned his top button, and rolled up his sleeves. He had muscular forearms.

He followed Brophy out of the lot, across the Fox Point Bridge, and up College Hill to Benefit Street. Brophy parked and joined Duncan in the VW.

"Benefit Street." Duncan smiled. "That's where I'd live if I were single."

"It's a pretty street. And it's close to the hospital," Brophy said. "I like all those old-fashioned streetlamps and brick sidewalks." They were roaring down Wickenden Street, past the Portuguese bakeries and onto I-195.

They turned onto the Wampanoag Trail, which runs along the Barrington River. Brophy watched the cars flash by as Duncan accelerated past them.

Duncan lived in a pretty colonial house built in 1779, with the Barrington River Cove for its backyard. His wife was visiting her sister on Cape Cod with the kids. Duncan changed while Brophy packed a bag with food and beer. They they went out to Duncan's boat.

It was a Typhoon, and sat halfway out of the water on a makeshift launch—just two long planks covered with canvas to protect the keel.

Duncan put his shoulder to the bow, Brophy pushed from the other side, and the Typhoon slid easily into the water.

They had to run after it and were in up to their waists before they could pull themselves on board.

Brophy had no idea how to hoist the sail. Duncan was busy down below. He came out of the cabin, lugging an outboard, which he eased down on the rear outboard seat. He told Brophy how to hook the sail to the wire that ran to the top of the mast. The sail came out of a nylon bag, hook by hook, and was up in a minute.

Brophy was very proud of his sail-hoisting.

"Good job," Duncan said.

"I'm making all kinds of progress here at the university," Brophy said.

Duncan started the motor and they puttered out into the middle of the cove. The wind picked up. Then he cut the motor and told Brophy to let out the sail.

Brophy looked around at the brilliant blue sky. There was a chop, and now and then a fine salt spray blew across his face, leaving a salt taste on his lips.

"They don't pay us much," said Duncan, grinning. "But then again, we don't work too hard either."

Duncan had wavy brown hair. His skin was taut and he looked very young.

"How do you like endocrinology, so far?" asked Duncan.

"Don't know. It seems I know less and less about it, the more I read."

"Know the feeling. Why'd you pick it?"

"Went through all the options. Hated the smell of GI bleeders, so gastroenterology was out. Cancer was out, too—everyone dies and there's nothing to do about it."

Duncan's smiled faded momentarily.

"Endocrine looked good. Most everyone gets better. Give 'em insulin, thyroid, whatever—they improve. It seemed, as they say, like a good idea at the time."

Duncan laughed. "What do you think now?"

"I'm nowhere."

"Beg to differ. You're at the world-famous University Hospital. You're a Fellow in Lionel Addison's program. You've come to the mountain top, big boy."

"I'm in a big-time research center and I don't know squat about research." Brophy drained his beer can. "Only question

Addison asked during my interview: 'What're your research interests?' What could I say?"

"You must've said something right."

"Well, here I am."

"Is that all that's bothering you? I thought you had real problems."

Brophy looked at Duncan and smiled.

"There's a million projects," Duncan said, letting out the sail. "Do one you like."

"You're working on cancer . . ."

"Now, that's something you could get in on. There's plenty to do," said Duncan, looking up to his spreader at the top of the mast. "Of course nobody gets better."

Brophy looked at Duncan's face, trying to read it. But it just smiled back at him. "And nobody ever will," said Duncan finally. "If we don't do something about it."

Duncan headed the boat out into the Bay. Brophy handed him a Narragansett beer. Duncan tried hard to relax, but he had the metabolic rate of a terrier.

"It can get to be a pain," Duncan said.

"Checking the calciums?"

"Yes. But then you get some results and you're walking in the footsteps of the giants." He looked over at Brophy, trying to see how Brophy felt about walking in the footsteps.

Brophy tried to look enthusiastic, but visions of Joe Heimler and the Whipple Cancer Wards kept bobbing up before his eyes and sinking to his stomach. The very mention of the words carcinoma, lymphoma, or acute myelocytic leukemia triggered neurons in Brophy's midbrain nausea center.

Duncan could see it in his face. "Jethro's got another project," he said. "I was going to talk to someone about it tomorrow. Jethro's all excited about it: the pregnancy project."

"Pregnancy?"

"He's been dying to get it off the ground, but he hasn't had a Fellow to get it going. He's studied five women on his own. They're just pouring out calcium in their urine."

"Like Dianne Tamborlotti?"

"She's one of the reasons Jethro got interested in what happens to calcium in pregnancy. Women who have hyperpara just go bananas if they get pregnant."

"And make kidney stones?"

"You saw Dianne," said Duncan. "Jethro's hot to study

some normal pregnant women, then go back and study Dianne and figure out what the hell's happening."

"Jethro's doing the study?"

"He wants to do it but he doesn't have time to get it all organized."

Brophy asked what that meant.

"Getting the women to come in for their studies. Keeping them happy."

"And Jethro would let me do it?"

"He'd love it."

The sky was turning a bright pink. It had been a hot day, but it was cool on the Bay, with water jetting by a foot below Brophy's outstretched hand.

"Where do I find the pregnant women?"

"That's all set up. Jethro tied in with this old OB doc, Sol Zigelman."

"Sure Jethro'll let me have it?"

"He'd be delighted," said Duncan. "It's a nice group of subjects to work with, too. Not to mention working with Sol. And he's got a nurse with him make your eyes bug out. Clarissa."

Brophy turned to look directly at Duncan. "Clarissa?"

"Beautiful girl. Redhead."

Brophy stared at him with an attentiveness that made Duncan suddenly uncomfortable.

"Sol's wonderful. Every private OB in Providence hates his guts," Duncan informed him cheerfully.

Brophy chuckled and relaxed.

"Why?"

"Because he's a giant and they're all midgets. Because he isn't afraid to run around with us academic docs. And he uses midwives."

"Quite the radical."

"Definitely . . . for Providence. Anything newer than Lister and antisepsis is considered subversive in Rhode Island."

So it was decided, right there on the Narragansett Bay. Brophy would march into Jethro's office the next day and enlist in the calcium-in-pregnancy effort.

A warm breeze picked up, driving them along. The sun was no longer visible at the waterline, and everything went from pink to crimson. Ten minutes later it was night. Not dark, but night sky, blanketed with stars, more stars than Brophy had ever seen.

"This redhead. You know her?" he asked, opening another beer.

"Works with Sol's all I know."

"It's not a common name."

"She's English or something."

Brophy smiled.

"You know her, don't you?" said Duncan. "From New York?"

"We were neighbors."

"I like her," Duncan said. "Lot of class."

"Yes . . ." said Brophy, far away.

Duncan had one hand on the rudder; the other held the lines and his beer. "Research ain't such a bad life," he said, looking at the sky.

Brophy said nothing. He was drifting someplace else entirely.

12

Brophy spent Friday morning struggling through the papers Duncan had given him from the Section reprint files. The papers divided neatly into two groups. The first emanated from Dick Cecil and the carbohydrate and catecholamine people. Catecholamines like adrenalin oppose the action of insulin, and Dick had the cunning to call them anti-insulin hormones, assuring him a place in the hearts of the editors of the *Journal of Clinical Investigation*.

If there was any practical usefulness to the concept of anti-insulin hormones, it escaped Brophy. It had been useful to Dick Cecil: it got his articles published and it got his name in print. Brophy couldn't imagine how a single patient could benefit from any of Dick's papers. Brophy knew he had to stop thinking like that.

The importance of the second group was easy to see: the papers were all about cancer and the relationship of calcium metabolism to various types of tumors. The calcium articles were fascinating but depressing. There was even an article by Duncan in the *Annals of Internal Medicine*. Duncan had recruited patients into his cancer crusade: they had volunteered for biopsies.

The findings were intriguing: the bones were dissolving, yielding up their calcium. The pain in all those pelvises must have been exquisite. Brophy had done bone marrows with a thin needle back at Manhattan Hospital, on the cancer wards. Getting a hole poked in your bone could really smart. And these patients were already full of cancer and misery.

Brophy could get no further with the papers. Fortunately,

there was a Section meeting that afternoon, so he could leave the library without guilt.

The Section meeting was in the Endocrine Library, which Brophy found after only five wrong turns. The Fellows were all in place, eating sandwiches out of brown bags. The faculty arrived, then the chief walked in and the meeting began.

Lionel Addison worked hard at being informal. He realized he intimidated everyone simply by being Lionel Addison and he wanted people in his Section to relax, to think, and to be critical, but he realized no one could do any of those things with him around. So he slid down in his chair, clasped his hands behind his head, lowered his eyelids, and managed to put no one at ease.

"Jethro," he opened. "You have some cases?" Jethro Brown was not only Duncan's mentor, he was head of calcium for the Section. Brown took out a manila folder. "This is Dianne Tamborlotti," he said, and read off a long series of numbers that evidently described Dianne Tamborlotti to the Endocrine Section.

"Tell the new Fellows something about Dianne," Lionel prodded. "Some history."

Jethro looked blankly at him. Jethro thought his numbers had said all there was to say about the patient. "Dianne's a hyperpara who got fixed by a surgeon, and once her hungry bones blew, damn near crashed and burned."

Somehow that did not clarify things, and Brophy had the feeling Jethro didn't mean it to.

"Now she's pulling a flanking action on us," Jethro was saying. "Went out and got herself knocked up."

It went downhill from there. Jethro employed a mix of martial imagery—they had used all the "big guns" on Dianne—and a bewildering array of numbers, interspersed with letters, the sum of which was totally incomprehensible.

Jethro was particularly amused by Dianne's numbers because they suggested that several rival calcium groups were all wrong in their disagreement with him about calcium dynamics in pregnancy.

"This just leaves them with a gaping hole in their flank." Jethro chortled. "You could drive a tank through it."

Brophy didn't know about all those unfortunates with the bad luck to be at another university, but he did realize that he was no longer listening to what Jethro said, but how he said it.

And he was beginning to dislike the man intensely. He was just too much. Tassled loafers, monogrammed oxford shirt, khaki pants. He had Brophy outprepped, outflanked, and totally in the dark. Remembering that he had told Duncan he would sign on with Jethro for the pregnancy project that very afternoon, Brophy plunged into his own private abyss.

One of the other new Fellows asked a clinical question about the Tamborlotti case. Something about the woman's painful joints. Brophy thought it was a good question and waited for someone to answer. But all around the room, eyes glazed over. The chief started examining his fingernails. Brophy listened for the answer, but the entire mass of faculty had plunged into an acute and profound stupor.

An hour after the conference ended, Brophy stood before the door to Jethro's office, which had JETHRO BROWN, M.D., PHD., lettered on the opaque glass. Brophy went in. It was just big enough to hold Jethro's file cabinets and the desk at which he was working, and it was filled with smoke from Jethro's cigarette and high-decibel Brahms from his cassette player. Screened by the smoke and sound, Jethro sat, his attention riveted on the papers covering his desk.

Brophy cleared his throat with a great roar during an interlude in the Brahms, and Jethro looked up, acknowledging his presence.

"I wonder if I could talk with you about the pregnancy project," Brophy said. "Duncan suggested I might."

Jethro reached over to the cassette player and turned down the volume. "Do you have time now?" he asked. He spoke so softly that for a moment Brophy wasn't sure that he had said the words at all. But he sat down.

One of the lights on the phone started to flash and the intercom buzzed. It was Jethro's wife. "Hi, Tiffanie," he said.

Brophy tried to look as though he weren't listening, but he kept thinking, *Her name's Tiffanie* . . . Tiffanie was fuming about their daughter's ballet teacher. Something had to be done; Jethro had to call. Yes, he would call. . . . He put his hand over the receiver.

"This may take a while," he said. Brophy was already standing. "Would you be good enough to go over and talk to Sol Zigelman? He runs the recruiting. Then we can talk—later."

"Sure," said Brophy, and he walked back across the hall to the Fellows' office, where he called Sol's office. Sol was on Labor and Delivery. His secretary told Brophy how to get there.

13

Brophy pushed through the swinging door on L & D and faced
the floor clerk, perched behind her desk opposite the door. He
asked for Sol Zigelman.

"Room D," she said, nodding at the long hall. "You can
change in there." She nodded to the locker room.

Brophy changed into the blue scrub suit and nonconductive
booties he hadn't worn since medical school. The scrub masks
and caps were in boxes beside the piles of scrub shirts and
pants. He checked himself in the mirror. A real doctor.

Room D was a delivery room. A baby was crowning as
Brophy slid through the door. Clarissa Leonard, gloved and
gowned, was doing the honors. All Brophy could see was her
eyes and ankles.

The father was stroking his wife's hair. Sol Zigelman was
standing behind Clarissa, fingers forming a tent, looking at the
mother.

Then, with a good loud yowl, came the main event. A boy,
looking most indignant. Clarissa handed him to the circulating
nurse, who rated him a 9 Apgar and placed him, squirming, on
the mother's belly. Mother smiled at her son, who went straight
for her breast while Daddy looked both terrified and elated. A
nurse squeezed some yellow antibiotic from an aluminum tube
into Baby's eyes and took him over to the heating lamp. She
put a knit cap on his head. He still looked indignant, even more
so after being taken from the nipple. But he was getting his
required heating. Daddy came over to inspect his son, who
promptly peed an impressive arc of urine right into Daddy's
glowing face.

Sol Zigelman was tearing off his gown and gloves.

"Boys will do it every time," he said to Brophy, as if they had been talking all along. "Pee right in Daddy's eye." Sol pulled off his scrub mask.

Clarissa was suturing the episiotomy.

The nurse wrapped up the baby and carried him off, followed by Daddy, who plainly was not going to let his son out of his sight.

Sol looked after them, then spoke again to Brophy. "They call it bonding." He winked. "Horse manure—love at first sight."

A nurse was pressing on mother's belly. Clarissa was chatting with mother as she sutured.

"She's Clarissa's patient," Sol said. "I'm just a formality. A requirement of the Obstetrical Practice Committee."

"Dr. Brown asked me to come over about the pregnancy project," Brophy said.

Clarissa looked at him. Her hair was tucked up under her scrub cap, and the mask left only her eyes exposed. They were so blue they seemed almost white.

Sol looked at Brophy, not understanding. "Oh—Jethro sent you!" he said suddenly. "You mean the *calcium* project." He laughed and put a big arm around Brophy's shoulder. "*All* our projects are pregnancy projects."

"Of course."

"You're going to help?"

"Yes."

"And what is your name?"

Brophy told him. Clarissa looked over and stopped suturing.

"Jethro's a good man," Sol was saying. "All he needed was a good Fellow to get this thing going. I'll call you tomorrow, with five women," he said, stripping off his nonconductive booties. "Then you call and give them the pitch. It'll be a great project. You'll see."

Clarissa finished suturing the episiotomy and came over, pulling off her rubber gloves. The white powder from inside the gloves dusted her hands. The nurses were helping the mother onto a stretcher.

"Hello, Dr. Brophy," she said, offering her powdery hand. "Hi."

"You two know each other?" Sol inquired.

"We were neighbors"—she spoke to Sol but looked straight

at Brophy—"when I was at Manhattan Hospital. I used to see
Dr. Brophy on the lift every morning."

"The lift?" Sol asked.

"The elevator," Brophy translated. "I lived on twenty-one.
She lived on fourteen."

"You've got quite a memory," Sol said.

"The elevator was the high point of my day."

Clarissa wrinkled the corners of her eyes.

"Come have coffee," she said.

They went out to the nurses' station, Sol still telling Brophy
about all the women he was going to send him.

Clarissa held the mother's chart to her chest, under her
folded arms, while she sipped coffee from a Styrofoam cup.

"Can you *bear* Providence after New York?" She was trying
to talk inconsequentially.

"Haven't been here long enough to say, really."

"Do you live in the City?"

"Benefit Street."

"We're practically neighbors. I shouldn't be surprised to see
you on the lift tomorrow morning." She sipped coffee and
looked over the rim of the cup at Brophy. "Sad, my apartment
doesn't have one, don't you think?"

"You live on the East Side?"

"Yes, off Thayer. Have you found Thayer Street yet?"

"Yes. It's a busy little street."

"It's a lovely little street. The coffee houses with those
sidewalk cafés open Sunday mornings in the summer. You can
see everyone in Providence at the La Maisonnette."

Sol started talking about the project again and Brophy
watched Clarissa.

14

Saturday morning Lars was up early; inflating inner tubes on the lawn in back of the garage—one for himself and one for each of the boys. He intended to devote the day to the care and soaking of his hernia, and he knew that if he spent time bobbing in the Bay in an inner tube, his sons would want to do the same.

Olaf was the first one out. He could see that his father wasn't dressed for tennis, which meant sailing had to be on the Saturday-morning schedule. It was always tennis, sailing, or, rainy Saturdays, shopping. But this morning his father informed him that he would be floating in an inner tube. There was one for Olaf if he wanted it.

"We're not going out?"

"In the boat? Not me. Maybe your mother will take you."

"She never wants to go without you."

"That's up to you and her."

Olaf went back inside to find his mother.

"Why aren't we going out in the boat?"

"Your father's got to soak his—" Beth cut herself off, realizing that if she said "hernia" she'd have to explain what a hernia was, and by the end of the morning, reports of Lars' hernia would be all over Barrington. "—Body," she said finally. "He's aching this morning."

Lars came in to collect some papers and the waterproof floating box, which had an attachment on the side that could hold a glass. Lars filled a glass with tonic water and put the papers in the box, clipping the watertight seal closed.

"How is it this morning?"

"Better. Really . . . it feels better. If I just relax in the water for a day it'll be gone. Water cure."

"Did you pump up tubes for the boys?"

"Pumping hurts, you know? But, yes."

"I may go into Providence this morning. Apex is having a sale."

"What're you looking for?"

"Electric garage-door openers."

"For Chrissake . . ."

"Chrissake nothing. What began all this anyway?"

"I had it before that. I've had it for years."

"Well, I hate getting out in the winter anyway. I want one where you just sit in the car and push the thing and the door opens."

"I can't believe we're buying appliances for my hernia."

Lars went down to the water with his inner tube. Floating was a very pleasant way to spend the morning. The boys decided not to join him and went to the neighbor's house, leaving Lars to soak in peace. The sun was ascending; the sky was blue and cloudless and the water cool. The memos were a bore, but Lars was behind and had to get through them. The past week had been a shambles, mostly because of the pain. It wrecked his concentration and dominated his days. And the pain triggered something else. There was something that happened after the pain—some kind of reaction to it.

But he felt fine now, soaking in the Bay, floating and reading and aching only a little down below.

Beth got home at noon and came down to the dock. She skipped across to the boat and sat above Lars, dangling her legs over the bow.

"No electric garage-door openers."

"Good."

"I met Clarissa on South Main."

"Did you thank her?"

"Yes. She was pissed that Waters was so high-handed with you."

"Did you tell her how much we liked Nancy Barnah?"

"Sure." Beth laughed. "She was saying Nancy is really quite a honcho over at the U.H. She's older than she looks."

"What did we figure—thirty-four?"

"Thirty-seven, Clarissa says."

"Looks younger."

"We have to have Clarissa and Lynn over."

"Call 'em."

"Don't tell Lynn about your run-in with Waters. She'll do an exposé and have him run out of town."

"Now that's a thought."

They had lunch on the deck in back of the house. Lars sat in a canvas chair and Beth talked about playing doubles. After Lars' hernia troubles they hadn't played tennis much.

It was warm on the deck, with the sun beating down. Lars roused himself to get back to his soaking. He walked down to the water and waded out to the inner tube, which floated on its rope off the bow. The water felt cold now after the baking on the sun deck. It numbed his legs, and Lars felt his heart take off, full gallop. He turned back, trying to get out of the water. He was having trouble seeing; his pupils were dilating despite the bright day and the glare off the water. Suddenly he was afraid he might fall into the water and be unable to right himself.

But he made it ashore to the grassy bank. It was only eight steps. Seemed like miles. He knelt on one knee and lowered his head, fighting for consciousness. It all passed in less than a minute. Lars looked around for his watertight floating box filled with memos. He had dropped it in his retreat to shore, and now saw it floating toward the inner tube.

He went after it, easing slowly into the cold water.

There was something about abrupt temperature changes that started things off. Lars thought about it as he pursued the box. There was that time downtown when he had gone out into a scorching afternoon and then returned to the air-conditioned building. It was the same panicky feeling; that's what it felt like, like being very afraid for no reason, until he became afraid of the very feeling, the sweaty, heart-pounding, neck-tightening, inexplicable grip that came out of nowhere.

Lars devoted the rest of the afternoon to intensive soaking. After dinner, he and Beth went out to the deck, sent the boys to bed, and drank gin and tonics until the stars came out. It had been an entire day with only one bad siege. Lars reflected on how long it had been since that had happened.

Beth was wearing old blue jeans, faded, tight, and worn in all the right places.

"Want to go for a swim?" she asked.

Lars thought for a moment about the frigid water and the

impact of that sudden temperature change. "Want to crawl off to bed with me?"

Beth smiled. It was nice to hear. He hadn't been himself since the hernia had flared.

Lars was standing close to her now, unzipping her Levi's, slipping a hand down the back, into the very wet spaces.

"Let's check the boys," Beth said.

They were asleep.

Lars was undressed and between the sheets when she came in. She dropped her clothes on the floor and lay down beside him. His leg slid up between hers, and she reached down to console his sore parts.

"Poor boy . . . feeling better?"

"Don't even notice it."

Lars was in fact noticing very little at that moment except what was going on in front of him, between Beth's legs. She rolled onto her back and Lars shifted on top. As he began to move, he tried to ignore the increasing pain as the thumping and bumping below him accelerated.

He was no longer in control, any more than a boat controls the sea that carries it: she moaned and moved beneath him, slowly building. She was rocking, swelling, falling. He would have no rest until the agitation accelerating within both of them became unbearable. Pain and sweat and squeezing tightness gripped his chest and head, all ignored. He would not stop the pounding, thrusting, deeper, deeper—then stopping, rolling with her, fixed in place. He would not stop for chest or head or whatever might explode within him. Lars held on tight until the storm broke and they lay breathing in the dark.

He didn't sleep that night. He watched his wife sleep but he knew he could not. He was paying the price. The pain, soaked away in the saltwater during the day, had returned to claim him.

15

Sunday morning, Brophy was up early for a run.

It had rained the night before and the street was still wet. Brophy could hear the cars coming from behind, their tires making a swooshing sound. Not that there were many cars at that hour.

Down Benefit Street, with its town houses and expensive restorations, and up George to the campus, all green and lush; through archways and empty quadrangles. Out to Thayer Street, tree-lined and verdant. Nobody stirring except a custodian putting out garbage behind the college refectory. Brophy wondered who produced all that garbage with the students gone for the summer.

He chugged past the dormitories and the science library. At the commercial end of Thayer, a man was selling Sunday papers: the *Times* and the Providence paper. Brophy could see the papers stacked to the ceiling of his station wagon. He looked up as Brophy jogged by, but he could see Brophy wasn't buying. There was a sidewalk café on one of the side streets, and Brophy turned off to see its name. It was La Maisonnette. A waiter wearing a white jacket and blue jeans was drying off the tabletops.

Brophy turned back to Thayer Street. Past the three-block stretch of movie theaters, bookstores, and restaurants, the university began again. He swung around the Thayer Street dorms, vacant in summer, and headed home, where he took a wonderful shower from steaming to cold, then dried, shaved, and dressed. He felt clean and virtuous after his run and shower.

He walked back up to Thayer Street. The station wagon man gave him a *Times* and a Providence paper and change, then said, "You were by here before."

"Yes. Are you here every morning?"

"Just Sundays."

Brophy went to the café, where he was the only one at any table. A waiter came over. He looked as if he'd just rolled out of bed.

"We don't open until nine."

"Fine."

"Would you like to see a menu?"

"Sure."

The trouble with the great American breakfast, Brophy reflected, is the essential choice between carbohydrate and cholesterol. This place had European aspirations. They had a trout and Bloody Mary brunch.

"The cook isn't in yet," the waiter said, "but I can get you the Bloody Mary."

"Hold the vodka."

So Brophy read the *Times* and drank tomato juice. But he couldn't keep his mind on the paper. He kept seeing Sunday morning on Columbus Avenue. They used to walk across the park from the East Side in the summer and sit at tables at Rúelles or at the Museum Café. All he had of New York now was the *Times*.

Thayer Street was coming alive with newspaper buyers, joggers, early morning people. Brophy pretended to read. It was better to watch the street flow. There were women in jogging shorts and T-shirts, and older men—professor types.

A dark-haired coed walked by his table. She was about nineteen and wore high heels and stockings. She was trying to look inconspicuous despite her clothes. Brophy thought she must be wearing what she had on the night before. She had spent the night and now she was walking home. It was a new experience for her and she felt marked. She hadn't gone home for the summer: she was staying in town and growing up. Brophy had done that one summer, after his freshman year.

Brophy folded the "Week in Review" section to control it in the breeze. He watched people for half an hour, searching. Then the waiter brought the trout, which was perfect. After Brophy finished it, the waiter took his plate and brought coffee.

Brophy picked up the Providence paper and started to

separate the sections. There was a headline on the first page, second section, that he couldn't resist: WHERE CARING COMES SECOND.

It was about the General Medical Clinic at U.H., a by-lined story by Lynn Ann Montano: "PROVIDENCE. Mary Giordano worked thirty years in a Providence jewelry factory until the pain in her fingers forced her to retire. Now she sits in a waiting room at University Hospital's General Medical Clinic and the pain is worse than ever."

Mary Giordano was sixty-three, grandmother of six, and had osteoarthritis, which Brophy was sure was somehow going to turn out to be the fault of the General Medical Clinic. It was all so predictable, so humanly interesting. By the end of the first paragraph, Lynn Ann was in high gear: "'It started in my fingers, now it's in my knees. They say it might be in my neck,' said Mrs. Giordano, twisting her handkerchief in her gnarled hands."

It was getting warm and the breeze gusted pleasantly. Brophy wasn't sure he wanted to keep reading, but he was hating it too much to stop. By the second paragraph there was the mention of the shining cars in the doctors' parking lot. Mrs. Giordano had been kept waiting three hours, only to be told that all the doctors had gone home for the day and she'd have to settle for a nurse. The doctors were getting in their shining cars and driving off to their golf clubs, leaving Mrs. Giordano to languish in pain for another day. Lynn Ann didn't say that. She didn't have to.

The University Hospital had hired a hundred brilliant young doctors since the opening of the medical school ten years ago. But they weren't in the business of helping the Mary Giordanos of the world.

If only she had gotten the attention she needed sooner. . . . "If they had caught it in time . . ." Mrs. Giordano was quoted as saying. Had they caught it sooner they could have told her even earlier that there was absolutely nothing they could do for her except give her Motrin and aspirin and all the other drugs that were failing so miserably now, which she said she took faithfully but never did.

The osteoarthritis would have progressed from hand to knee to neck just as relentlessly and probably no less painfully. Of course Lynn Ann didn't mention that. Not much human interest there. Brophy thought he might throw up his good trout all over Lynn Ann's nice by-lined article. He'd roll it up and mail it to her at the paper.

A three-hour wait in a clinic was inexcusable, though—if it were true.

"How can you read that on a full stomach?"

Her voice had come from behind him. Brophy spun around to face Clarissa Leonard. She was fresh-faced, and wearing shorts and a T-shirt, making them look very good.

"Good morning," Brophy said, pushing out the chair opposite him with his foot and motioning.

Clarissa sat down. "I mean it," she said. "It's enough to make you throw up. And Lynn Ann's a friend of mine. I'm being charitable."

"I was ignoring it, really. Just watching the street go by."

"Is there much to watch?"

"Everyone in Providence. But I was hoping to see you."

"So you wouldn't have to ring me up?"

"I wouldn't have to."

"Well, one of us would have. I guess I would have, if you held out." She smiled. "Did you know I was in Providence when you came to see Sol?"

"No."

"And I didn't know you were here."

"No way you could have."

"How long have you been here? July first?"

Brophy nodded and began playing with his coffee spoon, not meeting her eyes.

"Let's not be awkward," Clarissa said finally. "I was glad to see you even though I nearly sewed that poor woman's vagina completely shut."

"You looked pretty composed."

"Did I?" she replied a little distantly. "Did you know it was me under all the masks and gowns?"

"Of course."

"You looked like you knew. But how could you? I mean, all you could see was my eyes. And you were so cool."

"You looked pretty unruffled yourself."

"This isn't getting us anywhere."

Brophy smiled, started to speak, then closed his mouth. Finally he said, "How have you been?"

The corners of her eyes wrinkled.

"I'm fine. Love my job. Sol's a wonderful man. My patients are wonderful. It's worked out."

Brophy thought madly for something to say, running through a half dozen possibilities, discarding them all, finally just saying he was glad to see Clarissa was doing well.

"I lost track of you," he said, "after you left New York."

The waiter came and asked Clarissa if she wanted to order. She asked for coffee and a bagel with cream cheese.

"Went to Yale, straight off. They did a marvelous job of certifying me at Yale. Got a diploma with Yaleness Universitas—masters in nurse midwifery. But no job." Clarissa met Brophy's eyes. "Looked all over for a job. Only places interested in midwives were Indian reservations and Appalachia—and England, of course. I'd rather Appalachia."

Brophy had the feeling he should apologize for her having had such a hard time.

"Finally I gave up. U.H. had a job as head nurse—Labor and Delivery. I grabbed it." The waiter brought her coffee. He said the bagel would be delayed—the toaster was on the fritz. "First night, Sol was there. I liked him. He stomped around like a panda. But he was very nice to his patients."

Brophy laughed—Sol *was* bearlike. Clarissa animalized people: so and so was a ferretface or a toad. She'd called Brophy a stallion, once.

"We got to talking. Sol heard about the midwifery and later called me into a labor room to examine a patient. Asked me how dilated I thought she was. I told him. It's three A.M. He had me assign myself to his delivery. Had me do it. Simple vertex. Nothing to it. The next day he offered me a job."

"Quick."

"Took a year fighting it through the hospital. Obstetricians fighting for deliveries didn't take kindly to Sol's opening doors to midwives. Wouldn't be safe for the good women of Providence, they said—the good women they had in their palms for so many years, you understand."

"Sol must've got popular in a hurry."

"Not with the good physicians of Providence." Clarissa snorted. "Had his malpractice insurance suspended. Suspended his admitting privileges, too, for a while. They were really out to fix him." She shook her head. "They should have known. It only made it a crusade. Lots of university women around here. They weren't about to be cowed by a bunch of private OB docs."

"So Sol won."

"Well, I got privileges. He got a midwife. But they kept after him."

"Everyone I've met speaks very highly of Sol."

Clarissa said nothing.

"Everyone's really excited about the project."

"So is Sol."

"What I can't figure," said Brophy, shifting in his chair, "is what Sol gets out of it."

"Out of the research?" Clarissa laughed. "Sol's sixty-one. Been in practice over thirty years. He's younger-minded than any obstetrician in Providence. First one to use ultrasound. First to invite fathers into the delivery room. Never did knock his patients out for deliveries."

"And the first to use midwives?"

"That too," Clarissa said, appraising Brophy's tone, looking for an irony that wasn't there.

The waiter brought her bagel.

"Well, I'm happy about the project, too," said Brophy, struggling to keep things neutral. "Sure is one hell of a lot happier than the malignancy stuff I'm doing. . . ."

Clarissa met his eyes and waited for him to continue.

"We went to see this patient the other day. The guy didn't know he was in a hospital, much less understand what Duncan was telling him. But there he is, signing to have a hole punched in his pelvis."

"Very informed consent there."

Brophy laughed. "Duncan says that's what we go to church on Sunday for. Lots of consent—not much informed." He shook his head and blew out some air. "These cancer patients are so sick to begin with, and I'm supposed to go in there and have them sign for something that's just going to make them feel worse. For what? So the Section gets another paper published."

"New Knowledge."

"Oh, you've heard that one, too."

"It's a university hospital."

"And who pays the price? Poor suckers."

"Sounds like you're going to have a splendid time."

"Well . . . the pregnancy thing's good."

"We'll be working together."

"I'll like that."

Brophy played with his coffee cup and looked past Clarissa down to Thayer Street, where people were walking, carrying newspapers.

"Sol called me Friday afternoon with four names. I've already talked to three of them. They're all willing. Apparently, if Sol says it's okay, they'll do it."

"It'll be a piece of cake for you," Clarissa said. "At least as far as working with the women. Working with me may be another matter."

Brophy met her eyes, but it was like looking at a photograph.

"It's fate, of course," he said finally.

"Don't think that. It's just a small world—that's all."

16

The earliest Nancy could see Lars on Monday was three-thirty. Her secretary called her at the OR at ten A.M. and left a message that Lars was coming to see her that afternoon. She called her secretary and told her to make sure Admitting held a bed for him.

Nancy had three cases that morning.

She finished by three o'clock and walked back to her office in the main hospital building. Lars and Beth were already there.

"We're back," Beth announced.

Nancy laughed. "I couldn't help but notice."

"It's worse, if anything," Lars told her.

"Are you telling me you want it done, then?"

"You really know how to hurt a guy." Lars smiled. "You want me to say it."

"You've got to make the decision."

Lars asked if she could do it in the ambulatory surgery clinic.

Nancy looked at the blood pressure readings her nurse had taken. No, she wanted him seen by an internist about the blood pressure, and she wanted him prepped properly the night before.

Lars shrugged. "Let's get it over with."

Nancy's nurse drew the admission bloods and sent them to the chem lab. Her secretary sent Lars and Beth over to Admitting to get his forms filled out and to get his plastic ID bracelet.

It was nearly five-thirty. The technician in chemistry was

new to calciums and was just getting around to repeating the high ones. She was running Lars' blood a second time. She had found a high reading the first time.

Brophy was in the Fellows' Office reading *Endocrine Reviews* when Steve Reynolds came in at ten o'clock. Brophy glanced up at the clock as Reynolds set down his briefcase.

Reynolds caught the look and said, "This Fellowship's cutting into my moonlighting."

Reynolds was reputed to be the moonlighting king of U.H. While he was an intern and resident he had acquired a dozen moonlighting jobs which he subcontracted to new Fellows who hadn't been in Providence as long. The new Fellows filled in for Reynolds, who couldn't possibly be in twelve places at once, for which Reynolds allowed them the first 80 percent of whatever the job paid, the remainder going to him. "Finder's fee," Reynolds explained. "Nursing homes. I got all the nursing homes north to Woonsocket and south to East Greenwich."

"Emergency rooms?"

"No. I don't get involved in ERs," Reynolds continued, cleaning his nails with a paper clip. "You spend twelve hours working one of those ERs and you're shot for the next day. Nursing homes are what you want. Take your journals out there, sit in your room, and get paid for reading."

"Don't they call you for things?"

"The nurses bug you a little. Most of it you handle over the phone. I hold the record at Spacious Manor: twelve days running never left the on-call room. Told the nurses how to put down an N-G tube on some old gomer got distended, all over the phone."

Reynolds beamed, proud of his accomplishment.

"They pay your malpractice?"

"No, you have to take care of that for most of these places. Ran me about two thousand last year." Reynolds smiled. "It's a tax writeoff. I made as much off the homes as U.H. paid me to be a resident last year."

Brophy said nothing.

"This year I figure I'm doing pretty bad if I don't double my Fellow's stipend."

"That's real impressive," Brophy said. "Where do you get the time?"

"Well, as I said," grinned Reynolds, "there's always the danger the Fellowship'll cut into my homes. But I've been doing most of Dick's infusions over the weekends, and that makes for a little free time during the week."

"Dick doesn't mind?"

"You have to finesse it," Reynolds told him, looking through his briefcase. "Dick's a real wild man about spending time here."

"Tough to get away?"

"He's always on my ass." Reynolds shook his head. "Getting so bad we may have to live on my wife's income."

Reynolds' wife owned a boutique on South Main Street. She was a great entrepreneur—another shrewd investment, his wife.

But Reynolds was having trouble with Dick Cecil. Dick was one hard system to beat. Dick kept a hawk eye on all his Fellows, and he knew just where to find each one: they had to be up on the CRU, mostly in the infusion rooms.

Reynolds managed to convince Dick that the infusion rooms were too crowded during the weekdays, but Dick couldn't keep an eye on Reynolds when Reynolds wasn't in the rooms. And that made Dick uneasy—he wanted to see his Fellows around. He liked hearing how hard he drove them. And he didn't like the idea that a Fellow might spend less time in the hospital than he did. Dick claimed he never left the Stanford University Hospital for the entire two years of his own Fellowship, and he wasn't about to let his Fellows off easy.

"He always gets in at seven-thirty," said Reynolds. "First one here, last one to leave. Comes in nights. And he really lets you know it."

"He does advertise his dedication."

Reynolds brightened at Brophy's remark. "Dick works harder than anyone in the Section . . . according to Dick."

"How'd you get hooked in with him?"

"Went to medical school here, you know. Dick was my senior-thesis adviser. Got some great results. Wound up getting published in the *J.C.I.* I guess Dick was pretty impressed, senior thesis getting published."

"So you stayed here for internship and residency?"

"The wife has her store and we have a house on the water. You'll have to come out and see us. And Dick was so hot to keep me here. Boy wonder, you know. I'm sort of his protégé . . ."

Brophy smiled.

"So I figured, why go off to Harvard for two years, give up the house and the store, just to move back again for Fellowship?"

"Sounds like you're all set, then."

"Oh yeah. Except Dick's got to be educated. He was a real sweetie all through med school and internship. Now I'm a Fellow, he wants me to win the Nobel Prize by August."

Brophy shook his head and turned his attention back to *Endocrine Reviews.* He hoped Reynolds would just go away— off to some nursing home.

"Now he's got me doing his scut work," said Reynolds to the top of Brophy's head.

Brophy looked up, trying to look less than totally indifferent. Reynolds went on, bemoaning the paperwork Dick had given him. Dick had been asked to review a paper submitted by another endocrine group to a journal where Dick was on the editorial board, and gave it to Reynolds to write the rejection. Brophy couldn't help getting the feeling he was being told all this because Reynolds was subliminally pleased Dick had shown that much confidence in him.

Reynolds hadn't just written a rejection, he had demolished the paper, and he was escalating the description of megaton damage he'd wrought when he was cut short by the door to the office swinging open. Clarissa Leonard came in. She was wearing a white lab coat over her blue scrub suit. The blue looked very striking against her bright hair. Reynolds sat there appreciating her conspicuously.

"Sol gave me this for you," she said, handing Brophy a list of pregnant ladies.

"Sol doesn't waste a lot of time."

Clarissa turned to go, then looked back. "Be sure and get lots of informed consent."

Reynolds crossed and uncrossed his legs. Clarissa didn't seem to know he was there. She left.

"What was *that?*" Reynolds asked.

"Midwife works with Sol."

"Sol Zigelman?"

"Yes."

"You're doing something with Sol? And her?"

"Yes."

"I wouldn't mind doing something with her myself."

"I'll introduce you next time."

"She likes you."

"She's just foolin' around."

"No, she likes you."

"We're old friends."

Duncan came bubbling in and landed in the swivel chair in his office, spinning around with it. Brophy thought the temperature rose a few degrees whenever he entered a room.

"You knew her from before?" Reynolds persisted.

"From New York."

"You've got an in, then," said Reynolds, smiling. "You go out with her?"

"Neighbors . . . we were neighbors."

"That must've been some neighborhood." Reynolds did not look good when he smiled. He had almost no cheekbones, and when he grinned, he looked all teeth.

Dick Cecil stuck his head in the door.

"Hey—where you been?" he barked at Reynolds, glancing at Brophy. "Let's get moving!"

Reynolds jumped out of his seat and left with Dick.

"Yassir!" Duncan rasped when the door had closed behind them. "Jas call me step-'n'-fetch-it!"

Brophy smiled but said nothing.

"That's your Irish smile."

"My what?"

"Your Irish smile. All the potato eaters learned it soon as they got to this country and learned some politics. When you don't want to say it, you just smile."

"Oh."

"Reynolds likes Clarissa," said Duncan. "Licentious bugger."

Brophy looked startled.

"He's married, you know."

"He says his wife's a boutique queen," Brophy commented. "Maybe she's a liberated woman." He stretched and yawned. "It's a new age."

"I've never jumped in the sack with anyone else since I got married." Duncan made the statement without bombast, just simple declaration. "Not that I haven't been tempted. Jesus— I'm not asleep. And have I had the opportunity. . . ."

Brophy wondered why he was being told all this, and marveled at the difference from New York, where anyone who was not having affairs would never admit it.

"He's just talk," said Brophy finally.

"No," said Duncan, shaking his head. "I've heard it from a lot of people."

He looked hard at Brophy. "What I can't figure," said Duncan, "is why noboby's snapped her up."

"Who?"

"Clarissa."

"Maybe she doesn't want to be."

"All it takes to change that's the right guy."

"Maybe the right guy hasn't happened," said Brophy, trying to sound breezy but not managing.

Duncan looked uncomfortable.

"Well," he said finally, "she's young yet."

"She's thirty-two."

"Thirty-two?" said Duncan. "Looks like a kid." He crossed his arms and leaned back in his swivel chair. "What's she been doing?"

"She's been busy."

"She a midwife in England?"

"Grew up there. Her daddy got made chief of Surgery at Michigan when she was about to start college."

"Her daddy's a surgeon?" Duncan said, shaking his head. "No wonder she's screwed up."

"You didn't turn out too badly," said Brophy. "Big-time researcher. Papers in the *Annals*. Of course, you do biopsy a Heimler occasionally."

"You didn't really think I'd go ahead and do that, did you?"

"Didn't you? You got the permission slip signed."

"Brophy, the guy didn't know where he was: *Non compos mentis*. Consent is not enough." He opened his desk drawer and pulled out a paper ripped down the middle and handed the two parts to Brophy. It was the slip Heimler had signed. "This ain't Tuskegee, Brophy."

"Then why go through the whole charade?"

"I get carried away sometimes," smiled Duncan. "But you can't *let* it be a charade. It's just not worth it to risk a whole project trying to learn something from one guy." Duncan smiled. "Remember, big boy, you're still a doctor and these are still patients."

"And I thought you just wanted another case for a paper in the *Annals*, to make Daddy proud."

"Daddy doesn't read the *Annals*," said Duncan, somewhere between apology and bitterness. "He reads the *Dartmouth Alumni Monthly*."

"Now why would he read a rag like that?"

" 'Cause it's got writeups on his dead friends and on his second son. Plays linebacker for the Big Green Machine. Dad played end."

"Don't tell me: second son's going to be a surgeon when he grows up."

Duncan laughed. "He's got too much sense to do that." He was happy again, thinking of his brother. "Dad never got to him. He's an English major."

Brophy looked at Duncan, too small to play football.

Duncan went on about his brother. "He'll be editor of the New York *Times* someday."

"That's what Clarissa did."

"She worked for the *Times?*"

"She was an editor at Random House."

"Editor?"

"They call everyone editors at those places."

"She left that for nursing?"

"She wanted to see the real world."

"But *nursing?*"

"What did she know? She was an editor."

"That when you met her?"

"She was in nursing school."

"And you were a big honcho intern?"

"She wasn't impressed. She'd just got divorced. She wasn't exactly looking to be swept off her feet."

"What'd her husband do?"

"Business. Told her how to dress and how to look and how not to look."

"So they split?"

"And she went to nursing school."

"He probably fucked around on her," Duncan said suddenly. "Like Reynolds."

Brophy looked at Duncan, amused.

"You're kind of tough on Reynolds."

"He deserves it."

"He's having a time of it with Dick."

"Dick's done him a favor. He did a nice project with Dick back in medical school, but he still would've wound up in East Jesus for internship if Dick hadn't put in the word."

"I thought he could've done his internship at Harvard."

"Hardly." Duncan snorted. "From what I hear, he spent his entire four years in med school telling people what a genius he was. Only person who believed him was Dick."

"I thought you said U.H. was a weak place to do your internship."

"Better than what he would've got. And of course, what really counts is he got the U.H. Fellowship, in the end."

"Not a bad deal."

"Lionel almost never takes a U.H. intern for a Fellow. Doesn't think they're well enough trained."

"I still think you're pretty tough on Reynolds."

"I like his wife. Sweet little Italian girl."

"Maybe they have an understanding."

"Don't think so."

"Maybe she understands more than you think."

"Maybe."

"People usually pick up more than they let on."

"How do you know that if they don't tell you?"

"Eventually," said Brophy, "one way or another they tell you."

17

There was a Section conference every Monday afternoon at two-thirty, usually devoted to research topics. One Monday a month there was a clinical case presentation. This Monday, the presentation was by Duncan—a case of thyroid tumor.

He stood at the head of the long conference table with the patient's history outlined on the blackboard behind him. Brophy sat next to Jethro at one side of the table. The chief, Cecil, Reynolds, and some other Fellows sat opposite them. Other Attendings, private practitioners, and Fellows filtered in as Duncan began.

The patient was a forty-year-old bartender who noticed a lump in his neck one morning while shaving. He went to the emergency room at U.H., which referred him to the Endocrine Clinic. Duncan did a thyroid scan, which showed the mass as an area within the thyroid that did not absorb the radioactive iodine tracer, as normal thyroid tissue does. The mass looked ghostly white sitting in all that healthy dark thyroid.

Duncan sent the patient for an ECHO, which revealed the mass was solid, not cystic. That was enough for him, and he called Nancy Barnah, who promptly took the patient to surgery and cut out the tumor. It was medullary carcinoma of the thyroid.

All during the description of the case, there was much shifting about in seats, and several of the Attendings shot furtive glances in Brophy's direction, which made Brophy more and more uncomfortable until he realized they were aimed not at him but at Jethro. It was all very quick and subtle,

76

until Brophy, wondering what the hell they were all looking at, started staring back, which ended it.

Duncan began a review of the literature on medullary CA. Medullary CA was of interest because nobody could say anything really insightful about it, though many had tried. It arose from cells normally present within the thyroid, but which were not involved in making thyroid hormone. In fact, it was not at all clear what those cells were doing in the thyroid gland in the first place. They made a hormone called calcitonin, which was a very nice hormone because it was amenable to measurement, although it had no apparent function in human beings.

"So here's a tumor arising from cells that have no business being in the thyroid making a hormone of indeterminate function," Duncan said. "And the tumor is unpredictable, sometimes killing the patient in months, sometimes lying around indolently for years."

Lots of shifting in seats.

"But with a totally encapsulated tumor, and negative lymph nodes, survival is probably that of the normal life span."

Lots of smiles around the room.

What Duncan really liked about medullary CA, or MCT, as he called it, was its propensity to pour out calcitonin. Any tumor that makes a hormone couldn't be all bad, as far as Duncan was concerned. It was a very nice thing to measure in patients after the MCT had been cut out of their neck, since high levels told you the patient still had tumor smoldering, even if none was visible or palpable. On the other hand, if the calcitonin levels stayed low after surgery, it was very reassuring: no smoke, no fire.

Duncan went on about MCT, eyebrows leaping. Usually MCT popped up as an isolated misfortune, but there were several obscure syndromes in which it surfaced as one of a collection of endocrine gland tumors. One group had the MCT, parathyroid adenoma and a very rare bird, pheochromocytoma.

Brophy knew about pheo, and the word catapulted him back to internship at Manhattan Hospital. Duncan was talking about all the unsubtle ways pheo could kill you, but Brophy was seeing his resident's face turn gray when he heard that Mrs. Philby had a pheo. Unaware she harbored one, they had wheeled Mrs. Philby off to heart surgery, where her pheo exploded. They found the tumor at autopsy.

Duncan was saying that patients who had pheo were usually written off as first-class hypochondriacs because their symptoms—sweats, palpitations, sense of impending doom—were such classic anxiety-attack, nothing-wrong-but-neurosis, symptoms. Mrs. Philby had had palpitations but nothing else.

It was a real one-two-three punch, Duncan was saying; if the pheo didn't get you, the medullary CA eventually would. The parathyroid adenoma wouldn't kill you, but if it raised your calcium high enough, it could do nasty things to your kidneys. It all sounded very exciting, and Brophy would have gone right to the library after conference to read all about it, but he had a date with Clarissa.

It was supposed to be business: they were going to talk about the pregnancy project. Brophy was looking forward to seeing her. He kept telling himself not to be, but she got Reynolds all worked up and Duncan liked her: it was hard to resist all that good press.

Clarissa was heading to the cafeteria to meet Brophy when Lynn Ann Montano showed up on Labor and Delivery. Lynn Ann invited herself to lunch despite Clarissa's discouraging noises.

"Can't I see your new flame?"

"Brophy's an *old* flame. From New York. He's doing a Fellowship here."

"Small world."

"Isn't it?"

They were through the lines and at a table when Brophy arrived, lunch tray in hand. He was properly introduced and took a chair between them. Brophy tried to be subtle about looking at Lynn Ann. He wasn't the only male in the cafeteria having trouble being subtle, but he was the only one annoying Clarissa by his ill-concealed appreciation.

Lynn Ann was dressed simply enough—just a white blouse opened four buttons to the breast and a navy blue skirt. But she was glossy, high-heeled, and distinctive among all the women at the tables—nurses in blue scrub dresses with watches safety-pinned on, and women doctors in white lab coats stuffed with pens.

Brophy looked at her eyes and thought he hadn't seen a woman like her since leaving New York weeks and ages ago. She sparkled beside Clarissa and Brophy didn't stop to analyze how the glitter was achieved, whether it was the gold

necklace or the rings or the eye shadow and long lashes; he just
enjoyed the total effect.

Trying to concentrate on business, Brophy talked about the
project and the women he'd recruited.

Lynn Ann followed him intently, and though he spoke to
Clarissa, his eyes kept wandering back to Lynn Ann, who
looked even more absorbed when he glanced her way. Brophy
got the impression that she was dazzled by his display of
technical vocabulary. She made him feel very accomplished
and important simply by her rapt attention.

"These women," Lynn Ann asked finally, "have to go for
ten days without their milk or vitamins on low-calcium diets?
Each trimester?"

"Sorry to talk shop," Brophy said, thinking she was just
trying to be included.

"No, no—I'm really interested. How can they do without
the calcium? Doesn't it hurt the babies?"

No, Brophy explained, it does not hurt the babies, since the
mother is able to absorb as much calcium as she and the baby
need because her calcium-absorbing hormones are all pumped
up.

"But if she's not eating any calcium . . ."

"Even a low-calcium diet has eight hundred milligrams a
day. You only absorb about three hundred anyway," Brophy
informed her, not totally sure he had those numbers correct.

"This calcium cocktail you give them," Lynn Ann pursued
after some more talk. "How do you know that's not doing
anything to the mother or baby?"

"It's got about as much calcium as four glasses of milk,"
Brophy said, wondering why she was so interested. "The
current dogma is that pregnant women should drink four
glasses a day.

"Jethro wants to know how many women Sol thinks he can
come up with," Brophy said to Clarissa. "We want to be able
to tell the calcium nurse so she can plan her week."

He turned to Lynn Ann. "Sorry. This must have been a bore
for you." He pushed himself away from the table.

"Not at all—I'm all ears."

Brophy looked at his watch and said he had to get going,
although he really had nothing more pressing than his visit to
the library. It just seemed like the thing for a busy researcher to

say. Clarissa was becoming quiet and unresponsive and made Brophy uncomfortable with his impress-Lynn effort.

"Nice to meet you," he said to Lynn, glancing at Clarissa with a weak smile.

"Oh," said Lynn Ann. "Yes. Really."

Lynn Ann looked after him. "Nice teeth," she said. "Delicious mouth. Lies convincingly, too. That's so important to a man."

Clarissa laughed. "I don't think Brophy's ever lied in his life," she said. "He's not dishonest. He's just polite."

Lynn Ann looked doubtful.

"Brophy's a gentleman," Clarissa said. "A romantic and a gentleman."

"I just kept waiting for him to get a little mad."

"I know. He's so nice and sweet and holding-doors-open. I thought he had to be the most boring man I'd ever met."

"So you didn't like him that well?"

"He grew on me." Clarissa laughed. "Finally dawned on me he hated as many people as I did. Often hated the same ones. He just didn't indulge himself by saying anything about it."

"How'd you come to such an insight?"

"Aren't you the investigative reporter?"

"Funny you should say that," said Lynn. "Actually, I wanted to talk to you about some business or I wouldn't have butted into your lunch date."

"Business?"

"The very business of which we just spoke: this project."

"Don't tell me—"

"I've heard things."

"What things?"

"Questions about how safe all this is."

"For Chrissake," Clarissa said, angry now. "They're out to get Sol. You know that."

"Who is?"

"You know damn well who. The same little bird who told you about this dangerous project we're subjecting our patients to. Do I have to guess?"

"I protect my sources," laughed Lynn Ann.

"And we protect our patients," said Clarissa. "The HIC reviewed this project. It's been cleared."

"The Human Investigation Committee—how many consumers on that?"

"Give me a break—consumers. . . ."

"The HIC." Lynn sniffed. "Some group. All of them on staff at U.H. They want to see that research gets done, not stalled."

"Come off it, Lynn," said Clarissa, crumpling her napkin. "There's plenty of privates on the HIC—one of whom is your source. Privates have no stake in research. Half the time they act like they've got a stake in preventing it."

"You're right about one thing," Lynn Ann said. "Your project was not approved unanimously."

"Then you know more about it than I do. And the only way you could know that is if someone on the committee told you. Wouldn't take much to figure out who."

"I'm not saying anything about that," Lynn Ann said quickly. "But that's not the issue."

"Don't give me issues," Clarissa shot back, reddening. "This is an important project—and a safe one. Sol wouldn't do it if he had any doubts and I wouldn't help him if I had any. You're really being used on this one, getting led down the garden path by someone with an ax to grind."

Lynn Ann listened quietly, observing her friend closely.

"You want dirt on research?" Clarissa continued. "Ask Brophy—he's working on a project—cancer—he's got qualms about. But not this one. This one's clean. And it's a good one."

Lynn Ann was smiling now. "Fierce when aroused," she said. "Calm down. I was just probing. It's my job. I know when there's an ax being ground out there when I get a tip. But I had to check it out. Don't worry about your project."

Brophy left the cafeteria and headed directly to the library with his list of references on MCT, Multiple Endocrine Adenomatosis, pheochromocytoma and hyperparathyroidism. He had the articles photocopied within half an hour. Whatever one might think of the University Hospital, the medical school attached to it had a wonderful library.

Duncan was working on his notebook for the hypercalcemia and malignancy project when Brophy got back to the Fellows' Office, where he tossed the articles onto his desk and dropped into his swivel chair, spinning to face Duncan.

"Was it my imagination or was everyone squirmy at conference today?" Brophy asked.

"They were squirmy."

Brophy waited for Duncan to say more, determined to not ask why, but Duncan kept working without looking up from his notebook. Brophy sat there, trying to stare holes in Duncan's head.

"They always get squirmy when medullary CA comes up," said Duncan finally.

"Why?" asked Brophy despite himself.

"Jethro had a thyroid nodule last year. Nancy Barnah cut it out." Duncan looked up, holding Brophy riveted with his smiling blue eyes. "Turned out to be a medullary CA."

18

"He's a private patient." Duncan was looking at the floor number unhappily. It was late Monday afternoon, and they were checking calciums in the chem lab. Brophy was still thinking about Jethro Brown and his medullary CA.

"Don't you feel funny talking about MCT with Jethro sitting there?"

"He loves it," Duncan told him distractedly. Duncan was wavering between calling the floor about the private patient with the high calcium or just going sailing.

"What do you mean, he loves it?"

"It makes everyone so twitchy," Duncan said, looking up the telephone number of the ward with the hypercalcemic patient.

"Did they check his calcitonins afterward?"

"Bet your ass they did! Checked before and after. Worked him up for pheo and hyperpara, too."

"They thought he had MEA?"

"You heard the talk, big boy."

"But his blood pressure and calcium were okay?"

"You heard it. This year he's got MCT, next year, a pheo. Jethro gets checked every six months," Duncan said. "Should we see this one or not?"

"Sure. It's the only one."

Duncan called the floor and asked whom Lars Magnussen belonged to. His face lit up. "Nancy Barnah!" he yelled, slamming down the phone. He charged out of the lab with Brophy in hot pursuit.

"That's good?" shouted Brophy from behind.

"Couldn't be better." Duncan was flying down the stairs. "She does all the endocrine surgery here. Full time." Duncan called back over his shoulder. "Don't even have to ask. We've got *standing* permission."

He was already reading the chart when Brophy arrived, breathless, at the nurses' station on JB-4. Duncan didn't look so happy now. "Thirty years old. In for a hernia repair," he said, shaking his head. "In good health. Probably a hyper-para."

"Thirty?"

"Guy's young, healthy. Of course you can't be sure from these fucking surgical workups. Nancy's note isn't in here yet."

Duncan held up the chart. The note was not conspicuous for its detail; it was less than a page long.

"Not much in here," Brophy commented, looking over the surgical intern's note.

"No past medical history, no review of systems, no medications," Duncan added. "That's surgery for you."

"Surgical intern's not going to knock himself out writing a hernia."

"Not at the *University* Hospital," Duncan said.

"They don't write much at Manhattan Hospital, either, for something like that."

"Surgeons," Duncan went on, shaking his head sadly, "don't know squat about the people they cut on."

"He could have a bleeding disorder for all *they* know," Brophy chimed in, catching the tune.

They were playing "Rag the Surgeon."

"Well, they got a PTT and protime for that," Duncan said. "But this isn't your basic university hospital. Half the time they don't even match in surgery." He looked at Brophy to be sure Brophy showed the proper contempt.

They went to see Lars, who was still dressed in his street clothes, standing by the window and looking out. Beth was in the chair by the bed. The anesthesiologist was leaving as Duncan and Brophy walked in.

Brophy watched Beth scrutinize Duncan while Lars dealt with him. She was smiling, but her eyebrows were pinched together, appraising. Duncan wasn't wearing a white coat, just a pink oxford-cloth shirt, with ragged collar and tie, tugged loose. He hunched his shoulders, shifting his weight from foot to foot like a shortstop about to spring. He was talking fast.

Lars waited for them to take his blood pressure, but Duncan kept asking about his blood calcium, and did he know it was high? Had it ever been high before?

"What calcium? I thought you were here about my blood pressure."

"No, we're here about your calcium."

"Who sent you?"

Duncan took a step back, hesitating. "We check the lab every afternoon for high calciums," he said, tugging on his collar.

"You mean, Dr. Barnah didn't send you?"

"We work with Dr. Barnah," said Duncan, turning very pink. "But she didn't send us to see you specifically."

"I thought you were the doctors Dr. Barnah mentioned. Someone was supposed to see me about my blood pressure."

"No, she hasn't talked to us today," Duncan admitted, edging toward the door. "But maybe she knew about the calcium and was going to call us."

"No. That's not it. It was for my blood pressure," Lars insisted, with an edge. "What do you guys do?" Lars looked Duncan, then Brophy, right in the eye. "Research?" He made research sound like a very embarrassing thing to have to admit to.

"Well," Duncan said, moving closer to Brophy, who blocked his path to the door, "we check out all the calciums and follow up patients who come to the hospital with high blood-calciums." He saw that wasn't having the desired effect—"To find out what's wrong."

"What could that be from?" Beth asked. "Drinking too much milk?"

"Not usually," said Duncan.

"What's the harm of high calcium?" she persisted.

"Well, if it's from hyperparathyroidism, which is a glandular abnormality, it can cause kidney stones, sometimes thinning of the bones—"

"I've never had either," Lars said. "It's just the calcium in my vitamin pills. . . . What do you guys want to do?"

"We could do some tests . . ."

"You mean make me a guinea pig?"

"Lars . . ." Beth began.

"Not interested, guys." He stepped over to hold the door open, through which walked John McCullough. McCullough was the internist Nancy had asked to see Lars, as a consult.

Duncan nodded to McCullough and shot out of the room, dragging Brophy behind him.

"Who were they?" asked McCullough, looking after them.

"Wanted to make me a guinea pig."

McCullough laughed. He was in a hurry. Nancy had called him as he was going out the door. He was trying to get home. He took Lars' blood pressure.

It was 130/90.

McCullough shrugged. "It's a little high. They got it much higher before. You must have been upset."

"Sure was."

"Well, just come see me after you get out. We'll keep an eye on it."

He handed Lars a card and stepped into the hall, where he noted Lars' name and Blue Cross number so he could bill him for taking his blood pressure and giving him his card.

Lars threw the card in the trash can.

19

"Win some, lose some," Brophy told Duncan, who was consoling himself with a Tab and oatmeal cookies in the cafeteria, where they had retreated straight from Lars' room.

"We're never going to get enough tumor," Duncan moaned. "Even if we'd got him, he'd just be a control. He didn't have anything, 'cept maybe hyperpara."

"Things are just slow in the summer."

"No." Duncan shook his head pitifully. "Nobody wants to help."

"Things'll pick up. We'll get patients."

"We'll never isolate the Albright factor," Duncan wailed. Fuller Albright was the chief calcium icon of all time. He'd been dead for years, although nobody in the calcium world would admit it. He'd predicted the existence of a tumor-produced hormone, that raised blood calciums.

"It'll come," Brophy consoled him.

"But we need tumor! Scads of it. Tumor that makes *tons* of factor. My assay's so crude I lose half the cells every pass."

"If you had plenty of tumor, how long before you could isolate the factor?"

"Who knows? Not that long."

"It would be nice to get it," Brophy said, trying to get Duncan enthusiastic again. It was such a departure to see him down.

"Nice? Nice! It'd be fantabulous!" squawked Duncan. "It'd be a tumor marker, like calcitonin. All we'd have to do is draw a little blood to know if Heimler or whoever had tumor, before you could see it, before X ray could pick it up."

Brophy smiled. "You mean a patient might even benefit?"

"This is *very* clinically applicable," Duncan huffed indignantly, "not just as a tumor marker." He raised an eyebrow. "Peter Legos over in Oncology tells me he's got a way to hook antibodies to platelets. And you know what *that* means."

Brophy did not know why hooking antibodies to platelets was so exciting. Duncan looked around for spies from rival calcium groups, then back to Brophy, and said in hushed tones, "If we could make an antibody to the factor, and Legos could hook it to a platelet loaded with chemotherapy, it'd seek out cancer cells like a heat-seeking missile."

"No shit?" Brophy said, eyes widening, unable to be more eloquent in the face of Duncan's stunning revelation. Any tumor cell making the factor would be identifiable and could be destroyed. It wasn't just seeing his name on papers or even walking in the footsteps of the giants: Duncan was in pursuit of a weapon that could turn the tide.

"But hooking antibodies to platelets and all the rest must be pretty far off," said Brophy.

"Every journey begins with a first step," said Duncan. "You don't think I'm putting patients through biopsies 'cause I enjoy sticking people with needles."

Brophy looked at Duncan's pink and for once totally serious face. "We're not making money here. It's not much fun. But we're the last best hope."

20

At seven A.M. Tuesday morning, Nancy Barnah opened Lars Magnussen's chart on JB-4 to check the pre-op workup she had meant to review the night before. The note from McCullough was there, only a paragraph long, with the final line in big letters: PATIENT CLEARED FOR SURGERY. McCullough had done her a favor, seeing Lars on such late notice, but she still didn't like him. The note was inadequate. No mention of the high blood pressure, no physical exam. Just a "BP: 138/94," which Nancy supposed was McCullough's passive-aggressive way of suggesting that she didn't need the consult at all, and, in fact, was just playing "cover your ass" with a hostile-type lawyer patient.

To her surprise, the surgical intern had written a note listing all the tests she told him to order, which were standard pre-op checks:

1. CBC:WBC: 13.1
           Hemoglobin: 14
           Hematocrit: 42
2. Protime: 11.0 with a control of 11.0
3. Pulse 90: Blood Pressure 150/95

He had even written in the numbers to show he really had checked those things, instead of the "WNL" favored by the bulk of the house staff. WNL meant "within normal limits," and at U.H. usually meant the intern hadn't looked up the results at all. Having it all there saved Nancy the time of digging through the chart for the lab slips.

The white blood-cell count was a little high. Probably that was just the stress. Could be Lars was infected. She didn't want to think about that possibility. If he was infected, or became infected later, it would mean prolonging the admission, giving him IV antibiotics, and having him percolating in his room, where she would have to deal with his hostility every day on rounds. Lars had been pleasant enough with her, but he was a man holding himself under control with great effort. He'd get nasty if things didn't go right.

He had no fever, so there was hope.

She checked the order sheet, and, beyond all reasonable expectation, the intern had even written the pre-op orders correctly. In fact, even as she read, Lars was being injected with 50 milligrams of Demerol and given his pre-op enema. Nancy was running behind schedule. She put the chart next to the clerk's telephone so the clerk couldn't miss it, and hurried off to the OR, never noticing what the intern and McCullough had also failed to notice—that Lars had a calcium of 11.4.

A eight A.M., Lars was rolled down the long corridor to the Operating Room Suite. He was met at the door by the anesthesiologist, who rolled him into the induction room, slipped a syringe full of Fentanyl into the rubber hookup on the IV, and asked him to count backward from forty. Lars got to twenty. It was the last thing he remembered.

Just after Nancy Barnah finished exploring Lars Magnussen's inguinal canal, the anesthesiologist told her Lars' blood pressure was soaring. What he actually said was "Uh-oh," a phrase abhorrent to surgeons and scrupulously avoided in the OR. Nancy looked up, not pleased.

"We've got a problem," the anesthesiologist said, collecting himself. He told her about the blood pressure.

"One-ninety over one-twenty?" Nancy repeated. They waited a few minutes to see what the blood pressure would do, and when it fell to normal she went ahead and finished the procedure. The surgery went very smoothly, but the blood pressure surprised her. McCullough, with his magisterial "cleared for surgery," should have had to witness this.

Nancy let the resident close the skin incision and broke scrub, stripping off her rubber gloves and taking Lars' blood pressure herself. It was 90/60. Five minutes later she got 60/40. Now she was really worried. She was really worried because she had no idea what was happening and the anesthesiologist wasn't any comfort. He was pouring in saline and starting a Dopamine drip to bring the pressure back up. There was no reason for all this. Lars hadn't lost more than 50 milliliters of blood; he couldn't be dropping his blood pressure from blood loss. And what about that 190/120 reading? Hard to believe. Lars had been given some Demerol and nitrous oxide, and the Fentanyl, any of which could have played little tricks with blood pressure—but Lars was doing big tricks with his blood pressure.

Lars was waking up.

"How do you feel?" said Nancy, shaking his shoulders as he lay prone on the stretcher.

"Hurts."

"Good," Nancy said before she could edit her own response. He was conscious, feeling pain, and hypotensive. Better than hypotensive and unconscious.

They rolled Lars to the recovery room instead of taking him directly back to his room, where Beth was waiting. They wanted to watch his blood pressure.

Nancy called McCullough, but his secretary said she didn't expect him in until after noon. No, she could not reach him. He was probably sailing. Lars' blood pressure was bouncing around like a yo-yo, and McCullough couldn't be reached.

"Listen," Nancy told the secretary, "I've got to give Grand Rounds in Boston this afternoon, so I won't be able to speak with Dr. McCullough myself. We've had some trouble with Mr. Magnussen. I'd like Dr. McCullough to see him before he's discharged this afternoon. I won't be around to talk to him, but I'll leave a note in the chart."

She considered getting Chuck Mersault or one of the staff people to see Lars. But she had called McCullough in and he'd be properly irate if she switched internists just because she couldn't reach him immediately.

Nancy went back to see Lars, who was still groggy. She told him they had had some problems with his blood pressure, but she had fixed his hernias. She said she wanted him seen by Dr. McCullough before he went home. She wasn't sure he was awake enough to understand, and considered running up to talk to his wife, but her next case was in the OR already and she had to leave Providence by eleven to make the Mass General Conference by noon. She went to do her next case.

At ten forty-five, Nancy got out of the OR and stopped in to say hello to Lars, who was sitting up in the recovery room,

looking pink and happy. She told him to wait to be cleared for
discharge by Dr. McCullough and explained about the blood
pressure. He smiled and said, "Sure, sure." He looked
perfectly fine and his blood pressure had been rock steady at
140/90. Nancy wrote an order to not discharge Lars until
McCullough saw him, then wrote McCullough a note about
what had happened in the OR.

It was five past eleven, and Nancy hadn't even changed out
of her scrub dress. She tore off her clothes in front of her locker
and pulled on her dress, thinking about the fastest way to get to
her car in the hospital lot, then ran out of the Operating Room
Suite.

McCullough didn't get her message until three-thirty, and he
had two patients to see in his office. At four o'clock, Lars
walked out of his room, suitcase in hand, trailed by Beth and
by the head nurse, who wanted him to wait for McCullough or
sign the Against Medical Advice form.

Lars had no intention of doing either. "I've got an
appointment to see him next week," he lied.

He and his wife walked slowly off the floor, into the elevator,
out the door of the hospital, and into the parking lot.

It was a bright, sunny day.

"Born again!" Lars said, inhaling deeply.

"Maybe we should have waited for McCullough," Beth
said.

Lars went on as if she hadn't spoken. "First time in weeks
there's no spasm down there. The lady does nice work!"

"How do you feel?"

"A little nauseated but otherwise great."

They climbed into their Volvo and he stretched out on the
back seat.

"I wish you'd waited for McCullough."

"What's that old fart going to say? 'Here's my card—come
see me—I'll bill you later'?"

Lars lay back in the car with fixed hernias and a great sense
of relief.

21

Lars spent Wednesday basking in his canvas chair on the deck. Nancy called once to ask how he was. She did not upbraid him for skipping out before McCullough could discharge him, and extracted a promise he'd see McCullough about his blood pressure. On Thursday, he was able to have a bowel movement without fear. And Friday night he felt like himself again.

"Jesus, but you were just *foul*," Beth told him, "when you were sick."

"I wasn't sick. I was in pain."

"You just regressed. It was like dealing with a sick child. You were worse than your sons."

"And what's wrong with my sons?"

They were on the sun deck, in canvas chairs, looking out at the Bay and their boat, drinking gin and tonics and watching the sun set.

"You have marvelous sons."

"Princes, both of them."

Beth looked over her shoulder, through the glass door behind her at the boys' room. They were supposed to be asleep.

"You just got so hostile. Not just hostile—paranoid. Downright paranoid!"

"They were trying to cut my belly and take my money."

"Who was? Nancy?"

"'Dr. Barnah' to us mere mortals. Yes, her too. But she can have my money. She was worth it."

"Waters wasn't so bad. He just came on a little strong."

"Arrogant son-of-a-bitch."

"Maybe you didn't regress," Beth said. "Maybe you really are hostile and paranoid. . . ."

Lars reached over and ran his hand from her shoulder down her arm to her breast. She was wearing a sundress, with no bra.

"Tell me I'm hostile."

Beth smiled. It was the first time since his surgery that Lars had acted like his normal horny self.

"You really have to behave better," Beth was saying, still trying to conduct a serious lecture on the virtues of cooperating with doctors, despite Lars' hand, which had slipped down the front of her panties and now roamed between her legs. She glanced over her shoulder again to make sure the twins were still in bed. The sun was almost gone, swallowed by the Bay.

"You might need them again," she said, conscious of her own shortness of breath, induced by Lars' hand between her legs.

"Lars," she said, starting to laugh at her own breathiness. "I'm trying to raise some important issues here."

"You're raising 'em," said Lars, whose erection stiffened his tennis shorts impressively.

"You think they're asleep?"

"My sons? Certainly."

Beth leaned over and unzipped his shorts.

"Think it's all right?"

"Looks fine to me."

"No," laughed Beth, "I mean . . . I don't want you to have a relapse."

"I'll take the chance."

She shifted to his chair, her head in his lap, Lars reaching down over her back, one hand slipping in behind, driving her faster, and the other hand traveling through her fine gold hair. She was being careful—no teeth, all soft parts. She could feel her face turn hot. Everything below her waist was warm, engorged, and moving. But Lars' hand on her head was cool, and the other hand wasn't moving as it had been.

Beth looked up. Lars was pressing his hand to his head. His face glistened white in the moonlight and his lips were colorless. His eyes were squeezed shut.

"Lars!"

"Uh."

"You okay?"

"Okay."

Beth could see the pulse bounding in his neck, and his knit shirt was soaked through with sweat.

"What's wrong? You in pain?"

"Headache . . ." He tried to laugh. "Just started. Isn't that the damnedest . . . oh, dear, I can't—I have a headache . . ."

"Open your eyes."

His eyes fluttered open. The pupils were enormus.

"Oh, God!"

"What's matter?"

"Your eyes . . . and you're all wet. I'm calling a doctor."

"Yeah? Like who?"

"Dr. Barnah."

Lars laughed—a panting laugh. He was breathing thirty times a minute, more than twice the normal rate.

"What're you going to tell her?"

Beth stared at her husband's face in the moonlight. He was not right. He looked as if he'd been bled.

"It's just the moonlight," said Lars. "Let's go inside . . . I'll feel better."

"I'll get you some aspirin."

"Thanks."

When Beth returned with the aspirin, Lars was at the kitchen table with his head resting on his folded arms.

"How is it?"

"Much better," he said, without raising his head.

"Let me call someone."

"Sure," said Lars, with that tough inflection creeping back. "Call McCullough. Tell him your husband's got a headache."

22

Friday night, Brophy did not feel like checking the calciums at eight o'clock, but the prospect of finding a new subject for Duncan to study propelled him labward.

Not that he really cared about walking in the footsteps of Fuller Albright or about harvesting a parathyroid-like hormone-tumor factory. But Duncan was a prince. And Duncan would be overjoyed if Brophy dug up another subject.

He had unearthed five so far, and each time Duncan got more and more excited. He'd hug Brophy's shoulder and say, "We're doing it, big boy. You're making it happen."

He would run around joyously, telling Jethro and Lionel and anyone who'd listen how Brophy was churning out subjects, how the malignancy project had taken off since Brophy arrived, how the team was scoring again and again. Duncan was proud of Brophy.

So Brophy trudged up the stairs to the lab, to check the calciums, when all he wanted was to escape into the soft summer evening. But with each step, he became more disquieted. Brophy truly loved Duncan—but he hated cancer. Why couldn't Duncan work in a nice happy area like pregnancy? Pregnancy was such a happy neoplasm. The women were all rosy, and their growths were welcomed.

But cancer was full of Joe Heimlers. Or, worse, people you could really get to like, hard as you tried not to. What Brophy needed was a way out, some other project to draw him away from cancer, calcium, and all those catastrophic case histories. But so far all he had was Duncan—and Duncan had a cancer fetish.

Daniel Dumfy was spooking around the lab when Brophy arrived.

"Just one tonight," Dumfy said. "I've checked 'em out."

"Oh."

"Heimler," Dumfy said. "I think you already know about him."

"Yes. I saw him just before I came up here."

"He can't last long. He was fifteen today."

Brophy tried to remember if he had written his phone number in Heimler's chart.

Yes, he had left the call-any-time-he-does-it note. Any time, day or night, page Dr. Brophy. And Dr. Brophy would hustle in, hound the intern to call the family for autopsy permission, then rouse the pathology resident to come in and do an autopsy and dig out the tumor.

The next morning, Duncan would dance around when he discovered the tissue frozen on dry ice, waiting for him, waiting to yield up its Albright factor to Duncan's always improving but not yet perfect assay. The assay that could turn the tide in the cancer wars.

Brophy left Dumfy in the lab and took the stairs down to the parking lot. He saw Clarissa walking along the sidewalk ahead of him. She was in her blue scrub dress and wore a navy blue sports jacket. Her legs looked white in the evening light. Brophy walked faster. She heard him coming and turned around.

"Aren't we a pair? Working late."

Brophy smiled. They were not a pair at all.

"Were you in Labor?"

Clarissa laughed. "I was assisting a mother who was in fact in superb labor."

Brophy couldn't think of a thing to say. It was Friday night. He had no plans and doubted she did at that hour. But for all he knew, she was going home to a live-in boyfriend.

Clarissa wrapped her arms around herself and looked at the sky.

"It's going to be a lovely night, don't you think?"

Brophy agreed.

"*Will* you ask me for a drink?"

Brophy hesitated.

"You don't have to, you know."

"I know."

Clarissa turned to go.

"Where can we go, dressed like this?"

"Follow me."

Brophy followed her to the Rusty Scupper, on North Main Street, overlooking the State House. Clarissa didn't look at all self-conscious in her scrub dress. They sat in a booth and watched the white State House dome go purple in twilight. She had a martini. Brophy drank beer.

"You must stop me after one," she said. "My mother always told me to never have more than one martini with a man, unless you don't care *what* happens."

"Do you?"

"Do I what?"

"Do you care what happens?"

She smiled and touched his hand.

"I never stopped."

Brophy met her eyes for a moment, then looked away.

"I know you don't believe that," she said finally.

Brophy smiled and looked past her. He went a long way away.

"Don't be unhappy again," she said.

Brophy looked at her. He was back again.

"Déjà vu," he said.

"You brought it up, talking about caring."

"That *was* asking for it."

"No. It was normal and nice."

"I wasn't trying to be nice."

"I know."

"I was trying to figure out what to do."

"Don't figure. That's always been trouble," she said.

"You're one to talk. You kept the calendar. You were doing the figuring."

"Oh, stop."

"What I could never understand," Brophy said, "was I the blue stars or the gold stars?"

"Stop. Or I'll leave. I really will."

"I just can't remember."

"You remember. You just remember the wrong things."

Brophy sighed.

"I missed you," he said. "New York got lonely after you left."

"I hope you missed me. I hope you weren't lonely."

"Those things are connected."

"They don't have to be."

"But they are, for me," Brophy said, trying to be calm. "I'm just a small-town boy. Never ran around with a crowd."

"My crowd's gotten smaller," Clarissa said. "Walk me home. One martini's done me. I'll leave my car in the lot. Pick it up tomorrow."

"It's a long walk," Brophy said, "and I have a car."

"Give me a lift then."

Clarissa let Brophy pay and they went out to the lot and got into Brophy's car.

"I've never seen your place," she said.

She liked Brophy's place. It was a warm, breezy night, and he opened the windows. The curtains puffed inward with the gusts.

She walked around the living room, touching things she remembered—his old brown couch and the wooden rocking chair with the wicker seat. She looked at the aerial photo of Manhattan which Brophy had framed and set on the mantel above the fireplace. She stopped briefly at the far end of the living room to look out the dormer window and walked into the bedroom, where she patted the old brass bed and looked around at the framed pictures of ducks covering the walls.

She stopped to look at the books in the six-foot-tall bookcase, then went back out to the living room.

"It's got all the equipment," she said. "Even a fireplace. Your stuff looks right here. Not like New York. Those ducks never looked right in city apartments."

Brophy smiled.

"What a lovely view," she said, sitting in the dormer window and looking out over Providence. Brophy turned off the lights so she could look out into the night. For a while she watched the headlights of the cars stream by below on South Main Street, around the traffic circles, and up to the West End, across town.

Then she stood up and unwrapped her scrub dress and let it fall to the floor. Brophy watched her glide across the hardwood floor to where he stood on the oriental rug. She was wearing just panties.

She stood in front of him and began opening his shirt. She concentrated on the buttons as if she were studying how they worked. They were very straightforward buttons.

"It's the martini," she said. "I'm just a simple girl. Not at all flashy. It goes to my head."

She kept undressing him slowly, and quietly, while he stood there, wondering what to do.

"Flashy?" he said finally.

"Not like Lynn Ann."

"She's not all that flashy."

"You liked her."

Brophy couldn't think of a quick and clever reply with Clarissa kissing his chest. Finally he slipped her panties from her hips and watched them slide down her legs to the rug.

She was smooth and silky as ever, inside and out.

"Just a taste of you," she said. "It all comes back."

23

Brophy looked at his watch. It was ten-thirty, Monday morning. He hadn't checked the calciums all weekend, and he was feeling guilty. There might be four hypercalcemics sitting up there on the printout next to the atomic absorption machine, and Brophy hadn't investigated one of them. Duncan was in the lab, working on a technique for growing tumor extracts in cell culture. He had run in and out of the office distractedly and hadn't asked whether or not there were any new prospects on the wards.

Brophy decided the calciums could wait, since he hadn't enlisted any new pregos lately either. He called a name from Sol's list. No answer. The number for the second name was busy. The third was a Mrs. Addinizio. Brophy explained who he was, emphasizing that Sol told him to call.

"Oh, sure. Been waiting to hear from you."

They always sounded like that. Delighted to help. Delighted to come in for a whole morning and sit around urinating on command, drinking distilled water to keep everything flowing, getting veins punctured, trying to keep the toddlers they brought with them from destroying themselves and the calcium room. They were delighted because it was for Sol.

This was Mrs. Addinizio's first pregnancy. She was at the end of her first trimester, and she agreed to come in the next day so they could get one calcium absorption test for each trimester. She was a policewoman on nights, so mornings were no problem.

"Isn't Sol something?" said Mrs. Addinizio. "Complains about everything, trying to act tough."

"He's all bark."

"He's a sweetheart. Just trying to cover. He delivered my sister. He's real excited about this research. Says you're doing a real good job on it."

"Sounds like you had quite a discussion."

"Sol and I are old friends."

"Oh?"

"Stopped him once for rolling past a stop sign. This's before I was pregnant. Get out and see his driver's license and see 'Sol Zigelman, MD,' and say, 'Hey, you delivered my sister!' He says 'Well, give me the ticket anyway if you think I didn't stop.' Let him off with a warning. Told him I figured he was on his way to a delivery. He says, 'I'm going to my daughter's piano recital.'"

Brophy hung up and called the calcium nurse to set up for Mrs. Addinizio. Then he went up to Chemistry.

Daniel Dumfy was spooking around the lab in his Hush Puppies when Brophy arrived.

"Checking the calciums?" Dumfy asked with his benign smile.

Brophy stared at him. What else could he be doing, going through calcium print-outs? Dumfy was like a big friendly kid who had nobody to play with. How could you get snide with Dumfy? How could you say, "No, I'm looking for the racing results. I'm checking my stocks?"

"Yes, Dr. Dumfy—I'm checking the calciums," Brophy said, writing down the name of the one high one.

"Oh," smiled Dumfy, looking very pleased.

He put a hand tenderly on the spectrophotometer. "Ever seen a calcium machine like this one?"

No, Brophy had to admit, he hadn't seen a calcium machine like Dumfy's. Dumfy was very proud of his atomic spectrophotometer, which his technicians hated because it was so tedious.

"How did they do calciums where you were trained before?"

"Don't know," said Brophy, who had never set foot in the lab at Manhattan Hospital. Dumfy started showing Brophy the workings of his wonderful machine and Brophy started edging toward the door.

"It's really the state of the art . . . ." said Brophy, as Brophy disappeared out the door.

It wasn't that Brophy was trying to avoid Dumfy. How could you dislike a man who loved an atomic spectrophotometer so? But Brophy had to get to JB-5 before the house staff discovered that one of their patients, Mr. Sipple, had a calcium of 13.2 and tried to do something about it.

Mr. Sipple was a sixty-four-year-old man with crab in his lung and calcium climbing higher daily, who had been put to bed to die. He had been an investment banker until two weeks before. Mr. Sipple had been driving around in a Mercedes, smoking three packs a day and spending weekends at the Cranston Yacht Club. Then he started to cough up blood, and he spiked a temperature to 100.3 F. He shook violently and got admitted with what everyone thought was a simple pneumonia, until antibiotics cleared the infiltrate in his lung and the big bronchogenic carcinoma became clearly visible on the X ray.

Nobody wanted to have anything to do with him. He was a dead man, just waiting for the chariot to come carry him home.

Brophy, however, wanted something to do with Mr. Sipple. Mr. Sipple had a tube in his penis going to a sterile Foley bag, which would make collecting his urine a snap. He was semi-comatose, which meant there would be no problem keeping him fasting overnight. And he had an IV, which could be turned off for a few hours before Brophy collected the blood in the morning. He even had veins. He hadn't been in the hospital long, so they hadn't clotted off under the daily assault.

Brophy felt very tender toward Mr. Sipple, who was being very cooperative about the whole thing.

There was nothing Brophy hated more than having to wait around a ward all morning while a patient tried to urinate. The bloods had to be collected at the same time the patient urinated, and old men with cancer often kept Brophy waiting all morning. Big prostates. Fear. Who knows why? They just couldn't pee on command. Mr. Sipple, however, had a Foley catheter in. He could just have the urine collected from that. He was a delight.

Consent was a problem. Mr. Sipple was certainly not about to sign. Brophy called Sipple's private doctor, who was trying to see patients in his office and who said, "Sure, anything," and hung up. Brophy paged the intern on Mr. Sipple's case, who was relieved to hear it was just a Fellow who only wanted him to write a few orders. Brophy told the nurses what he needed done and left a note for the night shift.

Duncan was back in the Fellows' Office when Brophy returned. He was overjoyed to learn of Mr. Sipple, and kept pumping Brophy's hand, repeating, "What a team! What a finder!" He took down all the information Brophy had copied from Sipple's chart and entered it into his big black notebook.

"This is your sixth since you started," Duncan said, impressed. "Your first half dozen." He went over the honor roll of Brophy's finds: one breast CA, one renal-cell CA, two lungs, one head-and-neck CA, and a multiple myeloma.

"Can we get a post on this one?" Duncan asked.

"We'd have to get it from his wife."

"Get to know her," Duncan said. "You can't expect to get permission if she's never seen you before and you walk up ten minutes after her husband dies and ask for permission to do an autopsy."

Brophy went to Sipple's ward, put his name and telephone number in the chart, and Duncan's too, so the house staff could call any time Mr. Sipple died. Duncan needed fresh tumor. It began to autolyze within minutes after death. He was trying to extract the parathyroid-like hormone he knew that tumor produced. And Brophy had to get it for him.

"Just think," Duncan said, his face glowing pink, "this guy's got the hormone Fuller Albright predicted. And we're going to extract it! Fuller couldn't do it. They didn't have the filtration columns in those days."

Duncan was gazing off into the distance—toward Calcium Heaven.

"Just think! Fuller Albright's probably up there somewhere looking down at us saying, 'Go for it, Duncan! Go for it, Brophy! Get that hormone. It's in there. That tumor's loaded with it. Prove me right. It's the first step toward the end of the tunnel.'"

Brophy opened his mouth to say something, but Duncan had drifted off, smiling, to a world where only Duncan—and maybe Jethro and the chief—could go.

24

Everyone in the office asked Lars how he was feeling. He had called in before the surgery and said only that he was having "a little operation" and would be in the hospital overnight and back on Monday. So here it was Monday, and he was in the office, and everyone was acting as though he had had major surgery.

"How's the back?" Collier inquired.

"Fine. I'm fine."

"Such a bitch," said Collier. "Having a back go out on you. My doctor gave me Valium. Knocked me on my ass. Didn't do a damn thing for the back."

"They feel useless if they don't give you something," said Lars.

"Didn't do a damn bit of good." Collier wanted to meet with Lars for lunch.

Lars worked through the pile of papers on his desk until eleven-thirty, when Beth called.

"I know you're busy, first day back. But I don't know what to do."

"What is it?"

"Olaf's sick."

"Sick?"

"He was still in bed at nine, all sweaty and feverish."

"Did you take his temperature?"

"A hundred and four."

"Jesus," said Lars, standing up. He sat down again. "Call the pediatrician."

"She said to give him aspirin and fluids."

"When was that?"

"Nine-thirty. He couldn't keep anything down. Threw up most of the aspirin."

"Did you call the doctor back?"

"She said to mash up the aspirin in applesauce."

"So?"

"He threw up the applesauce."

"Is she coming to see him?"

"She wants me to bring Olaf to her office," Beth said, voice quavering. "He's like a rag doll. I don't know what to do. At this point I'm thinking of calling an ambulance."

"Son-of-a-*bitch!*" croaked Lars. "She doesn't make house calls. Drives a fucking Mercedes and can't get in it and drive a couple of miles to our house."

"She said to bring him to her office or take him to the emergency room," said Beth. She was crying now.

"Did you ask her to come to the house?"

"I don't remember what I said. He's really sick. I just took his temperature before I called. It's a hundred and four! His hair's all wet."

"Listen," said Lars, standing up again, running a hand through his hair. "Call her back again and tell her you want her— No, give me her number. I'll call."

Lars got the pediatrician's nurse, who wanted to hear the whole story and then told Lars the doctor had already spoken to his wife and told her to give the child aspirin.

"I *know* what the doctor told my wife," Lars said, "and I asked to speak with the doctor. Are you telling me I can't talk to her—or do I have to drive over there myself, right now?"

The doctor got on the phone. She had a calm and reasonable voice. It was a voice which said she had heard it all before, knew just what the matter was and if you would only calm down, everything would be all right. She dealt with children all day and couldn't make the transition to adults.

"Yes, Lars," she said ever so engagingly. "What can I do for you?"

Lars struggled to bring his voice under control, but it rose an octave and sounded as if someone were strangling him.

"My wife could not get Olaf to keep the aspirin down."

"I asked her to crush the tablets, then mix the tablets—"

"With applesauce. You know what happened to the applesauce. His temperature's a hundred and six."

"My," the pediatrician said with her Romper Room tone. "That *is* high . . ."

"I think he needs to be seen by a doctor."

"It sounds like that might be necessary."

"Will you go see him?"

"I asked your wife to bring him here."

"He's too sick to travel."

"Mr. Magnussen, I have a waiting room full of children."

"Any of 'em got a fever of a hundred and eight?"

"If he's *that* sick, he *has* to travel—either to me or to the hospital."

"You can't go to him?"

"What could I do for him at your house? I couldn't even do a blood count."

Lars said nothing. He hadn't expected her to say she couldn't do anything. When he was a kid, the doctor came to his house. He usually got an injection, and by the time the doctor left, he felt better.

"So you won't see him?"

"I'll be glad to see him—here in my office or at the emergency room," said the pediatrician, sweetly. "Where I can best help him."

Lars slammed the phone down.

His secretary buzzed him. Collier's secretary was on the line, asking if Lars was ready to go to lunch. Lars ran over to Collier's office.

"Jack, I'm going to have to reschedule. My wife just called. My kid's got a fever of a hundred and nine. I better run home for a few minutes."

"Did she call the doctor?"

"She called. I called. The bitch drives a Mercedes; won't even make a house call."

"Jesus."

"The kid's too sick to travel."

"When it rains, it pours. First your back, now this."

"I'm really sorry, Jack," he said. "I shouldn't be long."

"Hey"—Collier laughed—"don't apologize. Go see your kid!"

Lars ran back to his office and put on his suit jacket. His pulse was racing and his temples were throbbing.

The phone buzzed. It was Beth.

"I got hold of Clarissa."

"What'd she say?"

"She'd have a pediatric resident see Olaf in the ER."

"I'm coming home."

"Could you pick up a prescription on the way? Dr. Snyder called it into the Medi Mart on Wampanoag."

"What is it?"

"Compazine suppositories."

"Can't he get that at the hospital?"

"Clarissa said to give him the Compazine, just as Snyder said. If he feels better, he might keep some aspirin down."

That Lars wasn't stopped by the ever-watchful Rhode Island state police was, as he later put it, "providential." He did set a new record for the trip home despite the ten-minute stop at the drugstore.

The Compazine was spectacular. Lars sponged Olaf with a cool washcloth for twenty minutes and then had the boy sip some water.

He was actually drinking. And he got some aspirin down and held it.

An hour later he had a big sweat and his temperature was 99.

"How do you feel, champ?"

"Tired."

"How's the stomach?"

"Okay."

Olaf was drinking broth by two o'clock. Beth watched him gulping down the fluids and sat down next to Lars on Olaf's bed. She buried her face in her hands and cried. Lars put his arms around her shoulder and looked at the flushed face of his son. Olaf handed him the mug and laid his head on his pillow, falling asleep instantly.

"Poor little bugger."

Lars drove back to the office at two-thirty, thinking unkind thoughts about pediatricians and about doctors in general. He had had too much to do with the medical profession and with being unwell, lately. And maybe it was Beth's call when she said it was about "Olaf," but for the first time in a long time he thought about his dead brother.

BOOK TWO

1

Brophy was on Clinical Service during August and September. August first was a Sunday. He offered to take over Friday, and the Fellow who was on service for July was most grateful: he could go directly to his laboratory Monday morning.

Friday morning Brophy arrived at the Fellows' Office, expecting to meet the team of interns, residents, and medical students that was doing the three-week endocrine elective. Instead, the Fellow he was replacing showed up with fifteen 3 × 5 cards. Each had a patient's name stamped on it. He sat down with Brophy and said a few words about each card.

"We're not going around to meet them?" Brophy's voice was incredulous.

"You mean, you and me?" the Fellow asked, not understanding.

"Yes. In person, I mean."

"Why?"

Brophy blinked and tried to think of what to say. Tradition? Courtesy? What could he say without sounding critical and waspish? He considered saying he wanted to be introduced personally to each patient because that's the way they did it at the Manhattan Hospital.

"They've all got interns and residents," said the other Fellow. "Most of these patients aren't going to miss me. Probably don't even know who I am. They see so many docs. Half of 'em aren't smart enough to know an Endrocrine Fellow from an intern."

"Sure," said Brophy. "Thanks."

When the medical students drifted in at nine-thirty, Brophy

111

informed them of the change of command. He asked them how they had done things, how the consults were divided, and about rounds. There were no rounds, except with the Attending to present new cases. The students and house staff never saw the patients or discussed the cases before attending rounds. Brophy informed them they were going on rounds.

"What? Right now?"

"Now."

"But half the group isn't here!"

Brophy told the students to round everyone up, and half an hour later they all went around to meet each patient in the flesh.

The Endocrine Service acquired new patients as consults from interns and residents on the various wards of the hospital. Calls came in to the secretary at the Endocrine Section office from all over the medical, surgical, and obstetrical wards. The consults were entered into the consult book, and the residents, medical students, and Brophy signed off the patients as they saw them. They presented the patients to the faculty attending each morning at attending rounds, which ran from ten-thirty to noon.

Jethro was attending for August.

Brophy spent Friday afternoon reading the charts on his patients and wondering what people in Providence did on weekends. The Fellows rotated weekend call, no matter who was on Clinical Service for the month, and Brophy had this weekend off.

At three o'clock he went to the Endocrine Office to check his mailbox and noticed that a consult had been logged in at two. He was surprised and annoyed that the intern who called it in hadn't paged him about it.

"It's a medical intern, too," Brophy told Duncan. They were in Jethro Brown's lab, where Duncan was running an extraction column, looking for parathyroid-like hormone.

"I could understand if he were a surgeon and had to get back to the OR. But to just call it in to the secretary and not to tell me about it doctor to doctor . . ."

"That intern's probably already cleared out for the weekend," Duncan said. "This ain't the Manhattan Hospital."

"But it's only three-thirty!"

"Here at the University Hospital, doctors are what you call laid back." Duncan snorted. "They start thinking about the weekend on Wednesday."

Brophy was looking at the name of the consult patient on his card.

"How's Heimler doing?" Duncan asked.

"Still alive. I've talked to everyone. They're supposed to call me when he goes."

Duncan twirled his pipette. "You call John Bleir?"

"Who's he?"

"Chief res in path. The path residents aren't usually real eager to come in at two in the A.M. for a stat autopsy just so we can get the tumor before it dies. They're not used to doing anything stat in Pathology. Bleir's been real interested, though. He'll lay down the law for the rest of 'em."

"Okay," Brophy said, shaking his head and laughing. Duncan went over all this tumor-rescue rigmarole three times a week, as if they'd never discussed it before. Then, once a week he'd add some new fail-safe. "But the guy on call this weekend didn't sound like he needed a lot of arm twisting," Brophy added.

"He sounded reasonable?"

"Yes. I told him we needed the tumor within an hour of death. Told him either Heimler or Sipple might buy it this weekend."

"What'd he say?"

"Said okay."

"Even if it happens at two A.M.?"

"I asked him that. He said okay. He's sailing Saturday, but he'll have a beeper."

"Fine," Duncan said, disgusted. "That's terrific: it'll take him two hours to get ashore when Heimler crumps. All the tumor'll autolyze."

With the possible exception of Brophy, nobody at U.H. cared about curing cancer or unlocking the secret of hypercalcemia in cancer patients: not the nurses on the floor, who would forget to call Brophy when Heimler died, taking his tumor with him; not the pathology resident, who'd be sailing hours offshore when they needed him to dig out Heimler's carcinoma; not the interns; and not the residents. None of them had read the original article in the 1943 *New England Journal of Medicine*, in which Fuller Albright set down the postulates Duncan was now attempting to prove. It wasn't their quest.

"How's the cell culture?" Brophy asked soothingly.

"Good. It's good. But we need tumor."

"How about the mice?"

"We'll give them a shot, too." Duncan was growing tumor in special bred-to-grow-tumor mice. So far none of the tumor from human patients had taken. The mice all died of infection, presumably from bacteria carried with the tumor.

"We really need sterile crab to plant in the mice," Duncan said. "We'll have to get some at Surgery."

"I've been checking the OR schedule," Brophy said right on cue, assuring Duncan he hadn't forgotten to look for cases of cancer resections. Then they could have their own tumor garden, and if some of the tumors made the mice hypercalcemic, they might be able to grow their own parathyroid-like hormone.

"I told you about Prizilli," Brophy said. Duncan winced in pain. It was a gnawing, black, burning pain deep in his duodenal bulb that burned whenever he was reminded of lost opportunity. Brophy had called Prizilli twice the past week because two of Prizilli's patients were going to the operating room to have lung tumors cut out—a perfect setup to get clean tumor to implant sterilely into Duncan's mice. Prizilli said no both times. Prizilli had his private practice and his gym privileges. What did he need with Duncan's research? So the mice had to wait in their special sterile cages in the special sterile-cage room at sixty dollars a day sterile-cage-room fee, paid for by Jethro's cancer grant, and no tumor got implanted.

The nude mice had no hair. They had big floppy ears and looked like miniature Dumbos. They had no immune system to defend themselves against implanted tumors; they also couldn't defend themselves against the most innocuous infections. Duncan wouldn't let Brophy in the sterile-cage room, even masked and gowned, if Brophy had so much as sneezed in the prior twenty-four hours.

"You'll kill my mice! You'll *kill* 'em," he would scream. "Go find some tumor. *Stay away from my mice.*"

"It's really discouraging, trying to get tumor from the operating rooms," Brophy said.

"It'll happen," Duncan rasped. "It'll happen—and we'll be there."

"I can't believe I have to see this consult," Brophy said. "I still haven't seen Heimler or Sipple today. And I haven't checked the calciums yet."

"Patients do get in the way," Duncan said slyly, looking up from his pipetting.

Brophy turned red. One month at the University Hospital and he was already trying to figure out how to dodge the living patient so he could dig up some tumor.

"Look what you're doing to me," Brophy rasped.

Duncan cackled maniacally. "What's wrong with this consult?"

"Don't know."

"Maybe he's got tumor," said Duncan, hopefully. "Tumor, hypercalcemia, and a strong desire to contribute his body to medical research."

2

Lars Magnussen hadn't had a chance to think about the weekend, until he woke up Saturday morning and realized it was a beautiful day, and he didn't have to go to work.

"Doesn't feel like August," he said. He was standing by the open window of his bedroom, looking out at his boat bobbing in the water behind his house. Beth was still in bed, and opened an eye.

"It's not humid at all. Feels like September. Look at that sky."

Beth closed her eyes. Lars was in their closet, looking for his tennis shoes. Five minutes later he was dressed, ready to play.

"Rise and shine, star," he said, shaking Beth's shoulder. "We're going to hit the courts."

They dropped the boys off with Beth's mother and were at the tennis courts at ten. The sun was bright, the sky was an intense blue, and there was a cool breeze off the water.

Beth was a superb athlete and kept Lars moving with two-fisted backhands. Her shots came over the net low and hard.

"Twenty-five returns!" Lars announced after one rally, kneading an ache in his left flank. He was soaked with sweat. Beth had him all over the court.

"I can't believe you were counting!"

"No backhand. But I count real well," he said.

Beth headed back toward the base line to serve, and Lars watched her ass, and marveled. Two kids, seven years of marriage, still a splendid ass. She was coming out the bottoms of her shorts.

116

When Beth turned around to serve, Lars was holding his head in both hands. He had dropped his racket and swayed in the sun.

Beth took the net like a high hurdle, reaching him just before he pitched forward. She caught him by the shoulders and eased him to the ground.

"What is it?"

Lars wasn't talking. He just held his head and the blood drained from his face. It took three minutes for him to come around.

"We're going to a doctor."

"I'm fine."

"I'm not listening to 'I'm fine.' We are going to see a doctor."

"I'm okay now. Really. Just haven't played in a while. You're no pushover for an old guy like me."

Beth walked with him to the car, watching him. He looked pinker. Maybe it was just the heat and the overexertion.

But on the way home, Lars was jolted by a pain even he couldn't ignore. Fortunately Beth was driving, although she swerved almost off the road when Lars howled. She pulled over and stared, horrified at her husband, who was arching in the seat next to her.

"Lars!"

"It's my back," he gasped. "Unbelievable."

It was the worst pain he had ever experienced: it began in his back and shot down to his penis. He shook with a violent chill.

"I'm going to be sick."

He did not manage to get the door completely open before he vomited, splattering the inside of the Volvo.

Beth waited for him to be done. As soon as he slumped back into his seat, she reached across, closed his door, and without a word headed for Route 195 and University Hospital.

They didn't even stop him at the emergency room desk.

An orderly helped her get Lars onto a stretcher and wheeled him off to an examining room, while a no-nonsense nurse asked Beth a string of questions with such precision and purpose that Beth didn't have time to panic.

The ER clerk had a dozen Blue Cross-Blue Shield questions. Then they left Beth alone in the waiting room, where she sat down and cried, collected herself, and confronted the clerk again. She asked the clerk if she could see her husband. The clerk was a black-haired, hawk-faced woman of forty, who wore purple-tinted sunglasses. "When the doctors are finished, honey, they'll come for you."

Beth went to the pay phone in the corner of the waiting room to call her parents, but she realized she had left her purse in the car.

"Can I use your phone?" she asked the clerk.

"That's the phone for families." The clerk pointed to the pay phone. "We'd tie up all the lines if everyone used our phones."

There were only three people in the waiting room.

"I left my purse in the car."

The clerk shrugged.

Beth ran out to her Volvo, which was being inspected by a security guard.

"You better move it or we'll tow it."

"My husband's in there!"

"Pull it around back of that building or we tow it."

Beth moved the car and got her purse.

She ran back into the ER waiting room, afraid the doctors had looked for her and left.

"They'll come for you when they're ready, lady," said Hawkface wearily, resting her chin in her hand. She was watching the color television suspended in one corner of the waiting room. The screen was filled with Cary Grant, in some old movie. Beth glanced at it. *North by Northwest* she thought, amazed she could register that detail when her husband was dying in the back of the ER.

Her husband was, in fact, not dying. A medical intern had decided that within minutes after seeing Lars, getting the history of a hot tennis court, no water breaks, pain from back to penis accompanied by a shaking chill. The intern asked Lars to urinate. The urinalysis had blood. Lars was having a kidney stone.

"We'll see if we can see it on a simple belly-film," the intern said. "If not, we'll get an IVP."

Lars didn't ask what an IVP was. He didn't like the sound, but he wasn't in much shape to argue, especially after they gave him the Demerol.

Five minutes after the Demerol, his blood pressure dipped so low he could barely maintain consciousness, an observation which eluded the attention of the orderly who trundled Lars off to X-Ray, down the hall from the ER. The X-ray technician noticed that Lars wasn't helping much when they asked him to lift his hips onto the X-ray table, but they got the film, which showed the stone, and Lars managed the transfer back to the stretcher in a twilight of semiconsciousness. Then they rolled him back to the examining room, where the orderly left him, hypotensive, semicomatose, forgetting to tell the ER nurse that Lars was back. The intern was busy in another room with a young woman who had injected some angel dust into her neck vein.

So Lars was left alone.

Beth was nearing frenzy in the waiting room, trying to call her parents, Clarissa, Dr. Barnah, and Dr. McCullough, in that order. Her parents' line was busy—they were calling around, wondering where Beth and Lars were. Clarissa was playing tennis with Brophy. Dr. Barnah was out of town, but a Dr. Samson was covering for her and the answering service lady said Samson would call back to the ER if they could raise him by beeper. (They thought he might be sailing. If so, he would take a while to call in.) McCullough was being covered by a Dr. White, who was also on a beeper somewhere and hadn't been heard from all morning.

On her way to the lab, in the rear of the emergency room, the nurse peeked in and noticed Lars. On her way back from the lab she went in to ask how he felt. He didn't answer. She tried to take his blood pressure but couldn't hear it. She tried again, got 80/60, and called the intern, who thought it was probably the Demerol, because he couldn't imagine what else it could be.

Beth by now was making enough noise at the clerk's desk that the clerk was moved to buzz back and demand that the intern talk to the wife, stat.

The intern told Beth he thought her husband was passing a kidney stone and disappeared. Then Dr. Samson called back. Beth told him about the kidney stone, and he asked her to ask the clerk to put the intern on the phone. The clerk asked Beth to take a seat until the doctors were finished talking. About five minutes later, the intern came out again, to say Dr. Samson had told him to call a urologist, Dr. Witherspoon.

Beth had had enough. She brushed past the ER clerk, who was too absorbed with Cary Grant to notice. Beth waited with

Lars in the examining room. His blood pressure had normalized, and he was in less pain.

Witherspoon came in about an hour later.

He looked at the belly-film, holding it up to the light over Lars' stretcher, and pointed with a fat finger to the offending stone.

"Doesn't look like much, does it?" He laughed. "But it can cause the worst pain known to man. Worse than labor, they tell me. Of course I couldn't say about that for sure . . ."

Lars tried to smile, but he still had some pain and he hated Witherspoon for being so cheerful.

"We'll put you on the Urology Service upstairs," Witherspoon said happily. "Give you some fluids, painkillers and, hopefully, watch you pass it on your own. Ever had one before? No? Good. Let this be your last."

"What if he doesn't pass it on his own?" asked Beth, afraid to hear the answer.

"It's low enough we can get it without surgery, from below."

Neither Beth nor Lars knew what Witherspoon meant by "from below," but Lars did not like the sound of it. He could imagine several possibilities, and none made him feel any better.

"We may need an IVP," Witherspoon added.

Lars thought he looked pleased by the prospect of the IVP.

"But we can wait on that decision. Right now, it's wait and see."

Witherspoon disappeared, and they rolled Lars off to the elevator, his tennis clothes in a paper bag stamped UNIVERSITY HOSPITAL and his papers from the emergency room shoved under his pillow. On orders from Witherspoon, the nurse started an IV and there was blood on the white blanket under his arm.

Beth rode up in the elevator with him and sat around his room for an hour, making phone calls, until he started to doze off. Then she kissed his forehead, told him she'd come by that evening, and drove home, where she tried calling Clarissa again but got no answer.

3

Beth got no answer because Clarissa was at La Maisonnette with Brophy, drinking sangria from a glass pitcher crammed with fruit and ice. She was having a nice day. She had called Brophy that morning for tennis. Very casual. Brophy told himself it was the wrong thing to do and agreed immediately.

She had played Brophy even, but she had the feeling he could have blown her off the court any time.

She asked him if he missed New York.

"All the time—don't you?"

"At first. Don't think I could go back now. Couldn't take that level of craziness again. Besides"—she laughed—"I like Providence."

Brophy smiled behind the rim of his glass.

"You laugh," she said. "Quite true, though. I love my job. I have friends."

"Who?"

"Lynn—you met her at lunch—and Beth."

"You met them here?"

"Beth was practically my first patient with Sol. Inauspicious start: she miscarried at twenty-two weeks. Lynn was her friend."

"Was?"

"Still is." Clarissa plucked a strawberry from her glass and popped it into her mouth.

"Old school chums," she said. "Now Beth's got a home and kids—she already had two when she miscarried with me—and she's on the PTA and Lynn's a local celebrity."

"She was the one who wrote that awful piece on the medical clinic."

"The same."

"I didn't make the connection at the time, or even when you mentioned her later. Then I picked up the paper this morning, saw her name, and realized who she was. And she's a friend of yours?"

"She's not so bad. She thinks she's doing a service, propagating her misconceptions. Considers herself an investigative reporter."

"Was she investigating the other day at lunch?"

"Sad to say, yes."

"Not sure I want to hear this."

"She's been tipped off the pregnancy project's a fiendish plot to maim and cripple pregnant ladies and their unborn children. You have to watch what you say."

"Who told her that?"

"One of the private OB boys, no doubt. Apparently it was someone on the HIC. I checked to see who was on the committee when they reviewed the project. Had to be Clinton Marsh, one of the real old-time OB boys who hates Sol's guts."

"Did Lynn Ann ask you about it?"

"That's why she was at lunch."

"What did I say at lunch?" Brophy said, agonized, slapping his forehead.

"Nothing. You were fine."

"Think she believed you?"

"Probably."

"Did you tell Sol?"

"Not yet. He'd just fly off the handle."

"Should I tell Jethro?"

"No. Not unless she really gets serious. For now, just cool it or everyone will get nervous and drop the project like a hot potato."

Brophy shook his head.

"Wait till she starts on the malignancy stuff."

"Is she after that, too?"

"I may have let the cat out of the bag," Clarissa said slowly.

"How?"

"Nothing really. I just got hot and told her that the pregnancy project was the one project you really liked. And she immediately asked if you were working on any you didn't like. She may bug you. So be warned."

"Thanks a lot," said Brophy unhappily.

"Well, don't act so betrayed."

"I'm not," he said hostilely, "acting betrayed."

"Besides"—Clarissa sniffed—"at the time, you couldn't take your eyes off her. I'd imagined you'd be happy to hear from her."

"Really?"

"Stop being like that. I didn't tell her anything."

"I didn't say you did."

They finished the sangria and had some small talk, and went home separately.

It wasn't the way either of them really expected the afternoon to end.

4

Monday morning, Brophy checked the consult book at nine-thirty. There was a consult: Urology, Magnussen. And there was a yellow notepad message in his mailbox to see Jethro.

Jethro was in his office, compulsing over his data sheets. "Witherspoon, the urologist, called me about a guy on JB-Three: kidney stone and a calcium of eleven something. No phosphate yet: came in over the weekend. Why don't you see him and present him this morning?"

Brophy couldn't figure whether Jethro didn't like patients or just didn't have the time to fool with them.

"He doesn't get paid to see patients," Duncan had once remarked.

Jethro could spend all day on the phone and in his office with patients, but then his research would die and he'd never get tenure or published or produce New Knowledge.

Brophy went back to the Fellows' Office to put on his white lab coat. He always wore his white coat to see patients, although none of the other Fellows or house officers did. The house staff went to patients *sans* lab coat, wearing just shirt and tie—sometimes without the tie. That was a castratable offense at Manhattan Hospital, where patients were seen in white coats, period.

One of the medical students was reading with his feet propped up on Brophy's desk. He was a "fifth pathway" student. Brophy had never heard of "fifth pathway." Duncan told him the student hadn't been able to get into an American medical school so he had gone to school in Mexico. From there he had transferred to the university when the government decided to withhold funds from any medical school that refused to admit a fixed number of American students studying abroad.

"Fifth pathway students are almost as good as grants," Duncan told him. "They come in for the third and fourth years, and they make every one else look smart."

This fifth pathway student also made everyone else look conscientious. He missed rounds, came late, forgot to look up lab results, and never seemed to know anything about his patients.

"Going to see the new consult?" he asked, seeing Brophy take his white coat off the hook.

"Yes. Just a hypercalcemic."

"Can I come?"

"Sure, Wendel," said Brophy. Why hadn't Wendel already seen the patient if he was so interested? Why wait for Brophy to take him by the hand?

Wendel was dressed as he always dressed: corduroy pants, short-sleeved shirt with an ink stain on the pocket, and Topsiders.

"Want to get your white coat?" Brophy asked.

"I don't have one."

Wendel considered white coats authority symbols potentially damaging to doctor-patient sympatico.

They ran up the stairs to Chemistry. Brophy hoped the six flights might shake Wendel's resolve to tag along, but he just smiled and never asked why Brophy didn't just telephone the lab. They checked the phosphate on Lars Magnussen, which still hadn't been run. He had two calciums back however: 11.2 and 11.4.

Brophy asked Wendel what he thought Magnussen might have.

"Don't know,' shrugged Wendel. "Hypercalcemia, I guess."

Hard to argue with that, Wendel.

They looked over the chart at the nurses' station. It was a typical urology chart: nothing in it. There was a brief note from the Attending and a two-line scrawl from some illegible hand Brophy presumed belonged to a urology resident.

"Now what would we expect to see in a chart on a patient like this?" Brophy asked Wendel.

"A history and a physical exam," Wendel said brightly.

"And what in particular might the history mention?"

That was more than Wendel could fathom: "Now we're playing 'What Am I Thinking.'"

You know all the answers, Wendel.

"Not fair? Okay. I'm thinking I'd like to know whether or not this guy's ever had a stone before or is this his twelfth?"

"Why?"

"Because some otherwise normal people get a single stone and never have another. That wouldn't justify a big-time workup. But if this is his twelfth stone, he might have one of the conditions that are thought to cause stones."

"Oh," Wendel said, already regretting his decision to accompany Brophy.

"And what might those conditions be?"

Wendel considered which conditions might be associated with stones and then brightened. "We're playing 'What Am I Thinking' again."

"Hyperparathyroidism, Wendel," Brophy said. "We are doing endocrine this month. Hyperuricemia, and any condition that can cause the sudden release of urates—like massive tissue breakdown, as following chemotherapy for tumors." Brophy felt a little rush of pride, recalling that last fact from a paper he'd read on the subject Sunday night. "Any of the syndromes that feature hyperpara, like the MEA," Brophy continued happily. "And any of the conditions that cause increased absorption of calcium from the intestine, like sarcoidosis."

Wendel wrinkled his nose. "I could look all that up."

They went to see Lars Magnussen, who was sitting up in bed, feeling better. He hadn't needed Demerol since the injection in the ER. And he had passed the stone Sunday. Brophy recognized him from their previous encounter, when Duncan and he were thrown out.

"We're from Endocrine," Brophy said, introducing Wendel and himself.

"Didn't I meet you last time?"

"Yes. I think I was with Dr. Gordon."

"You do research."

"Yes. But that's not why I'm here now."

"Witherspoon call you?"

"Dr. Jethro Brown asked me to see you because Dr. Witherspoon wanted you seen by an endocrinologist." Brophy felt a little silly going through the chain of telephone and third-hand connections.

"Witherspoon didn't say anything to me about this."

"It was over the weekend, I suppose. But if you'd like to speak with him first, we can come back." Brophy was hoping mightily that Lars would throw him out again.

At that moment, Beth walked in. Brophy saw his chance to escape: "Oh . . . we'll be getting out of your way."

"I'm Beth Magnussen," Beth said, offering her hand and standing between Brophy and the door.

"Witherspoon sent them," Lars said, from behind Brophy. "Never even told me."

"We're with Endocrine," Wendel chimed in happily. Brophy had an impulse to whirl and beat Wendel to the ground, but he smiled and said, "We were just leaving."

"Why did Witherspoon want you to see Lars?" Beth asked. Then, looking at Brophy: "Weren't you here the last time? You told us Lars might get a stone because of his calcium."

"Actually, Dr. Gordon mentioned that. I was with him."

"Is his calcium still high?"

"Yes."

"What's causing that?"

"That's what Dr. Witherspoon and I would like to know."

"You're doing research?"

"I do research. But this is a clinical question."

"I'm not sure I get the distinction."

"I mean I'm not here about a research project this time. I'm here about a specific patient with a specific problem."

"You mean why Lars got this stone?"

"That's one question. There're others. Why should your husband have a high blood-calcium? Does the calcium have anything to do with his stone? Are they both manifestations of the same process?"

"Witherspoon told me it was just from getting dehydrated, playing tennis."

"Could be," Brophy said eagerly, inching toward the door.

"What would you have to do to find out?" Beth asked.

"Research," answered Lars. Beth waved him off, and looked to Brophy.

"I'd need to take a history, and do a physical exam, and then we'd know what we'd need. Usually it's blood and urine tests.

Sometimes we ask patients to swallow calcium and then we draw blood to see how much they've absorbed."

"We're going home today," Lars declared.

"Would this have to be done in the hospital?" Beth asked, ignoring him.

"Some of the urines could be collected at home. The calcium-absorption test has to be done on the CRU outpatient floor."

"CRU?" Beth asked.

Brophy paused, wondering whether or not he should translate or just flee.

"Clinical Research Unit."

"Then it *is* research," Lars said triumphantly.

"Some of the tests are paid for by a research grant. But they are all standard tests for patients with stones."

"They why does a research grant pay for them?"

"Putting them together to study large numbers of patients can qualify as research."

"I'd be studied?" Lars asked.

"Every time you give in a urine for analysis you are being studied."

"But a research grant doesn't pay for my urine test."

"That's true." Brophy was angry himself, now. He was face to face with the legal mind.

"Listen," he said. "Why don't you discuss this with Witherspoon? If you want to investigate this stone, he knows our number."

"Fine," Lars nodded. He had no intention of discussing anything with Witherspoon other than the hour he could be discharged.

Brophy pulled Wendel out of the room and headed back for the Section Office. On the way, he stopped off at Jethro's office to tell him Lars didn't want to be seen.

It was ten-fifteen. Brophy checked his mailbox in the Endocrine Office. There were no messages. Lionel stepped out of his office, which opened into the secretaries' area where the mailboxes were.

"How's that pregnancy thing going?" he asked Brophy.

"We've got about five women, so far."

Lionel went back into his office.

Brophy went to the library. He looked up three articles in the underground stacks and brought them up to the photocopying room at the front of the library. There were eight machines in constant use, but there was no line, and Brophy signed the sheet, filling in the spaces labeled "Grant Number" with the code for Jethro's malignancy grant. It felt good to have credit at the library. Brophy sat down with his three photocopied articles in the sunny newspaper room.

He read the first article and kept an eye on the people reading the papers. The Providence paper was lying on the floor. Someone was reading *The New York Times*, and someone else had *The Boston Globe*.

Brophy looked through the Providence paper. There was nothing by Lynn Ann Montano. While walking back toward the hospital his beeper went off. It was the Section Office. Brophy recognized the secretary's voice. It was Rona. Duncan called her "Wrong Way Rona." Duncan insisted that Rona did not know how to read or write. She could type, however, and the first grant application she typed was accepted, so Lionel kept her on out of superstition. Most things in life were simply beyond her capabilities, especially phone calls. Phone calls required her to talk and push a hold button at the same time. Every time she buzzed Brophy with a call, he'd ask who was calling, and Rona could each time seem puzzled by the question and come back with the name of the caller, having disconnected him in the process.

Brophy could tell Rona was really panicked this time—she had a caller whom she couldn't discourage by disconnecting.

Brophy answered the page from a wall phone just outside the library.

"Where are you?" Rona demanded, her voice rising hysterically.

"Who wants me?"

They went back and forth like that a while until Brophy finally broke down and told her his number.

It was Lynn Ann Montano.

"Donald?" Nobody called him that except people who didn't know him.

"I wonder," Lynn Ann said, low and sweet, "are you free for lunch?"

"I usually don't have time for lunch."

"How about a drink? After work?"

"I presume this is business."

"Half and half." Then, lower, "I'd like to talk to you," she said. "Without a chaperone."

"What's on the agenda?"

"I need to clear up some things—about U.H. You struck me as an articulate, straightforward guy. And you're on the inside."

"I haven't been here long."

"That's one reason I think you'd be reliable. You haven't gotten into the politics. I think I can trust you."

Brophy laughed.

"What's so funny?"

"*You're* worried about trusting *me*."

"I'm just checking sources. If I don't check things out with you, I'll check elsewhere." Then her voice dropped lower. "Of course, I'd like to have that drink. . . ."

"I'm on Clinical Service now. I'm pretty tied up." He thought about Lynn Ann. She was very good looking. She was also a woman who lived in Providence—and not Clarissa Leonard. "How about Friday?"

She paused. Brophy could visualize her checking her calendar.

"Five-thirty?"

"Okay."

"Why don't we meet at La Cantina?"

"Where's that?"

"West End. Little Italy. Very nice. Quiet."

Brophy agreed and hung up, wondering whether or not he should tell Jethro or Duncan.

5

Sweat was pouring out of every pore on his face. A river coursed down his back. Lars sat wet and cold in his air-conditioned office on the fourteenth floor of the Hospital Trust Building with the big window overlooking Providence to his back, and shivered. His secretary buzzed him for an incoming call.

It was Beth, reminding him about her dinner party that night: Seven-thirty—not to be late. He wouldn't be. Lars wasn't working late so often as he used to. He had a raging headache. It had arrived earlier today—this one began at noon.

Lars closed the door to the outer office, then went back to his desk. He opened a drawer and removed a fresh white shirt, undershirt, and towel. He stripped off his wet things, toweled down, and pulled on the dry ones. He changed shirts two or three times a day now.

He wiped off his chair and sat down, feeling better, and swiveled to look out over Providence. He could see down Route 95 all the way to U.H. It looked dark and lifeless from this distance. As he swung around to read the memo on his desk, he caught sight of the picture of Beth and his sons. His boys twinkled back at him from the photo. If people would just leave him alone until five, he could get the memo read. He hoped Collier wouldn't call him in. He hated that now. It made him sweat. And he was out of fresh shirts.

No one bothered Lars until five o'clock, when his secretary buzzed to say goodnight. Happy day—he'd finished reading the memo and the headache was subsiding. He dictated his response to the memo at five-thirty and packed up his attaché case.

He met Collier at the elevator.

"How's the back?"

"Fine. No problem."

"I threw mine out couple years ago. Had me on my back for six weeks. Ever tried to stay on your back for six weeks?"

"Sounds awful."

"Unimaginable. Cruel and unusual punishment. After the third week I though they'd have to commit me."

The elevator came with merciful celerity and released Lars on the first parking level.

"You must get in early," Collier said, holding the door open from inside. "This level's always full by the time I get here in the morning."

Lars smiled and said he got the last space when he was lucky. False modesty, and he knew Collier knew it. Lars had been getting in early because he wanted to make partner at an early age and because most days he was awake by six A.M., heart pounding, feeling as if the world would end momentarily.

"You're putting in too many hours," Collier said. "Get out and get some sun. You're white as a ghost."

Lars smiled and waved. People kept saying that: "White as a ghost . . ."

When Lars got home he found his sons driving Beth crazy. She immediately pushed him out into the backyard with them.

"Just hold them off," she said. "This kitchen's a disaster." She thrust a brown bag full of sandwiches and soda into his hands and commanded him to go for a sail and to take his sons with him. Beth could be very housewifey, especially before a dinner party, and now she was in her put-upon, slaving-over-a-salad-all-day snit.

The boys shot down the dock like hounds who've heard the master taking down the leash, and within seconds were at work in the boat, lugging out the sail and pulling on their life vests.

Lars went to the shed and pulled out the barbecue spit, getting his hands sooty. He unbuttoned his white shirt, smudging charcoal all over it.

"Oh, no!" he heard Olaf wail. He looked at his kids. Olaf was pointing at him. "Aren't we going?" they bellowed in unison.

"In a minute."

He had the coals going quickly and rolled the barbecue onto the patio, below the elevated sun deck. He called to Beth to watch the hot coals.

By the time he reached the boat, Olaf was standing on the bow with the line in his hand and Per was at his station aft. Olaf released the bowline.

Lars sat down in his customary place, to the chagrin of his sons, who wanted him to bring the outboard up from the forward hold.

"We going to drift out?" demanded Olaf.

"It'll take all night," rasped Per.

"What kind of sailors are you guys?" Lars said indignantly. "This is a sailboat."

Two faces clouded simultaneously. Called down for lack of sporting spirit.

The truth was, Lars was afraid to wrestle with the outboard motor. Unconsciously at first, now deliberately, Lars avoided lifting, running, any significant effort. It seemed to trip things off.

Olaf asked permission to run up the colors, which Lars gravely granted, and up went the Stars and Stripes, followed by the red Norwegian, then the white Rhode Island flag.

As soon as the colors were unfurled, Per started digging around in the bag Beth had packed and came up with a beer for Lars and a Dr Pepper for himself and his brother.

Lars looked at the bag, which was brimming with cans. "Who's going to drink all that Dr Pepper?"

The boys averred they would have no trouble finishing the Dr Pepper.

"How can you guys drink that stuff?" their father asked. "Got prune juice in it."

"Terrific stuff," said Olaf, gulping some.

Lars laughed. Olaf had picked up that phrase from him. Lars looked around contentedly at the purple sky, the gray water, and at his two mates.

"You guys ought to learn how to drink beer. Put hair on your chests."

Olaf made a face.

As soon as Lars finished his beer, Olaf dug into the bag and flipped him another.

"You guys trying to get me drunk?"

"Mom said to keep you drinking," Per said. "So your kidneys won't dry out."

"So you won't get another stone," Olaf added.

"So that's it."

"I think *I'm* getting a stone," Per said, digging in the bag for another Dr Pepper.

"Get hydrated," Olaf advised him. Getting hydrated with Dr Pepper was a very appealing notion to the boys.

"You're not getting a stone." Lars laughed. "If you were getting one," he said more seriously, "you'd know it. Nothing subtle about a stone."

Per looked at him solemnly.

"You know what 'subtle' means?" Lars asked.

"Not obvious."

"Correct," Lars said, impressed.

"It hurts, doesn't it?" Olaf asked.

"Yes."

"A lot?"

"Yes."

"Like a broken leg?"

"Worse."

The boys were most impressed by that big a pain. A friend of theirs had fallen off a dirt bike and broken a leg and they had seen him carried off.

"Did Uncle Olaf have a stone?" Olaf asked.

"Why?"

"They took him to the hospital too."

"They take people with all kinds of problems to the hospital."

"Why'd they take him?"

"Because he died."

"Mom told Mrs. O'Neill she thought you were a goner for a while," Per said.

"She did, huh?"

"You turned all pasty white," Olaf said.

"Stones don't kill you," Lars told them. "They just hurt."

The boys continued to ward off stones with Dr Pepper.

"How old were you and Uncle Olaf when you got your own sailboat?"

"Older than you guys." This was a new campaign. "At least eleven."

"Buddy O'Neill got a Sailfish. He's our age," Olaf said.

"Buddy O'Neill's parents haven't always shown the greatest wisdom."

Buddy O'Neill was the kid who fell off the dirt bike.

The boys' shoulders rounded and they heaved a defeated sigh.

They sailed for another half an hour, drinking faithfully and talking about sailing down to Newport. Then they headed for home.

6

Clarissa and Lynn Ann were there when the three Magnussens tied up. The boys were fed and sent off to bed.

Lynn Ann had brought a flaccid-looking editor with horn-rimmed glasses whom Lars hoped for her sake she was not screwing. Clarissa came alone.

They sat out on the patio and drank gin and tonics. The editor started talking about Lynn Ann's articles on U.H. Lars didn't hear how it came up, but he said he was glad to see the newspapers were keeping them honest at the University Hospital.

Clarissa eyed Lynn Ann, who became engrossed with the lime slice in the bottom of her glass. Lynn Ann got up and walked into the kitchen to help Beth while Lars basted the chicken on the barbecue and talked to the editor.

Clarissa pulled up a canvas chair next to them.

"They speak their own language," the editor was saying with a wave of a white, hairless hand. "That's what I love." He rolled his eyes. "A simple itch becomes 'pruritus.' Cold symptoms are 'coryza.' Even a heart attack gets blown up into a 'myocardial infarction.'" He spoke with a lot of motion about the mouth. "Of course, I suppose you can charge a lot more for a myocardial infarction than for a plain ol' heart attack!"

"You're way off base." Clarissa laughed, shaking her head. She sipped her gin.

"Clarissa's being loyal," said Lars.

"Hardly." Clarissa snorted. "What do I owe doctors?"

"But you do take exception?" asked the editor, crossing his legs and leaning forward behind thick-lensed glasses.

"The truth isn't that simple," Clarissa said. "It makes a nice piece to say they're talking medicalese to keep everyone else in place, but I don't believe it. Besides, people can learn a little medicalese if they want to."

"But why should we have to, to talk to the doctor?" the editor demanded, throwing up his hands.

"Every job generates its own language," laughed Clarissa. "Ever try talking to a post office clerk about what class mail you want? Or a mechanic? Or even an insurance salesman?"

"We've got Clarissa's back up," Lynn Ann said, coming up from behind Clarissa with a tray of fresh drinks.

"Far be it from me to defend doctors," said Clarissa. "But if you're going to fire a shot, you might as well aim it."

"Clarissa thinks I'm barking up the wrong tree," Lynn Ann said, winking at her editor. "She wants me to lay off her research."

"*You're* doing research?" Beth asked.

"It's not *my* research," Clarissa said. "I just help out. It's Sol's project." She turned to Lynn Ann: "And Brophy's."

"Brophy?" Lars asked, surprised.

"Know him?" asked Lynn Ann.

"I've had the misfortune," said Lars, caught. "Had a kidney stone. Wound up at U.H. This guy Brophy comes by and tries to rope me into a research study."

Clarissa stared at Beth, amazed to be hearing of this only now.

"And you're just in for a kidney stone?" said the editor, raising an eyebrow.

"I told him to look elsewhere for his guinea pigs."

"Looks like we're barking up precisely the right tree," said the editor. "Of course you weren't intimidated by the white coat," he added, expanding his remarks to the group. "But think of all the other patients. This is a blue-collar town. Doctor comes in and says, 'Do this, bend over, give blood,' most of the poor schnooks ask no questions."

"I don't know when was the last time you had to ask people for permission to do research on them," Clarissa said, draining her drink, "but that hasn't been my experience."

The editor turned to look at her, eyes magnified behind his lenses.

"Most people ask plenty," Clarissa continued. "They just don't listen to the answers."

"What's Brophy doing?" asked Beth.

"Don't know everything he does. He's doing one study with Sol on calcium metabolism in pregnancy."

"I don't think that's what he wanted me for," Lars said dryly.

"You never know . . ." the editor shrieked.

You are the soul of wit, Clarissa thought.

"He said Lars' calcium was high," Beth remarked. Lars shot her a look, but she didn't catch it and she pressed Clarissa: "What could that mean?"

"Probably means he wanted to scare Lars into signing up!" The editor snorted, then looked around for the others to join in. No one did.

Clarissa shrugged. "I'm just a humble nurse-midwife. What did Brophy say?"

"He started talking about some kind of thyroid glands. I couldn't follow."

"She couldn't follow," the editor said. "There you are. . . ."

"Parathyroid glands," Lars said. "I looked it up."

"Is Brophy a mad scientist?" the editor asked with a lilt. "Running around in the dead of night, trying to cut glands out of unsuspecting patients?"

"Hardly," Clarissa said.

Lynn Ann glanced over and caught Clarissa's eye.

"He's a decent guy," Clarissa continued. "He's not eager to push anyone into anything."

"Was he pushy with you?" the editor asked Lars.

"No," Beth said quickly, before her husband could answer.

"No . . ." Lars echoed, still looking at Clarissa.

"He was very polite," Beth said. "I had the feeling he was almost relieved we turned him down."

"Really?" Lynn Ann said. "How curious."

7

There were three pituitary protocol patients scheduled for admission to the in-patient part of the Clinical Research Center, Friday afternoon. Brophy had been on service a week, and these were his first protocol patients. They were coming in for "pit stops"—the routine follow-up done on all patients at yearly intervals after pituitary surgery. It was part of a study to evaluate the safety, long-term effects, and effectiveness of surgery for various kinds of pituitary tumor.

The patients had firm and incontrovertible instructions from the pituitary nurse to get to the in-patient CRU by three o'clock. The pit nurse considered Endocrine Fellows unnecessary and burdensome. Her name was Sylvia, and she had platinum blond hair and dark roots. She was not happy to hear from Brophy at four P.M. because Brophy was an Endocrine Fellow and because she knew he was going to complain about the absent protocol patients, just as every Endocrine Fellow before him had complained.

"Sorry to bother you, Sylvia."

Sylvia rolled her eyes. "Brophy, if you were so sorry, you wouldn't have bothered me."

"The thing is, none of the pit patients have shown, and a fourth just got penciled in on the admitting list."

"What can I do, Brophy? I tell them. What do you expect me to do?"

Don't mouth off. This isn't New York. You're upset because it's Friday afternoon and you have to meet Lynn Ann Montano at five-thirty and that's going to be tough if you have to wait for all the patients to show up.

"Sorry," he said. "I guess you get tried of hearing about it, too."

"That's okay, Brophy."

She actually sounded friendly. Almost sweet. *The soft answer turneth away wrath.*

Sylvia told Brophy there was nothing she could do. She had asked them to be in their rooms by three o'clock, but most people wanted to finish their day's work and come in after five. Some of them even went home for dinner and wouldn't roll in until nine or ten. They did that no matter what Sylvia said. Most of the protocol patients had had at least one pit stop and knew nothing happened the first night except that they had a physical exam and got some blood drawn. Those who arrived early enough went to Eye Clinic. There was no big rush as far as the patients were concerned.

Brophy sat there, acid forming in his stomach. Didn't the patients realize that someone had to examine them? Didn't they realize the later they came in, the later Brophy would be there, writing his note, signing all the pre-printed orders?

"Write your note now," Sylvia advised. "The history's in the chart. Fill in the physical exam later. And don't forget to write passes for the weekend for them or you'll get paged first thing Saturday morning when somebody wants to go shopping with her family.

"These people aren't sick," she added. "Don't make them feel sick. They've had their surgery. Now they're having their follow-up. No big deal."

"Then why do I have to hang around and admit them?"

"It's the protocol. If they do it by the rules, we all get paid. The grant covers it. Do it as an outpatient, it'll cost somebody a bundle."

"It's costing somebody a bundle this way."

"It's not costing Neurosurgery. It's not costing Endocrine. And it's not costing the patients."

Brophy closed his mouth with a truly heroic effort and said nothing.

"Look," Sylvia said, "you don't have to wait around for them. Come back after dinner, around eight, and see them then. They'll all be in by then."

"What if one of them has an MI before then?"

"Brophy"—Sylvia laughed—"these are four young women under the age of thirty-five. Nobody's going to have a heart attack. These ladies had little tumors in their pituitary glands. Relax. Go eat dinner."

Brophy waited until five-thirty and realized she was probably right.

"Do the other Fellows see the patients as soon as they hit the floor or do they come in late in the evening?" Brophy asked the charge nurse.

"Usually, the patients get in to eat dinner. Then, around eight, the Fellow rolls in."

They couldn't all be wrong. It wasn't the Manhattan Hospital way, but it was hard to argue with. So what if a patient sat on the ward for two hours before a doctor even shook her hand just to see she was still breathing? This was research. These were subjects.

Brophy went out to the doctors' parking lot, testing his beeper several times along the way just in case. Just in case one of those sub-thirty-five-year-old ladies hit the floor and had a cardiac arrest and they had to reach him fast.

No one beeped. Brophy headed toward the West End. One of the Endocrine secretaries had given him the directions to La Cantina.

The parking lot was full, but the place looked quiet from the outside. A tuxedoed maître d' showed him to Lynn Ann's table, and kept saying, "Oh, yes, *Doctor* Brophy. Right this way, *Doctor* Brophy. . . ."

Lynn Ann was sitting in a booth, wearing a white blouse, opened very deep. She was drinking a Manhattan.

"That's quite all right," she greeted him. "Don't apologize."

Brophy looked at her blankly.

"Doctors are always late"—she smiled—"and always forgiven."

"Good to hear, coming from you."

A woman in black mesh stockings took Brophy's order.

"Have any trouble finding this place?"

"No. Just got held up at U.H."

"What is it you do over there, exactly?"

"Right now I'm on the Clinical Service."

"Meaning?"

"Meaning I take care of all the endocrine patients."

"How is that different from what you normally do?"

Brophy laughed.

"Do you always ask questions when you already know the answers? Or just when you're checking up?"

"What makes you think I know what you normally do?"

"You're Clarissa Leonard's friend."

"I know what Clarissa does. I don't know what it is *you* do."

"When I'm not taking care of patients"—Brophy smiled—"I am pushing back the frontiers of medical knowledge."

Lynn Ann laughed. "Is that it? I imagine that noble pursuit allows for all kinds of license."

"Why?"

"It's so important—such a quest."

"Most people seem to think of it as a career."

"Who do you work with?"

"Funny you should ask that."

"Why?"

"Everyone else has been asking me the same thing."

"And what do you tell them?"

"Recently I've been saying Jethro Brown and Duncan Gordon."

"They're on the faculty?"

"Jethro is. Duncan is a Fellow, like me."

"They do research?"

"Whenever possible."

"And you work with Sol Zigelman on the pregnancy thing?"

"There you go again—asking questions when you already know the answers."

Lynn laughed again. "You seem so candid. That always worries me whe I'm looking for the truth."

"What is it you want to know?"

"People call me all the time. Most of them have axes to grind." She sippepd her drink again, peering over the rim of her glass at Brophy.

Brophy's beer arrived.

"Sol Zigelman's got lots of people who don't like him much in this town."

"And lots who do."

"Like who?"

"Like me, and Clarissa, and Lionel Addison."

"Addison doesn't count. He's chief of your department. Anyway, he's no help. Never returns my calls."

"Call often?"

Lynn smiled and went back to Sol.

"He's a maverick. I hear about everything he does. Now it's this pregnancy research."

"What do you hear?"

"That Sol's telling pregnant women to not drink their milk. That they're getting some radioactive drink each trimester so Sol can study the effects of calcium privation."

Brophy laughed, relieved. "Is that all?"

"Sounds like quite enough, doesn't it?"

"If it were true."

"It's not?"

"Just a matter of doing your homework."

"I'm doing it now."

"Get the protocol. Read it."

"Protocol?"

"Any time research is done on any human being, the researcher has to submit a proposal detailing what he or she wants to do to the patients, the risks, and the reasons," said Brophy, watching Lynn, who appeared quite absorbed. "The protocol has to be approved by the Human Investigation Committee, which certifies everything's safe and sound."

"Who's on the committee?"

"Don't ask me. I've never seen it."

"Then how do you know there even is such a committee?"

"Because I've seen the protocols. They're pages long. Nobody'd bother to write 'em if they figured nobody'd read 'em. And there's a front page with approval and disapproval signatures all over it. There's a committee, all right."

"Where would I get the protocol for the pregnancy project?"

"Call the hospital. I imagine they're a matter of public record. . . . Look," Brophy said, "I don't understand why you called me. You could have gotten all this from Clarissa."

"Maybe I just wanted a date."

"You're looking for something," he said, "but not for that. Not from me."

"What makes you so sure?"

"My rich and varied experience with women."

"I see." Lynn Ann laughed. "You're at least half right. Nobody over there will talk to me. I don't think you're all a bunch of mad scientists."

"Well, that's progress."

"I never thought that. There's no change in my opinion."

"What do you think?"

"That U.H. is no different from any other place in Providence. There are stories there, good and bad. But they look so damn suspicious, stonewalling when they don't have to."

"I hear they've been burned, being cooperative."

"I'd very much like to hear the particulars. When? Who burned them?"

"I'm new here. I just hear things."

"What things?"

Brophy shrugged. "And I read things. Like your piece on the General Medical Clinic."

"Yes?"

"You made the clinic the villain. They didn't give that old woman her arthritis."

"I didn't say they did," Lynn Ann said, a little indignant. "You know much about the clinic? Know anyone who works there?"

"No."

"Maybe you ought to do some homework," she said without anger. "It's run by the Department of General Internal Medicine. Bunch of deadbeats trying to pass themselves off as some kind of experts in 'ambulatory medicine.' There are six doctors in that department—the chief, the head of the emergency room, the head of the clinics, and three young guys just out of residency. The chief and his two heads never lay a hand on a patient. They were hired to see patients and get those outpatient areas going. They spend their time giving lectures to undergrads or doing 'consult work,' moonlighting really, during working hours."

"Sounds like a fine bunch," Brophy said.

"That's not the half of it," Lynn Ann continued, her neck growing blotchy red. "You think I wanted to write that human interest garbage about Mrs. Giordano and her thirty years in the jewelry factory?" She leaned forward. "I wanted to blow those bastards away. But I couldn't. I got the tip from someone on the inside."

"A doc?"

"It was confidential, off the record. I couldn't use it, and it was good stuff. But I couldn't risk getting my source in trouble."

Brophy grinned. "I feel much safer now."

"I suppose I deserved that. . . ."

She pulled back her chair and sat straight up, chin rising.

Brophy thought about the patients arriving at the CRU. He glanced down at his watch.

"Am I keeping you?"

"I've got time. Have to be back at eight."

"Do you like your Fellowship?"

"Haven't seen much of it yet."

"Where'd you train? New York, Clarissa said. Where she went to nursing school."

"Yes."

"You knew her?"

"It was really a small town, the hospital."

"Miss New York?"

"Mostly at night."

"And you like research?"

"Not really. I hated the whole idea at first. But I'm on Clinical Service now. Only research I do is calling up the pregnant ladies to come in and harvesting cancer patients with high blood-calciums."

"Harvesting? What an expression. You sound like the grim reaper."

Brophy laughed, relaxing.

"Feel like it sometimes. The patients are usually pretty far gone by the time I get to them."

"What do you do with your crop once it's harvested?"

"Usually help the interns and residents treat the high calciums and ask the patients to give blood and urine for our studies."

"Do they go along?"

"Sometimes. Most of them have read the newspapers about being guinea pigs." Brophy eyed Lynn. "But if we take the time to explain things, they often agree to the tests."

"You think they really understand what you tell them?"

Brophy thought for a moment. "You know, that's hard to say. . . . There was a study done about patients going to surgery. Before the operation, the surgeon tape-recorded himself warning the patients of all the possible risks. The patients all said yes, they understood. Afterward the surgeon went back and asked the patients what they had been told about the risks, pre-op. Not one remembered ever having been told anything."

"I find that difficult to believe."

"I don't," Brophy said, taking a gulp of beer.

"So you think it really doesn't matter what you do or don't tell them?"

"I didn't say that."

"But you implied it."

"I try to make the patients understand what I'm asking them to sign for."

"What if they just can't understand?"

"That's a problem sometimes," Brophy said, looking Lynn Ann directly in the eye. "But Rhode Island isn't Tuskegee. . . ."

Lynn Ann smiled and tilted her head. She looked very good in the light of the bar.

"Tuskegee . . . nice touch," she said. "Very disarming."

8

Saturday morning, Brophy woke up unhappy. It was already warm at nine o'clock, but a cool breeze blew across his bed. The phone rang and he remembered: he was on call for the weekend.

It was the emergency room. They wanted him to come in and see a little old lady with hyperthyroidism who was "jumping all over the place." He took a shower and got dressed.

By the time Brophy was in his car on the way to U.H., Lars was under sail with Beth and his sons. The sun was climbing in the brilliant sky over the Narragansett Bay, and the only thing wrong was that Beth had forgotten the beer and soft drinks. They had the food bags and were well out from shore before Beth noticed the missing fluids.

"We better go back," said Beth. "Witherspoon warned you about getting dehydrated. I could just spit. I left that cooler next to the refrigerator."

"We'll make Prudence by lunch," said Lars. "Maybe we can get some soda there."

Witherspoon had warned that the best way to get another stone was to become dehydrated, but Lars looked at his wife and kids, faces pinking in the sun and wind, and shrugged. "To hell with it." They were having too good a time to turn back.

The ER nurse looked relieved to see Brophy. "Oh—the endocrinologist . . . She's in Room D—all over it."

Brophy went to Room D, and in it he found a sixty-nine-

147

year-old wisp of a lady who was pacing from one wall to the other. She jumped as Brophy slowly opened the door.

"Oh-you-startled-me. I'm-just-so-nervous-lately-things-seem-to-be-happening-so-fast-it-all-runs-together." This was all said in a single breath, by a very breathless lady: a 33 rpm on a 78 turntable.

Brody studied her ER sheet. They had a thyroid level on her that was twice normal. It had been done the previous Thursday in General Medical Clinic. The rest of her chart wasn't available, probably still sitting in clinic, where it could do no one any good. The note from the ER intern said, "Hyperthyroid 79 y.o. White female with goiter." That was all. No physical exam. No temperature.

Brophy excused himself and stepped out of the room. He asked the ER nurse to take the patient's temperature and went to look for the intern. He was in the ER, smoking a cigarette, with his feet propped up.

"What did you find on Mrs. Liddle?"

"No chart," the intern said, blowing his smoke ceilingward. "But she's got that thyroxine they sent down from Medical Records. And that goiter."

"She febrile?"

"Isn't it on the sheet?"

Brophy handed him the ER sheet. The space for temperature wasn't filled in.

"Hey, Dot!" the intern shouted, leaning sideways in his chair so he could direct his voice down the hall. "Get a temp on D!" He smiled at Brophy, satisfied that he had solved that particular crisis.

Brophy decided not to pursue things with the intern and went back to Mrs. Liddle.

The ER nurse had managed to get an oral temperature with the IVAC thermometer despite Mrs. Liddle's nonstop chatter and constant motion: "One hundred point three," the nurse announced.

Mrs. Liddle did indeed have a goiter—a large, lumpy goiter. She also had a wide-eyed stare and nasty noises in her right lung, which Brophy presumed signified a pneumonia.

"What brought you in this morning?" he asked her.

"A-1971-Buick-never-had-a-bit-of-trouble-with-it."

"I mean, why did you come to the hospital? Were you feeling badly?"

"Can't-sleep-at-all. Came-last-night-they-gave-me-some-sleeping-pills-but-they-didn't-help-a-whit-so-I-came-back. And-do-I-need-sleep-I've-never-been-so-wrung-out."

She had had her goiter for years. Lately her heart pounded and raced. "Like-it-does-with-good-sex." She winked at Brophy. But she wasn't feeling well. Life had become an effort. She couldn't even drag herself over to the East Side Women's Club. The cough had begun Friday.

Brophy took her over for a chest X ray, which showed an infiltrate in her right middle lobe. Then he went to see the intern.

"She's got to come in," Brophy said.

"Think she's that bad?"

"You listen to her lungs?"

The intern shook his head, not at all chagrined he had missed a pneumonia. He had called the consult.

"She's in storm. Pneumonia probably triggered it. She's got to come in."

"We don't admit pneumonias . . ."

"You better admit storm. Know the mortality for thyroid storm?"

"Oh—*thyroid* storm." He nodded. "Sure, we'll put her in."

It was dark and quiet in the emergency room. Brophy phoned Jethro, who was playing tennis in his backyard and arrived at the phone out of breath. Brophy told him about Mrs. Liddle.

"I'll be there in an hour. Just need a shower. And I want to do some reading. Got a file on storm I've never even looked at. In an hour I'll be a veritable resource."

Brophy laughed. He liked Jethro for not trying to fake it. He was a lab mole and he admitted it. Brophy, on the other hand, knew what had to be done for Mrs. Liddle because he had read a storm article he had found on Duncan's desk three days earlier.

While they waited for Jethro to arrive, they put Mrs. Liddle in the Intensive Care Unit on a cooling blanket. She hated the cooling blanket, but her temperature had risen to a hundred and two.

Brophy went up to the CRU for some coffee while he waited for Jethro. Walking past the outpatient area, he noticed the lights were on.

Steve Reynolds was there doing an infusion. He had a big undergraduate hooked up to the infusion pumps and was drawing the bloods, running them in the analyzers himself. He seemed glad to see Brophy.

"Morning," Brophy said.

"You on call?"

Brophy was wearing his white coat and a tie. He nodded. Why else would he be here on a Saturday? "You're doing an infusion?" he countered.

"Yep."

Brophy shook his head and walked out of the room, feeling sorry for Reynolds. If he had time, he'd try to buy the wretch some lunch, as Duncan had done for him.

Finishing his coffee, he went to the medical school library, where he looked up two recent reviews on thyroid storm and made copies for Jethro. Then he went up to the ICU.

"Hey, hey," Jethro sang, breezing in. "Are we well versed?" He had presented a paper in Norway, where everyone said "Hey, hey." Now he said "Hey, hey," at every opportunity.

Brophy handed Jethro Mrs. Liddle's chart, and they sat down in the conference room, where Brophy told him what he knew about their patient.

They went to see Mrs. Liddle, and Jethro told her she had a serious problem so they would have to use some pretty big guns to subdue her storm.

"You're-going-to-do-what? Shoot-me?" she asked, more to Brophy than to this strange man who spoke of guns.

"We're going to use strong medicine to get you well in a hurry," Brophy told her.

"Oh," said Mrs. Liddle, looking relieved.

Jethro wasn't happy about using iodides because it would delay definitive treatment, which in this case meant radioactive-iodine ablation of the gland.

So they used propranolol and blocked Mrs. Liddle's heart off from the effects of the hormone typhoon. They gave the drugs IV so they would work faster, and by the time they left, her heart rate had slowed and she was less febrile.

"Wonderful field, endocrinology," Jethro said, disappearing out the ICU door.

Brophy went to the cafeteria, arriving just before they closed the door. He bought two peanut butter sandwiches and trotted back to the infusion room. It was one o'clock. Reynolds would be in serious need of glucose and probably in worse need of a urinal.

Reynolds wasn't there. The equipment was drying, all in place near the sink, but no sign of Reynolds or the undergraduate.

Brophy walked down to the nurses' station and asked the nurses if they had seen Reynolds leave. They hadn't even known he was doing an infusion.

Brophy drove home thinking about Mrs. Liddle and the wonders of propranolol and wondering how Reynolds had finished so quickly.

9

Sunday morning it rained. Brophy's bed was by the window, and he watched the storm move in, listening to the thunder. The lightning lit up the room in flashes. Then the rain came, heavy and loud, drumming on the roof. He sat up and looked at the rain on the street.

The rain was so loud he almost didn't hear the knocking at his door.

It was Clarissa. Soaked.

"Monsoon season," she said. "It was sunny when I left five minutes ago."

Brophy looked at her, dripping on his doorway. Her apartment was only five minutes away. If she had come from there, she would have waited it out. She must have started out much earlier, from farther away, and got caught in it. She hadn't spent the night in her own apartment. And she had lied.

"Invite me in or send me away," she said. "But *do* end the suspense."

Brophy invited her in.

Her white sundress was soaked and clinging. She wore no bra, and her nipples stood out hard against the dress.

"Hang that up in the bathroom," Brophy said. He went to make coffee.

Clarissa came out wearing his white terry cloth bathrobe. She was very tanned for a redhead.

She sat at the kitchen table with Brophy and drank coffee in gulps. The rain was letting up.

"It wasn't so bad living in Providence not knowing where

you were," she said, smiling. "Since you showed up, I miss you all the time."

Brophy smiled.

"That's your Southern smile," she said.

"What sort of smile?"

"It's what you do when you've just thought something nasty but don't want to say it. So you smile."

"I do that?"

"Frequently." Clarissa laughed. "And you think you're being inscrutable."

"I guess I'm easy to figure," said Brophy. "Not like you."

"Oh, I'm very easy to figure."

"Then why do I have so much trouble?"

"I'm deceptively simple."

"Deceptive, yes. Simple, no."

"I am not deceptive," Clarissa said, angry now, trying to not show it. "Never have been. You may have felt deceived, but that wasn't my doing. You asked no questions. I told no lies."

"You just kept a calendar."

"Good Lord, are we back to the *calendar* again?"

Clarissa fixed Brophy in a blue-eyed vise.

"I never understood why"

"Why?"

"Why you kept it. Did you want me to find it? Was that your subtle way of telling me?"

"Christ," she said, disgusted.

Brophy said nothing. He got up and rinsed out his coffee cup at the sink.

"As if everything were done with reference to you." She shook her head. "I wanted to know," she said, very steadily, "if my IUD let me down, who the father was."

"How could you tell?" Brophy asked evenly. "Some days had three different-colored stars. You'd have done as well drawing lots."

"Those were rare," Clarissa said tightly. She drew in a breath and stood up. "It was a neurotic calendar," she said, "for a neurotic time."

Brophy stood by the sink and watched her. She stood with her hands in the pockets of his bathrobe, crossing her legs.

"Do you have some blue jeans and a T-shirt? Just so I can get home?"

"You know where the closet is."

She came out with the cuffs rolled up, wearing a shirt that said AMHERST RUGBY.

"If you don't behave," she said brightly, trying to lighten things up, "I might not give this one back." She was trying to leave on a pleasant note. "I look so nice in mauve."

"Violet," said Brophy. "American T-shirts are violet."

"It's a British game," she said unhappily. She turned to go. She was carrying her dress. Then she turned back. "Do you remember a man named Lars Magnussen? A patient? You saw him at U.H."

"Sure. He had a kidney stone and hypercalcemia."

"His wife's a friend of mine. I've told you about her—Beth, Lynn's friend."

"Yes."

"Beth called me this morning. He's having some twinges in his flank. They were out all day sailing yesterday and he probably got dehydrated."

"Now he's paying the price," Brophy said. "She called you at home?"

"Yes," said Clarissa, confused. "What do you mean, 'At home?'"

"You were soaked when you got here . . ." Brophy waved. "Forget it. What was the problem with Magnussen?"

"Sounds like a stone, no? I told Beth to have him drink gallons of water. Was that the right thing to say?"

"Won't do any harm."

"What should I have said?"

"That's all you can say. If he has a stone, it's not going to dissolve, but it may break up, and maybe the urine flow will move it along."

Clarissa was holding her dress, in a wet ball. It was dripping on the hardwood floor. She was looking hard at Brophy, trying to see past his eyes.

"What did you mean about Beth calling me at home?"

"Why did you come by this morning?"

"I told you." She smiled tightly. "I miss you. Can't imagine why. You can be most difficult. What did you mean about Beth calling?"

"I didn't think you were home this morning."

"Did you call?"

"No."

"Then why . . . ?"

"You looked like you came from a long way off."

"You mean you thought I'd spent the night with someone else?"

"That's what I thought."

"Christ," Clarissa said, blotching red. "You are a royal, bloody pill." She was twisting her dress in her hands, and water splashed on the floor. "I've done nothing short of throw myself at you since I found out you were here. And all you can think of is whether I've got any outside business."

"Can't imagine why I might think that."

"What if I do?" shouted Clarissa, hurled her balled-up dress at Brophy. It hit the cabinet and dropped into the sink. "Oh, of course. You've found me out."

Brophy said nothing.

"It's not important that I come over here. What's important is where else I've been."

Brophy opened his mouth, but closed it.

"You really hate me, don't you? I wasn't your little dream of chastity. I wasn't your one and only."

"You weren't mine."

"No, I wasn't yours. I wasn't anybody's."

Brophy looked at her glistening eyes.

"I know you find it hard to believe, but I had a life before you." Clarissa swallowed and continued speaking with effort. "There were men. And a husband. A husband who just couldn't get me quite perfect. Then there was you." She took a deep breath. "And you couldn't get me perfect either. You couldn't have me your way."

"That's not the way I remember it."

"And how was that?"

"You were already perfect. You were it."

"*It*," Clarissa echoed. "That's what I was, all right!"

"What's that supposed to mean?"

"Brophy . . . you meant a great deal. But you weren't everything and you couldn't stand that."

"That's called love. . . ."

"No," Clarissa said, sounding very tired. "That's what *you* called love." She turned to go. "This was a big mistake."

"Tell me one thing—if I had been the father, by your infallible calendar, what difference would it have made?"

Clarissa smiled a Southern smile and backed out the door.

10

Monday morning Brophy met with the gaggle of medical students and residents taking the endocrine elective. He called them the Team, with an irony that was lost on every one of them, for he had been struck by the absence of teamwork among the interns, residents, and medical students on the wards at U.H. Interns went around seeing patients by themselves, often without an accompanying resident. It was the antithesis of The Manhattan Hospital, where the entire medical group went from patient to patient, discussing each patient in turn so every doctor on the service understood what was happening.

As the Fellow at U.H., Brophy ran the service, more or less.

He decreed Monday morning as time for Mega Rounds: they would all see the patients together before they met with Jethro at ten-thirty.

"Bedside teaching," Brophy said happily.

"Sore feet," countered Robin Pullman, who would rather have been sitting and reading about gene splicing.

By ten o'clock they had arrived at the ICU to see Mrs. Liddle. Brophy presented her story and asked Wendel for his diagnosis. Wendel thought hyperthyroidism, which Brophy took as a sign of progress, and turned to Robin Pullman, resident, sore-footed future gene splicer, who said, "Thyroid storm." She even knew how to treat storm. Brophy was impressed.

"Don't be," Robin said. "I heard there was a case of storm in the house. We're in the Intensive Care Unit seeing a patient with hyperthyroidism. Not too many endocrine cases wind up in the ICU, but storm would."

It was disturbing to Brophy that sharp doctors like Robin were not uncommon in this ragtag residency program at U.H. They didn't do rounds together; they didn't do anything the way they did it at The Manhattan Hospital; but they had a sizable number of impressive docs like Robin.

They stepped in the room to see Mrs. Liddle. "So many of you. Is this my wake?" She wasn't jumpy at all. The PTU and propranolol had done their work. Everyone looked at Brophy accusingly. This woman didn't look hyperthyroid, much less in storm.

"You should have seen her Saturday," was all Brophy could say. His beeper saved him, going off just as everybody started to hoot. It was the ER intern. He had a woman with a vanishingly low blood thyroid level they couldn't wake up.

"Let's go see her," Brophy said.

"Tell me about her at Jethro's rounds," said Robin.

They all went off in different directions. Robin said she was going to the library. Brophy watched the two medical students head in the direction of the cafeteria, which had excellent doughnuts but closed at ten-fifteen. Wendel was standing next to Brophy.

"Can I come?"

Brophy looked at him but didn't have the heart to say what he was thinking. He turned on his heel and they headed for the emergency room.

The woman was lying propped up on a stretcher in Room C. She was puffy-faced and a classic shade of lemon-yellow. Her name was Mrs. Gull. She had an old clinic chart as thick as a telephone book. Brophy flipped through it, stopping at the typewritten summaries, which were the only readable parts. She had been hospitalized for a variety of uninteresting ailments years prior and had been seen in Endocrine Clinic for hypothyroidism. Her last visit to the clinic had been two years ago.

"How are you, Mrs. Gull?"

Mrs. Gull raised her eyes very slowly toward Brophy. Her eyelids were so swollen Brophy could barely see the eyeballs.

"I'll . . . talk . . . to . . . you," she croaked, "if . . . you . . . give . . . me . . . time."

Mrs. Gull was not about to do much talking, which was

fortunate for Brophy, who could not have tolerated more than thirty seconds in the same room with anyone who spoke that slowly. Her eyballs rolled heavenward and her eyelids drooped. Brophy looked at her ER sheet, which, once again, did not have a temperature recorded. This time there was a three-line note from the same intern who had called Brophy for Mrs. Liddle. Brophy looked at his watch. It was ten twenty-five.

He asked Wendel if he knew how to do blood gases.

"Well . . . not exactly . . ."

"Wendel, either you know exactly or you don't know."

Just then Robin Pullman walked in, saving Wendel from having to defend himself.

"Okay, okay, Brophy. You've done it. I'm guilt-stricken. What am I missing?"

Brophy nodded at Mrs. Gull, then shook her, not having seen her breathe during the past minute.

"Holy Mother . . ." Robin gasped.

"Robin, we need gases, a temp, chest film, admission bloods. And make the CBC stat with a diff, an IV, and some oh-two. I'm calling the ICU."

"Okay," Robin said vacantly, still staring at Mrs. Gull.

Brophy darted out of Room C and ran past Lars Magnussen, who had just been brought in and lay writhing on a stretcher. At the nurses' station Brophy called the ICU resident and said he was sending up a myxedema coma. He knew Mrs. Gull was in myxedema coma because all the articles he had read about Mrs. Liddle's thyroid storm had mentioned the other thyroid emergency, which was coma. Then he called Jethro to tell him he'd be late for rounds. Jethro was overjoyed since he was busy in the lab. He said he'd go over Mrs. Gull that afternoon.

Brophy hung up. He kept trying to remember the myxedema coma parts of those articles. All he could recall was that people died in large numbers from coma, especially if their temperatures were elevated.

He hurried back to the coma lady, past Beth Magnussen, who looked after him. Robin had the IV going. She had taken Mrs. Gull's temperature. Ninety-nine.

"Well, that's good, at least," Wendel said with a smile.

"That's bad," Brophy said grimly, trying to think of which antibiotics to put her on, not knowing the source of her infection.

"I got a urine culture by cath, and they're taking her for a chest X ray in a minute," said Robin.

"We'll get it in the unit," said Brophy, swinging into gear. This was real medicine. It was a matter of organizing thoughts, taking steps.

Brophy examined Mrs. Gull. She had it all: creaking, slow reflexes; dry skin; and a scar across her neck where someone had sliced out her thyroid. They wheeled her into the hallway. Brophy sent Wendel ahead to get the elevator.

Beth Magnussen touched Brophy's elbow. "Excuse me, doctor."

Brophy remembered her. She was tanned and athletic-looking and Brophy definitely remembered her.

"Your husband back?" he asked, pushing the stretcher.

"He's just in agony . . ."

"Another stone?"

"I think so." Beth trailed after Mrs. Gull's stretcher. It was the fastest Mrs. Gull had moved in months.

The ICU resident came down with the elevator and met them as the door opened. "I can take her up with Robin," the resident said, seeing Beth.

"Okay," Brophy said.

Brophy walked back to the ER with Beth. Lars had been up all night, and Beth had taken him to the ER that morning, when neither of them could take it anymore.

Brophy was considering what to say, when Clarissa arrived, answering Beth's frantic pages in person.

"Am I ever glad to see you," said Beth, throwing her arm around Clarissa's neck.

"I see you got ahold of Brophy," said Clarissa.

"He warned us this might happen again," Beth said, nodding at Brophy. "Lars just wouldn't listen."

"He doesn't like doctors much," Brophy said. "Can't say I blame him."

"He'll like *you* well enough," Beth said. "We can't find anyone to see him," she added.

Clarissa looked over at Brophy, who shrugged.

"What do you think?" Clarissa asked.

"I'd be glad to admit him to the metabolic ward, the CRU, the Clinical *Research* Unit. . . ."

"At this point I think he'd go along with even that," Beth said. "He's just in agony."

"Didn't they give him anything for the pain?" asked Brophy.

"He wouldn't let them. Last time they gave him Demerol, he went off the wall. He's afraid of it."

Brophy, Clarissa, and Beth went to see Lars, who was lying curled up on his left side, his eyes squeezed shut. He opened them when they came in.

"We can't keep meeting like this," Clarissa said. She reached for his hand and winced—it was ice cold.

"Uh," was all Lars could say.

Brophy thumbed through his chart.

"You got pretty hypertensive during this hernia surgery in July. Did you know that?"

Lars nodded, hating Brophy for bringing up that irrelevant information.

"How long have you had high blood pressure?"

Lars grunted and pointed to his side.

"I know you're in terrific pain. I can't admit you to a private room since I'm not an Attending. All I can do is what I offered the last time we talked. I can put you on the Clinical Research Unit, which is run by my Section. We can take care of you there."

"Okay," grunted Lars, eyes closed. "What will you give me," he managed to get out, "for the pain?"

"I understand you had a bad reaction to the Demerol last time."

Lars nodded.

"What exactly happened?"

"I think . . ." Lars said, grimacing, "I passed out."

"Did anyone take your blood pressure?"

"No . . . they left me alone."

Brophy told him all the strong painkillers were opiates that were related structurally and in their side effects, but he could try morphine and hope for the best.

"At least," Lars rasped, "you're honest . . . let's go."

Brophy called the CRU, then wrote an order for morphine and watched while the ER nurse injected it under Lars' skin. He took Lars' blood pressure.

"How do you feel?"

"Lightheaded . . . but the pain's better."

Brophy kept taking the pressure until he was satisfied that it wasn't going to drop any lower. Then Clarissa, Beth, and he rolled Lars to the elevator.

Beth stood at Lars' head and stroked his hair while they waited.

"You drive a hard bargain," Clarissa told Brophy, smiling.

"Informed consent," he said. "Pure and simple."

—

11

Brophy dropped Lars off on the CRU, wrote a few holding orders, and called Nancy Barnah, Witherspoon, and Jethro. Only Jethro answered. Brophy told him about Lars.

"Eventually," Jethro said, "if we just sit like spiders, they come to us."

Then Brophy went to the ICU, where the house staff was busy with Mrs. Gull. Robin was looking at Mrs. Gull's urine, under the microscope, talking with the ICU intern about giving her antibiotics.

Brophy felt superfluous and went back to work up Lars.

The CRU nurses were wonderful. They had started the IV, gotten the belly-film, and checked Lars' blood pressures just as Brophy had written in his orders.

Lars was asleep. Brophy took Beth into the conference room and went over the history of the high blood pressure.

"But other than that," he inquired, scrutinizing her, "he's been perfectly healthy? Just the hernias, the high blood pressure, and the stones?"

"And the calcium."

"And the calcium. Other than that, he's been fine?"

"Yes. He's in great shape."

Brophy went through the standard workup: History of present illness (the two episodes of kidney stones); past medical history; review of systems—no gastrointestinal complaints, no cardiovascular complaints. But he did have headaches.

"He never had headaches until this summer," Beth said.

Brophy looked up from his paper and stopped writing. "What happens exactly when he gets his headaches?"

Beth told him about the time on the tennis court, and about how pale Lars had turned.

Brophy went on to family history, and Beth told him about Olaf Magnussen.

Brophy had been drawing the family tree, with squares for the males and circles for the females. He had written "A&W" under the square representing Lars' father, and another "A&W" under the circle for his mother. He had a square for Olaf Magnussen and blackened that in. He had been concentrating on getting the drawing right; then it struck him that Lars had a brother who had died. He looked up from his paper.

"How old was his brother when he died?"

"About thirty, thirty-one."

Brophy wrote "31" under the blackened box on his family tree drawing.

"That's an odd age to die. What'd he die from?"

"The doctors never could really say. Heart attack, probably."

"At thirty-one?"

"I don't know. They never were sure."

Brophy scratched the back of his neck, then looked at his watch. He had a lot of things to do. He had to get back to Mrs. Gull, and round up Robin and organize rounds. And there were the calciums to check.

"Why do you keep asking about Lars' brother and all these things?" Beth asked.

"Had a professor once." Brophy smiled. "Every morning he'd do rounds with us, he'd say, 'Better thorough than brilliant.' I never thought I had much choice."

Brophy went to see Lars, and reviewed the history of the stones, the blood pressure, and the calcium. Lars was in less pain, but he was in no mood to talk.

"I know you feel lousy right now," Brophy said, "but I wonder if you'd mind telling me about your brother."

"What about him?"

"He died when he was thirty-one?"

"Yes."

"Do you know what from?"

"Nobody knew." Lars shifted himself painfully. "Why?"

"It's not common for a thirty-one-year-old man to die."

"It's not common for a thirty-one-year-old guy to get two kidney stones one on top of another."

"You're getting my point, counselor."

Lars lifted his head and looked directly at Brophy. He took a deep breath. "Nobody knew what he died from . . . He just collapsed at his office."

"Where was he taken? What hospital?"

"What difference does that make?"

"We might be able to get the records."

"Manhattan Hospital."

Brophy's eyes opened wide. "Was an autopsy done?"

"No."

"As far as you know, did your brother have any serious medical problems—or was it all a shock to you, his dying like that?"

For a fleeting moment, Brophy looked and sounded like the skinny-necked intern who had interrogated Lars years before.

"What the hell do you think?" croaked Lars. "Of course it was a big shock!"

"Sorry," Brophy said. "Didn't mean to press you about a bad memory. But sometimes calcium problems run in families."

"He never had a kidney stone," Lars said. "That I know."

Beth had been standing at the door, listening, and she followed Brophy out to the nurses' station.

"He's in a lot of pain," she said. "He didn't mean to be crabby. It was really awful with his brother. He had to go through it all alone. He still hates hospitals."

"No problem." Brophy winked. He was sitting at the writing ledge, with the order book. Beth smiled nervously and walked back to Lars' room.

Brophy was hearing hoofbeats and told himself to think of horses. Common things occur commonly. Kidney stones were common. Parathyroid adenomas were not uncommon. Pheochromocytomas and familial Multiple Endocrine Adenomatosis were zebras.

But pheos could kill you. Miss a parathyroid adenoma, it would wait until next year. Miss a pheo, the next time you'd see the patient might be at autopsy. That had been the message at Duncan's conference.

Brophy couldn't remember which tests Duncan had finally said were the best. There had been some argument about that.

He wrote an order to collect all Lars Magnussen's urine and to send it for free catecholamines. Then he took an X-ray requisition from the file and wrote for an IVP. Another for a CAT scan of Lars' abdomen.

"Who are you trying to kid?"

Brophy looked up. It was Clarissa.

"He'll never hang around long enough for all that stuff. He's already convinced you want to make him a guinea pig."

"I'm going to give him the opportunity to say no a lot," Brophy said.

Clarissa was playing with the stethoscope around her neck.

"Nobody grows up in one day," she said.

Brophy's beeper went off. It was an outside call—Lynn Ann Montano.

"Hi, Brophy. Busy?"

"I'm always busy."

"I can call back, but I do have to talk to you."

Brophy watched Clarissa as he talked to Lynn. "Go ahead," he said. Clarissa put her hands in the pockets of her scrub dress and looked down at the floor.

"I've tried to get a story of that protocol," Lynn Ann said, "but the secretary in the HIC office said the protocols don't go out of the office."

"That's what you get for talking to secretaries. Why didn't you ask to speak with her boss?"

"He's conveniently out of town."

"He's not conveniently out of town. He's just out of town. I have a photocopy on my desk. I'll send you one."

"That'll help. But the heat's building on this thing."

"What's that supposed to mean?"

"The *Fox Point Focus* has got wind of it."

"The what?"

"One of those local freebie alternative rags. The People's Paper."

"And how did they pick up the scent?" Brophy demanded. He rolled his eyes ceilingward for Clarissa's benefit. She still didn't know to whom Brophy was talking.

"Probably the same way I did. I guess some people got impatient when I didn't print the story the next day. Checking sources does slow one down."

"You mean you're going to print that trash?"

Clarissa's eyes narrowed. She came closer to Brophy and mouthed, "Lynn Ann?" Brophy nodded. She walked over to the clerk's desk and picked up the receiver to listen in.

"Who's making the allegations?"

"That's confidential for now."

"That's kind of basic, isn't it?"

"What?"

"I mean you're entitled to hear the charges and to confront your accuser in this country."

"You're not on trial, Donald."

"I thought we're reported to be giving radioactive drinks to pregnant ladies."

"Let's talk this evening," Lynn Ann said. They hung up.

"Can you believe this?" Brophy hooted.

"What protocol?" asked Clarissa.

"The protocol for our project."

"You'd better check before you go giving out protocols to the press."

"They've got to be public property," he said. "They're N.I.H. government documents."

"Did you write the protocol?"

"No."

"Then it's not up to you to give it away. It's got everyone's name on it—Sol's, Jethro's, and mine. I'd talk to someone before I'd be handing out protocols to Lynn Ann."

"Wouldn't hurt to ask, I guess."

"Cover your ass," Clarissa warned him. "You saw what she did with the medical clinic story."

Brophy said nothing.

"You're going to see her this evening?"

"Guess so."

"Where?"

"Don't know. La Cantina, probably."

"Well, well," Clarissa said. "This won't be the first time, then."

Brophy looked at her inquiringly.

"It's Lynn's favorite place. Sounds like you've been before."

"What's it to you, lady?"

Clarissa said nothing. She just shook her head and walked out of the nurses' station.

12

Lynn Ann did not suggest La Cantina for Monday evening. She paged Brophy at five, but he was busy with Mrs. Gull and said he'd have to call back. Mrs. Gull was giving them fits. She just wasn't waking up and she kept forgetting to breathe.

By six-thirty they decided to not intubate her, and Brophy left the unit to check on Lars Magnussen.

Lars was still in plenty of pain and he was relatively pliable. He was cooperating with the urine collections and behaving himself.

Lynn Ann paged Brophy again at seven.

"Dr. Fantastic," she said, "you sound all out of breath."

"Saving lives is strenuous," said Brophy, who in fact had just run up the stairs to the chemistry lab to check the calciums, and found, to his great joy, there were no new hypercalcemics.

"Where are you?" he asked.

"Still at my desk."

"You must be starved."

"I'm faint," Lynn Ann said in her peculiar flat, inflectionless voice. Brophy had heard voices like that before on psych wards. Sometimes Lynn Ann sounded breathy and exciting. Tonight she sounded as if she were on Thorazine. "I need some immediate oral gratification," she said. There was more life in that.

"Where?"

"The Ming Garden."

"Where is it?"

"Downtown. Near City Hall."

* * *

There was nowhere to park. Downtown was just minutes from the hospital, but Brophy circled the square for fifteen minutes.

Lynn was eating chicken wings dipped in Ming's special sauce when Brophy arrived.

"Have some," she said. "They're wonderful." She was very good looking in a *Cosmopolitan* magazine sort of way. "Jackie Kennedy used to send a Secret Service plane up here for them."

"To Providence?"

"The Kennedys knew Rhode Island. They got married in Newport. Jackie also liked the banana cream pie at the Providence Airport restaurant. Sent the plane for that, too."

Brophy studied Lynn Ann's false eyelashes while she nibbled. She had a dramatic face, more so in the shadows of the restaurant. Fine high cheekbones. She was model-thin and she wore pearly eye shadow.

"What's a fast girl like you doing in a town like Providence? You belong in New York."

"I ask myself that about twice a week," said Lynn flatly. "In college, everyone said I'd wind up driving a Mercedes in Scarsdale."

"And here you are in Providence. What do you drive?"

"A Datsun."

They shared a laugh.

"It's not forever," she said. "I had lunch at Yellowfingers with Fletcher Daemon just last week."

"Fletcher Daemon . . ." Brophy repeated blankly, biting into a wing. The sauce splattered his shirt.

"The *Times,* Brophy. Jesus, doctors don't know anything but medicine. Fletcher Daemon's an editor with *The New York Times.*"

"He looking for a hot young investigative reporter?"

Lynn Ann rolled her eyes and smiled, stripping another wing with her straight white teeth.

"And Candice Flynn comes in. Christ, what a huge ass."

"She's an ass?"

"Well, probably that, too. No, I meant her anatomy. She has a huge ass. They must shoot around it."

"Oh," Brophy said cleverly. What could you say about a movie star's ass?

"Oh, well," Lynn Ann said in her flattest tone. "She gives the best head in New York."

"Now how would you know that?"

"Brophy," Lynn Ann said, smiling, "information is my game."

"But here you are in Providence. Who's to know here?" he asked, picking up another wing. "I mean, what's the scoop? Factory closing in Cranston?"

"'Research at University Hospital Runs Unchecked.'"

"Yes, indeed!" Brophy grinned and waved his chicken bone in the air with a dramatic flourish. "I forgot: 'Pregnant Women Poisoned at U.H.' How could that have slipped my mind?"

"I can understand."

"How'd you wind up here?"

"I got a job."

"No jobs in New York?"

"Sure. I could have been a schlepper at the *Daily News* for a few years and hoped I was balling the right guys."

"And here you're big time?"

"Nobody's big time in Providence. But I started as a reporter, right out of college."

"Where'd you go?"

"Missouri," she said, looking around for the waiter. "School of Journalism."

"Missouri?"

"It's known for its School of Journalism. Walter Cronkite went there. Actors go to Northwestern. Journalists go to Missouri. . . . You still sleeping with Clarissa?"

Brophy caught some Ming Wing in his windpipe and coughed it free.

"Have some water." Lynn Ann patted him on the back. "Didn't mean to asphyxiate you."

"Sometimes I forget you're the inquiring reporter."

"Oh, you don't have to tell me. I already have my answer—from Clarissa."

"What did she say?"

"It wasn't what she said—it was the way she didn't say it. She usually says, 'Oh, what a grotesque thought,' or something like that, if she isn't or hasn't. I asked about you and she changed the subject."

Brophy started playing with his tea cup.

"They haven't taken our order," he said.

"See, you're changing the subject, too," smiled Lynn. "I've already ordered for both of us."

"What are we having?"

"You'll love it. Tell me about you and Clarissa."

"What on earth for?"

"That's just what she said. Why on earth not?"

"Oh, I get it: 'Doctor's Ties to Nurse Queried in Research Probe.'"

"This isn't on the record. I'm just curious. I always suspected there was someone in her past," said Lynn Ann. "Someone who meant"—she searched for the word—"everything."

Brophy almost laughed, but didn't. "Maybe her ex-husband."

"No."

"You have someone like that in your past?"

"I had," she said, her eyes opaque. "If he walked in here right now, I'd leave with him."

"Where is he?"

"Stapling earlobes in Hollywood. Or doing acupuncture. I can't keep up. He's a doc. Got a lot of fat movie people seeing him."

"You met him here?"

"Boston. His wife was on the Cape for the summer. I was eating salad at Faneuil Hall. There was nowhere to sit. He offered me his place and said, 'Would you like to go to the Chinese delicatessen?' With a line like that, I was helpless."

"What's the Chinese delicatessen? Big hot spot in Boston?"

"No, he really meant a Chinese delicatessen."

"Well, at least he took you places."

"We used to go down to Newport, during the week. He had all these curls. Salt and pepper. Gold necklace. Spoke about ten languages."

"And you were smitten."

"In love."

"What kind of doctor?"

"I think he started out in dermatology. He had the most beautiful eyes."

Brophy could feel himself pulling away. Something in Lynn Ann's voice had sounded very unbusinesslike when she paged earlier. He didn't think this dinner was really about the story.

But he didn't expect to hear about Lynn's wounding in love, either. She was miles away.

"It wasn't you then?" she said, coming back to planet earth.

"What wasn't?"

"Clarissa. It wasn't you?"

"Why don't you ask her?" said Brophy.

The waiter finally came and cleared away the empty wing bowls.

They brought the next course: some kind of peanut, cashew, and chicken thing with bamboo shoots. It was almost equal to the wings.

"I'll come by for that protocol Wednesday. Okay?" Lynn Ann said suddenly.

"Okay," said Brophy, not knowing what else to say. He'd have to check with Lionel.

"What're you doing this weekend?" Lynn asked.

"It's only Monday."

"Ever been to Moonstone Beach?"

"Moonstone?"

"Beautiful place. Nudies." Lynn Ann rolled her eyes and laughed. "Gorgeous beach. You have to know someone to get in."

"And you know someone."

"Let's go Saturday."

Brophy searched furiously for a reason why he couldn't go to the nude beach.

"I'm on this weekend," he said. "I was thinking of going to the RISD museum. Someplace within beeper distance."

Lynn Ann smiled. "We'll go when we know each other better."

They began that process after dinner. Lynn Ann followed Brophy home and parked in front of his building. They walked down the hill to South Main Street and had drinks at Elizabeth's, next door to the boutique owned by Reynolds' wife. Elizabeth's looked like someone's living room. There were no booths, just sofas, coffee tables, and an oak bar in the rear. It was dark and unhurried. Lynn Ann ordered a Manhattan. Brophy had an Irish Mist.

"Oh, Donald—how *can* you?" Lynn Ann laughed. "An Irish Mist—how corny."

"I like Irish Mist." He shrugged. "Irish coffee, too."

"You must try to resist the impulse."

"I like them. I once spent an entire weekend in pursuit of the best Irish coffee in Manhattan."

"Did you find it?"

"O'Neal's, across from Lincoln Center."

"Why don't you have one now?"

"No, not now. Once you've had the best"—Brophy smiled —"it's hard to settle for anything else."

"Keep an open mind," said Lynn Ann. "There's life after New York."

"I don't know . . ."

"Was Clarissa on this great hunt?"

Brophy looked at Lynn Ann. He could never understand the intense female interest in the sex lives of other women.

"No," he said finally. "That was after Clarissa."

Lynn Ann smiled and finished her drink, then signaled the waitress for another. "I'm doing a piece on *you* . . . Dr. Delicious. . . ."

She crossed her legs, causing the slit in her skirt to rise up to her hip. Brophy could feel the stiffening in his pants. They were sitting side by side on a deep sofa, and she shifted her body slightly so that her thigh brushed against his. He wasn't sure that she had intended to touch him, but if so, it had the desired effect.

13

Mrs. Liddle got sent to a regular ward floor, but Mrs. Gull did not do as well. Despite 500 micrograms of thyroxine, despite Ancef and Tobramycin, oxygen by mask and constant electrocardiographic monitoring, and despite the fact that Brophy brought Jethro and the entire endocrine group around twice, she died.

Lars passed the stone in the wee hours between Monday night and Tuesday morning, and was feeling wonderful by breakfast. He had felt it move through his penis and caught it in his special urine strainer. He was very proud of his stone. The nurses wanted to send it off to the lab, but he wanted Beth to see it. It looked like a shriveled brown pea. It was hard to imagine an insignificant pebble like that could cause such devastating pain. On the other hand, there it was; you could hold it, feel it, and know what had been there creating all that agony. It was more satisfying than, say, Collier's low-back pain, which just came and went and you never could really see why.

Brophy presented Lars as the first case, at ten-thirty Tuesday morning. He lingered over Olaf's unexplained early death and the high blood pressure that had gone even higher during surgery. He hoped Jethro would rise to the bait, but Jethro looked unimpressed. So did Robin. Wendel looked at Jethro and Robin and decided to look unimpressed, too.

"Common things occur commonly," Jethro said. "A young man with hypercalcemia and kidney stones: hyperparathyroidism. I'll buy that."

"What about the hypertension?"

"Thirty percent of hyperparas are hypertensive," Jethro said. "The thing I'd worry about is whether or not his stones have wrecked his kidneys. That'd be a lot more likely than an MEA syndrome."

"I hope he'll let us get an IVP."

"Why wouldn't he?"

Brophy explained about Lars.

"Kidney stones usually whip patients into shape," Jethro said. "The most ornery bastards get just as meek as kittens when they get whalloped by the stone pony."

They went to see Lars, who was completely dressed, packed, and ready to walk out when they arrived. Beth was with him.

"Leaving so soon and only just arrived?" Jethro said. Lars didn't laugh. Beth bit her lower lip.

Brophy hadn't discharged Lars. He had simply decided to walk off the floor. The nurses were at that very moment trying to page Brophy and tell him.

Brophy asked Lars if they could all just talk for a minute in Lars' room. Lars nodded yes but stayed near the door with Beth.

Brophy waited for Jethro to take charge, but Jethro turned and smiled at Brophy.

"I brought Dr. Brown here to meet you. He's our director of the Renal Stone Clinic."

"Pleased to meet you," Lars said, shaking Jethro's hand but looking not at all pleased.

"This is your second stone?"

"Yes."

"Are you interested to know what's causing them?"

"Of course I am," Lars said, tight-mouthed.

"Working up stones requires some rather delicate orchestration," Jethro said.

Brophy shook his head. He was tempted to cut in to translate for Jethro, but Lars said, "Does that mean I'd have to stay in the hospital all week?"

"There are in-patient and out-patient protocols," said Jethro calmly, so quietly it was hard for even Brophy to hear him. "But either option requires substantial cooperative effort. We usually start with an appointment to Stone Clinic."

Brophy buried his face in one hand, sweating, then gathered the courage to look up at Lars.

Lars was leaning forward, trying to hear. He glanced over to Beth, then straightened up.

"I asked the nurses to page Dr. Brophy this morning at nine A.M. They said he was in conference and couldn't be bothered."

Brophy opened his mouth, but Lars continued.

"I waited until ten-thirty, and still no doctor. Beyond eleven, I have to pay for another hospital day."

"Dr. Brophy was presenting your case in some detail. In any given case there may be X, Y, or Z mechanisms. We try to suit our armaments to the pathology."

"And what did you decide?"

"There are a number of posibilities, some likely, others remote. We'd like a chance to winnow out the real culprits."

"Well, give me the appointment."

"I wanted to start you on some medicine for your blood pressure," Brophy said.

"I'll take the prescription."

"I wanted to give you the first dose here." Brophy looked at Jethro and added, "Prazosin."

Jethro nodded.

"Why can't I just pick it up on the way home?"

"There's often a reaction to the first dose," Brophy said. "I wanted you to take it right here, with me here."

"I've never heard of anything like that."

Brophy didn't know what to say: *I want you on Prazosin because I think it's possible you have a pheo, and this drug just might protect you until we have time to make or rule out the diagnosis?*

"We could stay—" Beth began, but Lars cut her short with a quick flash of his eyes.

"Look," he said. "I'll see you in clinic. Until then, I'll sip, sip, sip."

That was how Brophy had put it to Lars the day before. It was the way Jethro said it to all his clinic patients, but it sounded ludicrous the way Lars said it.

Brophy called in the appointment to the clinic and wrote the date on a slip of paper, certain that Lars would never show up.

The group stood by the door of Lars' erstwhile room and watched as he and his wife walked down the hall and out the door.

Jethro shook his head. "He's a tough nut. . . ."

"Prazosin?" Robin asked when they arrived at the conference room. "You don't think he really has a pheo, do you?"

"Well . . . he had that episode during surgery . . ." Brophy said haltingly.

Jethro rolled his eyes toward the ceiling. It was all pretty diffuse: pounding heart, sweating, pallor, even high blood pressure—the kind of things that anxious people complain about all the time. Brophy felt foolish.

"Now, just suppose the guy's an MEA two," Jethro said. "What would we have?" He looked at Wendel, who had heard Brophy talking with Robin before rounds.

"Pheo, hyperparathyroidism, and medullary CA of the thyroid!" Wendel announced proudly.

"Correct," Jethro said in his understated way that made everything he said sound ominous.

"And how would you go after the diagnosis?"

That stumped Wendel—Brophy hadn't said anything to Robin about that. Then he remembered Duncan's conference.

"You could do a calcium infusion for the medullary CA," said Wendel, brightly.

Jethro turned to Robin. "You agree?"

"No."

Wendel looked at Robin, betrayed. "Why not?"

"If he had a pheo sitting in his adrenal gland and you go pumping in IV calcium, what could happen to that high explosive, lurking deep within Mr. Magnussen's retroperitoneum?" whispered Jethro.

"Blow him sky high," said Robin, getting caught up in the imagery.

"You've always got to approach MEA thinking of the pheo first," said Jethro. "The medullary CA is no blessing, but it's not going to detonate suddenly. The first thing to nail down or exclude is the pheo."

Wendel nodded sagely, agreeing it would be better to not blow away such patients.

"What other things do you not want to give to people with pheos?"

"Glucagon," said Brophy.

"That can do it."

"Anesthesia, histamine, just about any kind of surgery," Robin added.

Jethro continued: "Last pheo at U.H. was a year ago. Kid

with a tonsillar abscess. They were putting him to sleep and his blood pressure just went through the roof. They found the pheo at autopsy. . . ."

"Jesus," said Robin. "That happened here?"

"Even at U.H. such things happen," said Jethro. He turned to Brophy: "You could get a calcitonin."

Brophy said he'd sent one.

"Good—we'll have it cooking."

"Dumfy sends it off to Chicago," Brophy added. "It won't be ready for six or seven weeks."

"Chicago?" Jethro asked. "Who does calcitonins in Chicago?"

Brophy had no idea. But of course, to a laboratory animal like Jethro, the interesting thing wasn't that it would take that long, but who had set up an assay for calcitonins in Chicago.

"Let's get back to cases," Robin said. "This guy sweats a lot in the summer. Half the lawyers in Providence sweat a lot in the summer. You don't go doing urines for catecholamines on all of them."

Brophy was about to protest, but Robin insisted on presenting her argument: "So he's a little hypertensive," she went on. "His calcium's up. Maybe if we repeat the calcium and it's still up, he's got hyperpara. But if Duncan hadn't given that talk on MEA two, would any of us have thought of pheo?"

Wendel and Jethro looked to Brophy. Robin had him. He turned crimson.

"Suppose he has it?" Brophy asked.

"We could any one of us have it," Robin said.

14

"At least you could have taken the prescription," Beth said as they drove home. "You know you need something for your blood pressure."

"I don't need Brophy's experimental pills."

"Experimental?"

"Ever heard of a pill the doctor has to watch you take?"

"He was just trying to get you to stay."

"Either way it's a sham."

"I thought you liked Brophy."

"He's okay. But I almost forgot until this morning—he's one of them."

15

It had been a long day.

At four, Brophy was sitting at his desk in the Fellows' Office. Duncan danced in.

"Any new crab in the house?"

"Haven't checked today."

"It's been a long dry spell since you went on Clinical Service," Duncan said, chewing his lip.

"I've been checking every day," said Brophy, defensively. "There's just nothing, except Heimler and Sipple."

"They're both still with us?"

"Saw Heimler yesterday. Haven't seen Sipple since Friday. But I saw his calcium yesterday: fifteen-six."

"What's Heimler's?"

"Heimler is currently number one on the list: sixteen-two."

"How's he look?"

"Pretty dead."

"Still conscious?"

"How can you tell?"

Duncan looked at Brophy, eyebrow raised.

"He's in and out," said Brophy.

"I should really get my ass over to the wards," said Duncan. "I've dumped it all on you."

"No problem."

"You're doing a great job, really. I should be helping."

"You don't have to. I can do it."

"It's just that the assay is almost there. Christ, I thought I had it last week. It's just not very sensitive yet. I lose grams of tumor every pass." Duncan was sitting at his desk. One leg was bouncing up and down. His knee kept thumping on the underside of the desk.

"I just need time in the lab," he said. "It's been such a godsend to have you beating the bushes for tumor. I just can't chase them down and do the assay, too."

"It's good for me. I *want* to do it," said Brophy. "I've found a home at U.H."

Brophy left Duncan thumping in the Fellows' Office and ran off in search of tumor, up the stairs to Chemistry.

"Calcium maven," sang the lab tech when she caught sight of Brophy. "We're running late," she said. "There's only two high ones so far."

The high ones were Heimler and Sipple. Brophy sat down to wait for the last run to come off the machine.

"There won't be anything for you in this run," said the tech. "It's all pediatrics." Brophy was not interested in pediatric hypercalcemia. The tech knew that. All the techs knew Brophy now. They rotated doing the calciums. They all said hi when they saw him in the cafeteria or in the halls. Harvesting hypercalcemics had established Brophy's place at the U.H. He was the new calcium maven.

And it wasn't just in the lab. Interns and residents knew he was on the prowl for cancer patients with big calciums.

All around U.H. nurses, doctors, and technicians knew Brophy had inherited Duncan's mantle. Medical students stopped Brophy in the hall with inside tips on cancer patients whose calciums had blasted off.

"Half the people here don't even know my name," Brophy told Duncan. "They just know I'm the calcium maven who looks for crab."

"That's all the name you need, big boy."

Brophy pushed through the swinging lab door. He had to go see Heimler and Sipple. He had to show up and smile and be ingratiating and remind everyone to call when autopsy time came.

Brophy nearly knocked Daniel Dumfy over with the swinging door.

"Checking the calciums, huh?" Dumfy asked.

"Yes."

"We got a urine from you today."

Brophy looked confused. "From me?"

"Morgenstern," said Dumfy. "From the CRU."

"Magnussen," said Brophy. "Rule out pheo." He kept walking toward the stairwell, afraid Dumfy might decide to show him his wonderful urine catecholamine machine. It broke Brophy's heart to have to tell Dumfy he didn't have time to marvel at the workings of the clinical chemistry lab. Dumfy tried to not look hurt when people said, "Sure, Daniel, later," and ran off. But Dumfy did look hurt underneath the brave face, so Brophy ran toward the stairwell before Dumfy could ask.

"He wasn't taking any drugs, was he?" Dumfy shouted after Brophy.

"No," Brophy called back over his shoulder, disappearing into the stairwell.

Dumfy hated drugs, whether or not the patients needed them. Drugs floating around in blood or urine befouled his assays. "Good," said Dumfy to the door closing behind Brophy. "Drugs screw up the VMA every time."

16

When Lars arrived home he threw his bag on the bed and went directly to the closet, stripping off his clothes. Then he put on his swimming suit.

"You're not going into the water?" said Beth. "Not with those stitches."

"I'm going sunbathing on my deck. For the last two days, caged in that hospital room, all wound up, I'd been imagining sitting on my own deck, in my own backyard, looking out over my boat."

"Take along some lemonade. You don't want to get dehydrated."

"Sip, sip, sip."

"Why don't you call McCullough?"

"Yeah, I'll do that," said Lars, disappearing out the bedroom door, heading down to the kitchen.

Beth followed him. He poured pink lemonade into a canteen and started out the door.

Beth jumped in front of him, blocking his way.

"Call McCullough."

"You call him if you're so interested."

"You're the one with the high blood pressure."

"You're the one worrying about it."

"Very responsible of you."

"What's that supposed to mean?"

"You've got two sons, you know," Beth said, lips quivering. "At least you might think about them."

Lars got McCullough on the phone and told him about the high blood pressure.

"That's acting up again?"

"So they tell me."

"Well, come in and see me about it. I'll give you my secretary back. Make an appointment for next week."

"Maybe I better take something in the meantime?"

"I'll call something in for you. What pharmacy?"

Lars gave him the name of the pharmacy in Barrington and made an appointment with the secretary.

"Could you pick the pills up when you go to get the boys?" Beth kissed him on the nose.

"Leaving me a widow doesn't bother you a bit. But mention your sons and you swing right into action."

"You can take care of yourself," said Lars. "My sons would wonder what happened to me."

17

It was hard to know what to do about Lynn Ann, and Brophy had his feet propped up on his desk in the Fellows' Office, considering his options, when Reynolds came in with Dick Cecil.

"Five or six more and we'll write it up," Dick said, pounding Reynolds on the back. He glanced over at Brophy and continued speaking to Reynolds. "You'll be published by the end of August. And it's a pretty study." Dick squeezed the back of Reynolds' neck and left.

"He looks pleased," said Brophy.

"He's all excited. The athletes' study's turning out. It's just like Dick said: they're all supersensitive to catechols."

"How many have you studied?"

Reynolds hesitated. "About four."

"So you'll have a paper out of it."

"Don't feel too bad." Reynolds smiled. "I'll be second or third author—and you would have been too if you'd stuck with Dick."

"Second author?"

"Dick's always first."

"But you did the study."

"His idea. So it's 'Catechols in Athletes,' by Dick Cecil, Lionel Addison, and Steve Reynolds."

"Lionel Addison?"

"Sometimes they list him last, as senior author emeritus."

"What did he do?"

"It's his department. He goes on all the papers."

Brophy looked incredulous.

"Really. Most places do that. People might not know Dick Cecil, but they say, 'Oh, that's Lionel Addison's group.'"

"Well, you're in famous company."

"You will be, too, when you get a project ready. When the pregnancy thing's ready. That'll be nice."

"Sure."

"It will be. It's a clinical study; people'll be calling you up about it. Maybe even the newspapers. Not like what I'm doing with Dick. We'll publish it and it'll disappear. Next year somebody'll publish showing just the opposite results. It'll go like that, back and forth."

"No."

"Sure."

"Why work on it if you feel that way?"

"It's a challenge." Reynolds smiled. "Besides, two years from now I'll be Board Eligible in Endocrine, in private practice with a big house in Barrington, shopping for my Mercedes. What the shit."

Brophy swung his feet to the floor and walked next door to the Section Office.

"Is the chief in?"

"He's on the phone," said Rona.

Seeing the light on Rona's phone extinguish, Brophy propped his head into Lionel's office.

"Do you have a minute?"

"What is it?"

"I think we may have some problems brewing on the pregnancy project."

The chief pushed a chair by his desk toward Brophy. "What is it?"

Brophy told him about Lynn Ann.

"What exactly does she have?"

"She thinks we're giving pregnant ladies radioactive drinks."

"And you told her it was just unlabeled calcium?"

"I even offered to show her the protocol to prove it."

"Don't do that."

Brophy looked at the chief, astonished.

"Why not? She'll really think something's wrong if we don't show her," Brophy blurted, regretting it immediately.

"She may not think anything of the sort," said Lionel. He wasn't angry, but he wasn't smiling either. "She's just trying to get a look at the protocol, especially at the 'Possible Hazards' section.''

"I thought the protocols were a matter of public record."

"They are," said the chief. "She can get a copy if she's really persistent."

Brophy looked at the chief uncomprehending.

"She's not interested in simply getting her hands on the protocol," said the chief, smiling, "she's interested in getting some quotes for her story. She's interested in you."

"But if I plead the Fifth, it'll look like we've got something to hide."

"We've got nothing to hide and she knows it. If you don't talk to her, she's got no story at all."

"Just tell her I can't talk to her?"

"That's right," said Lionel. "If she publishes the stuff claiming we're dosing up pregnant ladies with radioactive stuff, we'll call her on it. But I don't think she's that dumb. She's been around this town a while."

"But if she did print it," said Brophy, unable to restrain himself, "there wouldn't be a woman in Providence who'd sign on. Retractions won't mean a thing."

"Let's take the chance. Call her bluff," said the chief, turning back to the heap of papers on his desk, effectively closing the discussion and dismissing his Fellow.

Brophy backed out of the office and headed up to Chemistry to check calciums. Lionel was as cagey as they come. Lynn Ann had done work on medical subjects before: she probably knew all about protocols and HICs, and Brophy had stepped right into her trap. Now he'd have to tell her he couldn't show her the protocol. It was all pretty stupid.

18

When Beth went to pick up Lars' prescription for propranolol, the Medi-Mart pharmacist told Beth the pills might make him feel weak the first few days he took them. Dr. McCullough had said that too.

Lars didn't feel weak, but he did develop a roaring headache during the afternoon of the second day he took his medicine.

"You're white as a sheet," his secretary told him. He had taken six pills, 80 milligrams each, over a day and a half. About a half an hour after swallowing each dose, he noticed a pulsating in his temples and neck, then a feeling that his skull was too tight for its contents.

He went to the water fountain and took two aspirin. One of the other associates was there, taking some pills.

"High blood pressure," the associate said.

Lars smiled. You didn't tell people in the firm about things like that. The firm might not see fit to make a partner out of someone who was likely to be at the doctor's office a lot.

"First ones they gave me really threw me—couldn't even get it up," said the associate. "I thought it was all over. Then I tell the doctor about it and he tells me it's the pills. Never even warned me about it. Switches me to these and no problem."

Lars went back to his office and threw his pills into the trash.

That same morning Lars dispensed with his propranolol, Brophy, Robin, and Wendel were making rounds on Mr. Heimler, who was breathing three times a minute and looking very dead. Brophy couldn't stand the stench longer than the sixty seconds it took him to count Mr. Heimler's respirations.

He told the nurses to call him, as soon as Heimler died. And he left a note Scotch-taped to the aluminum cover of the chart.

Mr. Sipple was breathing better and looked like he might last the day. Brophy wrote a note in the chart, printing his beeper numbers in one-inch letters below his signature. He left without reminding anyone to call when Sipple died.

Mrs. Liddle looked ready for discharge. She wanted to know when she could go home. Brophy said that was up to her doctors, meaning her intern and resident, but told her to be sure to make an appointment with him in Endocrine Clinic.

He was glad to deflect the tiresome details of discharge planning. Prescriptions, transport home, were all someone else's job now. Consulting was gentlemen's work.

Rounds were going smoothly, and Brophy hadn't been paged all morning, a fact which had him worried. Quiet mornings meant things were percolating. It could be a very bad afternoon.

It didn't wait for afternoon. He got three pages within two minutes. The first was Rona, saying that a woman was on the line, but Rona disconnected whoever it was. The next was a call from Ob-Gyn Clinic. The clerk said it was Clarissa Leonard but she couldn't come to the phone. The third was Jethro, wanting to know when Brophy wanted to meet for Attending Rounds.

Then Clarissa paged again. When Brophy called back, Sol Zigelman answered the phone.

"Have we got problems."

"I know."

"How do you know already?" said Sol. "She only came in this morning."

"Which problems are we talking about?"

"I'm talking about Maria Addinizio. What are you talking about?"

Brophy realized Clarissa hadn't told Sol about Lynn Ann.

Clarissa got on the phone.

"Remember Mrs. Addinizio? The policewoman. She's in clinic. She's big for dates, but that's not why we're calling."

Brophy was glad to hear that, because he had no idea what big for dates meant. He was hoping nothing was going to happen to her. She was a nice lady, which should have been the clue bad things were in store.

"The problem is," Clarissa said, "her thyroid's big. I'm no endocrinologist, but she looks pretty jumpy to me."

"You think she's hyperthyroid?"

"That's what I'm telling you, doc."

"Terrific," said Brophy, unhappy because that couldn't be good news for either Mrs. Addinizio or her baby, and because he knew not the first thing about managing hyperthyroidism in pregnancy except that it was tricky and you had to know what you were doing.

"Be right over," he said, yielding to his clinical instinct to show up first ånd read later. Then he remembered he was the Fellow now, and would be expected to answer questions and say something intelligent, or at least to say something other people didn't already know. That's what consults were for.

"Clarissa?"

"Yes?"

"Would you mind if I sent over a medical student and a resident to see her first?"

"I don't care if you send over the bloody National Guard as long as she gets seen and we know what to do!"

"And, Clarissa—"

"Yes?"

"Is Sol there?"

"He's talking to someone."

"Good. I spoke to Lynn Ann."

"What's she want?"

"I'll talk to you later," said Brophy. "But I'm not smiling."

Brophy told Wendel and Robin to go see Mrs. Addinizio, and headed for the library, where he photocopied two articles about hyperthyroidism and pregnancy. He read them as he walked back to the clinic.

Sol was standing in the hallway, talking to Robin and Wendel.

"Ah, there he is!" said Sol when Brophy pushed through the door.

Brophy offered his hand, which Sol took in his two big paws.

"Now, what do we do for this lady?"

"Are you going to let me see her first, Sol?"

"Come," said Sol, pulling Brophy by the sleeve of his lab coat into the examining room, where Mrs. Addinizio sat on an examining table in a white paper gown.

"This pregnancy's getting to be more than you bargained for," said Brophy.

"Really," said Mrs. Addinizio, shaking her head. "Clarissa thinks I may have twins."

"Are we making you nervous, dragging all these doctors in to see you?" asked Brophy.

Sol beamed. Brophy was establishing rapport.

"I've felt so nervous lately," said Mrs. Addinizio, "I'd hardly notice the difference."

Brophy ran through his hyperthyroid questions, and Mrs. Addinizio said yes to every one: she had difficulty sleeping, felt warm when everyone around her was comfortable, and couldn't seem to sit still or concentrate. And she was losing weight rather than gaining. She also had a small goiter.

Brophy examined her under Sol's happy observation. Brophy felt he had to do something Wendel and Robin hadn't done, so after all the standard things he listened for bruits over the collar bones—something he had just read about in the articles he'd copied at the library. Sol asked him about it, and when Brophy explained that bruits over the clavicles were actually a more consistent finding than thyroid-gland bruits, Sol said, "See, a true maven."

When Brophy was done, he thanked Mrs. Addinizio for letting him examine her—something they had drilled into him at Manhattan Hospital. He told her he'd talk to Dr. Zigelman about what to do, but he thought she did have hyperthyroidism. Then he led Clarissa, Sol, Wendel, and Robin out to the hallway, closing the door behind them.

Robin and Clarissa said nothing, but they were both impressed. Brophy had been hewn in a clinical place and it showed.

"So what do we do, doc?" Sol asked.

"We'll have to present her to Jethro, of course," said Brophy.

"But I want to know *your* opinion."

"It's controversial; depends on who you read. The surgeons pretty much argue for surgery in the late first or early second trimester. They say it's better for the fetus that way. The medical docs say you can probably do just as well with low doses of antithyroid meds. No iodides, and of course no radioactive stuff."

"And what does Dr. Brophy say?"

"Dr. Brophy has never seen a case personally, Sol. But I'd give her a trial of medicine before I'd call in the blades."

"You see why I like Brophy," said Sol, taking Robin by the arm like a daughter. "He's never seen this problem personally. So he knows he doesn't know enough about it. He knows that reading about it isn't really the same thing as having to deal with it in a living patient."

Robin laughed.

"Why do you laugh?"

"I don't know."

"When will you show her to Jethro?" Sol asked.

"Let's get some numbers back on her," said Brophy. "We'll bring her to clinic next Tuesday or Thursday and Jethro can meet her then."

"No treatment? Why can't he see her now?"

"Try to drag Jethro out of the lab."

"But she'll be untreated."

"Nobody's going to treat her until we have some numbers."

"Okay," Sol said.

Brophy told Robin to draw the usual thyroid bloods, plus serum for antithyroid antibodies and for calcium.

"Why calcium?"

"Because we're presenting her to Jethro. And Jethro knows calcium."

"But the lady's got hyperthyroidism."

"Robin, people get hypercalcemic when they get hyperthyroid."

"So what?"

She was right. It was of no clinical importance. As soon as the thyroid normalized, their calciums normalized.

Brophy thought for a minute and called Duncan, who was, happily for Brophy, easy to find nowadays—always in his lab with his assay. Brophy explained about Maria Addinizio's pregnancy, her hyperthyroidism, and said that Jethro was the Attending.

"I see the problem," said Duncan, who had seen the problem frequently during the four months he was on Clinical Service. "What you have to do is get an opinion from a clinician without hurting anyone's feelings."

"That's it."

"When in trouble, don't forget the Vet."

Brophy waited to hear the rest, but Duncan was being silent.

"What's that supposed to mean?"

"It means call Chuck Mersault at the V.A."

"I thought he just took care of vets."

"They let him take care of real people whenever there's a problem over here."

Brophy called Mersault and explained the problem, pausing every few words to allow Chuck to ask, "So why call me?" But Chuck never asked. He just listened, as though he got this kind of call ten times a day, which in fact he did. Then he told Brophy what to do.

"Depends on who you read, of course," said Chuck. "But I believe Gerry Burrows. He says to use as low a dose of PTU as you can, say a hundred Q eight, then back off to fifty, BID."

Brophy thanked him.

"Any time," he said. "But, Brophy—you know I don't see a lot of pregnant vets, much less pregnant, hyperthyroid vets. Why don't you call up Burrows or Mazzaferri and ask them what they'd do?"

Brophy hung up, started to dial long distance information, then hung up again. Jethro was still the Attending on the case: it might be politic to ask him first, even though there wasn't a real calcium question to be had.

Brophy walked toward Jethro's lab, thinking about Mersault—and thinking about U.H. At U.H., Mersault had the social status of a small-town undertaker. He just wasn't polite company—necessary but ostracized. At Manhattan Hospital he'd have had medical students hanging all over him, emulating, adulating, massaging his ego into a state of perennial erection.

But no such luck at the University Hospital, where cases of egotistical priapism were found only among those who saw their names enshrined on the covers of *The New England Journal of Medicine,* and the *Journal of Endocrinology and Metabolism.*

Brophy walked down to Jethro's lab.

"Got a great case for you!" Brophy shouted over the Beethoven. "Hyperthyroidism in pregnancy."

Jethro groaned. Then he recovered.

"Fine," he said. "And Brophy?"

"Yes?"

"What I know about hyperthyroidism in pregnancy you

could put in my little finger. Why don't you call Massi at St. Louis? Ask *him* about this. . . ."

Massi agreed with Mersault about using the low-dose PTU, but he was worried when he heard Mrs. Addinizio was big for dates.

"Have they ECHOed her belly?"

"No, why?"

"Moles, choriocarcinoma can pump out enough HCG to make someone hyperthyroid."

Brophy ran back to OB Clinic, but everyone had left. The clerk said Clarissa and Sol were having lunch in the cafeteria.

Brophy found them at a corner table.

"She's scheduled for an ultrasound tomorrow," Clarissa said. "It's part of the workup for big for dates."

"Oh."

"You had to call St. Louis to learn that?" laughed Sol. "Academic medicine in action."

"I was calling to ask around about how the mavens would handle her."

"Very impressive," Clarissa said. She really meant it.

Brophy bought a roast beef sandwich and went back to the Fellows' Office, where he sat down at his desk and made a list of all the things he had to do:

1. Check Heimler and Sipple for signs of life
2. Check Addinizio's ultrasound tomorrow
3. Check Addinizio's thyroid tests
4. Check the lab for Magnussen's free catecholamines
5. Check the lab for new hypercalcemics

Brophy prayed there would be no new hypercalcemics that day. He was too busy to come in and wait for someone to urinate the next morning.

19

"She really adores you," said Clarissa. She was talking about Mrs. Addinizio. Brophy was on the phone in the Fellows' Office, trying to get Burrows in Toronto. He slammed down the receiver. "Damn. He's out of town."

"Who is?"

"Burrows." Brophy sifted through papers on his desk, looking for another authority to call. "Thyroid maven. Wanted to ask him about Mrs. Addinizio."

"You were really nice to her today."

"I'm just a nice guy."

"You didn't used to be."

"When was I ever not a nice guy?"

"In New York." Clarissa was sitting on a desk, swinging her legs. "You never even looked at patients when you talked to them, then."

"I was an intern," said Brophy. "By definition psychotic."

"And you never would have gotten upset not being able to get someone on the phone to ask them about a patient."

"Interns don't get upset about things like that."

"You never would have even called in those days."

"I had thirty patients sometimes, on Service. I didn't have time to take a shit, much less call long distance tracking down mavens. That was for Fellows."

"So now you have the time, you're a nice guy?"

"Yes."

"No. I think you've changed."

"I haven't changed. I've just graduated. I'm not an intern."

"No."

"People shouldn't be held responsible for their behavior when they're interns," said Brophy. "It's a case of temporary insanity, open and shut."

"No, Brophy, you've changed. You're a better person. Be gracious and say, 'Thank you for having noticed.'"

"I was always nice. You just knew me at a strange time."

Clarissa stood up. "Have it your way," she said and left.

Brophy leaned back in his swivel chair, hands behind his head. It was almost like going home again, being with Clarissa. He felt like such a different person now, miles away from New York, light-years away from Manhattan Hospital. But she made him remember the standards he'd been judged by. He was the same. Only the circumstances had changed.

20

Lynn Ann arrived early. She knocked on the door of the Fellows' Office at five-fifteen and looked through the window in the door.

Brophy let her in.

"Found it with no trouble. You always keep it locked?"

"Have to keep the secrets safe."

She looked around. The room filled with her perfume. "Nice big sign on the door. Little crowded, isn't it?"

"We don't believe in wasting the government's money here at the U.H.," said Brophy. "You can quote me."

Lynn Ann took a cigarette out of a gold case.

"Can I smoke? Or would it use up all the oxygen?"

"We can open the door."

She lit up and looked at her reflection in the window in the door to the hallway.

"Well," she said, blowing smoke ceilingward, "what can you show me?"

"Not a whole lot," said Brophy quietly.

"Pardon?"

"I talked to the powers that be around this place and was told that since we have nothing to hide, we have nothing to show."

"What are you *talking* about?" she said, blinking. She wore silver eye shadow. Brophy wondered if the lashes were real.

"I can't show you the protocol."

"What?"

"There's no use of radioisotopes. The thing is clean. But if you want to find out what's in it, you'll have to get it from the sources who tipped you off in the first place."

"I can't believe this. You said I could come and get it off your desk. You were so open."

"That was before I got told to keep away from inquisitive reporters."

"Who told you to do that?"

"I have to protect my sources."

"Now I *am* getting mad."

"Sorry."

"*You're* sorry . . ."

"You said you had sources: use them."

"What are you so afraid of?"

"Hey, I just work here."

"Look, this smells of rat. Why do you suppose they told you to stonewall?"

"Ours is not to reason why . . . just churn out New Knowledge."

"And don't care who you hurt."

"I know enough to know when I'm hurting patients and when I'm not. That's the difference between me and you."

21

Thursday morning Lars woke up with a lump on his throat. He noticed it while shaving. Brophy had poked around his neck pretty aggressively when Lars was on the CRU, and at first Lars thought it might be just a tender spot from that . . .

But this was a short distance from where Brophy had been prodding. And it was rock hard.

He wiped away the shaving cream and watched himself swallow in the mirror. He could see it bob up and down under the skin.

His mouth went dry and it was hard to swallow. He swallowed again, watching. He saw the lump float up, then sink down. Lars felt he was watching something entirely unconnected to himself. It just didn't belong there. He felt it again. Solid. He could slit the skin with his razor and tear it out.

There was only one thing it could be: cancer.

How could Brophy have missed it?

Well, he wouldn't give him the chance to miss it again.

Lars knew he had to do something.

Driving to work, Lars thought about what he would say to get past McCullough's secretary, to get seen that day. He hadn't told Beth about the lump. He drank orange juice, careful to turn away, so she wouldn't see it bob up and down; so she wouldn't get hysterical. He'd see McCullough today. There'd be time for worry later.

McCullough spoke to him right away. There was no need for lengthy explanations.

"Well, if it's just popped up, it's probably nothing to get

alarmed about," said McCullough. "You say they didn't feel it just a few days ago in the hospital?"

"They weren't feeling in this area. It's pretty big. Like a pebble or a small rock."

"Rock hard?" said McCullough. "Why don't you come by this afternoon? Let me see if we have an opening.

McCullough didn't have an opening, but he scheduled Lars for eight-thirty Friday morning.

22

Brophy was sitting in clinic, looking through the lab reports folder. The nurses there had collected all the numbers on each patient scheduled to be seen that day in Endocrine Clinic.

Brophy had four sheduled: Mrs. Liddle, Mrs. Addinizio, Lars Magnussen, and one new patient. Mrs. Addinizio was scheduled first, and hadn't shown. Her thyroid tests were high. Brophy remembered she was supposed to have had her ultrasound that morning. He called Ultrasound.

"Addinizio?" said the technician. "Who is this?"

"Dr. Brophy."

"We did her about an hour ago."

"Yes?"

"She got admitted."

Brophy paged Clarissa.

"She's got one," Clarissa said. "Sol's going to evacuate it this afternoon if we can get her on the OR schedule."

"A mole? She's got a mole?"

"That's what the ECHO showed. Think there'll be any problem with the hyperthyroidism?"

"No. In fact, her mole might be what's making her hyperthyroid," Brophy said, remembering what Massi had told him. Massi actually had been talking about tumors that sometimes follow moles—choriocarcinomas, which make a hormone capable of stimulating thyroid glands. Brophy didn't want to think about that possibility for Mrs. Addinizio.

"Stop by and see her," Clarissa said. "She's pretty low and she always liked you."

"Sure," said Brophy, hanging up, distracted. Mrs. Ad-

200

dinizio was turning into a great case. Two weeks ago she thought she was pregnant. But all she really had was degenerating placenta in her uterus.

Brophy had asked Sol to draw some blood for calcium studies on her. Jethro had never studied a hyperthyroid pregnant lady, and he wanted to run her blood through his assays. Now he had blood from a lady with a mole. He would probably be the first to report 1.25 vitamin D level in a patient with mole.

Today she would have all those grapelike villi sucked out with a vacuum suction, and tomorrow she could go home. And she had thought she was going to have a baby.

There was no report on Lars Magnussen's urine for free catecholamines. Brophy called the lab. Not that he thought Lars would actually keep his appointment, but Brophy wanted to check while he remembered.

The lab clerk answered on the second ring. She told Brophy the urine wouldn't be run until two o'clock that afternoon.

"He had it collected Tuesday," said Brophy, trying not to complain.

"They only do one run a week for cateholamines," said the clerk. "It's cost-effective that way."

"That what your computer says?" said Brophy, losing the battle for eternal pleasantness. "It's cost-effective that way?"

"That's what Dr. Dumfy says," said the clerk cheerfully.

Brophy hung up. He couldn't understand why he had gotten angry at the clerk. She was a fine clerk. It was a magnificent lab. It just didn't seem right for Mrs. Addinizio to have mole.

23

Brophy went over the consult list before going to check the chemistries. There was only one new consult. It was from Surgery, for "diabetic management." Robin had signed it off. Everyone hated those referrals, which basically meant the surgeons didn't want to take care of the patient once they were past the surgery and the fun was over. Robin was nice to have taken it.

Brophy made it up two flights of stairs before his beeper went off. He answered the page from the phone next to the atomic spectrophotometer.

"Dr. Brophy, this is JB-Three."

"Yes?" he said, wondering why people identified themselves as wards.

"There's a note here to call you about Mr. Heimler."

"Yes?"

"So I'm calling."

"He's dead?"

"Either that or he's fooled us all."

Brophy called the clinic, but Duncan had left. He called the Section Office, Duncan's lab, and the Fellows' Office. No answer. Then he remembered it was Thursday. Duncan moonlighted at the nursing home on Thursday evenings.

Brophy called the autopsy room. The resident on call for autopsies wasn't there. They gave him a beeper number, and Brophy phoned the charge nurse on JB-3, who told him the body was wrapped and Escort had already taken it to the morgue.

Brophy felt a little sick. *Who knows how long ago Heimler*

died? It usually took an hour to get the body off the floor. They had to pull IVs, wrap and label, close the doors to all the other patients' rooms, and call the elevator. Then they had to roll it down the hall and open the ward back up again.

Brophy ran down to the autopsy room in the basement and paged the pathology resident again. The resident finally answered.

"Remember that patient—Heimler? With the hypercalcemia and the tumor?" Brophy asked.

"You work with Duncan Gordon?"

"Yes."

"The melanoma? He ready for me?"

"Yes. What do I have to do to get autopsy permission?"

"Closest living relative. Wife, usually," the resident said.

"He was a vagrant bum. No known relatives."

"That could be a problem."

"We need that tumor before it autolyzes," Brophy said.

The path resident gave Brophy the name of the chief of the Autopsy Service, who knew all about Duncan's research and told Brophy to bring him Heimler's chart. Brophy got the chart from the morgue clerk and ran over to the autopsy chief, who examined the face sheet and to Brophy's embarrassment found "Bruce R. Heimler, brother," listed as "Relative." Brophy had never thought to look.

And now he'd have to tell Duncan the next morning that he'd blown it.

To Brophy's stupefaction, however, the chief not only found a Bruce R. Heimler listed in the Providence directory, but he answered his phone when Brophy called. The chief listened on the other phone.

"Mr. Heimler?"

"Who's asking?"

"This is Dr. Brophy from University Hospital."

"I paid my bill."

"I'm calling about your brother Joe."

"He in town?"

"I'm afraid I have some bad news."

"Yeah?"

"I'm afraid to say, he's died."

"That's too bad."

"Mr. Heimler?"

"What is it?"

Brophy could hear the television in the background. It was loud. Bruce R. was watching the Red Sox, and they were having a big inning when Brophy interrupted.

"It's very important we do an examination to find out why your brother died."

"Yeah," said Bruce R. Brophy could hear the crowd roar. Somebody had hit one out.

"We need your permission for an autopsy," Brophy said, this somewhat lower, and he wasn't sure Bruce R. could hear, if he wanted to.

"Okay."

"Can you send us a telegram, giving us—"

"I said okay."

Brophy looked over at the autopsy chief, who nodded.

"Thanks," said Brophy.

"No problem," said Bruce R. Heimler, hanging up.

"Really shook him up," said the chief. "You better work on your technique."

Brophy paged the autopsy resident, who said he would be there in fifteen minutes. Then Brophy dashed up to Duncan's lab, pulled on the asbestos gloves, and went to the walk-in freezer, where he hammered away at the dry-ice block until he had enough to fill two big, black, insulated tissue boxes. He grabbed four bottles of pink-cell-culture fluid, popped them into his lab coat pocket along with two bottles of fixative, and raced down to the autopsy room.

They had Mr. Heimler laid out and opened up. His abdominal organs were socked-in solid with tumor.

"Like cement," said the autopsy resident.

The diener was cutting a skin flap at the skull. He looked up from his work, peering around to see the abdomen. "Holy Mother," said the diener, shaking his head and going back to his scalping.

"I need tumor for cell culture and to freeze," Brophy said.

"It's not really sterile," said the resident.

The resident cut Brophy some tumor and they filled the cell-culture bottles, then the two big dry-ice buckets.

The diener started in with the electric power saw on the skull. Brophy hated that smell of aerosolized bone.

"Smells like when a dentist drills your teeth," Brophy said, feeling queasy. He could feel the microscopic bone dust drifting into his nose and eyes; dust from Heimler's skull settling, implanting on the mucous membranes of his throat.

"Got enough tumor?" the resident asked.

"Thanks," said Brophy. He had had enough of Mr. Heimler's airborne, ground-up skull.

He ran up the stairs, breathing in the clean air, unlocked the lab door, and spread out his take on the lab bench Duncan usually used.

He logged the tissue-culture vials into the lab book and placed them in the refrigerator, then put the dry-ice buckets into the walk-in freezer.

He called Duncan at the nursing home. They had to page him.

"Heimler got transferred to the Eternal Care Unit," said Brophy, trying to restrain himself.

Duncan groaned. "Oh, great. They do it every time. They wait till I get someplace twenty miles away and can't leave. *Then* they crump. Can you get somebody to come in and do the post? When'd he go? Probably too late, anyway."

"Four-fifty."

"It's six. Christ." Duncan sounded as though he might cry. "We blew our one chance."

"We got tissue."

"Maybe we can get Sipple when he goes, but it just kills me to miss . . . *What did you say?*"

"We got it. I got the resident to come in. We got permission and everything: tissue, cell culture, everything on dry ice . . ."

There was a long, loud cheer from the other end of the line. They must have wondered, at the nursing home.

"Brophy!" he shouted. "What a lifesaver!"

"He was *loaded* with it," squealed Brophy.

"How much did you get?" shrieked Duncan.

"Buckets! Pounds! But it wasn't easy getting permission."

"Permission? From who?"

"He had a brother."

"No!"

"Yes."

"How'd you ever get ahold of the brother?"

"Hey, Dr. Brophy gets his man. Dr. Resourceful," hating himself for taking all the credit.

"You are a *prince*. A true prince."

Duncan rattled on about what to do with the cell-culture things. He agonized about the nude mice. Brophy didn't know how to inject them. They could be growing Heimler's tumor like Kansas topsoil grows corn. But you had to do it right or they got infected and died before they could grow anything but staph and clostridia and whatever bacteria they got septic and died with. Duncan hadn't taught Brophy the technique for the nude mice yet.

Duncan congratulated Brophy a few more times and hung up, exhausted but happy.

Brophy sat down and considered going back up to check the calciums. And he had to see Sipple, who was probably about to make his contribution to medical science. And Mrs. Addinizio.

Then he thought about Mr. Heimler, or what was left of him, down there on that cold slab with the diener working on getting his brain out of the skull, with that electric saw, and the brain dust in the air.

The phone rang. It was Duncan.

"Be sure that path resident sends us a copy of the autopsy report."

"Sure."

"Hey," said Duncan, brightly. "How's Sipple doing?"

"Not quite there yet."

"Keep on it. He'll make it."

"He was seventeen yesterday."

"He'll make it. Soon."

"I know."

Duncan hung up.

Brophy stood up, and felt a little nauseated. He had that skull dust in his nostrils. He walked across the hall and hung up his lab coat. The calciums on the print-out machine next to the atomic spectrophotometer could wait until morning. Brophy was going home. There had been enough New Knowledge for one day.

24

It took a long, hot shower to finally expunge the skull dust from Brophy's nostrils and the autopsy room from his brain. Clean, and wrapped in his terry cloth robe, he suddenly became voracious and threw open the refrigerator door: nothing but Dannon yogurt.

He opened a beer and sat down on the couch, considered calling Clarissa for dinner, but told himself to be rational. She had made her choice in New York, and Brophy had to keep her from becoming a recurrent disease. Of course she was different now—he couldn't imagine her slipping from bed to bed anymore. But then again he hadn't been able to imagine it in New York, either. He reached for the phone, but stopped. She'd talk about Mrs. Addinizio or Magnussen or something medical, and eventually there'd be analysis or discussion of basic values. It would wind up tense and emotional and Brophy needed something different tonight.

He thought about going down to one of the bars on South Main Street where there were perfumed women, dark corners, and cold drinks.

The phone rang. It was Lynn Ann.

"Can I tempt you with wine and a steak?"

Driving over to her apartment, Brophy fought off a persistent erection. It was a sultry evening and as he drove along Benefit Street he smelled flowers—honeysuckle and lilac.

She was wearing something slinky and low-cut when she came to the door. It had a satin finish, and Brophy ran his hand over the rise below the small of her back before he could think.

"You're an eager one," she said, pushing away after a brief kiss.

"I just wanted to set the proper tone—all play, no business."

"Agreed.'

When she went into the kitchen, he explored her apartment. It was a lovely apartment, with a fireplace and ten-foot ceilings, but it did not feel like New England. Too much chrome and glass. And it was air conditioned. *Vogue, Glamour,* and *Cosmopolitan* were spread out on the coffee table in front of the plum-colored couch. There were hardwood floors and a lime-green area rug, and a big, bright wall hanging: a pair of toucans. The colors of the wall hanging picked up the plum and green. It was a glossy, New York place.

He walked into the kitchen, where she was pouring the wine. She gave him a glass and told him to go out on the porch, which was through the kitchen and overlooked the city: the State House, the renovated brick factory buildings, now fancy condos, all deep purple in the twilight. It was a splendid view. Brophy could smell the steak cooking.

Lynn Ann came out with her glass and they looked at the city, sipping. When they finished she said, "I need a refill," and handed him her glass, but as he stepped by her she put her arms around his neck and said, "Not that kind of refill," and kissed him and didn't stop. She kept at it, and when his hands roamed all over the satin finish, she pressed closer and her tongue picked up the tempo. Brophy reeled under the sensory bombardment, her perfume, the steak aroma, the satin feel, and the wine taste of her mouth. But most of all, there was the feel of her body through the dress—lean, muscled, willing, and very soft in places.

She broke away. "The steak will burn," she said. "It's getting very hot."

He watched her walk away from him, her heart-shaped ass moving in that silky satin. The steak was wonderful and they finished the wine.

"Would you like an apéritif?"

"Sure," croaked Brophy. The only apéritif he wanted was Lynn Ann.

"I got this specially," Lynn Ann said, holding up a bottle of Irish Mist.

Brophy laughed.

They drank it on the couch, where he made efforts to get

under the dress, hampered greatly by the liquor glass he kept placing on the table and almost kicking over with each attempt. Lynn Ann smiled at his difficulties and responded whenever he managed to set down his glass, get past her glass, and wrap an arm around her.

"Let's have dessert," she said finally, taking his hand and leading him to the bedroom.

Tell me you didn't say that.

She was more original in bed, and Brophy couldn't remember when he'd had more things done to him in a shorter time.

Brophy was most proud—he hadn't said a word about U.H.

Lynn Ann was very nice about it: "You're delicious to have in bed," she said, "even if you won't talk to me." She was lying on her stomach, stroking Brophy's eyelashes.

"I distinctly remember talking to you at dinner. I recall having a bona fide conversation."

"Not about what you do."

"But that's business," laughed Brophy. "You agreed tonight was not going to be business."

"Did it feel like business?"

"It felt wonderful."

"And I plied you with wine. . . ." She ran a finger across his chest. "Not Dom Perignon, but wine nevertheless."

"If I'd known this was business, I'd have let you take me out. You could deduct it."

"I like cooking at home."

"It was superb."

"But you didn't talk."

"All dark secrets are safe with me."

"Are they so dark?"

"The big one is that there are none."

Lynn Ann laughed. "Not likely."

"I'm serious," said Brophy. "Is that so hard to believe?"

"Yes."

"Why should people be willing to let you reduce their work to a five-inch column?"

"Oh, I get more than that. Some of my stories run ten."

"There you are."

"What's so bad about ten inches?"

"I can see it now: 'University Hospital: World of Shattered Hopes.'"

"Catchy."

"'*Providence. AP.* Behind door Two-fifteen at University Hospital lies Joe . . . Smith, age fifty-two, unemployed, a derelict, a Bowery bum. Life has not been kind to Joe. But like many of life's dispossessed, Joe knew he could turn to the hospital when he couldn't go on. His last best hope lay at University Hospital, on the cancer ward. . . .'"

"I may let you write the article."

"Or we could do it on the pregnancy project: 'Pregnant Patients Poisoned at U.H.' I like that alliteration."

"I like 'The World of Shattered Hopes.'"

"That's my favorite, too."

"You might be good at this."

"Might be? It'd be easy, from the inside," said Brophy, reaching for some wine. "I could write such a lovely article."

"You have to research it. It takes work, you know."

"Not for me. I'm living it." Brophy turned his glazed eyes back to the ceiling, where he could visualize the front page of the Providence paper, with his story. "' Dr. Donald Brophy, twenty-nine, Fellow in Endocrinology at U.H., smiles with warm, empathetic eyes and recalls how he got into cancer research.'"

"Empathetic eyes?"

"Human interest."

Lynn laughed. She had pretty, white teeth.

"'I interned at the Whipple Hospital for Cancer and Allied Diseases in New York City,' said Dr. Brophy, in his eyes, a far-off look, seeing it all again. 'I was rocked by what I saw: death, disease, disfigurement, despair, disillusionment. It was downright depressing. I knew I had to make it my life's work.'"

"Did you really?"

"Make it my life's work?"

"Intern at Whipple? I thought you were at Manhattan Hospital, with Clarissa."

"They were part of the same medical center."

"And now you're studying cancer again?"

"Not 'again.' I wasn't studying it in New York. I was watching it. There's an enormous difference."

"Which is?"

"When you're an intern at a cancer center, you're one of the victims," said Brophy. "When you become a Fellow, however, you are no longer concerned with the individual patient. That's what the interns are for."

"How specialized."

"The Fellow," continued Brophy, ignoring her remark, "is not just listening to the bombs fall. He is trying to learn from it."

"Are you?"

"Trying?"

"Learning?"

"I don't know," said Brophy. "I really don't."

25

Brophy groped for the clock in the dark. Lynn Ann shifted away from him, and he found it on the night table, next to her. It was six A.M. He had to get home, shower, change, shave, and be on the CRU to do an insulin-tolerance test at eight o'clock.

He did not feel like getting up. It was beginning to get light out, but he could not rouse himself.

Brophy rolled out of bed. The light was coming in from the window near Lynn Ann.

Brophy's bladder issued an urgent reminder of the two bottles of wine from the night before and he found the bathroom.

Brophy was sure Lynn Ann would have dental floss, with those teeth. She had very nice teeth. He opened the mirrored cabinet. There was no floss. There was, however, an impressive psychopharmacopoeia: Mellaril, Stelazine, Thorazine, Elavil, Valium. Everything for the well-appointed schizo. Brophy looked at the dates. July–August of the previous year must have been rocky. Somebody thought Lynn had real disease. You don't prescribe Stelazine just to smooth out the rough spots in life. . . .

Brophy arrived on the CRU at five minutes before eight. The patient was a thiry-year-old woman Brophy had admitted. She had had a prolactinoma, discovered a year ago: her breasts had started disgorging milk and she had stopped menstruating. They cut it out at U.H.

Now she was in for her follow-up tests. The nurses had her

IV in. Brophy took out his pocket calculator. The nurse told him the patient's weight in pounds. Brophy converted pounds to kilograms, figured out how much insulin to give a sixty-five-kilogram woman, and drew it up. The insulin looked very unimpressive in the syringe. Looked like water, just a thimbleful.

He injected it and started chatting. The woman was from Westport, Connecticut. She was the wife of a stockbroker who worked in New York. She was very funny about Westport.

"You see ten-year-old kids shopping in Pappagallo there. Looking for pocketbooks," she said. "Ten-year-old girls should be out running around in blue jeans—playing soccer and beating up boys. In Westport they're shopping for pocketbooks with Mommy's MasterCard."

About ten minutes later the sweat came. The CRU nurse came back with the reading on the blood sugar: it had dropped from 100 to 70. The drop had taken twenty minutes. It was a little fast: they may have taken out a little too much pituitary.

Brophy did not know this lady very well, but he was dropping her blood sugar to seizure levels. Still, he felt in control. He could always bring her back with his Bristojet of IV glucose. And, unlike the infusion he'd done on the athlete for Cecil, he understood perfectly why this test had to be done. They had to know whether or not she had enough pituitary reserve after her surgery.

"Fucking shame what they do to those kids. . . ." The woman was crying. She was very pale. Brophy drew a stat glucose and the nurse ran it down to the lab.

"You okay?" he asked, shaking her shoulder. She was hard to rouse—just what Brophy did not want to see. Wake up. No coma now.

She opened her eyes. "Say something?" she drawled, thick-tongued.

"Tell me about your husband. How did you meet?"

They had met at the Club Med in Cancún.

"But it wasn't like that," she said, laughing. She was getting better. Her pituitary had pumped out ACTH, which stimulated her adrenal glands to release cortisol and raise her blood sugar.

The nurse came back to say the blood sugar had been 40 when the patient was crying and sleepy. Brophy sent off another, sure it was higher now.

"I'm so embarrassed," she said.

"Everyone cries—it's the insulin." He took her pulse: 120. Her arm was wet; her skin soaked. The sweating was impressive; the whole reaction was impressive. Just a drop of clear liquid insulin had done all that. The power of hormones.

Brophy thought back to his clinic patient, Mrs. Kroc, with her nonhypoglycemia. She should be lashed to this bed for an insulin-tolerance test. Then she'd know what hypoglycemia was really like.

Sitting there with the nice, pasty-looking lady from Westport, Brophy suddenly recalled Beth's description of Lars Magnussen on the tennis court—pale and sweating.

If her description of her husband's drenching sweats, pallor, and dilated pupils was accurate, then Lars looked just like the lady from Westport did now—and for basically the same reason: he was awash in adrenalin. But nobody had injected Lars with insulin or anything else to provoke a cortisol-adrenalin tidalwave.

Brophy dialed the lab from the bedside phone and asked for the urine on Lars Magnussen. The clerk at the computer terminal punched MAGNUSSEN into her machine and the numbers appeared on her glowing screen.

"Magnussen, Lars," said the clerk. "One hundred twenty micrograms per twenty-four hours. Total volume: eighteen hundred ml."

"What's normal?"

The clerk punched in the request for normal ranges.

"Oh, my."

"What?"

"Upper limits of normal is one hundred. Definite diagnosis requires one-fifty."

"And he's one-twenty?"

"That's right, doc. One-twenty."

"Terrific," Brophy said unhappily. "Now what am I supposed to do?"

"Call Dr. Dumfy," said the clerk. "That's what we say around here: when in doubt, dial Dumfy."

26

Daniel Dumfy was happy to hear from Brophy. He'd been expecting Brophy's call because his systematic review of results with the chief technician of each lab section had revealed the borderline elevation in Lars Magnussen's urinary free-catecholamine level.

Brophy told him about the urinary catecholamines and about Lars.

"Brophy, you should always remember: call me as soon as you think of it. It saves time. Remember that—you'll never forget."

Dumfy explained the best test for pheochromocytoma was not urinary free-catecholamines.

"We get into trouble with it," he said. "We do a real nice VMA here."

"VMA, huh?" said Brophy, acid burning deep within his duodenum.

"Didn't we talk about this guy already? Larsmussen?"

"Magnussen," croaked Brophy.

"You told me you got a urine to rule out pheo. I thought you'd ordered a VMA," Dumfy said.

"I did send you a urine to rule out pheo: I sent you a free catechol."

"Not the best test, Brophy. You should always talk to me first. Now you've got a free catechol of one-twenty. What're you going to do with that? Flush it down the toilet, that's what you're going to do. Get me a VMA. That's a nice test."

"But that paper in the New England *Journal* from Harvard," said Brophy.

"Harvard? What do they know? We see one, maybe two pheos a year here. VMA made the diagnosis every time. The free cats were really up in only one of them—last year. If the tumor's real big, the VMA's a lot better."

"But I thought there were so many things that interfered with the VMA assay."

"You thought wrong, Brophy. That's why you should always call me first. Don't try to think, call. No, we got a good VMA technique now. We can band everything out. If he's got a pheo, we'll see it on the VMA. Send me another urine. We'll run it for VMA. What's the name? Larsmussen?"

"What were you saying about if the tumor's big?"

"Some pheos are so big they metabolize everything, so all you wind up with is lots of VMA. Everything else is borderline; the VMA's sky-high."

Brophy hung up, feeling depressed. He wanted a yes or a no. Now he had a big maybe. He'd have to call Lars and give him the chance to turn in a repeat specimen. Fat chance he'd go along with that.

Jethro didn't believe Lars had a pheo, anyway, and Robin said Brophy was being an alarmist. It was all clinical judgment. But that amounted to a big guess. You had to do the test to know anything for sure. Brophy laughed at himself—a few weeks doing infusions, collecting tumor and data, and he'd turned into a numbers man. What did Robin or Jethro know? Nobody had the numbers on Lars. Of course, now Brophy had some numbers: unfortunately the wrong ones.

Fortunately for Brophy, he was saved from having to think about Lars for the moment by a page from one of the wards. Mr. Sipple had died.

Brophy smiled and shook his head. Classic. Sipple had hung on all week, clinging improbably to existence in the face of truly celestial blood-calcium levels, heart beating in defiance of calcium flux, ion-exchange, and the laws of bioelectricity. Now he decides to die. Actually, he was a little early. *Late* Friday afternoon would have been the perfect time to ensure Brophy maximum difficulty. Late Friday afternoon Sipple could have died and been assured Brophy would never manage to round up Duncan, the pathology resident on autopsy, the relatives who needed to give consent. But now he had a chance.

It would be hectic, coordinating all the people and telephone calls to get tissue from Mr. Sipple for Duncan's assays. But Brophy knew he had a shot. He'd never have time to call Lars. But maybe they could get some tissue for the nude mice. Duncan would be so pleased.

27

When McCullough's secretary arrived at eight-fifteen Friday morning, Lars was waiting outside the office door.

McCullough got there at eight-twenty and took Lars right in to an examining room. He felt the lump.

"They didn't feel this at U.H.?"

"If they did," said Lars, "they sure as hell didn't tell me about it."

"I'm not sure it's in your thyroid," said McCullough. "There may be something in the thyroid itself, but this feels more like a lymph node."

"A lymph node?"

"A gland. You need a thyroid scan."

"When?"

"As soon as we can get it."

They could get it at eleven that morning.

"If this thing is cold on scan," said McCullough, "it's going to have to come out."

"What would being cold mean?"

"It could be a tumor."

"When will we know?"

"Late this afternoon," said McCullough. "If it's positive, I'll have you seen by a surgeon Monday."

"Who?" asked Lars, hoping McCullough would say Nancy Barnah.

"A thyroid surgeon . . . probably . . . Well, let's cross that bridge when we come to it." McCullough would have Lars seen by either of two men he did business with, depending on which one had the time.

Lars decided to drive directly to the hospital instead of going back to his office for the hour or two he could spend at his desk. He wouldn't get much done, thinking about the scan. It wasn't until he pulled into the parking lot that he realized it was Friday the thirteenth.

They gave Lars the radioactive cocktail. He sipped it in Nuclear Medicine just about the time Mr. Sipple died. Lars didn't like Nuclear Medicine. It was all very new and shiny and there were no green plants anywhere, as if nothing could live in this spaceship atmosphere with all the ionizing radiation.

The scan was painless but unnerving. He sat face to face with a very large metal machine that silently counted the radioactivity he could almost feel emanating from his neck. Lars wondered what the machine was learning.

It didn't take long.

"How is it?" he asked the technician.

"Your doctor will get a report as soon as the radiologist reads it."

"When will that be?"

"Later this afternoon."

Lars drove back to the office, hating the technician for not telling him what he already knew: he had cancer in his neck. It was gettitng bigger all the time, tracking in among all the muscles and nerves and blood vessels. Lars could feel it moving, expanding under his touch.

Brophy had really blown it. Brophy was negligent as hell. How could he miss a rock that size in someone's neck?

Lars walked past the secretaries on the way to his office. One was telling the other about her car troubles. Lars wondered how anyone could worry about anything so trivial.

At his desk, he tried to read, but he couldn't keep his mind on it. He kept imagining his family without him, trying to imagine what it would be like. Beth would remarry. His boys would grow up with another father. They were old enough to remember.

He didn't think about the details of dying from that inexorable malignancy in his neck, or how long it would take, or how painful it might be, or what exactly it would feel like. He wasn't curious about the details of destruction: tumors eroding through windpipes, cutting off air. None of that microvisualization passed before Lars' eyes. Until today he hadn't even realized he had looked forward to so many things, to growing old.

Without ever having thought about it, he had planned for those years. It was an underlying assumption. He had never seriously considered not being around. He had bought life insurance, set up trust funds, but none of that had stirred serious imaginings.

Then it struck him that he'd not thought once about his job. He never even wondered whether or not he would have made partner. He hadn't any real curiosity who would win any of the five cases he was working on.

And his parents. This will really do it. First Olaf, now Lars. What was it Brophy had said? Lars had been too concerned about the kidney stone pain at the time to listen. Brophy had asked about Olaf: he seemed to think there might be some connection. But Olaf died suddenly. They thought stroke or heart attack. This would be cancer. There couldn't be any connection.

28

Getting the tumor out of Mr. Sipple, into the mice, and frozen for the assays took all afternoon.

"Another hit!" Duncan said, pumping Brophy's hand.

"Thanks."

"This thing's really taking off!" Duncan's eyebrows were jumping.

"I know."

"I can't tell you how much it's meant to me. And doing it all, and Clinical Service, too. Really—it's just terrific!"

"Such praise . . ."

"Well, I wanted to let you know I really appreciate it," Duncan said.

"I know. But it's not like you to be so effusive."

"Clarissa says I don't tell you I appreciate you."

Brophy laughed. "When did you talk to her?"

"I don't know. Yesterday. But I mean it. You've really been a tremendous boost."

"I can't believe she's ragging my buddies."

"It wasn't like that," Duncan protested. "I think she really likes you."

"In her own way."

Duncan looked at Brophy with his friendly smile. He never would ask. He just waited, playing with the beeper on his belt.

"We used to go out," said Brophy finally. "In New York."

"She told me."

"Didn't work out."

"I guessed."

Brophy watched Duncan tug at his ragged collar, waiting to hear more. Brophy didn't say anything.

"She's really something," Duncan said. "There's something so . . ." He searched for the word. "*Refined* about her. And she likes you."

"She doesn't even know me anymore. It's been years."

"That's what she said."

"What? That she doesn't know me?"

"That it's been years."

"Maybe I improve with age."

"Maybe."

Whenever Clarissa showed signs she cared, it had the desired effect. She used to do that in New York—tell someone how much she loved Brophy, and it always got back to him as planned and it always worked.

Duncan got in a sudden hurry to get home. One of his kids was playing softball for Barrington Day Camp. On the rare occasions when he wasn't talking about the malignancy project, he was telling Brophy what a great ballplayer his nine-year-old was. Duncan went to all the games.

He had married his high-school girlfriend when he was a senior in college, over his father's objections.

"Her father wasn't a surgeon," said Duncan. "Sold used cars. She wasn't even pregnant at the time."

"She put you through med school?"

"Dad sure as hell wasn't going to, once we got married. He would've been real smug if we'd broke up trying to get through . . . like everybody else."

"Sounds like you're being a little tough on Daddy."

"Hardly," said Duncan, stuffing his journals into his knapsack. "I ran away from home about four times in high school. Dad went to Dartmouth, so naturally that's where I was supposed to go."

"You had other ideas."

"Didn't get in."

"You were better off. Gets cold and lonely at Dartmouth."

"So I went to Wesleyan. Dad still can't remember the name of the place. It's just 'that school Duncan went to.' First in my pre-med class. When time came to apply to med school, I got into Cornell."

"That where Daddy went?"

"Of course. He said the only reason I got in was because

he'd gone there." Duncan looked at Brophy, his eyes reddening. "*First* in my fucking pre-med class and he says that." Duncan shook his head. "I fucking went to Yale."

Duncan flew out the door. Brophy never got a chance to ask what happened to his wife.

29

Brophy hadn't checked the calciums. He hadn't called Magnussen. He looked at his watch: It was only three forty-five. He wavered, wanting to go home, and decided finally to do some telephoning. He might even call Clarissa.

He looked up Magnussen in the phone book. It listed a home phone only. Brophy thought about getting Lars' chart for his office number but decided it would be easier talking to his wife anyway.

Beth answered the phone on the fifth ring. She was trying to get in the door with her two raucous boys and a grocery bag. The door had been locked and the keys had been in her pocketbook.

"This is Dr. Brophy, from University Hospital."

"Yes, I know," said Beth, trying to hear above the racket rising up from her sons. "Silence!" she shouted. Then to Brophy: "Is anything wrong?"

"The tests I did on your husband have come back," he told her, pausing as dramatically as he could. "They fall into a suspicious category."

"Suspicious for what?"

Brophy was afraid she might ask that.

"For a curable form of high blood pressure," said Brophy. "But we need to do more tests, to confirm the diagnosis. I know your husband has reservations, and he's busy. But I think it's very important."

"Let me give you his number at work."

Beth recited it and Brophy thanked her.

He called Lars at work, but Lars' secretary said he was in

conference, so Brophy left a message to page him at the hospital. Ten minutes later his beeper went off.

It was Clarissa.

"You trying to scare the shit out of my friends?"

"His catechol level is borderline high."

"Speak English. I'm just a poor dumb midwife. Catechol?"

"I told you about the pheo, the MEA."

"Yes," said Clarissa, getting quiet.

"I can't be sure. It's still a long shot. But we've got to get another sample on him."

"I understand."

"Well, he's not going to like it."

"You think he really has it, then?"

"I think he *might* really have it. If it were me, I'd want to know."

"Lars unfortunately may not," said Clarissa. "Want to know, that is."

"Think his wife can put some heat on?"

"I imagine," said Clarissa. "But you're going to have to call him, too."

"I have. He was in a meeting."

"Keep after him," said Clarissa. "We'll help."

"I've only got so many hours in the day," said Brophy. "This isn't pediatrics. He's a big boy now."

"He's got two kids," said Clarissa. "Think about that."

30

Lars got back to his desk at four-fifteen, and went through his messages. There was one from McCullough and the one from Brophy. He called McCullough.

"It's positive," said McCullough. "I want you to see Dr. Chase on Monday."

"He the surgeon?"

"Yes. He'll see you in his office, next door to mine, at ten-thirty."

"Is the lump in the thyroid?"

"No," said McCullough. "But there is a cold spot in the thyroid. What you feel is outside the thyroid."

"So they missed it during my admission."

"Apparently."

Lars hung up. He picked up the pink message slip with Brophy's name and number, crumpled it into a ball, and fired it into the wastepaper basket.

"Little turd," he said.

The secretary buzzed. Beth was on the line.

"Donald Brophy, from University Hospital, Clarissa's friend, called."

"I remember Brophy."

"One of your tests came back 'suspicious.' He wants you to call. He wants you to get another test. A repeat."

"He say what kind?"

"Some kind of urine test."

"Okay."

"You'll do it?"

"Sure."

"No you won't. I can tell you won't. You're just trying to get me off the phone."

"I am sort of tied up right now," said Lars with an edge. "But I'll take care of it."

"Lars," said Beth desperately, "this is your health."

"I'll take care of it."

"Will you call me when you've talked to him?"

"I'm real busy right now." He hung up.

Brophy tried once more at five to five. The secretary had left and Lars answered the phone himself.

"Mr. Magnussen?"

"Yes."

"This is Dr. Brophy, from the University Hospital."

"Did you call my wife today?"

"I called you. Your wife answered."

"I work."

"I wanted to tell you about your tests."

"But you told my wife instead."

"I told her it was suspicious and that I wanted to do another."

"Anybody ever tell you medical information is confidential?"

"What did you want me to tell your wife? That I just called up to chat?"

"You could have said that you wanted to discuss some things with me and left it at that."

"Which is what I did say. She asked for more information— as most wives will."

"And you gave it to her—right between the eyes!"

"Mr. Magnussen," said Brophy, taking in a breath, telling himself to calm down, "your test was suspicious. If you'd like to pursue it, that's up to you. I'll be happy to help. If not, that's your choice. But what we're looking for is a tumor."

Brophy paused to let the enormity of that word sink in, certain that in Lars' case it would repel him even more strongly, since he was obviously nurturing a hostility born of cold, irrational fear and growing deep in the soil of denial.

"What tumor?" said Lars slowly.

"Remember? We checked your urine for catecholamines. Catecholamines are hormones: adrenalin is a catecholamine. Yours were high."

"Where is this tumor?"

"One of the things that can overproduce catecholamines is a tumor," continued Brophy, determined to get it all out. "It can cause high blood pressure, sweating."

"Where is it?"

"In your adrenal glands," said Brophy, adding quickly, "I'm not saying you have it, remember. I'm just saying the test was suspicious."

"Where are the adrenal glands?"

"They sit on your kidneys. One on each."

"In the belly, then?"

"Right."

"Brophy, let me tell you something," said Lars, starting to rise from his chair, trying to control his voice.

"Yes?"

"I don't think you'd know a tumor if it walked up and bit you on the ass."

31

Lars was still angry at Brophy when he got home that evening. Being mad at Brophy almost made the bad news about the scan tolerable. If he thought about Brophy, he could almost stop thinking about the scan and what was to come. The stiff jab carried by the word "tumor" had lost some of its force. Lars had been told twice in one day he had or might have tumor, and he was still alive. He was thinking about the impropriety of Brophy's telling Beth.

"What did he say to you?"

"That your test was suspicious—whatever that means. Jesus, I didn't want to ask!"

"Of course you didn't," Lars said, holding her and stroking her hair. "That's how he gets you. Rock 'em with a little fear— the more diffuse the better. And we're meek as kittens. Do whatever he says."

"You will go in for the tests, though? Say yes!"

"Don't worry about it. I'll be a good boy."

He'd go see Brophy, all right—to punch him out. Brophy missed the tumor he had and dreamed up one he didn't have. He started thinking of ways to get Brophy. He had violated medical confidentiality. He had tried to manipulate Lars, using Beth. What if Brophy had decided to call Collier or somebody else in the firm?

Just contemplating Brophy made Lars' temple throb. Why waste time on him? The boys were clamoring to be taken sailing while there was still light.

"Take them," said Beth. "They've been talking about it all day. Did you promise them?"

"I'm sure they think so."

The boys were on board, struggling into their life jackets. They scrambled for their positions as their father walked up to the jetty. Lars took his seat aft and Olaf heaved the bowline while Per struggled with the sail bag. They got the sail out and began hooking it up.

Lars went forward and lugged the outboard from the hold. He had to strain to lift it, which started his headache in earnest. He lowered it on its seating and yanked on the starter cord, forgetting to screw the motor on securely. The motor ignited and almost leaped off the boat. Lars caught it, cut it off, and screwed the thing fast before starting it again.

He sat down, heart pounding, and brought the boat around. They cut across the incoming waves, thwack-thwacking rhythmically out into the Bay. His hand on the motor was tingling from the vibration. Lars cut the engine and pulled it up. They were under sail.

But the tingling in his hand didn't stop. Instead, it spread. His other hand was tingling now, and his lips and nose. He felt nauseated although the sea was calm. The wind picked up and blew his hair away from his face. He took a deep breath and felt better.

The boys were staring at him. He smiled.

"Who brought the beer?"

Two solemn faces jumped into grinning joy.

Olaf tossed him his Narragansett, took out a Dr Pepper for himself, and threw one to Per.

"How come you two always hog the Dr Pepper?" Lars asked. He had had trouble pronouncing the "r" in Pepper.

Olaf said, "You okay?"

"Sure. Why?"

"You like 'Gansett."

"Can't I have Dr Pepper one time?" said Lars, laughing. "Christ, you guys are like a couple of old women. Change one thing and you get all out of joint. Toss me a Pepper, junior."

Olaf reached into the knapsack. A cold spray came over the bow, soaking Lars. He shivered. Olaf flipped over the Dr Pepper and Lars reached for it, realizing his fingers were almost numb. The can sailed by his outstretched hand.

Lars looked over his shoulder and watched the can sinking in the water. He couldn't understand how he could have missed it. He steadied the rudder with his elbow and rubbed his tingling hands. If Lars was surprised at missing the toss, Olaf was astonished. His mouth was open and he exchanged glances with his brother.

When they finally came about, the sun was almost gone and the stars were declaring themselves. The water and the sky were one color—very purple. Lars leaned back, feeling the breeze on his face and trying hard to smile. He couldn't enjoy it.

Unexpectedly, he jibed and almost knocked the boys overboard. His vision was coming and going, his tongue was heavy, and he was scrambling his words.

"Catch lat thine," he told Per, pointing to the line near his son's shoulder. "Cet's lome about." Then, slowly and with effort, he got it right: "Let's come about."

"Let's go in," said Olaf.

Lars opened his eyes. Olaf never wanted to head in.

"What's wrong, tiger?"

"Getting late," said Per.

Lars looked at his two normally gung-ho mates. They did not look happy.

"You cold?"

"Yeah," said Olaf. Per nodded.

Lars headed back home, disappointed. It was really a nice night for a sail. The moon was full and threw a great wide stripe down the Bay—a lighted avenue.

They got to the jetty and Olaf hopped out fast to tie the bowline. Per took down the sail and stuffed it into the bag. They worked silently. Lars sat in the stern, wondering what he'd done wrong.

"Let's go," they called from the dock.

Lars stood up and the boys held out their hands, pulling him up to the dock. He left the outboard on its seating, something he never did. Per started to say something, but Olaf shook his head at him. They followed their father back to the house and went directly to their room.

"What's with them?" asked Beth when Lars came in. "They went by me without a word. Went straight to bed."

"Did they?" said Lars, disturbed. "They wanted to come home early. Said they were cold."

Beth went to the boys' room.

Lars stepped out onto the deck and sat on one of the canvas chairs. A few minutes later Beth came out and sat next to him.

"They said you were acting funny. They said you scared them."

Lars looked up, startled.

"Am I?"

Beth took his head in her arms. "Go for the tests."

32

That same Friday the thirteenth Brophy was walking to the parking lot when his beeper went off. He looked at his watch: six-thirty. He was officially off for the weekend at five, but he answered the page anyway.

It was Clarissa.

"Do you know how to set fire to charcoal?"

"Buy a can of charcoal-lighting fluid."

"Done that. There are large warnings printed all over it. I'm afraid I'll burn down the entire neighborhood."

"Might do the place some good."

"I live in a very fine neighborhood. And I'm trying to invite you for dinner, but you're making it most difficult."

"You're making it difficult, not me."

Clarissa did in fact live in a fine neighborhood, two blocks off Thayer Street, across from the college engineering building. She had the top floor of a Victorian house, with gabled windows, turrets, and fancy woodwork.

"You realize this is the first time you've ever had me for dinner, either here or in New York?"

"I lived in a dorm, in New York."

"The fact remains."

"Bygones are bygones."

Brophy smiled and met her eyes, trying to read them.

"What are you thinking?" she asked.

"Where's the charcoal?"

"That's not what you were thinking."

"Terrific insight you got there."

"Don't be like that."

233

Clarissa handed him the charcoal and pointed him to the grill in the backyard. The people who owned the house were away, and Clarissa and Brophy had the garden to themselves.

Brophy poured out the briquettes into a heap on the grill and soaked them with fluid. He stood several feet away, flicking lighted matches at the pile until one hit and the coals ignited. Clarissa brought out a plateful of hamburgers.

"Are I housewifey?"

"No."

"Am I not? I've made salad and sangria. We are having a barbecue. How much more housewifey can I get?"

"You need an apron."

"Of course!"

"And a Country Squire station wagon."

"Beth used to have one of those before they got a Volvo."

"And a husband."

"Yes," said Clarissa, sitting down on a lawn chair opposite Brophy, putting her legs across his knees. "That *is* a problem. Rather does in my housewifey pretensions, doesn't it?"

"Rather does."

"Are you making fun of my English?"

"Never."

"Do you still want a woman who'll do all that?"

"I never said I wanted that."

"Not the apron, nor the Country Squire, but the monogamy—the little woman safe at home."

"When did I ever say I wanted that?"

"Don't let's talk what you wanted then. What do you want now?"

"What makes you think I want anything?"

"Everyone wants something."

Brophy looked at her, then stood up to turn the hamburgers.

"What do you want?" he asked.

"No fair. I asked first."

"Since when is life fair?"

"Is that a quote?"

"Yes."

"Then you got it wrong," she said. "It was, 'Since when is love fair?' "

Brophy poured himself some sangria, splashing the strawberries and orange slices into big Styrofoam cups.

"I would like a little less loneliness," said Clarissa, finally.

"Not a houseful of other people, you understand. Just a kind-hearted, intelligent, sensitive, understanding man."

"Or three or four . . ."

"Stop it."

"Sorry."

"That wasn't necessary."

"I thought you had friends: Beth, Lynn Ann."

"They are friends," said Clarissa with a slight smile. "But Beth has Lars and the kids. And Lynn Ann . . ." Clarissa smiled and looked at Brophy out of the corners of her eyes. "Lynn Ann has her own problems."

"Doesn't everyone?"

"Lynn Ann's going through now what I went through in New York."

"What's that?"

"Price fixing."

"Price fixing?"

"Like the morning gold prices. Every morning she tries to find out how much she can get, what she's worth today, who's bidding what."

"On what market?"

"All markets. The important thing is that other people set the price, not her. If a man wants to pursue her, she must be worth something today. If no one bids, she falls all to pieces."

"How dismal."

"You wouldn't know," said Clarissa. "You wouldn't know how dismal."

33

Dr. Chase, the surgeon, showed Lars the scan, Monday morning.

"Here's the lump you feel," he said, pointing to the photo. "And here's your thyroid—the big, black, butterfly-shaped thing. See that white hole in it? It's a 'cold spot.' We'll have a look at that, too."

"When?"

"Tomorrow."

"So fast?" Lars asked, more to himself than to the doctor. "I haven't even told my wife yet."

"No sense wasting time," said Chase. "You want an answer, don't you?"

"What's the question? You know it's tumor, don't you?"

"In all likelihood," said Chase. "But don't be disappointed. It could be cyst. I don't think so. Not with that hard lymph node sitting there."

"So what's the question?"

"The question is what kind of tumor," said Chase. "There's at least four possibilities. Two of 'em are pretty benign. A third type is some trouble. But if it's the fourth, anaplastic CA, you're a dead man."

Lars flinched.

"It's not anaplastic, though," said Chase. "Anaplastic behaves entirely differently. Rapidly expanding mass, pain, hoarseness."

Lars had to admit that it didn't sound as though he had anaplastic CA.

"No, this is papillary or follicular—probably papillary."

"You said it *might* be benign."

"Well . . . the cold nodules are worrisome. But even the malignant ones aren't going to kill you. You'll die from heart disease before the thyroid cancer kills you."

"Then why operate?"

"To make the diagnosis. Once we get in and get the frozen section back, we'll know how much more to do."

"How much more?"

"If it's papillary CA, which is my bet, I'll take this lobe." Chase pointed to the wing of the butterfly with the white cold spot. "And probably I'll take a few lymph nodes to see if it's spread."

"What will my neck look like?" Lars involuntarily felt his nodule. "Afterward, I mean."

"You'll hardly be able to see the scar, once it heals. I'll tuck it right in the existing neck folds."

"And you say the prognosis is . . . not bad?"

"I said it depends on the type of tumor. But chances are you'll live a normal lifespan."

Lars floated out of Chase's office. He might live, after all. A few years at least. Just to see his kids to high school. What a break he hadn't said anything to Beth! If he had broken the news before talking with Chase, it would have been one grim weekend. Now he could give her the bad news—and the good news.

He had to stop off at U.H. on the way home. Chase had told him to have blood drawn, to have a chest X ray, electrocardiogram, urinalysis, and then go home and pack. Into the hospital tonight, surgery tomorrow, and home by the weekend.

That's what Chase had said. Chase didn't waste a lot of time.

34

Brophy was making rounds with Robin and Wendel. He had tried hard to repress the whole idea of seeing Mrs. Addinizio, but Robin finally prevailed.

They sat in the nurses' station and went through her chart. The path report was hydatidiform mole, and choriocarcinoma.

"Lucky woman," said Brophy. "First she thinks she's pregnant; then she's got a little hyperthyroidism; then a mole. Now she's got cancer."

He turned to the laboratory section. The thyroid hormone level was lower than before the D&C, but still higher than normal. The HCG levels were still high.

"What's that mean, Wendel?"

"The tumor makes HCG," said Wendel, repeating what he had heard Duncan say once in a conference. "If she's still got high HCG, maybe she's still got tumor. Maybe it's metastasized."

"Or she may have some left in her uterus," said Brophy. "Chorio digs down deep and you can't always D&C it out. But she's probably got it in her belly."

"Or in her lung, or in her brain," said Robin. "Look at her calcium."

It was eleven. Brophy had forgotten to check the calciums Friday afternoon. He had called Labs, gotten depressed, and gone to dinner at Clarissa's, feeling guilty. He felt twice as guilty now, missing the calcium on a patient he was supposed to be following on Clinical Service.

"You can study her, now that her calcium's high," said Robin.

"Sure." Brophy was not eager to study Mrs. Addinizio. Mr. Sipple didn't even know he was being studied. Mrs. Addinizio was another matter.

"They're transferring me to Medical Oncology," she told him.

Brophy held her hand. "This didn't turn out the way we thought."

Mrs. Addinizio's nose began to run, and Brophy handed her a Kleenex. She was trying hard to hold it back, but the tears rolled down her cheeks.

"No," she said. "This isn't exactly what I expected."

"In six months, a year, this will all be just a bad memory," said Brophy. "You'll be past it."

"They said I have cancer."

"What else did they say?"

"I don't know."

"Did they tell you why they were sending you to Oncology?"

"For treatment."

"For *cure*, Maria," said Brophy. "This used to be *real* bad news."

"It still is."

"I know."

"Will you come see me on Oncology?"

"Yes."

"Every day?"

"Okay."

"I'm afraid of Oncology."

"Why?"

"I won't know anybody there."

"You'll know me—and Dr. Pullman and Wendel."

"Okay."

They walked out into the corridor and Wendel asked Brophy about her chances.

"She's going to get a cure," said Brophy.

"Cure?"

"The salient feature of choriocarcinoma is that it used to kill every last patient," said Brophy. "Now it's almost totally curable." He hiked up his pants. "They'll blast her with Methotrexate, actinomycin D or Cytoxan, whatever poison protocol they're pushing this month. And she'll survive."

"For how long?" asked Wendel.

"Forever. For a normal life," Brophy told him. "You should know about chorio CA. Every time someone in Washington asks what good all the money for cancer's done, the cancer mavens all shout 'Choriocarcinoma!'"

"Actual, *bona fide* cures?" asked Robin.

"Chorio's good news nowadays. The cancer industry needed some good news."

"Duncan says more people live off cancer than die from it," said Wendel.

Brophy shook his head slowly. "Unless things have changed since my internship, there must be legions living off it."

Brophy's beeper went off. It was Sol, in OB Clinic.

"Brophy, you just see patients and forget them?"

"We just saw her, Sol."

"We're transferring her to Medicine," said Sol. "Oncology."

"She told me."

"You'll follow her there?"

"Sure."

"They sent a Fellow by, over the weekend," said Sol. "Scared hell out of her."

"She didn't tell us."

"Guy starts talking about cancer. I never use that word. She went all hysterical."

"What did you tell her?"

"They told us mole on the frozen. I told her she was fine. Then they call me Friday afternoon. I had to come back and tell her not so fine."

"She'll do well."

"She'll go through some hell getting there," said Sol. "Stick around, Brophy."

35

Brophy had just returned to the Fellow's Office at five-thirty when his beeper went off.

"We had a late run," said Dumfy, excited.

Brophy began calculating how to get off the phone and out the door without wounding Dumfy brutally, when it dawned on him that he meant another run of serum calciums.

"That's great," said Brophy, trying to not hang up instantly, despite his own radical indifference to whether or not Dumfy had made an extra calcium run.

"There's a high one," said Dumfy, quivering, aroused. "I thought you'd want to know."

"Sure," said Brophy, unable to bring himself to say that he didn't care either the extra run or the high calcium. "I'll check it out in the morning."

"Oh . . ."

There was something so plaintive, so utterly dashed, about that "Oh" it sent Brophy crashing into a chasm of abject guilt.

"Give me the name," he said soothingly.

"That's why I called," said Dumfy, still hurt. "I know it's after five—but it's that Larsmussen."

"Magnussen?"

"Yes. Magnussen. He's twelve-one."

"I didn't order any calcium on him," said Brophy, more to himself than to Dumfy. "Where'd it come from?"

There was a pause while Dumfy checked his magic computer, which could tell the source of any sample submitted to the lab.

"Pre-admitting," said Dumfy. "That's why it was late. They

send their stuff over after four. I've told them how much
trouble that gives us. They're supposed to call if they're going
to be sending late samples . . ."

"Pre-admitting?" Brophy echoed, not comprehending.
"He's being admitted?"

"Apparently."

"By whom?"

Dumfy checked his wonderful, all-knowing computer.

"The report goes to JB-Four," said Dumfy, voice swelling
with pride. His computer had Magnussen all buttoned up.
"That's Surgery."

"Surgery? Who's the Attending? Nancy Barnah?"

Dumfy had that on the glowing screen.

"Chase."

"Chase? Chase who?"

"Arnold Chase," said Dumfy. "He's a surgeon."

"*Lars* Magnussen?" Brophy said. "You sure this is the
same guy?"

"Lars Magnussen—age thirty. That's all we have. Unless
you want his hospital number."

Brophy felt in his shirt pocket and came up with a set of 3 ×
5 index cards, each stamped with a patient's name and hospital
number.

"One-two-three-twenty-four-B" he asked.

"That's him!"

"Son-of-a-*bitch*," Brophy muttered.

"What was that?"

"Where is he? JB-Four?"

"JB-Four."

Brophy was silent for a moment, his mind swirling first in
one direction, then in several at once. "Did you . . . did you
ever get that urine on him? The one for VMA?"

"When?"

"I just called him Friday. It would have to be today."

Dumfy's fingers flew over the terminal keyboard, punching
retrieval by date, name, and hospital number.

"No," he said after a minute. "Of course, if it came in
today, it might not have got logged into the computer yet. You
didn't know he was being admitted?"

"No," Brophy answered, far away. Then he turned his
attention back to Dumfy. "Hey, thanks for calling."

Dumfy's voice got all choked. "Any time. Any time . . ."

Brophy had already hung up. He turned out the lights in the Fellows' Office, thinking about Magnussen and what this might mean. He was still thinking about Lars when he reached the stairwell. Why was he being admitted? What had Lars said on the phone? Something about Brophy not being able to recognize tumor? Had someone else found a pheo?

Brophy stopped abruptly. He could stop by JB-4. On the other hand, Lynn Ann was coming over for dinner and he had to go home and get things organized. Magnussen was a hostile lawyer—if someone else had seen him, it was because he had chosen to drop Brophy. Let Dr. Arnold Chase, whoever he was, deal with all that anger. Brophy started down the stairs again.

At the bottom of the flight, he paused on the landing, thinking about Duncan and thinking about being compulsive. Duncan would never just head for home. Duncan could be hard-boiled, but he never forgot what he owed patients. As he continued downward, Brophy felt he was descending into an abyss of criminal neglect.

There were echos in the stairwell: Jethro's remarks about operating on patients with pheo, unsuspecting. Pheos found at autopsy. Mrs. Philby. Depth charges. High explosives. Clarissa had said Brophy had changed. The old Brophy would walk away.

But what could he do on JB-4? Suppose Lars were there now? Just thinking about that hostile face was good for another flight of stairs, closer to the parking lot. . . .

Ten minutes later, Brophy was on JB-4, reading the admitting sheet on Lars Magnussen. There was no admitting note; no chart yet. Just one sheet of paper with the admitting diagnosis: thyroid nodule.

Thyroid nodule? Brophy swirled in deep chagrin. He had missed the nodule he had spent so much time prodding for.

He considered calling the surgeon—but what could he say? He had an equivocable urine for catecholamines. That and a little hypertension. Brophy got up and started to leave: Magnussen had consulted another physician. Brophy was off the case. If the other physician operated on Magnussen without evaluating him, and the depth charges went off, that was the surgeon's problem.

Spoken like the old Brophy, Clarissa would say. The Brophy who was too busy to care. Surgeons didn't evaluate people for pheos. Surgeons cut. Evaluation was for internists and for surgeons like Nancy Barnah.

All Chase had to do was read the old chart. Brophy's notes were all over it: Rule out pheo. Jethro didn't think Magnussen had a pheo. Robin laughed at the very idea. Brophy had heard Duncan give a conference about pheos, done a little reading; now he saw pheos behind every hypertensive.

But there was that episode during surgery when Nancy Barnah fixed Lars' hernias. Brophy should have checked with Nancy about that. He should have called the anesthesiologist. He should have found out exactly what happened. How high did the blood pressure go? How impressive had that episode been? It couldn't have impressed Nancy all that much: she would have had Lars evaluated by Medicine if she thought it was a real problem.

Brophy looked at his watch. Lynn Ann was due at his apartment at seven. He asked the clerk if Magnussen had arrived. Just as she said no, Brophy caught sight of him coming down the hall. He retreated into the head nurse's office and hid there as the clerk directed Lars to his room.

It was Brophy's chance to escape. He dialed Lynn Ann.

"I'm going to be a little late."

"Saving lives and killing rats?"

"There's a little problem with a patient."

"Patient care? I thought Fellows didn't get mired down in things like that. I thought you stayed aloof."

"I try," said Brophy. "I really do."

Brophy told her he'd meet her at eight, then hung up and dialed Duncan's number. Duncan's wife answered.

"This is Donald Brophy. I work with Duncan."

"I know," she said. She waited for Brophy to continue.

"Is Duncan home?"

"He's at a ball game with the kids."

"Oh." He tried to think, hoping Duncan's wife would say something like, "But I can go get him." She didn't. She just waited for Brophy to say something. Brophy needed Duncan to figure out what to do. Should he stop surgery on Magnussen? Brophy was about to make a flagrant fool of himself, and Duncan's wife wasn't being any help.

"I'll see him tomorrow," said Brophy finally.

"At work?"

"Yes." He slammed down the receiver.

As he stood there, considering what to do, a distinguished-looking doctor appeared and asked the clerk for Magnussen's chart.

"Dr. Chase?" said Brophy, trying to lower his voice into a register of authority.

Chase looked up. He looked like a man whose time cost money, and Brophy's throat went dry.

"Yes?"

"I'm Donald Brophy . . ." he began, trying to think of what to say next.

"Yes?"

"I'm an Endocrine Fellow who worked up Mr. Magnussen during his last admission for kidney stones. He'd had hypertension and hypercalcemia." Brophy was talking very fast. He saw Chase's eyebows pinch together. He was listening, assessing Brophy and following what he was saying. Brophy could see Chase examining him, became even more nervous, and spoke even faster.

"So we worked him up for pheochromocytoma and a urine catecholamine, which was borderline high. Then he got discharged, so we couldn't follow up with VMA. He's not very compliant. But before that he'd had Nancy Barnah fix his hernias and got hypertensive, then very hypotensive during anesthesia. I'm still not sure he hasn't got a pheo. But I'm not sure he does, really—"

Chase held up his hand. "Wait a minute." He closed his eyes, then slowly opened them. "You say you've been following this patient."

"Well, not exactly *following*," said Brophy, face red-hot, sweating now. "He never would follow up. But when he was in the hospital last time—"

"Then he's not your patient?"

Brophy saw his out. Chase was getting ready to shut the door. Brophy had done all he could.

"No," he said. "I only saw him during his last admission."

"For stones?"

"And hypercalcemia."

"So you thought stones, hypercalcemia . . ."

"Hyperparathyroidism," Brophy said, dispirited. *Yes, Dr. Chase, I am an idiot—hear-hoofbeats-think-of-zebras-Brophy.*

"And the hypertension," said Chase. "You thought was a pheochromocytoma?" Chase pronounced each syllable in pheochromocytoma very carefully, which made it sound very arcane and painfully absurd, a kind of unicorn of a diagnosis, existing only in some Endocrine Fellow's fantasy.

"Yes . . ." said Brophy, looking at the floor.

"And did you examine his neck?"

"Yes."

Chase looked Brophy directly in the eye, narrowing his focus to see him even more clearly, though Brophy stood no more than two feet away, now beginning to back away.

"You were thinking of one of those endocrine-gland tumor syndromes?" said Chase, sounding suddenly interested.

"Yes," said Brophy. "MEA two."

"I didn't know about the stones or the hypertension," said Chase. "Looks like I didn't get a very complete history. Just felt that rock in his neck, saw the scan, and admitted him."

Brophy blinked.

"So now you're here. Why?"

"I think the pheo thing has to be settled." Brophy's mouth felt dry. "Before he gets anesthesia."

Chase looked even more serious. "You want me to cancel him for tomorrow?"

Brophy swallowed. He could feel his Adam's apple go up and down. "I can't be sure he doesn't have one."

"How sure were you he didn't have a neck mass?"

"Look," said Brophy. "I missed the neck mass—unless it grew pretty fast."

"Doubt that."

"I came over here to tell you about this pheo thing. Maybe I'm just being an Endocrine Fellow, looking for freaky things. I can't tell you what to do—he's your patient."

"How long's this going to take?" Chase asked.

"If he collects the urine tomorrow, we could run it Thursday."

"Then we wouldn't know until Thursday night," said Chase. "The earliest I could do him would be Friday." He did not look pleased. "I wouldn't want to do him Friday, with nobody to watch him over the weekend."

Brophy was about to volunteer, but realized Chase meant there would be no *surgeon* to watch Lars if surgical complications developed.

"This is going to cost us a week," said Chase grimly. Brophy was more of a problem than he had first realized.

They arrived at Lars' door. Chase pushed it open and gestured for Brophy to walk in, then smiled a smile that clearly said, "This is your party, doctor."

Lars and Beth looked up. Lars was not smiling.

"You're getting to be tough to shake," said Lars. "I don't remember asking for an endrocrine consult."

"Like it or not," said Chase, "I'm afraid we've got one."

"Well, I don't like it."

"Look, when I saw you I wasn't aware you'd had a recent admission."

"For kidney stones," Lars said. "Nothing to do with this."

"That's where Brophy disagrees with you," said Chase, quite neutrally, not taking sides. "I must say, I don't know what to think. But whether or not he's right, the point he's raised is a matter of record."

Lars opened his mouth, then closed it.

"We'd better clear this up before getting at that problem in your neck."

"For crying out loud . . ."

Chase looked at Lars steadily. "Now, you can understand I'd be negligent to go ahead without looking into this."

"Into what?" Beth asked.

"Dr. Brophy—" Chase motioned for Brophy to answer her.

"I can't believe this," Lars said to no one in particular.

Beth turned to her husband: "I thought you talked to Brophy—you *said* you talked to him. . . ."

Lars waved her off.

She turned to Brophy: "I thought he checked with you. When he came home and told me about the neck tumor, I asked if all this could have anything to do with your tests."

"It might," Brophy told her, "even though there's only a small likelihood."

"You said the urine test was suspicious."

"Yes. This tumor we're looking for—"

"Tumor!"

"The pheochromocytoma."

"You didn't say tumor, before."

"That's what we're looking for. It's very rare—"

"How long will this take?" Lars asked.

Beth began to cry. "What difference does it make how long it takes?"

"Will you let me ask?" Lars said sharply.

"It's a twenty-four-hour urine collection," Brophy explained. "The results can be ready by Thursday."

"It'll take all week—all week in the hospital . . ." said Lars, not at all happy.

Brophy started to say that he could collect the urine at home, but realized that it was up to Chase to discharge the patient he had admitted.

"We'd better get it over with," Chase said. He spoke in a rich baritone. No one else in the room seemed to carry his authority.

"Okay," Lars said finally.

Beth took his hand.

Brophy and Chase walked out of the room and back to the nurses' station.

"Talk to the nurses tonight and again tomorrow," Chase said. "I don't want them flushing this test down the toilet or collecting it in the wrong container."

Brophy nodded.

"I want to come out of this thing with more than a bucket of warm piss," said Chase, striding off down the hall.

Brophy's beeper went off—an outside call.

"Hey, big boy. What've you got for me?" It was Duncan.

Brophy presented the case: "So I've delayed everything for the sake of the fuckin' VMA. The surgeon's pissed. The patient's pissed. The only one happy is the wife, and she'll be pissed too when the VMA comes back negative and she realizes I cost them a whole week for nothing."

"Nobody's ever angry to find out they don't have a tumor," said Duncan. "They can't crucify you for being careful."

"They sure as hell can make me feel like an idiot."

"That should be the worse thing ever happens to you."

"You think he's got one?"

"A pheo?" Duncan laughed. "Hell, no."

"Then why hold him off from surgery?"

"Look, you were worried enough to do the urine catechols. You were worried enough to call *me* after five o'clock. You were worried enough to stay after five o'clock, when you could've gone home. Let Chase get the ulcer. He's not a bad guy, Chase. You did your job. If he doesn't like it, fuck 'im!"

Brophy looked at his watch. It was five to eight. It took three minutes to get to the parking lot and seven to drive home if he hit the green light on the Fox Point Bridge. Lynn Ann would be sitting out on the front stoop if she didn't get mad and leave.

Brophy wouldn't have been all that disappointed if Lynn Ann did stomp off tonight. When his hormones were surging, she was a great release. But tonight he would have been glad to see Clarissa waiting for him. Clarissa he could talk to.

But Clarissa wouldn't be there. Tonight, he had a date with Lynn Ann. He wished it were Clarissa. But Clarissa was a problem, and Brophy had been causing problems for everyone tonight.

But Duncan made him feel better. Duncan said he was just doing his job.

36

Lynn Ann wasn't sitting on Brophy's doorstoop when he got home, but her car was parked out front. It was a silver Datsun 280 Z. Brophy was looking at it when she came walking down Benefit Street in high heels and sunglasses. She was wearing a starched blue Bloomingdale's work shirt and white slacks. You could see her panties through the cloth.

"How can you see anything in those?" asked Brophy. It was eight-thirty and the street was in shadow.

"If I didn't wear my sunglasses," she said, "who could tell I'm a star?"

She tilted the glasses back on her head and kissed Brophy, enveloping him in a cloud of Lily of the Valley. The perfume took control of the primitive parts of his brain, and her active body made him forget all reservations as she pressed her mons pubis into his stiffening crotch.

"I don't know if I can wait to get upstairs to undress you."

"Let's do it here then," she said, smiling. Her teeth were very white in the shadows of the buildings, and her skin was dark. She started unbuttoning Brophy's shirt.

"Let's go upstairs," said Brophy, taking her hands away. "I don't like sharing you with the whole street."

"It's hot up there," she said. "And what makes you think you're not sharing me already? I've got lots of friends on Benefit Street."

Brophy looked at her for meaning and she laughed. "Let's go for a walk."

"In those?" He nodded to her high heels.

Lynn Ann pulled off her shoes and they walked along Benefit

250

Street. At Waterman they stopped to watch the students tossing Frisbees on the front lawn of the Rhode Island School of Design.

Lynn Ann sighed. "I must be getting old—they look like such children."

"Wouldn't you like being their age again?"

"Christ, no!" she said, brows arched.

"I wouldn't mind being back in college again," he said, "knowing what I know now. . . ."

"What do you know now?"

"I know not to worry."

"Jesus, Brophy! You always want to go back. Back to New York. Back to college. Your're retrogressive."

Brophy shrugged.

She started to walk up Waterman, toward Thayer, but Brophy caught her arm and steered her down the hill, toward South Main Street, saying that he wanted to go to the Blue Point Oyster. What he wanted was to avoid running into Clarissa.

"I used to go to the Blue Point with my dermatologist," said Lynn Ann. "Place still turns me on like a Pavlovian response. No matter who I go with now, I just get wet in the pants and want to run home and tear off his clothes."

"Well," said Brophy. "I'm warned."

He could never understand women who insisted on telling him about all the other men in their lives. Lynn Ann said it as though she thought it made her somehow more exciting. Clarissa once called Providence the herpes genitalis capital of the world. For all Brophy knew, Lynn had it—if she was really such a genital champion. Clarissa never talked about her own vaginal exploits. Just the opposite. Of course, that had spelled trouble before, in New York. She came out looking worse for all the deceit. But now, listening to Lynn, maybe Clarissa had a point.

There was no line at the Blue Point. They sat at the bar and watched the barman pry open the oysters. Lynn Ann took one in her mouth, watching Brophy while she moved it with her tongue. Brophy looked past her. Lynn Ann could look stunning just walking down the street, but she could open her mouth and spoil it all.

"What's the matter?" she said, swallowing the oyster. "Am I a ballbuster?"

The barman looked up and smiled at Brophy.

You're not real intuitive, Lynn, thought Brophy.

"Brophy, what you need is to stop mooning over New York and Clarissa and things gone by and get on with it." She had finished her martini and was getting loud.

"Is that where you come in?" said Brophy, lowering his voice, hoping Lynn Ann would lower hers. Not much chance of that. She ordered another martini.

"If you'll let me, I'll come   . . ." said Lynn Ann, smiling. "In, that is."

The barman looked up again, first at Lynn Ann, then to smile at Brophy.

"You know," said Lynn Ann, "I'm not off the U.H. case yet. In fact, I just got a new lead."

"What's that?"

"You'll find out soon enough," she said. "But tonight's not business. Tonight you're going to get me drunk and take me home and not stop till morning."

This time the barman didn't look up. Nobody in the place was listening to Lynn Ann anymore.

37

At seven-thirty Tuesday morning, while Lars Magnussen was still sleeping in his room on JB-4, Brophy was in the nurses' station, going over how a twenty-four-hour urine ought to be collected with a nurse who couldn't understand why Brophy had come in at that hour to go over a routine thing like a twenty-four-hour urine. She was a surgical nurse, so she didn't say, "What's the matter, you don't think I know what I'm doing?" Any medical nurse would have said that. Surgical nurses treated doctors with respect. Instead, she just smiled pleasantly and said, "Yes, doctor," to everything Brophy said. For ten minutes Brophy was in love with her until he realized she was just trying to get rid of him.

Behind Brophy stood four surgical residents, listening to Brophy's instructions, and smiling at one another.

When Brophy felt he had the nurse adequately instructed, he sat down to write a note in Lars' chart.

"You the Endocrine Fellow who canceled the thyroid nodule?"

Brophy looked up. The resident who had spoken had a real down-home accent and looked like he had played linebacker without a helmet for Alabama.

"Guilty as charged," said Brophy.

"You really think this guy's got pheo?" The other residents were smiling smugly behind the linebacker.

"Not likely."

"Then why'd you cancel the nodule?" asked the linebacker, incredulous.

"You want to cut on someone with an elevated urinary

catecholamine?'' Brophy was playing his ace. It wasn't much
of an ace.

"Hell, I read the old chart," said the linebacker, sending
Brophy sprawling. Surgeons don't read old charts. If the
linebacker had read it, he knew Brophy had missed the thyroid
nodule. "I saw your Attending didn't think this guy had a
pheo. And his catecholamines were only 'borderline.'"

"If you read the old chart, you saw what happened when
Nancy Barnah fixed his hernias."

"Hell," smiled the linebacker, "I cut your hernia, your
blood pressure'll go up too."

"I'll remember that before I let you work on me."

"Brophy?"

"Yes?"

"You better try and learn how to *feel* those thyroids, boy.
You missed a nodule size of a cherry pit."

Brophy looked from the linebacker to the other surgical
residents arrayed behind him. None of them would have
missed that cherry pit. He could feel his face growing hot. He
was being made an example of. You don't miss a key physical
finding and strut around in a white lab coat. The residents were
standing there being glad they weren't Brophy, who was
wishing fervently that he could shrink rapidly into a speck on
his chair and blow away.

The group of residents trotted off to Surgery, leaving Brophy
looking after them. See how smart you guys will feel if
Magnussen turns up with a pheo after all, he thought.

Then he realized that wasn't really the point.

38

Dick Cecil was yelling at Steve Reynolds, and his voice carried down to the nurses' station all the way from the infusion room.

"Guess Steve hasn't got that infusion technique perfected," smiled Robin.

Brophy had halted rounds for a visit to the coffee machine in the nurses' station.

"Dick doesn't consider the technique perfected until Steve gets the results he predicted," snorted Brophy. "Lately, Steve's been getting the opposite."

The shouting continued, and Brophy escaped with the group to continue endocrine rounds.

The last stop on rounds every morning was Medical Oncology. This was last because the Medical Oncology floor was devoted to the care and nurturing of cancer patients. And cancer depressed Brophy almost as much as it excited Duncan, because Brophy knew there wasn't a thing you could do about it, even if there was a lot you could learn from it.

There were exceptions, of course, and Mrs. Addinizio's choriocarcinoma was one.

All the nurses on Medical Oncology knew Brophy. They called him the Calcium Vulture. At least it was an identity. They knew he was part of what U.H. did best. But he didn't like the oncology floor, which was in fact a very well run and astonishingly cheery place for a cancer ward.

There were bright Renoir and Van Gogh prints all around. They had an incredibly competent oncology nurse who gave all the poisons, knew all their toxicities, and never forgot to call

Brophy when someone's calcium went high, even for a day. But it was still cancer, and not a happy place.

"Who's got calcium today?" the oncology nurse asked when Brophy appeared at the head of the endocrine pack.

"We're not here for calcium," Brophy told her. "I'm on Clinical Service now. I'm following Mrs. Addinizio."

"Mrs. Addinizio has calcium."

"But that's not why we're here."

"You probably gave her her calcium," said the nurse. "Just looking at you, my calcium starts creeping up."

Brophy had been trying to think of reasons to not see Maria Addinizio since nine-thirty, when it became evident that rounds were going quickly and there would be plenty of time to check on her. Brophy didn't want to check on Maria Addinizio because she had cancer and was getting better, which meant Brophy had no excuse if she didn't do well. The weight of her optimistic prognosis depressed him.

Brophy was also depressed because Mrs. Addinizio was a bright and engaging person who asked questions and never believed the answers. She wanted to know why they did brain scans, lung scans, tomograms of her lung, and a liver scan before they began the chemotherapy.

"Why are they looking at my brain? Do I have tumor in my brain?"

"They look. That doesn't mean they find."

"But they think it could be there?"

"If they *knew* it was there, they wouldn't bother doing the scan," Brophy told her half-truthfully. The fact is, there was no indication from her neurological exam that she had any tumor growing in her brain. But if there had been an indication, they would have done the scan to follow the tumor size as it shrunk in response to therapy. The brain scan was part of the research protocol.

"I've had headaches," said Mrs. Addinizio, to herself but out loud.

"I get headaches," said Brophy. "That doesn't mean I have tumor in my brain."

"You never had tumor in your uterus."

It was hard to argue with that.

Fortunately, the scans all turned out negative, and then chemotherapy began. Brophy promised great things from the chemotherapy, which he immediately regretted, remembering the key rule of the cancer ward: only bad things happen. (If things go well, don't talk about it.) The prognosis was later modified by the oncologists, who said the outlook depended on how widespread the disease was to begin with.

Then they blasted her. The poisons could be a cure, but they were no pleasure. The chemotherapy nurse had given her a little card listing all the side effects of each drug, and Mrs. Addinizio watched, horrified, as each toxicity happened to her. The Methotrexate looked harmless enough, just some little yellow pills, but they made her hair fall out in great clumps and gave her bloody diarrhea, which smelled foul and scared her half to death.

She would have been more disturbed had she known, as Brophy knew, that the drug had also insulted her liver, which was already smarting from the chlorambucil.

She also developed a frightening rash over her legs and arms, which might have been either the chlorambucil or the Methotrexate, but Dermatology thought was more likely the actinomycin-D. They were dripping the actinomycin-D into her vein through IV lines wrapped in aluminum foil to keep the sunlight from despoiling the poison before it could despoil the tumor. The actinomycin-D also did nasty things to her bone marrow, wiping it clean of white blood cells needed to fight infections. Denuded of white cells, she got septic one night and almost died. And nobody called Brophy, for which he was secretly grateful, since a septic patient is very scary, especially in the middle of the night.

Brophy had seen many a septic patient die in the middle of the night at Whipple and did not want to be present if it happened to Mrs. Addinizio, whom he liked a great deal.

Apart from the rash, falling-out hair, bloody diarrhea, and sepsis, Maria hadn't done badly, and her tumor was melting away, judging from her HCG levels, which were now almost undetectable.

Even so, Brophy didn't want to cross Maria Addinizio's threshold, knowing he might find her stricken by yet another complication of therapy. He lingered over her chart and tried to engage Wendel in a Socratic exchange about the significance of the young white blood cells now appearing on her blood count. Robin finally put an end to Brophy's ploy and dragged them in to see Mrs. Addinizio, who was looking much better.

Brophy hardly noticed the fading rash, the brighter eyes. He hardly noticed because he was unable to draw his attention away from Lynn Ann Montano, who was beaming at Brophy from her post at Mrs. Addinizio's bedside.

"Well—look what the cat dragged in," Lynn Ann greeted him.

"You know each other?" asked Maria Addinizio, looking from Lynn Ann to Brophy.

"I was going to ask you the same thing," said Brophy.

"We're old friends," said Lynn Ann.

"She's a reporter," said Mrs. Addinizio.

"Is she making you famous?" said Brophy, looking at Lynn Ann.

"She's the famous one," said Maria. "Just visiting."

"Just visiting," echoed Brophy.

"Maria's my buddy," said Lynn. "She's my Inside Source at the Providence P.D."

"She's your inside source," Brophy repeated flatly.

"You'd think I gave away state secrets," said Maria Addinizio. "I'm not the only one downtown happy to do her a favor. She's done us a few."

"I guess you know when someone's just doing her job," said Brophy. "You're happy to help her out."

"That's it," said Mrs. Addinizio, a little thick-tongued.

"I just found out Maria was here Monday," said Lynn. "Got down to the station house and asked where Maria's been, and they said, 'Oh, she's in the hospital.' I thought she'd had her baby. Some friends I've got down there. Nobody tells me anything."

"Oh, they just figured, why tell you about that? You're looking for cops and robbers."

"Hey, they know I'm always looking to protect my sources. Especially when one of 'em winds up in the hospital," Lynn Ann said, giving Mrs. Addinizio a hug. "Is Dr. Brophy taking good care of you?"

"Oh, he's not my doctor anymore," said Maria. "I'm on Oncology now."

"I just check in to make sure she behaves herself," said Brophy. "I had to write a character reference to get her in here."

"I should've asked you for a letter on the oncologists," said Mrs. Addinizio. "They been working me over."

"You're getting better," said Brophy. "Really. I know you may find that hard to believe."

Mrs. Addinizio reached for Brophy's hand.

Brophy asked Robin to check Maria's tongue, which looked as big as it sounded. Then he smiled at Lynn Ann and led Wendel and Robin out to the nurses' station, where Robin wrote a note in Maria's chart about the tongue.

She was interrupted by a clattering in the hallway. It was Lynn Ann, in high heels, arriving at the clerk's desk. Robin looked her up and down, from her high heels to her tight white skirt to her white collared, blue shirt to her false eyelashes.

"How's she doing?" Lynn Ann asked Brophy.

"The therapy is not without complications."

"I couldn't help but notice."

"She's got a bad disease."

"Oh, not so bad for you," said Lynn Ann. "You got her in a study yet?"

Robin's mouth dropped open and she looked from Lynn Ann to Brophy.

"I just might consider it," said Brophy.

"You'll get lots of informed consent?"

"Tons. Always do."

"Always the consent, anyway," smiled Lynn Ann. "I'll have to read over the protocol for that one."

"Why don't you volunteer as a normal control?" said Brophy. "They'll give you one free."

"I'll bet."

"Think of it as your bit in the war against cancer."

"I gave at the office."

"Not like you'd give here."

"She said these drugs you're giving her are experimental."

"She's getting standard drugs for choriocarcinoma."

"She had to sign some kind of protocol."

"She's in a study."

"Then it *is* research."

"The drugs are standard. The tests they do to follow her, the doses, the combinations of drugs, are systematized and compared to other patients. That makes it research."

"I don't get it."

"Getting drugs on a research protocol doesn't mean the drugs are experimental."

"But it means there's some experiment. Something isn't known. You're trying to answer some question."

"It's not my protocol," said Brophy finally. "Ask the oncologists."

"What they want to know," said Robin, "is whether or not they can use lower doses with less toxicity for the same cancer kill, by using different combinations of drugs."

"Then the treatment might not work?"

"That's possible, study or no study. The only difference is how many tests are done to follow the tumor regression and who pays for them."

"That's the most sense I've heard since I got here," said Lynn Ann, smiling ingratiatingly at Robin, looking at her name tag. "You're Dr. Pullman?"

"Yes," said Robin.

"We've got a lot of patients to see," said Brophy, pulling Robin out of her chair. They cleared out of the nurses' station and moved off down the corridor. Brophy winked over his shoulder at Lynn Ann.

"You didn't have to pull my arm out of the socket," said Robin, rubbing her shoulder.

"You know who that was?"

"She was wearing enough perfume to start her own factory. She's a reporter, she said."

"That's Lynn Ann Montano. Considers herself watchdog over the U.H. and all its sinister research efforts."

"What the hell," said Robin. "We're not splicing genes. We're just treating cancer."

39

Brophy checked the calciums at four-thirty. The only high one was Mrs. Addinizio.

"Just one," said Dumfy.

Brophy spun around to face him.

"You know this Addinizio lady?" Dumfy asked.

"Yes."

"Her TFTs are still a little up. So's her HCG. Better, but still up. She's really something."

"Choriocarcinoma."

"I guessed. You're on Service, right? You should present her to conference. She's really something," Dumfy repeated.

"You ought to go down and see her. She's on Medical Oncology."

"Oh, I couldn't do *that!*" Dumfy said, shrinking away.

"I'll present her."

"She's a good case," Dumfy said, disappearing out the door.

"I know."

Duncan was in the Fellows' Office when Brophy got back.

"Tons of factor!" he screamed. His blue eyes were glittering and his face was a brilliant pink. "Heimler's tumor: *tons* of factor. The assay went right off the wall. . . ." Duncan was very excited about Heimler's tumor. "I just wish we'd gotten some into the mice!"

"We got Sipple's into the mice."

"He had shit tumor," said Duncan. "Hardly any factor."

"We're doing better than some guys," said Brophy. "You hear Cecil blasting Reynolds?"

"Poor Reynolds. Dick is really on his case. He even comes in weekends now."

"At least he can work in peace," Brophy said. "Without supervision." He looked meaningfully at Duncan.

"What do you mean?"

"Steve did one of the fastest infusions I ever saw last weekend I was here. He was out of here by one o'clock."

"Maybe he aborted it."

"Maybe," said Brophy. "But I saw the data sheet on his desk the next Monday: showed a regular five hours' worth of data. He must have started that infusion in the wee hours."

"You probably saw the data sheet from some other infusion."

"I saw the date."

Duncan took Brophy across the hall to his lab and closed the door.

"You said anything about this to anyone?"

"Just you."

"Good," said Duncan. "Don't."

"I thought I ought to say something to somebody. I mean, I don't really know what happened, but I couldn't very well ask."

"You should have told me. Now just consider your duty done. I'll handle it."

Brophy looked at Duncan for meaning, but Duncan's expression had changed entirely. He was smiling.

"We got anything else cooking?"

Brophy hesitated.

"Dumfy told me there's a high one on Medical Oncology," said Duncan, looking sidelong at Brophy.

"Oh," said Brophy, guilty, caught. "Her."

"Who's her?"

"Well, there's this lady. But she's only been hypercalcemic a few days. Maybe's she just dehydrated. I'm following her on Service."

"What's she got?"

"Chorio CA."

"Chorio!" thundered Duncan. His eyes were saucers, spinning with delight. "We've never studied a chorio! Where is she?"

"Oncology."

Duncan dragged Brophy to the Medical Oncology Ward, talking about choriocarcinoma, nude mice, the assay, and stopping off in the Section Office to pick up a permission slip for the bone biopsy and the malignancy protocol.

Mrs. Addinizio was happy to see Brophy again.

"Twice in one day," she said. "I must be really special."

Brophy smiled. *You don't know how special.* He introduced Duncan, who was standing beside him, barely able to restrain himself, bouncing, smiling.

"Dr. Brophy's told me all about you."

"He's been so nice."

"You were in his pregnancy study, I understand."

"Yes." Mrs. Addinizio's face clouded, remembering how recently she thought she was pregnant. It seemed she had always been a cancer patient. She was saddened to think of that happy, nonmalignant time.

"That makes you very special," Duncan said, "having had those tests Dr. Brophy did on you."

"How's that?"

"You had those special calcium studies before anyone knew about your tumor," said Duncan. "That almost never happens. Besides pregnant patients, Dr. Brophy and I also study patients with tumors who have calcium problems."

"Do I have calcium problems now?"

"Your calcium is a little high."

"Is that bad?"

"Not at this stage. And once you're treated, it'll come down to normal."

"Good."

"What Dr. Brophy and I would like you to do is to let us take a look at you again, before you've finished your treatment, and then again after the tumor's completely gone."

Mrs. Addinizio looked to Brophy, who tried to smile without looking sick.

"Another calcium absorption test?" she asked.

"That," said Duncan, "and some other things." He smiled. "I know this tumor's been a nightmare for you. It's bad, and there's no way around that." He put a hand on her shoulder. "But we're trying to find out how these things work. So we can help other patients with the same thing."

He explained about the special blood and urine collections, working up to the bone biopsy.

"We'll still love you if you don't want to get involved," Duncan said.

"No, I want to help," Mrs. Addinizio told him, to Brophy'a astonishment. *No, you don't*, he thought. Duncan had just finished telling her he wanted to jab a pencil-sized needle through her pelvic-crest bone.

She listened calmly as Duncan read the informed consent form for the biopsy. The language was very clear. The biopsy would hurt. She might bleed. She listened to it all, quietly and unperturbed.

She signed the forms and Duncan ran off to get his biopsy kit.

"Mrs. Addinizio," Brophy rasped, "you understand—this biopsy will make a hole in your bone. It's going to hurt."

"I know," she said. She was looking in a hand mirror, fluffing up her new wig.

Brophy cleaned Mrs. Addinizio's hip with Betadine and anesthetized her skin with Novocain.

Duncan arrived with the sterile drapes and sterile gloves, and reswabbed the hip and anesthetized down to the bone covering—the periosteum. Then he took out his special stainless steel French-made trocar. Brophy saw the light glint off the trocar as Duncan held it low, the way a matador conceals his sword, so Mrs. Addinizio would not see and be afraid. Then he drove it home.

"How was it?" asked Brophy afterward.

"Not bad."

Duncan held up the glass vial with the core of bone floating in the fixative.

"Perfect," he said. "You did fantastic!" he almost shouted, pinching Mrs. Addinizio's cheek. She smiled at him as he disappeared out the door. He had to get the bone core to the lab.

"You'll collect the blood in the morning?" Mrs. Addinizio asked Brophy.

"Yes. Then they'll give you more chemotherapy."

"I can't say I'm looking forward to that."

"It'll be over soon."

"You were surprised I had the biopsy."

"Yes."

"Why?"

"People who suddenly discover they have tumor usually don't want anything more done to them than necessary."

Mrs. Addinizio smiled, but her eyes were serious.

"Bad things have happened to me. I wanted to do something," she said. "To fight back."

40

"Brophy, what *are* you doing to my friends?" It was Clarissa. She sounded serious. Brophy was gripped momentarily with the panicky thought that she might be calling about Lynn Ann, then he realized it might be better if she knew. Clarissa, after all, was the one who had championed the free life in New York. Somehow, though, that now seemed like an old complaint. Clarissa had changed since then. She was more in control. And she was sensitive about Lynn Ann, which, perversely, Brophy decided to enjoy.

"Beth just called. She's beside herself. What kind of surgery are you doing on Lars?"

"I'm not doing surgery on anybody."

"Don't be difficult. You've admitted him for someone else to do it."

"Wrong again."

"What's the story, then? Beth kept talking about tumor. Has he got tumor?"

"That's the big question."

"What's happened? Last I heard, Lars was discharged. Now I get a call he's been admitted with a thyroid tumor which is making him hypertensive."

"He found a neck mass, shaving. But there's a question of pheo, still."

"*Lars* went to a surgeon?"

"Apparently."

"I'm amazed this is the first I've heard of it."

"I gather he didn't tell his wife until the day he had to go in."

"But this is the man we practically had to straitjacket to get a hernia fixed!"

"This time he thought he had cancer."

"Does he?"

"Don't know what's in his neck."

"Where did you come in?"

"I discover Magnussen's in the house, about to get some anesthesia, and we still haven't ruled out pheo."

"You want to get your tumor before the surgeons get theirs?"

Brophy struggled to check himself but he was angry enough to let it fly. "You sound like Lynn Ann."

"Lynn Ann? Aren't we familiar?"

"Maybe we are."

Clarissa was silent. Brophy waited.

"Look," she said finally, "I called about Lars. Beth is distraught. Why are your tests so important?"

"The first thing to be sure of is that there's no pheo. You anesthetize someone who's got pheo, you're apt to set off that depth charge—"

"What a colorful image."

" —so the first thing to do is rule out the pheo. Not because I'm possessive about my tumors—"

"I didn't accuse you of being possessive."

"—but because the pheo always comes first."

"So you weren't just kidding about that workup. You really think he's got it."

"I'm just not sure he doesn't have it." Brophy took a breath and tried for lower pitch. "It's not likely. I wouldn't give odds on it. I wouldn't even bet on it. But the catecholamines were high. And as long as those high cats are sitting on his chart without any followup, nobody's going to touch him."

"So you didn't stop the surgery? The blades wouldn't have done him anyway until the other tests."

"They never would've noticed the cats. When did you ever see a blade read an old chart?"

"Some of my best friends are blades," Clarissa said with an inflection that left no doubt about what kind of friendships those might be. "I know for a fact they read old charts."

"Well, anyway. He'll finish his twenty-four-hour urine tomorrow. We'll know by late afternoon."

"You'll call me?"

"If they're positive."

"Brophy?"

"Yes?"

"You're not fooling around with Lynn Ann?"

"What's it to you?"

"Oh, don't play games like that."

"What games?"

"She's really all wrong for you."

Brophy said nothing.

"She's just so *desperate*."

"I'll keep that in mind."

They hung up and Brophy thought about Clarissa and about Lynn Ann and about her shiny jet-set chrome-and-glass apartment.

41

Brophy sat down Thursday afternoon in the Endocrine Fellows' Office and tried to collect his thoughts. He took out a sheet of paper and wrote down everything he had to do, and what was bothering him, and whom to call.

First on the list was: "Why do I feel like I'm flying?"

He was elated because Dumfy had sounded so high when he called. It was Dumfy's fault, this shameful sense of euphoria.

"He's got it!" Dumfy had trumpeted. "Larmussen's VMA: ninety-six!"

"What's normal?"

"Seven, Brophy—seven!"

"Jesus," said Brophy, tingling.

"What a pickup . . ." Dumfy had rattled on about how the last positive came back on a patient who had already gone to surgery and died, and the VMA was ready the day after the autopsy.

"Ninety-six?"

"The second-highest VMA on record in this lab. I checked the computer."

"Is there anything else it could be?"

"He's not on Aldomet? No. Ninety-six, Brophy!"

"Jesus."

"You'll present it to conference."

"Sure." Brophy had thought about Lars and Jethro and Robin and Chase and the linebacker all in a swirl. He had had to sit down.

When he was a little calmer he wrote a list of all the people who had to be told: Clarissa, Jethro, Chase, Lars and his wife; Robin and Wendel and Nancy Barnah.

He paged Clarissa.

"Busy?" Brophy could hear the screaming in the background.

"Got a lady in labor."

"Can I drop by?"

"When?"

"Now."

"Brophy, can you hear that? This place is a madhouse . . ." Then her voice changed. "Is this about Lars?"

"I'll talk to you about it."

Brophy ran up to Labor and Delivery. Clarissa was sitting in the nurses' station, smoking.

"I've never known you to be so melodramatic," she said, blowing smoke in his direction.

"You're not suppose to smoke here."

"You got me upset."

"He's got it."

"Good Lord."

"His VMA is fourteen times normal," Brophy said.

Clarissa rested her forehead on her palm. "What now?"

"First I tell my Attending. Then I'll have to tell the patient."

"I wish I could be with Beth," said Clarissa, looking at her watch. "I've got a woman who's not likely to go for hours. She crushed her cigarette. "Of course, all I have to do is walk off the floor and she'll pop the kid out."

Brophy said nothing.

"They're not going to know what pheo means. They'll just know it's bad news."

"I'll explain."

"Lars'll get angry," said Clarissa. "Beth will panic. Tell her to call me."

"Okay."

"They were having *such* a nice life. . . ."

"People survive pheos," Brophy said, but Clarissa cut him off with her look.

"You don't understand, do you?"

"What?"

"This isn't all part of a day's work for them. This is the worse thing that's ever happened to them."

Clarissa waved him away, walked out of the nurses' station and back to the woman in the labor room.

Brophy sat down in front of the phone and took out his list. He called Jethro.

"Where are you?" asked Jethro. "Sounds like Dante's Inferno."

"Labor and Delivery."

"Close."

Brophy told him about the VMA on Lars.

"Well, well, well," said Jethro. "You really hung in there and saw it through. Nice going."

"Thanks."

"What are you going to do now?"

Brophy tried to settle down and think like an academic. "Probably ought to repeat the test just to be sure."

"Brophy: ninety-six."

He thought again.

"Better tell the patient."

"And then?"

"Guess we better find the tumor."

"That's better. See if they'll do a CAT this afternoon."

"Fat chance."

"Never hurts to ask."

"Okay."

"And better start him on some blocker tonight. Dibenzyline. Call the VA and ask Chuck Mersault about the doses and how to do it."

"Okay."

Jethro paused, thinking. Brophy could hear him turn down the Brahms.

"Dumfy wants me to present him to conference Tuesday."

"Good idea," said Jethro, still thinking. "Look, get Anesthesia and Cardiology. And tell Lionel. See if Dick Cecil will come. He's abrasive, but he knows about catechols. And remind Dumfy on Monday."

"He won't need reminding."

Jethro laughed. "He pretty excited?"

"It's unseemly."

"Well, pheos don't come along every day, Brophy. You're going to be part of an event."

Brophy said nothing.

"You're going to see the university machine swing into action," said Jethro.

"But we need a battle plan. And the first step is the big powwow."

"Okay, who else?"

Jethro named a few more. Just about everyone in the Section had to be invited for one reason or another. "And don't forget Chuck Mersault. And of course, Nancy. Nancy Barnah. Better call her today so she can clear her OR schedule."

"Oh," said Brophy, remembering. "That's another thing. He's still on Chase's Service."

"That's ticklish."

"Who would you want going after that bomb, if it were you?"

"No need to get personal," said Jethro. Brophy remembered about Jethro's medullary CA and felt stupid. Nancy had done Jethro's neck.

"If we could get him to the CRU, maybe we could pry him away," said Brophy.

"Does Chase want to do the pheo?"

"I haven't asked him yet."

"He's a pretty reasonable guy. He may bow out gracefully."

"What if he doesn't?"

"Let's not press it right now. Get Lars the CAT. Then tell Chase we want him on the CRU for the pre-op blockade. We'll play it from there."

"Okay," said Brophy, sounding not at all convinced.

"It's really up to the patient, who he wants."

"What if he wants Chase?"

"He'll want Barnah," said Jethro. "We'll see to that."

Brophy called Mersault, who told him the dose of Dibenzyline.

"Make sure they check his blood pressure four times a day," said Mersault. "That's about all you can ask the nurses to do. Then *you* check it four times a day. That's eight readings. Ought to be enough. Standing and lying. The Dibenzyline'll make him pretty orthostatic, so warn him not to stand up too fast. All you need is to have him fall on his head."

They had to get Lars blocked. All those catecholamine receptors had to be plugged with Dibenzyline so when they grabbed hold of that pheo during surgery and all the norepinephrine and epinephrine shot out, there was plenty of insulation from the shock.

"All those arterioles, heart cells, and kidney cells have to be packed tight," Mersault said.

"I feel like I'm forgetting something," said Brophy, looking over his list.

"That's because you haven't seen one of these before." Mersault laughed. "You're not going to be doing this alone. Wait till you see that conference Tuesday. All those guys come out of their cubbyholes and it's a well-oiled machine."

"I could use that."

"You'll get Nancy Barnah, right?"

"Chase is the surgeon at the moment," Brophy said.

"Get Nancy. They really have to yank and squeeze and pull on those pheos sometimes. It's like squeezing an inky sponge in clear water."

"We'll get Nancy."

"That's key. Don't worry about hurting people's feelings. You want Nancy."

"Okay," said Brophy, hanging up, realizing why Chuck Mersault was not in private practice or at the Main Hospital.

Brophy called CAT Scan.

"I have to schedule a stat CAT scan."

"In-patient or out?" the booking secretary asked, sounding very bored.

"In-patient. I said 'stat.' We need it today."

"Name?"

Brophy told her.

"Hospital number?"

Brophy told her.

"Diagnosis."

Brophy had to spell pheochromocytoma.

"He's booked for the second."

"The second case?"

"September the second."

"I'm afraid that won't do." Brophy felt the heat rise up his neck. *Be calm. Nobody responds to hostility.* "He needs it today—right now—stat."

"Please hold."

Brophy heard the click and considered running downstairs to the basement where he could beat the secretary into a greasy spot.

"I'm sorry, but September second's our first opening. You're lucky: it's slow in the summer."

"You mean there are no emergency CAT scans done in the summer?"

"Oh—you didn't say it was an *emergency*. . . ."

"It's an emergency."

"Hold," the secretary said, annoyed.

"I'm sorry, but we can't find that diagnosis on our list of approved emergencies."

"Who is we?"

"Me and the other girl."

"Can I speak to the radiologist?"

"He's in conference."

"What's his name?"

"Dr. Scali."

Brophy slammed down the receiver, looked up the Department of Radiology in the hospital directory, and asked to speak to the chief, who turned out to be Dr. Scali.

Scali listened to Brophy's remarks about the secretaries, the list of approved emergencies, and his case for doing an immediate CAT scan on patients with pheochromocytomas.

"This guy's got a pheo?" Scali asked.

"That's what I'm trying to tell you!"

"We'll do him tomorrow morning."

"But the secretary said—"

"Look, Brophy—you want something out of the ordinary, don't screw around with the secretaries. Call me. He'll be done tomorrow morning. Call the girl back in ten minutes."

Brophy waited ten minutes, imagining with pleasure what the chief was telling the scheduling secretary. Then he called back.

This time the secretary was cold and efficient.

"He'll be our first case. Seven-thirty. Have him ready. Don't wait for Escort. Have someone there who can bring him down as soon as we call."

Brophy called Chase, but the answering service said he was in Surgery.

"Where?"

"University Hospital."

Brophy ran down to the operating rooms, one floor below Labor and Delivery. The nurse at the desk looked at the blackboard above her head.

"Chase? Room D."

"Where's the locker room?"

The nurse nodded at the doorway across the hall and handed Brophy a combination lock.

"Use any open locker except the gold ones."

"Why not the gold ones?"

"Because I said not the gold—and because they're for the professors."

Brophy used a gold locker and changed into blue scrub suit, scrub hat and mask, and nonconductive paper booties with the black tape that gets stuffed inside the shoes.

He found Room D, but the door was locked. Then he remembered: you don't barge right into an operating theater, sweeping bacteria in along with the air currents from the hall. He found the entrance through the scrub room.

A group of people was standing around the table. The anesthesiologist was at the head, breathing the patient. Chase was at one side of the table and two residents, holding retractors, at the other. Chase was poking around in the belly, searching for a bowel perforation. He looked up when Brophy came through the door. All Brophy could see was the man's eyes, but he was certain it was Chase.

Chase looked at him inquiringly, keeping his hand in the belly.

"Donald Brophy—didn't mean to interrupt. I'm the Endocrine Fellow on Magnussen. We talked the other night."

"Didn't recognize you in that get-up," Chase said. "You look like a *real* doctor," he added—meaning a surgeon.

The scrub nurse glanced over, and the two residents turned a little to observe Brophy questioningly. They didn't allow themselves to turn too far, since backs are considered unsterile, and if their backs had approached the plane of the operating table, they would have to regown. The circulating nurse stationed herself between Brophy and the table, keeping him away from the sterile field.

"I thought I'd better tell you about the VMA on Magnussen—" Brophy began.

Chase continued to probe. "Don't suppose you'd go to all this trouble if it were negative."

"It's positive."

"How positive?"

"Ninety-six," Brophy informed him, trying not to crow. "Seven's upper limit of normal."

Chase looked up and stopped moving his hand around. "Good Lord."

The scrub nurse looked over at Brophy and so did the two residents, who had been watching Chase's hand.

"Aw, those VMAs get fouled up by so many things," said one of the masked residents. "Vanilla, bananas, whatever." Brophy recognized him. It was the linebacker.

"I checked with Daniel Dumfy," said Brophy, trying to sound neutral and academic and not at all smug. "And I checked with my Attending. They both think we ought to take it seriously."

"Ninety-six isn't vanilla pudding," said Chase, going back to his exploration, laughing.

The residents laughed obediently, even the linebacker. Surgical residents call Attendings "Sir."

"You'll get a CAT?" Chase inquired.

"Tomorrow morning."

"Good."

Brophy did not like the drift. Chase was planning for the next step as if he were still running the case.

"I talked with my Attending," Brophy said slowly, trying to maintain his disinterested air. "We really ought to start Dibenzyline now—tonight."

"Fine," Chase agreed.

"He thought it might be easier managing the blockade on the Clinical Research Unit," Brophy continued, all innocence. "The nurses on the CRU are a lot more familiar with the drug than surgical nurses."

"Who's your Attending?"

"Jethro Brown."

"Jethro? Oh, all right. Do what you want."

"No big rush," said Brophy, unsure of whether or not Chase saw through it. "We'll take him after the CAT tomorrow."

"Fine," said Chase, who was moving retractors around and concentrating on the belly again.

BOOK THREE

THE EXTIRPATION

1

All the way down to JB-4, Brophy kept formulating and reformulating exactly what he would say.

Lars was sitting in the chair by his bed. Beth was lying on the bed, reading *The New Yorker*. Brophy knew it was *The New Yorker* although he couldn't see the cover, and wondered how he knew and why it mattered.

"Did the test come back?" asked Beth.

Brophy opened his mouth, but nothing issued. He looked at Lars, sitting there, looking back at him.

"It's positive," Brophy said finally.

Beth sat up and moved toward Lars. Lars was expressionless, mouth open.

"What's this mean, exactly?" asked Beth.

"This has to be taken seriously," said Brophy, feeling foolish. Beth and Lars were serious enough. "It takes precedence over the thyroid."

"But what is it?"

"It's called a pheochromocytoma."

"I can't say I'm really surprised," said Lars.

Beth looked at him, stunned.

"What?"

"I don't know," said Lars, looking up to Brophy. "A lot of things. I just haven't been right."

He reached into the drawer of his bedside table and pulled out a Merck Manual.

"The sweating. The feeling of dread, for no good reason. Something's been happening."

"Oh, baby, why didn't you tell me?" said Beth, reaching over.

"What now?" Lars asked Brophy.

"You need a CAT scan."

"To locate it?"

"Yes."

"Where could it be?" asked Beth.

"In the adrenal gland," said Lars. He looked up at Brophy, smiling. "I've read that chapter over pretty well."

"It may be in both adrenals," said Brophy.

"Or maybe it's metastasized," said Lars.

"You *have* been reading," Brophy said with a flicker of a smile. "Maybe too much."

"No," Lars said. "What's dangerous is a *little* knowledge."

"This tumor," Beth said. "You can . . . treat it?"

"The short answer is yes," Brophy told her. He pulled up a chair and sat down. "It's not a tumor like a lung tumor. I wouldn't call it cancer, either. It doesn't behave like that. It just sits there and causes mischief by secreting hormones called catecholamines. Adrenalin is a catecholamine."

"That's what makes you feel so racy," Lars interrupted.

"You've been feeling *racy?*" said Beth.

"All you have to do," Brophy continued, "is find it, block the effects of the catecholamines with drugs, and then cut it out."

"All you have to do . . ." Beth echoed.

"These things are pretty rare, aren't they?" said Lars.

"Yes."

Lars stood up, wobbling a little. He'd noticed that lately he got dizzy whenever he stood up.

"You think my brother may have had the same thing?" Beth looked up at her husband, astonished.

"We still don't know what happened to your brother," said Brophy. "But if that lump in your neck is what I think it is, you probably have a syndrome which runs in families."

"I haven't been able to find much on that," said Lars.

"I'll get you some things to read."

"Our kids might have it?" asked Beth.

"Let's take one step at a time," said Brophy. "First we find out what your husband has."

"But I thought you knew."

"One thing this place has taught me," Brophy said, "is how

hard it is to be sure of anything. Let's take it one step at a time."

"This room's closing in on me," said Lars. "Is there somewhere we can all go and talk?"

Brophy looked at Lars for a long moment. Now that Lars had a pheo, he regarded him as a walking bomb. Any little jiggle, and boom . . . *Be rational, Brophy. The man's been walking around unprotected for weeks.*

"How about the solarium," said Brophy. At least if anything happened they'd still be on the ward, with the crash cart nearby.

They left the room, Lars between Brophy and Beth.

"You've been very nice about all this," Lars said. "I realize I haven't exactly been a model patient."

"I know you don't like hospitals," said Brophy.

"We want you to know . . . how much we . . . we really . . ." said Beth but she drifted off in thought.

There was an eighty-year-old-woman in the solarium, tied into a wheelchair, with a Foley catheter bag hooked up to the armrail. She kept saying "Mamma mia" over and over. The nurses had turned on the color TV and faced it toward her, but she wasn't watching. She just kept saying "Mamma mia" and rocking back and forth.

Lars, Beth, and Brophy stood there looking at her. Then Brophy went over and turned off the TV. He rolled the woman into a corner of the solarium, where she repeated "Mamma mia" to a plant.

"I'd like to ask you a question you don't have to answer," said Lars.

Brophy glanced at Beth.

"If you were the one with this tumor, would you have it removed here in Providence? Or would you go to one of the big centers? Like Boston?"

For weeks nothing would have made Brophy happier than seeing Lars pack up for Boston. Now, he wanted to see it through. But Lars had asked him to think as a patient, not as a doctor.

"I'm sure Clarissa's mentioned some of the problems at University Hospital," Brophy said, choosing his words carefully. "But for something like this, the most important thing is probably the preparation for surgery and the surgeon."

Lars was following Brophy intently.

"Even a place like Mass General probably doesn't see more than two or three pheos a year. The difference between three and one really isn't much in this case."

"So you think U.H. is as good as anywhere?"

Brophy thought about that.

"You can get lost in a big place like Mass General or Manhattan Hospital. . . ."

Lars reacted to that name. Brophy was sorry he'd said it, but he wanted the point made.

"What about the surgeon?" asked Lars.

"I don't know who'd you'd find elsewhere," said Brophy. "But I think Nancy Barnah is one of the best."

There was a clopping in the hallway. It was Clarissa, in her wooden clogs.

"Oh, thank God," Beth said, going to meet her.

They sat down together on a couch and Beth started crying.

"Chrissakes," said Lars. "I'm not dead yet!"

Clarissa looked up and smiled him. "Leave her alone—she deserves a good cry." Then, to Brophy: "I'll call you later."

The old woman in the wheelchair started crying, too. Beth looked at her and she stopped.

"I don't know what I'm going to decide," said Lars. "But whether it's Mass General or U.H., I want you to know I appreciate what you've done."

Brophy looked appropriately modest. "While you're making your decision, would you mind if we moved you over to the CRU?"

"Wherever you want me."

Brophy smiled. That sounded so odd coming from Lars.

"It might be a little easier to give you the medications you'll need over there."

"Fine," said Lars. "When will Nancy Barnah see me?"

Brophy smiled, unsure of what to say. It appeared Lars had made at least one decision.

"That's up to you. If you'd like, I can tell her you want to see her. But that's up to you. As far as I'm concerned, you're Dr. Chase's patient."

"Forget the protocol," said Lars. "Get me Nancy Barnah."

2

Brophy left Clarissa and her two patients and went down to the nurses' station, where he wrote the orders for the Dibenzyline, going over them with the charge nurse.

"Now, this stuff's going to make him dizzy when he stands up," Brophy told her, "so be careful getting him up. You're going to have to take his pressure lying, then standing."

The charge nurse said they'd never given Dibenzyline, but she'd order it up. Brophy was glad Lars would soon be on the CRU, where the nurses were familiar with the drugs.

Back in his office Brophy found Wendel, reading *Playboy.* Brophy told him about Lars.

"No shit!" said Wendel astutely. "No fuckin' shit."

Brophy told Wendel to meet him on JB-4 at seven the next morning, and to bring Robin. They would all go to the CAT with Lars and see the pheo take shape before their eyes. Wendel said Robin wouldn't be there; she was going to a Fellowship interview in Boston.

Brophy walked across the hall to Jethro's lab and told him Lars had asked to be seen by Nancy Barnah.

"Let's go with the first team," Jethro said.

Brophy grinned, but his moment of satisfaction was cut short by his beeper.

"You guys don't miss a trick." It was Lynn Ann.

"What's that supposed to mean?"

"Your friend Duncan Gordon got to Maria Addinizio. Poked a hole in her bone."

"She gave informed consent."

"Haven't you done enough to her already?"

"I haven't done anything to her."

"I asked her what it was all about. She hadn't the faintest. Some nice young doctor came in and had her sign a form and next thing she knows she's got a biopsy."

"I was there when Duncan explained things," said Brophy. "It wasn't quite like that."

"How was it like?"

"Oh, I get it: 'Confused Cancer Patient Made Guinea Pig at U.H.'"

"Come on, Donald. . . ."

"Duncan told her what he was doing."

"Did he?"

"He did. He explained why and how and that it'd hurt a little."

"A little? The poor woman was limping around."

"She was sore for a day. You make it sound like he crippled her. That your idea of accurate reporting?"

"Maria gave me her copy of the protocol. That's one protocol I don't have to subpoena."

"You never had to subpoena any protocol."

"Why are you going around punching holes in nice ladies with horrible diseases?"

"If you want to interview anyone, call Duncan. He's running that project. He'll tell you all about it."

"Donald," said Lynn Ann, trying to sound personal and exciting, "I don't know Duncan—I know you . . ."

"Look, Lynn—you're going about this all wrong."

"How am I going about it?"

"You don't know enough. You've got a little knowledge and you're making it into a dangerous thing."

"So enlighten me."

"You've got to listen to the answers."

"Just give me a reason to believe."

"You're not going to believe anything that doesn't make a good story."

"There's faith for you."

"It's true. How much of a story is 'Woman with Cancer Volunteers for Research'? It happens every day."

"Oh, you know all about it?"

"I read the papers. Good guys and bad guys."

"Now who's swinging half-cocked?"

"I can't talk to you, Lynn. I've been waved off."

"By whom?"

"By the powers that be."

"Lionel Addison?"

"I can't reveal my sources."

"Don't you see how that looks? You guys look like you've got something to hide."

"That's one interpretation," said Brophy, looking at his watch. "The other's that nobody trusts your paper to write about any of this in a fair light."

"You mean in a flattering light."

"I mean in an intelligent way."

"Well, thanks a lot," said Lynn Ann. Brophy heard the phone click.

Brophy had been talking from a phone in Jethro's lab. He went back across the hall to the Fellows' Office. His beeper went off again.

"Labor and Delivery," said the clerk.

"Dr. Brophy. Somebody page? Probably Clarissa Leonard." Clarissa got on the phone.

"Brophy? What can you tell me? Beth's just a wreck. Lars plays it tough, but they're both just reeling."

"I bet."

"Don't you care?"

"What can I do about it? It's bad news any way you cut it."

"I'm going to spend the night with Beth," said Clarissa. Brophy wondered why she was telling him this. Was he supposed to care where she was sleeping nowadays? "I'd like to get together with you so I can answer Beth's questions halfway intelligently."

"Call me tonight."

3

Brophy sat down in the Fellows' Office. Everyone had cleared out for the day. Reynolds' briefcase was gone and all the desks were clear. He began writing out a list of things to do.

The door to the office flew open and Duncan came steaming through.

"Now we know who the troupers are," he said. "Six o'clock. Everyone's gone home and Brophy sits working at his desk, pushing back the frontiers of science."

"Where is everyone?"

"Who knows? Sailing. Reynolds, of course, is at some nursing home."

"Well," said Brophy, "he does his work on weekends." Duncan smiled. "Enough said."

"You know who Lynn Ann Montano is?" Brophy asked.

"The reporter?"

"She called me today about Mrs. Addinizio."

"Oh, lovely."

"Seems some wild-eyed researcher poked a hole in Mrs. A. without getting what you call truly informed consent."

"Whatever that is," snorted Duncan.

"Whatever that is."

"I thought Mrs. A. liked us. What'd she go call the papers for?"

"She didn't call anyone. Lynn Ann keeps tabs on all the cops. She visits Mrs. A. in the hospital."

"I wish you'd told me that," said Duncan gravely, "before you roped me into sticking her."

Brophy looked at Duncan, astonished, waiting for him to

smile. Duncan grinned, and it was all right. "And Montano called you, asking questions, hearing no answers?"

Brophy nodded.

"If she goes to work on me, I may as well pack my bags. Providence is a small town. Nobody's going to sign up for a biopsy by Dr. Wild Eyes."

"What really kills me," said Brophy, "is that she's got *your* scent. Why doesn't she go after something around here that really stinks?"

"Hey—I meant it about not bringing that up."

"Maybe I ought to call Lynn back and trade Reynolds' ass for yours."

Duncan's face became as serious as Brophy had ever seen it. "You're just kidding around?"

"About Reynolds? No, sir."

"About talking to that reporter."

"I play dumb," said Brophy finally.

"Good." Duncan swiveled around in his chair and looked out his window at the Bay.

"Tell me you'd really care," said Brophy to the back of Duncan's head. "If I offered up Reynolds for sacrifice. It'd be Dick's own fault if he got burned, too. He's supposed to be supervising."

Duncan turned around.

"You think Dick can check every dot on every graph?"

Brophy looked at Duncan, trying to understand. Whatever Duncan wanted to do, Brophy could accept.

"What makes you think," said Duncan, "that if you handed her Reynolds, she wouldn't take me as well—and print *both* stories?"

"You're right," said Brophy. "Can't talk to reporters."

Brophy put his hands behind his head and considered how infrequently anyone checked his own data—he could be recruiting patients with normal calciums for all Duncan and Jethro knew.

Brophy shook his head, then snapped out of his thoughts. "Hey—we got the VMA on Magnussen. He's got it!"

Brophy told him about it, and Duncan got more and more excited, eyebrows jumping, grinning, dancing around.

Of course he wanted to study Lars.

"What study?" Brophy asked, not eager for him to latch on to Lars just now.

"Pheos cause hypercalcemia. Nobody knows the mechanism."

"Jesus, Duncan . . ."

"It wouldn't be any trouble at all. You just set him up like everyone else. I could do the biopsy when he goes to surgery."

"Duncan," pleaded Brophy, "the guy's just found out he's got big troubles."

"I suppose you're right," said Duncan, unconvinced.

"Remember the first time we saw him? He wasn't exactly eager to be a guinea pig."

"But this is his big chance to do his bit for science!"

"Somehow I don't think he's going to see it that way."

"Now's the perfect time to study him—before he's treated."

"Duncan, he's already talking about bolting for Mass General. You go in there with your biopsy needle unsheathed, he'll be on the next bus to Boston."

"We better wait," said Duncan. "But keep it in mind."

4

Brophy was about to leave the hospital when he remembered he hadn't checked the calciums with all the excitement about Magnussen. Sure enough, there was a high one, and, calling the ward, it turned out to be a banker with prostatic CA. Brophy trudged over to the banker's ward, and, much to his dismay, the patient was very willing to donate blood and urine for the malignancy study.

Brophy called Duncan to see if he could come in and collect the samples at seven the next morning, but Duncan had an assay he had to set up at six forty-five.

"Maybe we ought to pass on this one," Brophy said. "I'm supposed to go to CAT Scan with Magnussen tomorrow. I'll never be able to do it if I have to be collecting this guy's samples."

"Brophy, which comes first at U.H.? Patient care or New Knowledge?" said Duncan with his most ironic smile.

"Oh—priorities," said Brophy. "How could I forget?"

"What do you have to be there for, anyway? Send a medical student or someone with Magnussen."

"You really want to study this prostatic CA?"

"It's another brick in the pyramid," Duncan said. "Sometimes I think I must have been Fuller Albright in a former life."

"And before that, you recruited knights for the Holy Wars."

Brophy called Wendel before going home. Wendel was very impressed that Brophy had bothered to call him at home. It was a very important mission, taking Lars to CAT Scan, Brophy told him. Wendel swore he'd be on JB-4, ready to roll at seven sharp.

Brophy drove out of the parking lot, thinking about all the details he was trying to organize for Magnussen. He had the feeling he was keeping five balls aloft, but there were six balls.

The sixth was the Dibenzyline. Brophy had forgotten to check to make sure the surgical nurses were giving it on schedule.

They weren't. Lars' blood pressure had dropped so dramatically after the first two doses that they had held his next dose and paged Brophy to find out what to do. But Brophy had left his beeper in the Endocrine Office and never got the page. So Lars got only two Dibenzyline doses the day before his CAT scan. The rest was held for very good reasons.

5

At six-thirty A.M., Brophy called the nurses on Urology to remind them to wake the banker and have him empty his bladder. They had him drinking distilled water until Brophy arrived at seven. His bladder was full again and ready to empty into Brophy's special, acidified containers. Then Brophy filled six vacutainers with the banker's blood and plunked each one into his ice bucket with the urine. It was a model collection.

Duncan was in the lab when Brophy popped through the door at seven-eighteen.

"Good man!" roared Duncan, seeing Brophy. "Brophy has struck again."

Duncan was hopping around in front of his bench, setting up the glass and rubber paraphernalia for his assay.

"A dawn strike . . ." Duncan was chanting.

Brophy picked up the phone and called JB-4. To his astonishment, Wendel was actually there, waiting with Lars for the call from the CAT scan people.

"We're ready for blast-off," Wendel squeaked.

"I'll call the CAT people," said Brophy, "just to make sure there's no snafu on their end."

"I already went down there," said Wendel. "They're opening up. We're first case."

Wendel, showing initiative? Anything could happen this morning.

"How's Magnussen?" Brophy asked.

Wendel had even checked Lars' blood pressure—149/85.

"He got the Dibenzyline, then?"

"He says it made him dizzy."

"Good," said Brophy, happy everything was going as planned. "Is the Regitine taped to the stretcher?"

"The stretcher isn't here."

"Do they have the Regitine on the floor?"

"It's taped to his bed."

"Untape it, Wendel, and when the stretcher arrives, tape it to the stretcher. And don't leave his side."

"When will you be here?"

"I'm in the lab now. Maybe twenty minutes. I'll call first. If you're down in CAT, I'll meet you there."

"Okay," said Wendel. He sounded frightened: Brophy had scared him with the Regitine. "Wendel isn't so bad," Brophy said after he hung up.

"Your mission," said Duncan, still playing with the assay columns, "should you decide to accept it"—he spun around, waving his palms at Brophy like a minstrel—"is to spin down those bloods and urines and log them in and get to CAT in time for the Great Pheo Show."

Duncan raised one hand behind his head and held an invisible fencing foil in his forward hand, then advanced with two quick thrusts toward Brophy.

"Stick that pheo!" he cried. "Lo, these many weeks, only Donald Brophy, MD, has believed in Lars Magnussen's pheo. Now he has it—and on this very morning he has also pulled off a sneak attack on the mysterious fortress of prostatic CA, as it nestled in the bones of a Providence banker."

"This is sick," shouted Brophy. "I come in here, having roused some poor bugger out of sleep at six A.M., punctured his veins, commanded him to pee into an acidified plastic cup, and you're cheering. I should be arrested, and you're cheering."

Duncan crossed his arms and smiled.

"Now I call JB-Four," Brophy continued. "Wendel's really high. Something big's about to happen."

"Something miraculous is about to happen," said Duncan. "Through the wonder of modern Computerized Transaxial Tomography, that heretofore scoffed-at pheo will be visualized with photographs. Undeniable proof!"

Brophy's beeper went off. It was the intern on the Medical Intensive Care Unit. He paged when he woke up and discovered that his resident had decided to spend the day moonlighting for Steve Reynolds at a nursing home, leaving the intern all alone with a comatose, juvenile-onset diabetic amputee in renal failure, who had started throwing grand-mal convulsions as soon as the medical resident walked out the ICU door.

Brophy told the intern he'd be right up. Then he called JB-4. CAT Scan had called and Wendel had taken Lars on the stretcher. Brophy pipetted the serum from the vacutainers into the appropriate glass vials and put them in all the right places in the metal racks in the freezer, logging them into the lab book.

"I can't believe I'm pipetting here and there's a guy seizing and an intern wetting his pants up in the ICU," Brophy said.

"Guilt is a heavy burden," said Duncan. This from the man who never left for home without six medical journals in his bag.

Brophy put everything away in the freezer and ran next door to the Fellows' Office, where he got his white lab coat. He ran up the stairs to the ICU, thinking about Lars in the CAT scan room.

The patient was a thirty-four-year-old man named Sertoli, who had been diabetic for twenty years. He never much liked being diabetic and took his insulin erratically. He had had all the bad things happen that can happen to diabetics, with one or two exceptions: he had not yet had a major stroke and he was still alive. Brophy reserved judgment on the stroke until he could do a physical exam.

Down in the CAT scan room, Wendel was wondering what had happened to Brophy, and considered paging him. They were waiting for the radiologist to come in and start the test. One of the techs started an IV on Lars.

"What's this for?" asked Lars.

"They give you contrast later," said the tech. Her panties showed through her white pants, a fact not lost on Wendel.

"Contrast?" Lars asked him.

"It makes the pictures easier to read."

"Does Brophy know I'm getting contrast?"

"Oh, yes," lied Wendel, who had no idea whether or not Brophy knew. The tech smiled at Wendel.

Back up on the ICU, Brophy read rapidly through Sertoli's chart.

At age thirty-one he had stepped on a nail, but having diabetic neuropathy and no sensation in his feet, he didn't notice it for a few days, when he finally discovered the head of the nail sticking out of his foot. By that time he was shaking with violent chills, sweats, and fever. They had to cut off his foot. A year later he got retinal detachments. Through it all, he continued to work as a gardener.

Brophy called CAT Scan and asked to speak with Wendel, who told him about the contrast. Brophy said it was okay. Wendel did not mention that the radiologist had arrived and was opening a vial of glucagon, and drawing it up in a syringe. Brophy said he'd be a few more minutes and would be in the ICU.

He asked the ICU intern if he had given the patient glucose. The intern had. He had even thought to draw a blood sugar first so the diagnosis of hypoglycemic seizures could be established. The blood sugar drawn prior to the injected glucose was spectacularly low: 19. Sertoli had stopped seizing for a while after the first bolus of glucose, then started again.

"Why's he keep getting so hypoglycemic?" asked the intern.

"Because you're giving him the same amount of insulin he took before he went into renal failure. But now he can't pee out his metabolized insulin."

The intern hung a glucose drip, and Brophy went to write his note, feeling triumphant, like a real endocrinologist. Lower the insulin dose in renal failure. Brophy had just heard that in one of Dick Cecil's conferences. Dick wasn't much of a human being, but he could be useful.

Downstairs, Lars was ready for the CAT scan. The machine was intimidating, looming over him like a space module. They slid him into it and he could see the parts rotating around inside. It made a whirring noise.

Things went well, in the beginning. They were getting decent scout images, but the intestines kept moving and blurring the picture. So the radiologist walked into the room with his syringe of glucagon and pressed some into Lars' IV.

Thirty seconds later Lars shouted, "*What the hell did you do?*"

He tried to sit up, but struck the machine encasing him.

The radiologist, followed by Wendel and the technician, ran into the room. They had been observing Lars from behind a leaded-glass screen.

"Don't move!" the radiologist shouted. Lars was ruining the pictures.

Lars was also on the verge of stroking out his entire left cerebral hemisphere. He tried to speak, but his words wouldn't come. His head felt like it was blowing apart, and his heart was galloping out of his chest. His skin blanched a deathly white, and sweat washed over his body as though a dam had burst.

Wendel did not appreciate all the details of Lars' condition, but he perceived that he had big trouble, and he stat-paged Brophy, clinging to the phone, watching Lars erupt.

Brophy heard the operator call out "Six-four-three-one-three, STAT!", jumped out of his chair, and bolted through the ICU door. He sprinted down the hall to the stairwell and down the stairs to the CAT scan room in the basement. He knew 6-4313 was CAT Scan's number.

This can't be happening. What could they possibly have done to him in CAT Scan of all places?

They had pulled the stretcher out of the CAT and aborted the rest of the study. The technician was taking Lars' blood pressure. Wendel huddled, looking very pale, in the corner of the room, by a phone. The radiologist, who appeared to be on the point of joining Lars in cardiac arrest, was on another phone, frantically dialing a "code blue"—the alert for that emergency.

Brophy asked the tech about the blood pressure.

"Two-twenty over one-sixty. Is that possible?"

Not only was it possible, it was Lars' blood pressure. Fortunately for him, he wasn't conscious to hear it.

Brophy looked around for Wendel. "Wendel? Where's the Regitine?"

Wendel recovered just enough to point to the stretcher and say, "By his head. . . ."

In one sweeping motion, Brophy ripped the syringe from the underside of the stretcher, stripped it from the adhesive-tape anchor, and plunged the needle end into the rubber valve on the IV line. He squeezed the plunger, sending a bolus of 5 milligrams of Regitine rushing into Lars' bloodstream, and Lars' blood pressure plummeted to more civilized levels.

Two minutes later, Lars had a blood pressure compatible with life. There was a swirling, whirling very fast, and he could see nothing and know nothing. Not where he was, not even who he was, just that he was alive. He was able to hear and that was all there was. Then the deepest, most overwhelming sense of nausea, about which he could do nothing. A face flashed by. Then the swirling again. He was a long way away and there was nothing but the nausea. Gradually there was light, but still the sickness, still the whirl. Then voices. Still no memory of who or where or what. Consciousness only, and the pressing nausea. Then there was a face. Brophy's face. And Lars knew he had been very far away. And he was frightened.

"You had an episode," Brophy told him. "You're going to be all right."

Lars felt grateful. Profoundly grateful. It was the worst thing that had ever happened to him, and somehow he connected Brophy with his return.

Brophy told Wendel to call the CRU and tell them to get the room ready. As he wheeled Lars toward the elevator, he realized there had been a great many doctors in the room. When he arrived it was just the radiologist, Wendel, and the technician. Now, as he looked back over his shoulder, he could see all the members of the cardiac arrest team filing out. He heard them canceling the code on the overhead page.

"What happened?" Brophy asked the radiologist. The radiologist was blinking wildly.

"He sat up and started having a fit," said the radiologist, who couldn't stop blinking.

"Was he seizing?"

"Don't think so," said the radiologist, whose chest pain was only now subsiding.

Lars was listening to the radiologist, but watching Brophy.

"Did you do anything before he had it?"

"No. Just adjusted his position. Gave him some glucagon. Turned up his IV—"

"Gave him some glucagon?" said Brophy, evenly.

"He had some movement artifact: slows the bowel motility."

Brophy considered punching him out then and there in the hallway, but decided to do it after he'd seen the pictures.

"Did you see the pheo?" he asked, keeping his voice steady.

"Oh, yes!" the radiologist assured him, relieved to get back to the subject of radiology. "Come back down when you have him settled."

Brophy had his hand on Lars' wrist. The radiologist pushed

the elevator call button, waved good-bye, and darted back down the hall.

"How are you doing?" Brophy asked Lars.

"I'm soaked. . . ." Lars was getting some color back. "I felt like somebody cracked me over the head and stuck me on a very fast merry-go-round."

"Everything's under control now."

"I feel much better."

"You've had a morning of it."

Wendel handed Brophy a blood-pressure cuff just as the elevator arrived. "I called his wife," he told Brophy on the way up. "She was waiting on JB-Four."

"Thanks," Lars said.

"What'd you tell her?" Brophy asked.

"That the test was over. To meet us on the CRU."

"Did you call the CRU?"

"Yes. They said you had to call Admitting."

"Did you bring his chart?"

"Yes," said Wendel. "I'm not sure they have a bed for him."

"They'll have one," said Brophy. "Open that chart. Are the medications in there?"

Wendel looked. He opened the chart and placed it on Lars' abdomen. No med sheets.

"Once we get him in bed, I want you to go back to JB-Four and get those med sheets."

"They gave him the Dibenzyline."

"I'm sure they did."

6

At the fifth floor CRU the nurses helped transfer Lars from stretcher to bed, and flew around taking blood pressures and putting on EKG monitor wires. Wendel had phoned ahead to tell them what happened.

"Better call Admitting," the head nurse told Brophy.

"Sure."

"What happened?"

"They gave some glucagon to a pheo," said Brophy. "Nearly sent him into orbit."

"Oh, my."

"What I can't understand is why he wasn't protected," said Brophy. "He was supposed to be getting Dibenzyline."

Beth and Clarissa arrived. The change in plans and something in Wendel's voice over the telephone had tipped off Beth that something had happened. Then she heard them paging the cardiac team for somewhere. She had paged Clarissa, in a panic.

The nurses were rolling the stretcher out of Lars' room as Beth and Clarissa hurried in. Brophy was watching Wendel take Lars' blood pressure.

"You're white as a ghost," said Beth, seeing Lars.

"I'm okay now," said Lars, taking her hand. "It got a little hairy though."

Clarissa looked at Brophy and tilted her head toward the doorway.

They walked out of the room. Wendel and a nurse stayed behind, taking blood pressures.

"What on earth?" said Clarissa when they were in the hall.

"Never a dull moment at the U.H.," said Brophy. "I may go into Dermatology."

Clarissa followed him back to the nurses' station.

"I hear them page the cardiac team. Then I get a stat page from Beth and she's hysterical. And Lars looks like he's just back from the grave."

Brophy sat down and reached for a pad of paper and began making another list.

"Sorry it's been such a tough morning for you," he said, reaching for the phone.

Clarissa folded her arms and watched him dial Page.

"You're not talking to me?"

"When you calm down," said Brophy, listening to Page not answer his ringing, "I'll talk to you."

He asked Page for the neurologist on call. He held the receiver to his ear and looked up at Clarissa without smiling. The neurology resident came on the line.

"We had a little problem with one of our patients," said Brophy. "He's got a pheochromocytoma and had a hypertensive crisis a few minutes ago. He was aphasic for a few minutes."

Clarissa sat down and listened to Brophy answer the neurologist's questions. Brophy hung up.

"Did he have a stroke?"

"Haven't had time to examine him," said Brophy. "I'm just the band leader in this performance. This morning I dropped the baton."

"He couldn't speak?"

"His blood pressure was off the wall at the time," said Brophy, who was starting to shake and sweat. He felt a chill pass, sitting there in the air-conditioned CRU. Brophy took his own pulse.

"How high?"

"He set a new indoor record," said Brophy. "As Jethro would say."

"He was talking just now."

"I think he'll be okay."

"How do you know?"

"I don't know," said Brophy. "That's why I called the neurologist. His blood pressure was off the wall. Every artery in his brain must have just clamped right down in one big reflex to protect his gray matter from that blast."

Clarissa followed Brophy, getting teary eyed. "Poor Lars."

"The Regitine brought his pressure down and he woke up and started talking."

"No permanent damage?"

"That's what I got the neurologist for."

Brophy reached for an order sheet and started writing. Clarissa sat by him reading what he wrote.

1. Admit: CRU
2. Diagnosis: Pheochromocytoma
3. Activity: Bed Rest
4. Diet: Regular
5. Observations: Cardiac Monitor, Vital signs Q shift, Blood pressure lying and standing 1 Q hour.

"What did it show?" asked Clarissa.

Brophy looked up, startled. "What did what show?"

"The scan."

"Jesus," he said. "I forgot all about the scan."

Clarissa and Brophy ran out of the nurses' station just as the phone rang and the clerk answered.

"Dr. Brophy," the clerk called after them, leaning across her desk, shouting down the hallway. "It's Admitting. Do you want a bed for Magnussen on the CRU?"

They ran down six flights of stairs, down past messenger-service people who leaned back against the walls as they came barreling by. They reached the basement floor and burst through the stairwell door and flew down the hallway to CAT Scan.

The radiologist was looking at Lars' scan with some residents and Attendings when Brophy ran in. Clarissa arrived, breathless, a few seconds later. It looked like the whole department of Radiology.

The pheo was plain to see, big as day, in the left adrenal.

"Look at that mother," said the radiologist. The radiologist was very happy with his picture. It was very good work, despite the movement artifact.

The resolution was really very good.

They pointed out everything. The pheo was a smooth white circle sitting right where the left adrenal should be. It had a dark, crescent-shaped area across its center. The radiologist said that was an area of infarction. It made the pheo look like a smile button.

It all seemed so simple in the Radiology Suite. The CAT

scan was such magic. There was so little doubt. All the uncertainty, all the fussing about urine collections was miles away. It was hard to believe anyone had ever doubted Lars could have a pheo.

"It's a photograph," said Brophy grinning at the pheo smiling back at him. "A veritable portrait."

He felt Clarissa's eyes bearing into his cheek. He thought of Lars and Beth up there in the room on the CRU.

And he thought of what was to come.

"Can I have some copies?" asked Brophy. "I've got to show them to Jethro Brown and Nancy Barnah. And I'll need them for conference Tuesday." He was smiling broadly.

The radiologist sent a technician to make a copy of each cut.

"Wait till Dumfy sees these," Brophy told the radiologist. In the luminescence of the lighted wall boxes, everyone in the room looked like images on a black and white TV.

"How'd you pick it up?"

"Were you the guy who gave him the Regitine?"

The tech came back with the copies and they put the originals back up on the view boxes. They were pointing to the other adrenal, on the right side, thinking there might be something in that one, too.

"It's bilateral then?" asked Brophy.

"Can't be sure. Looks like it might be, from what we have."

Brophy was beaming, shifting from one foot to the other. "That's key. That's just key."

"Well," said the radiologist, "I'd definitely tell the surgeon to explore the right adrenal."

"You'll come to conference?"

"When is it?"

Brophy told him.

"The thing is," Brophy continued, "this guy had a brother who dropped dead for no good reason. If it's bilateral in Lars, then it's the familial form. They're not usually on both sides, except in the familial form."

"Well, it looks consistent with bilateral disease," said the radiologist with that greatest of radiological qualifications— "consistent with."

Brophy took his copies and strode off down the hall, followed by Clarissa.

"Where are you going now?" she asked. Her eyes were red and watery.

"Got to show these to Jethro," said Brophy, grinning. "And to Dumfy. Dumfy'll go wild."

"You going to tell the patient?"

"Of course."

"You might try calming down," she said. "You look like you've just won the Irish sweepstakes."

"I don't feel that way."

"Yes, you do. You're quite vindicated. A hero, even. The radiologists might vote you Endocrine Fellow of the Week."

"Lars will live through this," he said. "He'll see his grandchildren."

Clarissa had been trying hard not to cry. Now she laughed through her tears, stopping in the hall to wipe her eyes.

"Do you *really* think so?" she said. "Do you really think of that at all?"

"This could be a pretty depressing line of work," he said. "So I get happy when I find a tumor could have killed a guy didn't know he had it."

Brophy looked at Clarissa but couldn't read her expression.

"Are you going back to see Lars now?" he asked.

"Just for a minute. I've left Sol with one of my patients who's probably wondering where I vanished."

"Tell Lars I'll be by to show him the CAT scan."

Brophy watched Clarissa walk off down the hallway in her blue scrub dress and for some reason he pictured Lynn Ann clattering down the hospital corridors in her spike heels. Clarissa belonged here—and not just because she looked right. Brophy watched Clarissa until she turned the corner at the end of the hall, then he raced downstairs to show the scans to Nancy Barnah.

7

Nancy Barnah wasn't in her office, so Brophy had to run all the way back up to the Operating Room Suite.

Nancy was sitting in the cubicle off the recovery room, drinking coffee between her cases.

"Holy Mother!" she said, holding the film up to the fluorescent light. "This is Lars Magnussen?" she said, smiling to hide the pain, looking to Brophy to say it wasn't so.

Brophy nodded.

"I got your message that he was in the house. I was going to stop by today. But I didn't know about this."

She looked at the film again, holding it up to the fluorescent light on the ceiling. Brophy didn't need to point out anatomy to Nancy.

"And I operated on this guy," she said, shaking her head. "Hernia. He could have exploded on me."

"You were covered," said Brophy, smiling. "You had a medical clearance."

Nancy looked at Brophy and smiled. She said nothing. She had rosy pink skin and blond hair and looked about sixteen, and she smiled and said nothing, like a grown-up.

"Once you have him blocked, I'll need an arteriogram. Monday, okay?"

"Should I schedule it?"

"No . . ." she said, thinking. "I will. I'll ask Bob Lamphere to do it." She paused. "Let's make it Tuesday. I want to go over this CAT with Bob before he does anything. No screwups this time."

Brophy looked down at his shoes.

"I'll see Lars," Nancy said. "Oh, shit. I'm going out of town for the weekend. Forgot today's Friday. I'll see Lars Sunday night. Can you tell him that?"

Brophy nodded.

"We'll do the arteriogram Tuesday morning. What time's this powwow Tuesday?"

"Twelve-thirty. Can you be there?"

"I've got a gallbladder at eight-thirty. Should be no problem."

"Jethro wants everybody who knows anything about pheo there. You're the star, of course."

"I'm just the plumber," said Nancy. "You're the star. You found the thing."

"Jethro says we'll need a battle plan."

"He's right about that. You've got to get everyone there: Anesthesia, Intensive Care people, Endocrine. . . . Everyone talks before we touch him. I don't want anybody slipping him any more glucagon or Christ-knows-what just because they didn't know better."

"One thing, Nancy."

"What's that?"

"He might want to pack up and ship off to Mass General."

"After today." She laughed. "I couldn't blame him."

8

Daniel Dumfy was a real disappointment. He was impressed but curiously subdued as Brophy held the films up to the window light for him to see. Dumfy smiled wordlessly, like a grandfather. Brophy had the feeling Dumfy was smiling at him, not at the CAT scan and the discovery it documented.

When he finally held up the film which showed the pheo in all its shining glory, Dumfy merely smiled again and nodded and asked how big it was.

Brophy faltered, stunned by Dumfy's equanimity. Here was the man who became orgiastic over a high calcium now confronted with the actual visualization of the tumor his precious VMA had diagnosed—and he just smiled and asked about its size.

"I think one of the radiologists said something about a grapefruit, or an orange. I can't remember which. It's big."

"I knew it!" cackled Dumfy, pointing a finger at the film, then forming a fist and striking his other palm with it. "It *had* to be big. That's why the catecholamines were only borderline . . . This is a good case for conference—you should invite Ira Goldwasser from the medical school."

"We're going to need the auditorium for this conference," said Brophy. "There'll be more people than for grand rounds."

"That's what a place like this is good for."

Dumfy sat down at his desk and began pushing around stacks of lab reports.

"You're following that Addinizio lady, aren't you?"

"Yes." Brophy had almost forgotten there were other patients on the Endocrine Service.

305

"She's getting treated now, I presume."

"Yes—how did you know?"

Dumfy held up a computerized lab print-out.

"Number one: she's on the Oncology ward. That's a clue," he said. "Number two: her HCG's falling like a rock. It's almost undetectable. They'll cure her," he said happily, "if they don't kill her first."

9

Brophy headed for the CRU. He went directly to the nurses' station. Wendel was there, telling the nurses about the fireworks at CAT scan. Brophy pulled the med sheets out of Wendel's hand.

"Well, that explains it," said Brophy. "They held the Dibenzyline."

They held the Dibenzyline and the radiologist gave glucagon.

"Like an execution," Brophy said.

Brophy worte the orders for the Dibenzyline and went over them with Lars' nurse.

"No matter how hypotensive he gets when he stands up, give him the drug."

"Don't take it out on me," said the nurse. "I didn't hold the Dibenzyline."

"I just want to be sure everyone understands."

"Brophy," she said, "this is the CRU. We get pheos up here what? Once every two years. We're old pros."

Brophy's beeper went off. It was Lynn Ann, all sweetness again.

"Sorry I got pissed," she said. "I was having a bad day."

You don't know what a bad day is, honey. . . .

"No problem. It wasn't a great day for me, either."

"How about Moonstone . . . Sunday?" Her voice was low and breathy, but without effect. It sounded all wrong. "We won't go to the nude part. It's a gorgeous beach—really."

The idea of going anywhere with Lynn Ann struck Brophy as distinctly unappetizing at that moment, but the vision of a

307

pretty beach and the strong desire to get her off the phone asserted themselves, so he said okay. She told him to pick her up at nine. Brophy hung up. He considered calling her back and canceling, then calling Clarissa and asking her to go to Moonstone. But he had things to do.

He called Admitting and told them he wanted a bed for Lars Magnussen in Room 584. That satisfied the Admitting clerk quite nicely until she discovered there already was a patient in 584.

"Yes," said Brophy. "That's Magnussen."

The clerk was no longer pleased. She couldn't admit Magnussen to a bed when her computer screen showed there was already someone in that bed.

"Who's the computer show there?"

The clerk said the computer didn't show a name, it just said, OCCUPIED: NAME TO FOLLOW.

"Fine. The name to follow is the following: Magnussen."

The clerk was still confused, so Brophy told her to come up and ask the person in Room 584 his name. She said that wasn't her job. Brophy said he was sure she could handle it, that he had great confidence in her. Then he hung up.

He went to show Lars the CAT scan.

Beth was sitting in a chair close to her husband's bed.

"I come bearing CAT scans," said Brophy.

He pointed out everything: kidneys, liver, adrenals, and tumor.

Beth started to cry, just a reddening of the eyes at first, then a single tear rolling, traveling down her cheek, then sobs. Lars put an arm around her shoulders, keeping his attention on the scan.

"Fantastic pictures," he said. "Fascinating."

Brophy stared at him, amazed. Lars was actually smiling, looking at the scan.

"I'm looking right at my own tumor."

"Tumors," corrected Beth.

"Tumors," he echoed. Then he looked up suddenly. "Do you think Olaf had this?"

Brophy told him about the significance of having tumors in both adrenal glands—the pattern typical of familial disease.

"Then it's probably true. Olaf died of this too."

"Can our kids have it?" asked Beth.

"We'll check them when they're old enough."

"If the pheos are in both glands, then I probably have the MEA syndrome. And if I have the MEA syndrome then part of that syndrome is medullary carcinoma of the thyroid. So that's what I have in my neck."

"Very likely," said Brophy. "You've really studied that Merck Manual."

"And the calcium," said Lars, "that's high because of hyperparathyroidism, which is the third part of the package."

"That's the way I put it together."

"And the kidney stones were because of the high blood calcium?"

"Presumably."

"Why's that?" asked Beth.

"Urine's made from blood," said Brophy. "It's sort of a distillate. You have tons of calcium in your blood. It spills over into the urine. Get a high enough concentration and it precipitates out."

"When did you begin to suspect I had the MEA?"

"When you had your second stone and I brought you up here to the CRU."

"Even then?"

"Your wife told me about your brother," said Brophy. "I think that's what really hooked me. But I wasn't sure. It just seemed like something not to miss."

Lars and Beth laughed.

"I'd like to read up on this," Lars said.

"I'll take you over to the medical school Sunday, if you're well enough blocked. You can read all you want."

"Is this pheo"—Beth didn't know how to put it—"serious?"

"It's a problem," said Brophy. "But it can be managed. We just have to be careful."

"Could you bring me a few articles before Sunday?" asked Lars.

Brophy agreed and told Lars Nancy Barnah would be out of town until Sunday.

"Tell her to come at night," said Lars. "I'll be in the library in the afternoon."

Beth asked what happened that morning at CAT scan.

"The radiologists always give a hormone to quiet the bowels. Unfortunately, that hormone can arouse the pheo. It did that to Lars, and his blood pressure took off."

"That neurologist went over Lars for hours," said Beth. "He wouldn't tell us anything."

"I haven't read his note. If there's anything there, I'll let you know."

"The radiologist made a mistake, didn't he?"

"Evidently," said Brophy. It came out sounding more angry than he had intended. "I mean, looking back, we know the glucagon was an error." Brophy hesitated, realizing that wasn't the word he wanted either.

"Have you thought about where you want this whole thing done?" asked Brophy, who, after the day's events, was beginning to have his own doubts about keeping Lars at U.H.

"We were just talking about it before you came in," said Lars. "I'm happy with U.H. as long as you're with me. You found the thing. You can damn well do something about it."

"Lars was very grateful," said Beth. "For what you did this morning. That's his dumb way of saying it."

"For what I did?"

"The medical student, Wendel, told us how you gave the drug that brought down Lars' blood pressure."

"Regitine," Lars interjected.

"And how quickly you got there. And how fast you reacted."

Brophy laughed and shook his head. "See you Sunday."

"Drop those articles off tonight," said Lars, "before you go home."

10

The spirit who looks over Endocrine Fellows saw to it there were no new hypercalcemics on the Friday-afternoon calcium runs. Brophy checked calciums at three-thirty, then made rounds with Wendel.

They pushed along quickly because Brophy still had to show the CAT scan to Jethro and call the people for the big conference on Tuesday.

Mr. Sertoli in the ICU was sitting up drinking cranberry juice, keeping his blood sugar up and not seizing. Mrs. Addinizio was looking much better. Her balding head was covered with a new blond wig, and she wasn't at all nauseated.

"If I've got a new life to lead," she said, "let me live it as a blonde."

"You're doing much better," Brophy told her.

"I'm supposed to tell *you* that."

"Your HCG level is almost normal."

"That's good news, I take it."

"The best. When there's no more HCG, there's no more tumor. And you feel well?"

"Much better. This stuff they're giving me for the nausea is super."

Brophy looked at her tongue. It was a fine, normal tongue.

"Dr. Clark says my hair will grow back once they finish the chemotherapy."

"Maybe it'll grow in blond."

"I'll settle for mousey brown." She laughed, touching her wig without thinking.

"You look lovely."

"I do, don't I? I've lost fifteen pounds. Wouldn't recommend this method to anyone, but it's been years since I've been down to a hundred-five. My cheekbones look terrific. I could be a model."

Brophy laughed.

"Of course my arms look like I'm a junky," she said, examining the bruises from the blood-drawing and the IVs.

"When are you getting out of here?"

"About two weeks, maybe sooner."

Brophy and Wendel hustled down to find Jethro, who was sitting in a cloud of smoke in his office, working over his data sheets. Duncan was sitting next to him.

"No music?" said Brophy.

Jethro looked up. "Local pilferers. Stole my beautiful Brahms machine. Came back from lunch and it was gone."

Brophy looked at the envelope in his hands, wondering if Jethro would be in any mood to go over the CAT scan.

"You brought me something?" said Jethro, taking the cigarette from his mouth and reaching for the envelope. Jethro dug out the films and held them up to the light.

"What's the diagnosis, Dr. Gordon?" he said.

Duncan looked at the films, noting Magnussen's name in the lower left hand corner.

"There it is," said Duncan, pointing at the pheo. "There's something in the right side, too."

"Have you called everyone for Tuesday?"

"Just going to do it."

"Well, hurry up, man. It's Friday. Everyone's going to clear out for the weekend."

"Okay."

"And, Brophy," said Jethro, putting his cigarette back in his mouth and smiling. "Nice pickup."

Brophy sat down in the Fellows' Office and started calling. He lined up Anesthesia. (Nancy had given him a name.) He got through to Dumfy's man in Physiology, Ira Goldwasser, who was delighted to be asked. And he left a message with Lionel's secretary. Chuck Mersault said he would be there. Brophy went right down the list. Each honcho sounded flattered to be singled out and invited, and congratulated Brophy on making the diagnosis.

Clarissa paged at five o'clock.

"Wanted to say I'm sorry about this morning. I was a bit overwrought."

"Weren't we all?"

"Anyway, I'm sorry. You did a good job on Lars."

"There's a RISD museum show Saturday morning. Gilbert Stuart. Want to go?"

"You asking me for a date?"

"Yes."

"Maybe I ought to give you a hard time more often."

"Not necessary."

Clarissa agreed to go, and Brophy hung up, wondering why he had acted on impulse like that. He had to resist her or she'd get into his blood again. It'd be New York all over again. Lynn Ann was there for Sunday—an antidote. But Lynn Ann was wearing off. And things seemed different with Clarissa now. In New York, there was no thinking rationally about her—she had only to appear, and a thick cloud descended over Brophy's brain. But he was younger then, and led a glandular existence.

11

Brophy picked up Clarissa and they stopped off to see Lars before going to the museum. Lars became dizzy standing for Brophy's blood pressure check.

"I think I'm pretty well blocked," he said.

"You've been reading those articles," laughed Brophy. "Listen to him, talking about being 'blocked.'"

"I'll be through them by tomorrow," Lars said. "What time we going to the library?"

Brophy didn't want to get into a discussion about his plans for Sunday with Clarissa standing there.

"About four. But you'll have to be well blocked. I want your lying pressure no higher than a hundred-fifty over ninety."

"I'll be okay."

"Where you taking him tomorrow?" asked Clarissa as they walked to the parking lot.

"The medical school library."

"Think it's safe?"

"I'll have a syringe full of Regitine in my pocket."

They wandered through the museum, then walked up the hill to Thayer Street and had some sangria at a sidewalk table outside La Maisonnette. It was a sunny day and there was a nice breeze.

"I'm going over to see Beth this afternoon," said Clarissa.

"She must be a wreck."

"Lars made out a will."

"He's a lawyer and never had a will?"

"He's never thought of dying."

"But he's got two kids."

314

"Beth went to pieces after the will. I had to get Sol to write her some Valium."

"I could have done that."

"You've done enough."

"I'm not sure how you mean that."

"Gratefully."

Brophy relaxed and shrugged. "All in a day's work."

"Why can't you be gracious and simply say, 'You're welcome'?"

"It's no big deal."

"It was a *very* big deal. Lately I've seen a side of you I really respect, and you keep denying it."

"You didn't respect me until lately?"

"Oh, of course. But you were always so intent on being breezy . . . talking about gomers."

"I was an intern," said Brophy. "That kind of talk helped then."

"I'm glad to see you've got beyond it."

12

Brophy knocked on Lynn Ann's door at nine.

"It's open." She was in the bathroom, putting on her eyelashes.

There was a pile of things in the living room. Brophy looked around idly, wondering why she was housecleaning at this hour, Sunday morning. He noticed two aluminum beach chairs, a wicker basket, plum-colored towels and a thermos.

Lynn came out in a brown bikini, pulling on a bright-green terry cloth shirt-dress that ended just where it should; only the white underlip of her buttocks peeked out.

"We going on safari?" said Brophy, nodding at the pile.

"We are going to one of the world's most gorgeous beaches. So stop complaining."

She disappeared into the bedroom. After a while, Brophy called out, "Ready?"

"Carry the stuff down to the car like a good boy."

Brophy carried the towels and chairs and basket down the stairs. He could hear Lynn Ann locking her door.

He looked back up and watched her. Between the towels and the dress, she was color coordinated—the same green and plum as her living room.

Brophy piled her paraphernalia on the back seat and put down the top of his car while Lynn Ann pulled on a straw hat with a scarf that tied under her chin.

"I knew you'd want to drive with the top down," she said.

It was a bright day, already hot, and Route 95 slowed at the Route Four turnoff with beach traffic. The police were working the highway in unmarked cars, and the traffic flow was fitful.

"Take Route Two when you see it," said Lynn Ann.

"I thought we wanted One."

"The tourists take One. We'll take Two."

Everything slowed down until they were hardly moving.

"Go up the shoulder," said Lynn. "The turnoff for Two is right up there."

"The shoulder? You want a close-up interview with a cop? They're thick as locusts today."

"They don't work this stretch," said Lynn. "Don't be such a woosy."

"Your traffic cop information any better than your U.H. stuff?"

"Fuck you."

Brophy stopped the car and started to get out. Nothing was moving anyway.

"What're you doing?"

"You want to drive up the shoulder, drive."

Lynn Ann slid down in her seat and took off her hat.

"Forget it," she said, tilting her face to the sun. "We'll just sit here."

Route Two really was a good idea when they finally got to it. Along the way they passed a police car, lights flashing, behind a van that had tried to sneak by on the shoulder.

"He just didn't know how to do it," said Lynn.

You could really fly down Route Two. It was inland and farm country. They reached Moonstone at ten-fifteen. They had to park about a mile away in someone's driveway. Lynn said she knew the people and it was all right. It was a big driveway anyway.

They walked to the beach, Brophy loaded down with the aluminum chairs, the towels and the basket and Lynn carrying the thermos and a canvas beach bag full of makeup and Bain de Soleil. Brophy remembered going to Jones Beach with Clarissa. They used to drive out to West End Two, wearing their suits under their Levis, carrying just towels.

The beach was, as Lynn said, gorgeous. Very clean and white. The water was a single shade of blue. It looked like a painted ocean. Lynn set up camp. Brophy spread out a towel and occupied it, lying on his back, looking at the sky.

He looked out over the water at the white gulls in the air.

He could smell the iodinated baby oil and the tanning stuff Lynn was oiling herself up with.

After a half hour, he had to go in. It had become very hot.

"Go play without me. I'll watch," said Lynn Ann. She was glistening in the sun, reading Sidney Sheldon.

He should have known she wouldn't want to go in. Her false eyelashes would wash off.

There weren't any children on the beach. Brophy looked down the shoreline in both directions. Half a mile down was a cluster of bodies. He couldn't be sure, but he didn't see any bathing suits.

He worked on getting in up to his waist. The first time Clarissa took him to Jones Beach, she dragged him into the water as soon as they got there and made him swim out from shore, despite his shark phobia. And she wrapped her legs around his. Until then, he'd never touched her, and she wrapped her legs around his and he tingled all over. Brophy wondered what Clarissa was doing this Sunday. He thought he might see her when he took Lars to the library. She was spending a lot of time with Lars and Beth.

Brophy looked back at the beach. Lynn Ann was sitting in her aluminum chair reading _Rage of Angels_. She looked up and waved. Brophy waved back and thought about Clarissa and about Lars sitting in his room back at the CRU.

13

Brophy arrived at the CRU at four-thirty and went directly to
the nurses' station. He wanted to check the blood pressures
before he took Lars off the floor. No more screwups—Lars
wasn't going anywhere until he was blocked.

He was blocked. His pressures were running 130/85 lying
down, and fell to 110/70 when he stood up. If he could stand
up and walk without fainting, he could go to the library with
Brophy.

He was dressed and lying in bed when Brophy walked in.
Clarissa was not there. Beth was sitting in the bedside chair.

"You've got some sun," said Lars. "Where were you?"

"Moonstone Beach. Know it?"

"Sail by it with my binoculars." He laughed. "You can get
tanned in some painful places there."

"I kept my suit on."

"I'm all set," said Lars. "All blocked and ready to go."

"He's been talking about going to the library all day," said
Beth. "And he's been practicing walking all morning."

"I just have to get up slowly."

It made Lars very dizzy to lift his head. After a few minutes
sitting, he stood up.

They walked slowly down to the elevator. Lars leaning
against the walls along the way.

"Maybe this isn't such a good idea," said Brophy. "I don't
want you falling on your head before we get this thing out."

"I'm fine," said Lars, resting against the wall. "You know,
those articles you left me talked about using propranolol."

"Yes?"

"McCullough gave me propranolol once. For my blood pressure."

"Yes?"

"Made me feel awful. Headaches. Now I know why."

"Why?"

"Because it's a beta blocker and it can make people with pheos even worse."

"That's why you always give the Dibenzyline first," said Brophy.

"*Then* you give the propranolol," Lars said. "That clown McCullough could have killed me with that stuff!"

"It's a good drug for hypertension. He just didn't know you had a pheo."

"You knew. Why didn't he know?"

They were approaching the door to the street. Lars stopped short. "Uh-oh."

"What is it?"

"The heat. Is it a hot day out?"

"Blazing. Why?"

"I had trouble with changes in temperature. Now I know why, of course." He smiled bitterly. "They mentioned that in that article from Johns Hopkins."

Brophy opened the door and let the hot air mix with the cool air inside the building. Lars stood for a few minutes in between, where the temperature change was more gradual, then walked into the afternoon heat and down the stairs to the street, feeling fine.

"You got me well blocked, doctor."

They walked over to the library building and eased into the air conditioning.

"So why didn't McCullough even consider pheo? The article said, 'every patient with high blood pressure—' "

"Look," Brophy said, cutting him off, "those articles are written by guys who think pheo's the most important diagnosis in the world."

"The medical fraternity . . . I'm sorry. I shouldn't push you. I know you can't criticize a brother."

Brophy took him to the main reading room and deposited him at a table. "The stacks with the journals are downstairs. I don't think you should go tramping up and down stairs. Make me a list and I'll fetch them."

Lars seated himself at the *Index Medicus* with a sheet of

paper and pencil and went over all the articles on pheo written over the past five years.

He devoured the first article Brophy retrieved. "These tumors can make you diabetic until you cut them out," said Lars. "Am I diabetic now?"

"Your sugars are a little high."

"But I've never had one of these glucose-tolerance tests, have I?"

"No. But it's sure to be abnormal. So what?"

"You just expect it to be abnormal. Let's really show it," Lars said.

Brophy looked at him, horrified. Then he smiled, then laughed, shaking his head.

"What's so funny?"

"A week at the U.H. and we've turned you into a researcher."

Two hours later, Beth came to make them take a break. They eased out into the afternoon heat. There was a truck parked in front of the hospital entrance, selling lemonade to nurses coming out for dinner. Lars and Brophy sat on the brick wall in front of the library and Beth went for drinks. She came back with three big cups—ice crush with real lemons ground up in it. It was delicious, cold, and very refreshing in the muggy Providence heat.

"Now, what have you two been learning?"

"It's mostly old hat," said Lars. "Read one review, you've read 'em all." He slurped his lemonade crush and looked down at the sidewalk. A few drops of melted ice darkened the cement briefly, but it was quickly white again. "Mostly they argue whether or not to use propranolol and Dibenzyline or just Dibenzyline. It doesn't seem to make much difference what you do."

"Will they give Lars propranolol?"

"There's a big conference Tuesday," said Brophy. "That will be one topic for discussion."

"I don't suppose I'll get to be there."

"We might come by afterward," he told him. "But your opinion about how to prepare you for surgery will not be solicited."

"I might've known."

"No great loss," said Brophy. "After today, nobody'll be able to tell you anything you don't know about pheo."

"They do repeat themselves," said Lars, laughing. "About the only thing new we read today was about the brown fat."

Brophy laughed. "Fat lot of good that'll do us."

"What kind of fat?" asked Beth.

"Brown fat," said Lars. "It's amazing, the drive to publish. They'll write up anything to get their name in print."

"This old geezer from Columbia or somewhere," said Brophy. "A pathologist or surgeon or something published this three-page article on brown fat."

"I don't get it."

"Neither did we," laughed Lars.

"Apparently, people with pheos get brown fat, which is a kind of fat babies have a lot of, but usually disappears by adulthood. Anyway, the whole point of this article is that there's a lot of this fat in some patients with pheo."

"But what does it matter? What does brown fat mean?"

"Damned if I know," Brophy said. He turned to Lars. "Did you understand it?"

"Something about being more or less efficient as an energy reservoir. Doesn't seem to matter—it goes away once you cut out the pheo."

Beth glared at her husband. "That's what you've been reading about all this time? Brown fat?"

"That was just the last fifteen minutes," Lars said.

"We haven't gotten to the surgical journals yet," Brophy added.

"And what do they talk about?"

"How to do the surgery, I imagine," Lars said.

"The big issue is whether to make an abdominal incision or to go through the flank," said Brophy.

"What difference does that make?" Beth asked.

"The abdominal incision's a lot more cutting and it's rougher on the patient," said Brophy.

"Then why do it?"

"Because it lets you look at both adrenals. I think Nancy will use it."

"Because there's question about the right adrenal?" Beth asked.

"That, and because she can explore the belly through the abdominal approach."

"To be sure it hasn't metastasized?" Lars asked.

"Will you stop saying that," said Beth.

"Well, it may have."

"You don't have to sound so happy about it. You're just showing off your new word."

They went back for more reading.

Brophy's beeper went off at seven—Nancy was on the CRU, waiting to see Lars.

14

"You've been in the sun," said Lars. "All my doctors are out having a good time and I'm in the hospital getting dizzy on Dibenzyline."

"You don't look so bad," said Nancy. "We'll have you out soaking it up pretty soon."

"Can you believe this?" said Beth.

"Actually, yes," said Nancy. "Brophy showed me the CAT scan. Now I believe."

"I hear you've been educating yourself on pheochromocytoma," Nancy said to Lars.

"That's where we were," said Beth. "In the library."

"I guess Brophy has given you some idea about the plans."

"Arteriogram on Tuesday. Then the conference," said Lars.

"You'll have to sign a permission form for the arteriogram," said Nancy. It was needed to define the blood supply.

"They'll send around a radiology resident to explain the details," said Nancy.

Lars asked her which approach she would use. She said she'd go through the abdomen unless anybody at the conference had any big objections.

"I'd sure like to be at that big powwow," said Lars.

"They'd bore you stiff," laughed Nancy. "I like it 'cause I get to see all the big-name honchos. But you'd go right to sleep."

"I don't think so," said Lars. "They're going to be talking about me."

15

"Nancy wants to do an arteriogram on Magnussen," Brophy told Jethro Monday morning, hoping Jethro would get right on the phone to her and convince her to call it off.

"That," said Jethro, "is her prerogative."

"Just thought I'd mention it."

"Glad you did. If she's going to stick a catheter in his artery and go up the aorta, we might as well have 'em stick one in the vein and do a venogram."

"But why? Why take the chance?" Brophy asked.

"Suppose there's torrents from the left side and nothing from the right?"

"But Nancy's going to explore both sides anyway," said Brophy. "Besides, we'll never get the catechols back before surgery."

"Oh, yes we will."

"How?"

"Dick Cecil's going to do them for us. And Gertrude Rios is going to run anything we can give her on Tuesday afternoon."

"Look," said Brophy, taking a breath. "The venogram can do in this guy's adrenals. May not happen, but it's a risk. And what do we get for it? We find out if he's got pheo on one side or both. But Nancy's going to tell us that at surgery. So why do it?"

"Suppose Nancy gets in there and finds a couple of nodules on the aorta down low—say near the bladder. She picks everything clean, but we want to know postop whether or not he's really clean?"

"We follow his blood pressure—his VMA."

"All that tells is he's still got some pheo somewhere. The venogram tells us *where*."

"So, if that happens, we do a venogram postop."

"Nancy's doing an arteriogram on the guy. As long as she's getting a radiologist to go in there, we may as well demonstrate biologically what is already exquisitely clear anatomically. Anatomy is not biology."

It was impossible to argue with Jethro when he got abstract.

"I'll call Nancy. If she doesn't mind, we ought to get the studies," said Jethro. "You talk to Dick Cecil and Gertrude." He paused. "Or talk to Reynolds if you don't want to talk to Dick. I can understand your not wanting to talk to Dick. But have Reynolds get the stuff to collect the samples. They need some special containers. I forget what. I think Gertrude's stuff has to be on ice."

Brophy left to find Reynolds and ask about the specimen containers. Robin said Reynolds moonlighted at a nursing home in Woonsocket Monday mornings. Brophy looked up the telephone number.

Reynolds said he'd meet Brophy with everything he'd need at the CRU the next morning. He asked if Brophy had seen Dick Cecil that morning. Brophy said no.

"If you see him, don't mention you talked to me."

Brophy didn't know what to say, so he said nothing. *What am I going to do if Dick sticks his obnoxious head in the room and asks me if I know where Reynolds is? Lie?*

Reynolds listened to the silence and said, "This place is a real gold mine. I'll put you in for some time. You can come out here and read for twenty-four-fifty an hour."

"Good."

"I'll bring you that stuff tomorrow," said Reynolds. "You don't have to do a thing."

16

The radiology resident visited Lars Monday night and asked him whether or not he was allergic to angiogram dye. Lars told him he couldn't be sure, never having had any.

The resident was coming out of Lars' room with his signed permission slip when Brophy, Wendel, and Robin walked onto the CRU.

"He's a pretty sharp guy," said the resident. "Asked me if they had Regitine down in the arteriogram room. Knows all about his disease."

"He learns fast," said Brophy. "He sign the permission for both procedures?"

"Sure—we do them both at once." The resident hurried off.

"I think I just gave what's called informed consent," said Lars. "That character scared the living shit out of me."

"He's supposed to inform you of the risks."

"He did that. And then some."

"Well," said Brophy, "Nancy wants the study. She's captain of the ship."

"She told me you were the general."

Brophy laughed.

"Do you think I need this arteriogam?" Lars asked. "I mean, didn't the CAT show the damn thing?"

"I'm not doing the cutting," Brophy told him. "You give the surgeon what she wants."

"Well." Lars smiled. "We're certainly not denying her." Then he turned serious. "What about that glucose-tolerance test?"

"You know," Brophy said, "if you really want to study

327

mechanisms, why don't you give Dr. Gordon some urine and blood for his calcium studies? Your calcium's still high."

"Why's that? The parathyroids?"

"In you, it's not clear. Pheos can cause hypercalcemia all by themselves."

"How?"

"That's what Dr. Gordon wants to know."

"Well, send him by."

They walked out to the nurses' station, where Brophy wrote an order for the glucose-tolerance test.

"How could you do that?" Robin asked him.

"He's been bugging me about this glucose-tolerance test. He wants it. It won't do him any harm."

"I mean siccing Duncan on him."

"He's got hypercalcemia. Duncan's been wanting to study him."

"Christ," said Robin, "that poor guy's got enough problems without getting Duncan and his terrible swift biopsy needle into the act."

"He's at a research institution. And he has free choice."

"Right," said Robin. "I forgot."

"He's really gotten into this problem," said Brophy, smiling. "Really. He wants to go over all the results, see all the X-rays. He knows what he's doing."

"You really believe that?" said Robin.

Brophy looked at her, his face darkening.

"He's under the gun here," she said. "He's just trying to get some control."

"What am I supposed to do?" said Brophy. "Just tell me what I'm supposed to do."

17

Tuesday morning, Brophy walked into Lars' room at eight A.M., as they were getting him on the stretcher to go down to the angiogram.

"Glad you could make it, professor," said Lars.

"Wouldn't miss it for the world."

"I'll bet," said Lars, settling on the stretcher. "I want you around from now on."

They took the elevator to the basement and rolled Lars on his stretcher down the long corridor to the X-ray area.

Clarissa was waiting with Beth in the visitors' area on the CRU. They didn't know Lars was back until Clarissa caught sight of Brophy sitting in the nurses' station, going over the postarteriogram orders with the head nurse.

"They're back," said Clarissa.

Beth went to see Lars, and Clarissa stood beside Brophy as he wrote.

"How'd it go?"

"Sensational."

"No problems?"

"None. For once."

Brophy had an ice bucket full of tubes of blood the radiologist had drawn from the catheters he had guided into Lars' adrenal veins. He ran the samples up to Gertrude Rios' lab, then joined Clarissa back at the CRU. They headed over to conference.

"Who's coming to this party?"

"Everyone who's anyone," said Brophy. "And some of the people who're actually going to do something about getting these tumors out."

329

"Nancy?"

"She's invited."

"Who else?"

"Dick Cecil."

"Ugh."

"He knows about catechols."

The conference room was at the end of the hall off the clinic. It had a long table surrounded by two dozen chairs. Chuck Mersault from the V.A. was sitting there, taking his sandwiches out of a brown paper bag when Brophy and Clarissa arrived. Brophy was happy to see Chuck. Brophy went to the blackboard and started writing Lars' history in yellow chalk.

People began coming in as Brophy was writing. Clarissa sat by him in her blue scrub suit.

The radiologist came in carrying his films, and began putting up a few of the best shots of the pheos. Then he turned off the lights in the view boxes so the X-rays looked black and were unreadable until the radiologist was ready to show them.

Gertrude Rios came in, carrying her lunch in a brown bag. She smiled and waved at Brophy.

"Who's that?" asked Clarissa.

"Gertrude. The woman who's processing the samples from the venogram."

Reynolds and the other Fellows came in, carrying sandwiches from the cafeteria, talking about the Red Sox.

A white-haired man wearing scrubs under a white lab coat sat down next to Clarissa.

"This is Dr. Longstreet," she said. Longstreet was the anesthesiologist.

Dumfy came bubbling in with a small gray-haired man who turned out to be Ira Goldwasser, from Physiology. Dr. Goldwasser was very pleased to be invited to a conference with all these clinicians. Brophy tried to smile and indulge him as Duncan, Jethro, Dr. McCullough and Nancy drifted in. Finally Lionel appeared, wearing a white cotton turtleneck, carrying his brown bag. He went over and shook Goldwasser's hand and slid into a seat. Lionel looked around the table and said, "I thought I was the only one not on vacation in August."

The conference began.

Brophy went over the history, beginning with the episode during surgery when Nancy fixed Lars' hernias.

"That was really pretty impressive," Nancy said. "I'm

kicking myself for letting him sign out before we could get him seen."

McCullough's face was impassive. You could never have guessed that he had ever set eyes on Lars Magnussen.

Brophy continued, describing the history of high blood pressure, the sweating, the palpitations, the episodes of kidney stones. There were knowing smiles all around the table. Most of the Fellows and the faculty had heard all about this case and knew the diagnosis, but a few of the private Attendings didn't know, and everyone was being smug and quiet. Hearing about the combination of hypertension, the flareup of blood pressure during anesthesia, and kidney stones and hypercalcemia was enough. Every Fellow at the conference table knew there could be only one possible diagnosis. The Attendings still weren't so sure.

Brohpy gave the physical-exam findings during the admission for the kidney stone, then he presented the lab results for the free catecholamines. There was a massive stirring, and muffled laughter here and there. The Attendings began to smile. McCullough was not smiling.

Brophy told them about Lars finding the neck mass, and everyone began to laugh. It was just so obvious, all three components of the syndrome at once, staring them in the face.

"Well, I guess you know what we did next," said Brophy. He wrote the VMA value on the blackboard, big and bold. 96!

Everyone applauded. The radiologist jumped up and showed the CAT scan, pointing out the pheo on the left and the questionable mass on the right. Then he showed the arteriogram and everyone started whooping again.

Brophy looked at Clarissa. She was the only one in the room not smiling.

Brophy sat down and Lionel asked Ira Goldwasser to say a few words about the physiology of catecholamines. As he was speaking, Dick Cecil came in and sat down. Goldwasser explained about how the catecholamines were first discovered, and assayed. Then he went over Lars' symptoms, and explained how each one could be understood in terms of the specific known actions of epinephrine or norepinephrine on the receptors in the sweat glands, the arterioles, and the vascular tree. As Goldwasser spoke, Dick Cecil shifted in his seat, crossing and uncrossing his legs. Dick was the resident expert in catecholamine receptors, and he was being upstaged. When

Ira was finished he asked Dick if he had anything to add. Of course Ira had left precious little to be said. But Dick picked a point or two to show he knew as much about catecholamines as any physiologist from the medical school.

Jethro asked the anesthesiologists what kind of anesthesia they were planning on using, and whether or not they thought they could get away without pre-op blockade, the way they did at Cleveland Clinic. That started the major battle of the day. The anesthesiologists wanted to use one drug, Ira Goldwasser suggested another, and Dick Cecil a third. Finally they agreed on what the anesthesiologist wanted in the first place—he was the one giving the drug, after all.

They all agreed the Celveland Clinic might get good results in Cleveland, but no pheo was going to surgery at U.H. unblocked.

The people from the Intensive Care Unit said they wanted a Swan Ganz catheter put in, once Lars was under anesthesia. It would make the postoperative monitoring easier.

"As long as we're all putting in requests," said Duncan, looking to Nancy, "I've spoken with the patient and he's willing to have a bone biopsy once he's under anesthesia. I'll be glad to be there once you've got the pheo out."

"Okay, Duncan," Nancy said, laughing. "As long as you wait until we've got the pheo out."

Lionel asked Jethro if, during the arteriogram, they had obtained venous samples for epinephrine and norepinephrine from the adrenal veins draining the tumors. Jethro winked at Brophy and said yes. Gertrude would have them ready that afternoon.

Dumfy talked about the VMA and why it was such a good assay and Gertrude discussed her serum free catecholamines and why they would someday be the test of choice for diagnosis of pheo. She spoke very quietly, in a little, mouselike voice, and everyone had to lean forward to hear her. Dumfy became mildly indignant at the suggestion that anything might someday be better than his VMA.

"If that VMA's still high after surgery," said Gertrude, "you'll be plenty happy we did the serum CATS from that venogram."

"If it's still high after surgery," said Dumfy, "*then* you could do your venogram. You don't need to find residual tumor before the initial surgery."

"There won't be any residual tumor," Nancy added.

Everyone laughed again. They had forgotten there was a surgeon in the room.

There was another fight between Ira Goldwasser and Dick Cecil over some obscure point of catecholamine physiology that no one cared about except Ira and Dick.

Lionel held up his hand. That ended it.

The radiologist started taking down his X rays. Nancy and the anesthesiologists and the people from the Surgical Intensive Care Unit stood around and talked.

Brophy took Clarissa's elbow and they walked out of the room and up the stairwell to the cafeteria, where Brophy put quarters into the Coke machine and bought them each a cup.

"Hard to believe they were talking about Lars Magnussen," Clarissa said.

"They were talking science," said Brophy.

They walked down the hall to CRU.

"You made it all sound so easy," Clarissa said.

"What?"

"You weren't sure he had anything at all until that VMA came back. They all seemed to know what he had by the time you mentioned the kidney stones."

"That," laughed Brophy, "is the great advantage of advance notice."

"You think that whole exercise helped?" asked Clarissa.

"I know it did."

"They didn't say all that much about Lars, really."

"They all showed up. They got together. They decided about the propranolol . . . the Swan . . . the anesthesia."

"That took about ten minutes. Seemed like they spent hours talking about those wretched assays."

Brophy laughed. "You have to learn to be tolerant around here."

Brophy checked with Gertrude at four-thirty to find out the results of the venogram samples. She said they wouldn't be ready until five, but it looked like the only samples with very high catecholamine levels were those from the adrenal-gland veins, which drained the tumors. That was reassuring. If samples from lower down in the abdomen had high levels, it might mean tumor spread.

18

At seven-thirty that evening, Brophy stopped by the CRU.

Beth was watching Lars eat his dinner. She stood up when Brophy walked in.

"What'd they say at conference?" asked Lars.

"They think you ought to have your pheos removed."

"It's been arranged," said Lars.

"When will they take him?" asked Beth.

"He's first case. He'll probably get put on the stretcher at seven-thirty. At eight o'clock, anesthesia. Then we'll see."

"Will Nancy come by tonight?"

"I imagine."

"How long will it take?"

"Better ask Nancy that."

"Will you be there?" asked Beth.

"You mean in the Operating Room?"

"Yes," said Beth. Lars was looking at Brophy, too, waiting for the answer.

"Medical doctors aren't much help," said Brophy. "Not in the Operating Room."

"Oh," said Beth, plainly disappointed.

Lars looked down at his plate and started playing with his fork. Brophy looked from him to Beth and back again.

"If it'd make you feel better, sure, I'll go in."

Lars looked up. "Thanks."

The phone was ringing when Brophy arrived home. He was expecting Clarissa. It was Lynn Ann.

"Killed any rats lately?"

"We work with people now."

"How is Maria Addinizio?"

"Haven't you seen her lately? Or is your interest only journalistic where Maria Addinizio's concerned?"

"I've been busy digging into nefarious doings at U.H."

"She's almost ready to go home—'Woman Survives Cancer at U.H.: Research Protocol to Blame.'"

"How wonderful. She's really better?"

"Cured. But that's not news," Brophy said.

"Oh, I don't know."

"Yes, you do."

"Want to have a drink and ravage me?"

Brophy tried to think of something to say.

"Well, let's not all jump at once," said Lynn Ann.

"I've got to be at the hospital before seven tomorrow morning. I was just going to turn in."

"It's only eight."

"I'm wiped out. Tomorrow's going to be a long day."

"Okay, okay," said Lynn Ann. She was not happy. "Actually, I did have some business to check out with you. You know this guy Duncan Gordon? The one who punched a hole in Maria Addinizio?"

"Yes."

"What's he like?"

"A solid citizen."

"Well, we've heard he's been drilling holes in quite a lot of people and telling them it won't hurt a bit."

"You better check your sources."

"That's why I've been so busy."

"Lynn." Brophy tried to control the pitch of his voice. "The truth is, he does good work."

"I've been talking to people who say he's a lot better on consent than informed."

"Have you talked to him?"

"He won't answer my calls."

"Have you talked to anyone who knows what he's talking about?"

"That's just my problem. You guys say you know, but you won't talk to me."

"I think we've been through this before."

"Okay, I'll get off the phone. I wanted to tell you, though. We're going ahead with this."

"I'll be looking forward to it."

"You do that." Lynn Ann hung up. Brophy was sure she slammed the receiver.

Clarissa came over half an hour later.

"I stopped in to see Beth and Lars. They told me you're going to the OR with him."

"They ganged up on me. Don't know what they expect I'm going to do."

"They'd appreciate it."

"Okay," said Brophy. "I guess they're a little apprehensive."

Clarissa laughed. But it sounded more like a sob.

19

Wednesday morning it rained a steady, gray rain.

Brophy was up at five forty-five, before his alarm clock rang. He went for a fifteen-minute run, just to wake up. Brophy hardly noticed how nice it was to run in the rain. He was thinking about Lars Magnussen. He wanted to be in the shower and shaved by six-thirty and at the hospital by seven. He wanted to be there when they came for Lars with the stretcher.

Lars Magnussen had needed no alarm clock or prodding nurse to wake him at six o'clock. His eyes were wide open at five. He sat up slowly, reassured by his lightheadedness. Brophy had blocked his receptors well. He put on his bathrobe and went across the room to the shower, clutching his bottle of pHisoHex. He washed and lathered carefully, killing every last bacterium on his skin. With the water running, providing a covering noise, he knelt on the floor of the shower and prayed. Then he dried himself and went back to bed.

Nancy Barnah was the last to rise of the three. She sat up slowly, waiting for the low back pain that never came. It was six-thirty, and she walked naked across her apartment to the shower. She thought about her schedule. Magnussen was first, then a fifty-year-old woman with a gallbladder, and then a credentials committee meeting at two o'clock. She'd never have time for lunch with two morning cases like these. Magnussen could take three, even four hours.

The anesthesiologist was up earlier than usual, thinking about the pheo case. He wanted to get in early to set up the nitroprusside drip, which took time because he had to wrap the lines and the bag in aluminum foil to keep the nitroprusside from breaking down on exposure to light. He had checked the literature and phoned his old mentor at Harvard about handling pheos. But this was his first.

Beth arrived at six-thirty. The paunchy security guard held her up at the lobby. She made him call the CRU, and the nurses there told him to let her up: her husband was having surgery. She was pretty distraught, but in control. The boys were with their grandparents. She had not slept at all. She had gone out on the deck and looked at Lars' sailboat, and sat on a canvas chair and cried. Clarissa had spent the night. She woke up when Beth dropped the coffeepot in the kitchen. They had driven to the hospital together. Clarissa had scheduled herself for the day off.

The scrub nurse arrived at six-fifty, and the circulating nurse at seven.

The blood bank technician called the OR at seven-fifteen because she had five units typed and crossed for Lars Magnussen and nobody had called to confirm that he was going to Surgery. The OR secretary took the call, said she'd get back to the blood bank about that right away, and promptly forgot about it. The nurses on the CRU called Escort at seven-twenty, all hot and bothered because Escort hadn't shown up to take Magnussen to the OR, but not to bother, Dr. Brophy would do it.

Brophy found Beth holding Lars in her arms, in his bed. "We'd better not be late," he said.

Beth kissed Lars and started to cry.

"They shot me up with Valium this morning," said Lars, "just to relax me. Now you're climbing into bed with me, and crying, getting me all excited."

Beth mussed his hair and turned to Brophy, wiping her nose with a Kleenex.

"You bring him back all cured."

Brophy smiled. "It's almost over."

He helped Lars onto the stretcher, and he and Clarissa went out into the hallway to leave Beth and Lars alone together until they had to go.

Clarissa leaned against the wall.

"I'm scared to death."

Brophy smiled again and shook his head.

He rolled Lars down the hallway to the elevator. One of the CRU nurses was holding the elevator for them.

They were down to Four almost immediately. There, they pushed Lars' stretcher down the long corridor to the Operating Room Suite. There was a metal remote-control plate on the wall, which opened the doors, making the negotiation of stretcher and door very easy.

"Very nifty," said Lars, seeing the doors swing open.

"We're clever here at the University Hospital."

Brophy checked which OR Lars was assigned to, pushed him down to D, and left him in the hall.

"Don't go anywhere," Brophy told him. "I've got to change into a blue suit."

"You leave me alone and I'll bolt. I've only done this well because I've been under constant surveillance."

"You're doing very well."

Nancy Barnah came down the hall to the stretcher.

Her hair was pulled up under a green paper hair-hat, and a scrub mask dangled from her neck.

"Good morning," she said, very happy. "I'm glad everybody showed up for this party. I hate to be stood up."

"We wouldn't have missed it," said Lars. He sounded tight. He looked tight, seeing Nancy.

"This will take about two hours," she said. "Maybe more, depending on how easily things go. But you've gone through the CAT and the arteriogram, and this is just the payoff. Those other things will make this much easier."

Brophy went to change. He had trouble retying his shoelaces; his hands were shaking. *Glad I'm just here to watch.*

The anesthesiologist walked up to Lars and shook his hand. "I'm going to roll you into the induction room now," he said.

In the induction room, a surgical resident and an intern were lathering, washing, then scrubbing their fingernails with soapy disposable brushes at one of the two sinks. Nancy and another medical student were scrubbing at the other. Lars didn't know who the men with Nancy were. They all wore blue scrub suits. Above the sinks was a sign: SEVEN MINUTES ON EACH HAND.

The anesthesiologist had two assistants. He had set up a chrome IV pole on which hung four fluid-filled plastic bags. One of the bags was covered with aluminum foil, and the lines running from it were also wrapped in foil.

The anesthesiologist and his assistants were looking over an open attaché case filled with needles and glass vials, each in its own slot. He picked out a 14-gauge angiocath and said, "I'm going to put in an IV now."

He pulled a tourniquet tight around Lars' arm, just above the elbow. Lars could smell alcohol and became suddenly afraid. "Make three fists," said the anesthesiologist. Lars made the fists and held the last one. He looked at the ceiling. It had soundproofing tiles. "Oh, you have very nice viens," said the anesthesiologist. Lars kept looking at the ceiling. "Now, you'll feel a pinch." Lars felt it. It was more than a pinch. He could feel his heart pound and wondered whether or not Brophy had him completely blocked.

The anesthesiologist punched the needle of his syringe into the rubber part of the IV line and let the syringe dangle. He inserted the IV line into the angiocath and opened it. It ran freely.

He slipped a pillow under Lars' shoulders so Lars head dropped back, chin up.

"Now, I just want you to count backward from twenty, very slowly . . ."

Lars could feel someone wrapping a blood pressure cuff around his left arm—the one without the IV. He felt the cuff tighten and could hear the pumping sound the cuff made. "Count, please."

"Twenty . . . nineteen," Lars began. The anesthesiologist pressed the syringe very slowly and the drug ran down the IV tubing into Lars' vein. By the time Lars got to ten, his words were thick. By five, he wasn't counting anymore. The anesthesiologist tilted Lars' chin up a bit more and placed the laryngoscope perfectly. Lars' laryngeal cords popped into view, and the anesthesiologist slipped the intubation tube between them. It was a smooth, flawless intubation—the same technique Brophy had learned on Lars' brother, Olaf. He hooked the rubber breathing bag to the tube and took over the job of breathing for Lars.

They rolled the stretcher into the Operating Room and cranked Lars above the operating table. Then they lowered the stretcher canvas onto the table and slid it out from under him. Lars was on the table.

The surgical resident was scrubbed and gowned. He waited

while the circulating nurse poured Betadine over some big gauze pads, then he prepared the skin over the collar bone, working in concentrically larger and larger circles, painting the skin Betadine orange. When the Betadine dried, he draped the area, leaving a square of orange skin visible. Taking a 14-gauge needle, he attached it to a syringe, which he slipped under the collar bone into the big subclavian vein. In two minutes he had the subclavian line sutured fast and hooked up the Swan Ganz catheter. With the Swan, the anesthesiologist measured the pressures in Lars' heart chambers and his cardiac output.

At the other end, a nurse prepped Lars' penis and inserted a Foley catheter. Lars was now plugged in. The anesthesiologist could calculate how much fluid was going into Lars' vascular tree, and the response of the vascular system, and how much fluid was coming out. As long as the kidneys got enough blood, they would put out urine into the Foley bag. Seeing lots of urine would be very reassuring.

The nurse-anesthetist put in two more IVs, one in each arm. One was for the nitroprusside drip and the other was a fail-safe. In case something happened to the first IV, they'd have a spare through which to pump drugs and fluids.

Brophy walked from the locker room to the Operating Room. He opened the door to the amphitheater entrance and ran up the stairs. Calling it an amphitheater was something of a hyperbole. It was just three rows of seats, elevated five feet above the OR floor, with a glass window between the seats and the OR. Brophy was happy there. He always felt obtrusive in the OR and was forever contaminating things and getting caught by the ever-watchful scrub nurse. Once he contaminated an entire scrub tray by inadvertently touching it with an ungloved, unsterile finger. It had delayed the case twenty minutes while they got a new tray ready.

Of course, the OR nurses intimidated everyone. They were always watching and incontrovertible. If they said you'd broken the sterile field, you had to reglove, no matter who you were.

Brophy watched the team swirl around Lars. He had to keep reminding himself that the form on the table was the man he had put there—Lars Magnussen, father of two, avid reader of medical literature on pheochromocytoma.

Nancy had taken her place. A tall medical student stood beside her and the intern and resident across from her. The anesthesiologist and his nurse-anesthetist were at the head of the table, breathing Lars with the hand bag.

Nancy made a long incision, extended so she could get at both adrenal glands. Then she started the ritual of blunt dissection along cleavage planes—no cutting, just separating—prying apart.

Brophy couldn't see anything from the amphitheater perch— it was a good view over Nancy's shoulder, but too far away. And the tall medical student kept getting in the way. All he could see of Lars was his exposed abdomen spotlighted in the rectangular operating field in the green paper drapes.

Brophy walked downstairs and onto the OR floor. "Don Brophy," he said to Nancy.

"Who else did you think I'd take you for?" laughed Nancy. "William Osler?" She looked around the table and said Brophy could scrub in, but she thought he'd get a better view by climbing onto a stool and looking over her shoulder.

Nancy ran a very relaxed OR. There was Borodin playing on her cassette player this morning—Polovtzian dances. All Brophy could hear, aside from the music, was Nancy's soft voice asking for a clamp or suture ties. Occasionally she'd use the Bovie, the hot blade used to seal off bleeders, and he could hear the hissing, burning sound.

Every once in a while she asked for the blood pressures, and the anesthesiologist would call them out. They were fine. "Nice work, Brophy," Nancy said without looking up.

Brophy walked over to look at the anesthesiologist's graph of Lars' blood pressure readings. They formed a happy, straight line running right down the middle of the normal range.

Things wouldn't be so well behaved when they started squeezing tumor. But for now it looked good.

Once or twice Nancy pointed out something to the medical student, and, without turning to Brophy, who was sitting on a stool a few feet away and watching her back, she'd say, "I'd show it to you, Brophy—but you already know all this anatomy."

Everyone around the table laughed quietly. Medical doctors didn't know any anatomy. Surgeons knew anatomy. Surgeons and medical students. Not medical doctors.

They got through the abdominal-wall musculature and into the peritoneum, the membranous covering of the abdominal contents. The chief resident was doing most of the separating out of tissue layers, and Nancy was talking him through it.

Brophy listened to Nancy's comments and to the sound of the anesthetist pumping up the blood-pressure cuff and letting out the air.

They reached the omentum.

Then Brophy heard Nancy say, "Oh, Christ."

"What is that stuff?" the medical student asked.

Nancy didn't answer. She turned halfway around, looking for Brophy. He could only see her eyes and he didn't like the expression.

"This doesn't look good," she said.

Brophy brought his stool up directly behind her and placed it down carefully, heart thundering. Then he stood up on the stool and looked down into the belly.

Nancy rolled away from the operating field so Brophy could see.

The underside of Lars' omentum was studded with hundreds upon hundreds of golden-brown implants. They were everywhere and ugly looking.

"What are they?" the medical student kept saying. Nobody answered. "What are they?"

"They bleed," said Nancy, looking up at Brophy. "Just touching 'em with a sponge." She shook her head. "Just so vascular. I'm not sure I even want to biopsy 'em. Not much doubt what they are."

"What *are* they?" the medical student asked again.

"Metastases," said the resident. "He's just loaded with 'em."

Nancy was shaking her head, trying to decide whether or not to biopsy one or to just close up.

"He's inoperable?" asked the student.

"Looks that way," said Nancy. She sounded very low.

Brophy looked down dizzily from his perch, and was suddenly afraid he would pitch forward onto the open abdomen. He saw Clarissa and Beth swirl by. It was such bad news—and it couldn't have happened to a nicer guy.

Brophy stared at those cruel, plump little nodules—gold, brown and shiny—and tried to calm down and think. What could they possibly be besides what they looked for all the world to be? Tumor implants, metastatic seedlings, spread out all over the fat pad, riddling his omentum, and undoubtedly pasted all over his abdominal organs. They were impossible to remove: even if they could be picked off one by one, they had obviously invaded everything. It would be an exercise in futility.

Why hadn't they shown on CAT? They were probably too small and too numerous. And why hadn't they shown on the arteriogram? They had plenty of blood supply. But they were small . . . And the venogram samples? Why hadn't Gertrude's marvelous assay shown elevated catecholamines coming from anywhere else but the adrenal glands?

Brophy studied those little brown nodules. Those plump tumors. Plump, almost fatty. Like the globules on a lamb chop. Like fat . . .

"Fat!" he roared, startling Nancy and the others.

"What?" said Nancy.

"It's brown fat!" sang Brophy. "Biopsy it. It's vascular, but it's fat. I just read about it."

"Brown fat's in babies," said Nancy.

"And patients with pheo," said Brophy joyously, thanking God for the medical school library, for academicians who wrote about absurd things like brown fat, and for medical journals that published such eccentricities. There was no doubt in his mind. He entertained no other possibilities. It could not be widely metastatic tumor, which would have Nancy closing Lars' belly, unexpurgated, an inoperable case. Brophy was willing those nodules to be fat—and brown fat they had to be.

Nancy biopsied several of the meaner-looking nodules and gave them to the circulating nurse, who plopped them onto a gauze pad and handed it to Brophy.

Brophy raced to the path lab, down the stairs, flying with the specimens. He burst through the door to the lab and watched as the pathologist ran the nodules through the special freezing and slicing machine while Brophy kept up his none-too-objective lecture about brown fat and its well-described association with pheochromocytoma and why this had to be it because he'd just read about it.

The pathologist put the slide under a two-headed microscope so he and Brophy could examine it simultaneously.

"I have to call it as I see it," he said. "It won't help this guy if I call it fat when it's really tumor."

Then he leaned down to the intercom speaker, which was connected to the OR.

"Dr. Barnah?"

"Yes?" Brophy could hear Nancy's voice clearly.

"That specimen on Magnussen," said the pathologist, smiling at Brophy. "It's fat."

Brophy could hear them cheering in the OR. He would have cheered too, but he was starting to cry. He ran back to the Operating Room.

"Nice going, champ," said Nancy. "You can hang around my OR any time."

They were going down to the kidney on the left side. Nancy was working fast and the resident and the medical student were working hard to keep up.

Then Nancy said, "That's it."

"Now, that's pretty," said the resident.

Lars had a nice, smooth, encapsulated tumor, about the size of a large peach or a small orange.

Nancy was very careful about touching it. They were working all around it, trying to get it completely shelled out before she actually put her hand around it.

"Okay, Brophy," she said, wrapping her hand around the pheo. "Here's where we find out what kind of endocrinologist you are."

They both stared at the monitor screen. Nancy tightened her grip on the pheo and finished breaking the connections with her fingers. Lars' blood pressure rose from 140/90 to 160/100. She pulled it free and the blood pressure line on the monitor climbed to 170/104.

"It just shelled out," said Nancy triumphantly, holding it in the palm of her hand for all to see. It was orange-tan colored and round. Nancy wanted some of it for her tumor cultures. She was trying to grow pheochromocytomas in cell culture.

The resident carried the tumor over to a sterile tray and Brophy went over to look. The resident was slicing it up. He gave the circulating nurse a piece to run over to Pathology for an official microscopic diagnosis from frozen section. He minced up another part for Nancy's special cell-culture vials. He had another jar for Ira Goldwasser and one for Dick Cecil, and there was one with Duncan's name on it. Duncan wanted to grow some pheo and implant it into the nude mice to see if they became hypercalcemic. Everyone at U.H. was getting his slice.

Nancy got the tumor from the other adrenal in less than an hour. Lars' blood pressure went up, but not out of sight, and when the last visible pheo cell was cut from his body, his blood pressure fell and his heart rate compensated, keeping blood going brainward. The anesthesiologist poured in lots of volume, for which Brophy was happy, since all the articles said to do that. Apparently the anesthesiologist had read the same articles.

Nancy looked around for more tumor. She pressed here and there, checking the monitor to see whether or not Lars' pressure shot up when she pressed. Sometimes a bit of tumor could hide out.

"I've goosed him everywhere," she said. "If he's got any tumor left, I sure as hell can't find it. Brophy, why don't you call Duncan? Tell him we're coming out. He can get his bone biopsy."

Brophy paged Duncan, who answered immediately.

"How's it going?"

"Nancy's closing up, if you want to come up for that piece of bone."

"Be right up. How'd he do?"

"So far, so good."

"She got 'em out? Both sides?"

"Nothing to it."

"Hallelujah!" said Duncan.

Duncan arrived, wearing his blue scrubs, about ten minutes later. The nurses made him scrub in and gown and glove. Then they prepped the pelvic rim and Duncan punched his biopsy needle through.

"Perfect core!" he said, examining his specimen floating in the clear liquid fixative. "He didn't feel a thing, either."

They had Lars sewn up within half an hour.

Nancy took Brophy to the coffee room in the OR Suite. Brophy saw them roll Lars by, on his way to the recovery room.

"We'll keep him in the SICU," Nancy said, "after he gets out of the recovery room."

"His wife's waiting on the CRU."

"Oh, shit"—she looked at her watch—"I almost forgot. And I've got a gallbladder to do and got to get out by one-thirty so I can make it to a meeting by two."

"I'll go get her. You can just step outside the OR Suite and talk to her in the hall."

"Would you? That's really sweet of you."

Brophy smiled. Nancy could sound like a girl sometimes.

20

Clarissa spent the day with Beth, visiting Lars in the recovery room and then sitting around his room on the CRU when they sent him back. Brophy dropped in at five o'clock, took Lars' pressure, and reassured Beth that everything really did go well.

Clarissa followed Brophy to the nurses' station and watched him write his note in Lars' chart.

"They got it all?"

"Can't be positive until we repeat his tests." Brophy smiled. "But sure as hell looked like she got it all."

"You must be exhausted."

Brophy looked at her and felt the sudden urge to simply put his head in her lap and be petted. Instead he stood up and said, "Would you like to have dinner?"

They stopped off at Star Market to buy steaks and salad things, and Clarissa cooked at Brophy's place.

He opened a bottle of champagne. "To the extirpation," he said, holding up his glass.

"I thought you said it was too early to be sure."

"He's through surgery and out of recovery. That's enough to celebrate. We'll have another bottle when his VMA comes back normal."

Clarissa laughed. "I can't get over Dr. Donald Brophy. Is this the same man who once organized a pool to wager the number of deaths for a single weekend at Whipple Cancer Ward?"

"Same man. Different place."

They washed the dishes and Clarissa started collecting her

things to go. But Brophy caught her and pressed close. "The night's still young."

"That's why I'm leaving." She smiled. "You don't want me spoiling your fun. Lynn Ann called while you were in the bathroom."

"So what?"

"She didn't sound happy to hear me answering your phone."

"That's her problem," he said, undoing Clarissa's skirt.

"Look," said Clarissa, pushing away, speaking in even tones. "You've made your point. You couldn't have me when you wanted me, now you can have whomever, me included. You don't have to rub my face in it."

Brophy looked surprised. "But I wasn't trying."

"Then what was Lynn Ann all about?"

Brophy sat down and scratched his head. Then he went to the refrigerator and got a beer.

"Maybe I was trying to play catch-up," he said finally. "Tried out recreational sex."

"You'd never tried that?"

"No," said Brophy. "I went to medical school."

"I can't imagine you having uncomplicated affairs."

"You can't imagine me having fun."

"We had a good time," said Clarissa. "But it's always been complicated."

"It can still be fun."

"No," she said, putting down her stuff and unbuttoning Brophy's shirt. "But that's no reason not to do it."

21

The next morning, Brophy looked in on Lars. He was blowing into the incentive spirometer, trying to keep his lungs clean and free of pneumonia.

"I'm just afraid of popping the stitches," he said, holding a pillow to his belly as he blew.

"If you saw how they put those in," laughed Brophy, "you wouldn't worry."

Brophy finished rounds and went to find Duncan in the lab.

"How's Magnussen?"

"Sitting up, blowing on his spirometer like a good boy. Pressure's normal."

"You missed some excitement yesterday."

"I had plenty, thanks."

"No—I mean the Fellows' meeting," Duncan said.

"What was that all about? Rona gave me a hard time when I told her I'd be in Surgery. I had to see Lionel to get out of it."

"What'd he say?"

"That you'd tell me about it."

Duncan looked up from his pipetting. "Reynolds is out."

"Out?"

"Out of the program. Lionel axed him."

"What?"

"Seems he got caught fabricating data."

"What?"

"Lionel didn't like that."

"Kicked out of the program?"

"Completely."

"How'd they catch him?"

Duncan looked up and smiled. Brophy waited for him to say something, but he just continued pipetting. Finally he said, "They got a tip. Dick came in one weekend—no Reynolds. First thing that Monday, Reynolds shows up with a perfect data sheet from his weekend study."

"Jesus," said Brophy. "You saved Dick's ass."

"As you once said, Dick was supposed to be supervising Reynolds."

"But you never liked Dick," Brophy said.

"He's a good investigator. A royal asshole—but good."

"Dick have anything to say to you?"

"Don't think he even knows. Which, incidentally, is the way I'd like to keep it. He got the word from Lionel. Dick doesn't know who his fairy godmother is."

"What's going to happen to Reynolds?"

"He'll have to start his private practice a little earlier than anticipated."

"Jesus."

"He'll be okay," said Duncan. "Year from now he'll probably *own* every nursing home in Rhode Island."

22

By Thursday afternoon, Lars was able to walk to the end of the hall. He had the nurses collecting his urine in the big catecholamine jars, with the acid in the bottom.

"I told him there wasn't any order for it," Lars' nurse told Brophy, "but he was so sure you'd want it done. He says he's discussed it all with you."

"Won't hurt to collect it."

"Do you want it sent off for anything?"

"Send it for a VMA. I'll write the order."

Brophy had no idea how long the VMA and catecholamines hung around in the bloodstream and poured out in the urine after the tumor that produced them had been extirpated. He made a note to call Daniel Dumfy about it. Lars' blood pressure was down now, without any medication. That was the best sign.

"They drew a sugar this morning," he told Brophy.

"How do you know that?"

"I asked."

Brophy said nothing.

"How was it?"

"Lars, it's only ten A.M. They won't even run it until noon."

"When will my urine be ready?"

"They'll do a run on Tuesday."

"That's five days."

"The key thing is that your blood pressure's down."

"But that's not really test of cure. . . ."

"It's one test of cure."

"But the VMA levels. . . ."

"Listen to you"—Brophy laughed—"arguing like a professor."

"I know I'm a pest . . . and you're here on your time off."

"It'll take a while for your body to clear all the catecholamines and for your VMA to fall. Don't rush things."

"Besides," nodded Lars, "I've still got that little problem in my neck." He felt his lump reflexively.

"Compared to what you've just been through, it'll be a piece of cake."

"When will Nancy do it?"

"When do you want it?"

"Today."

"Let's wait." Brophy laughed again. "I need more time to recover."

23

Clarissa was reading the paper at the kitchen table Friday morning when Brophy finished his shower. He rummaged around the refrigerator and watched her.

"Orange juice?" he asked.

No answer.

"Miss Leonard? Paging Miss Clarissa Leonard . . . ?"

No response.

"Okay, ignore me."

"'Where Patients Pay the Price,'" Clarissa quoted. "'By Lynn Ann Montano.'"

"What?"

"'Providence: Mid-July: Maria Addinizio thought she was going to have a baby. Early August, Dr. Duncan Gordon was driving home a stainless steel biopsy instrument through her pelvis bone. The pain lingered a week.'"

"Let me see that," said Brophy, coming to the table.

"'The pregnancy turned out to be what doctors call a hydatidiform mole. It had to be removed, and the pathology report came back 'Cancer.' Not long after she was told her diagnosis, Maria was approached by a friendly doctor, who asked her to become a subject in his research. 'Mrs. Addinizio gave informed consent,' said Dr. Gordon. 'She signed the consent form.'"

"Duncan never told me she called him," said Brophy. "Lynn must've interviewed him."

"'But did she, or any of the other patients still reeling from the overwhelming news they had cancer really know what she was getting into? Are patients in such desperate positions, patients searching for someone to help, able to make informed choices, free of duress? Do they really feel free to refuse?' "

"Duncan'll die," said Clarissa. "I feel like an assassin."

"Why?"

"I bet Lynn got the idea from me, that time."

"No," said Brophy. "She wanted to pursue it."

They finished the article. There were quotes from the chairman of the Human Investigation Committee and quotes from relatives of patients who'd died horrible leukemia deaths. "If I'd known what they'd put him through," a widow was quoted as saying.

"First she talks about Duncan. Then she talks about chemotherapy research, then Duncan again," said Clarissa, "You can't tell who's doing what to whom. Sounds like Duncan's treating leukemics."

"In her mind, it's all the same."

"You notice she never quotes Maria Addinizio."

"Maria wasn't mad at us."

Duncan was in the lab when Brophy arrived.

"You don't look like a mad scientist," said Brophy.

"They're coming to take me away, any minute."

"I'm awfully sorry."

Duncan shrugged. "Maybe she'll write one about you: 'Hero Doc Saves Pheo Victim.'"

" 'Pheo Victim Manages to Escape with His Life,' more likely."

"No, people like clinicians."

"It's you wild-eyed lab types need to be taken away," said Brophy.

Duncan smiled, but he didn't look happy.

"I'm really sorry this happened, Duncan."

"You want to be an explorer," said Duncan, taking up a pipette, "you gotta take the lumps."

"They laughed at Columbus," said Brophy.

"I'm unappreciated."

"I appreciate you. So does Jethro. So does Lionel."

"That's the whole list," said Duncan, trying to smile. "My wife doesn't even really know what the hell this is all about."

"This'll blow over."

"But first, it'll blow away the malignancy project," said Duncan, getting red faced. "Some airhead had trouble passing college biology explains my research to the world."

"I'm really sorry."

"Not your fault." Duncan looked down to his pipette. "It's worse for you. I can always creep off to the lab. You're out a project."

"You've worked on it a long time, and it was just showing results," said Brophy. "And I've still got pregnancy."

"Wait'll she gets ahold of that one!"

Brophy looked a little shocked, and briefly considered calling Lynn Ann.

No, thought Brophy, *I'll page Robin and Wendel and we'll make rounds.*

24

Brophy walked into Lars' room carrying a bottle of champagne the day the VMA came back normal. He and Lars finished half of it when Beth arrived, and she finished the rest. Brophy discharged Lars the next day.

Brophy found a note in his mailbox. "See me," signed Lionel, and his mouth went dry. He stepped into Lionel's office and Lionel offered him a seat.

"Thought you might want to see this," said Lionel, handing Brophy a letter. It was Lionel's reply to Lynn Ann's article. Brophy thought it covered all the points.

"I misjudged her," said Lionel. "She wasn't as smart as I thought she was."

Brophy said nothing.

"Have you tried to recruit any new patients for the malignancy thing?" Lionel asked.

"Not since the article."

"Don't imagine you'll have much luck for a while."

"Probably not."

"How's the pregnancy thing going?"

"Fine."

"You're on Clinical Service?"

"Until October," Brophy told him.

"By then maybe this malignancy thing will have blown over."

"Yes."

"I've talked to Jethro. He's got a couple of other projects we thought you might find appealing."

"Thanks."

Brophy walked to the door and turned back to Lionel.

"Do you think anyone will ever find out why they get hypercalcemic?"

Lionel looked up. "We weren't the only group working on the problem." He smiled.

"But it won't be us."

"We might not be first. But there are plenty of questions need answering. Talk to Jethro."

Brophy stepped across the hall to the lab. Jethro wasn't there, but Duncan was jumping around in front of his columns.

"It's the ex-malignancy maven," said Duncan.

"I just found out," said Brophy. "He suspended the project."

"Lionel's right. We've got a snowball's chance in hell getting anyone to sign an informed consent."

"He says it'll blow over."

"Maybe."

"Should I still check the calciums?"

Duncan looked up from his columns. "Not for a while. January, maybe."

"What'll you do?"

"Try to extract factor," said Duncan. "We've got tumor frozen from eight patients."

"But you'll need more."

"We'll cross that bridge. . . ."

Brophy was astonished to find Duncan so cheerful, and said so.

"It's a setback, no denying," said Duncan, looking up from his column. "I had to send back my nude mice: Costs too much to keep 'em and we won't be getting any tumor for a long time. That was depressing. Hated giving up my mice."

Brophy shook his head.

"It's like having a grant rejected," said Duncan. "You just have to go on to something else."

Brophy's beeper went off. For an instant he thought it was Lynn Ann. He hadn't talked to her since the article, and had no intention of calling. It was Clarissa.

"We've been invited to dinner," she said. She wouldn't say where but she demanded he be ready at seven o'clock.

Brophy went back to his desk and looked through his pregnancy project notebook and made a few calls.

He came across Maria Addinizio's page and called her.

"Great to hear from you," Maria said.

"You sound good."

"I'm feeling fine. Hair's grown back enough to comb it. I look like a pixie."

"Say hello if you're ever back at U.H."

"I'm glad to hear you're still talking with me," she said, her voice serious, "after what Lynn Ann did. . . ."

"That wasn't your fault."

"I felt like a stool pigeon. I liked Dr. Gordon. He's fighting the good fight."

"Don't."

"I never expected that from Lynn Ann."

"I guess she surprised a lot of people."

Brophy said good-bye and hung up. Then he leafed through his malignancy notebook and checked his consult book, which had nothing new. He drove home.

Clarissa arrived, wearing a white sundress, which Brophy immediately tried to remove.

"Let's make an excuse," he urged.

"Oh, no . . ." she said, slipping away. "Dinner first."

She drove him to Barrington, down a tree-lined road to a house on the water.

Lars answered the door. "Glad you could make it."

Beth kissed Clarissa and pecked Brophy's cheek. The boys were introduced. They had their hair combed for the occasion, and they were very formal, and shook Brophy's hand. Then they were hustled off to bed. Beth came back laughing.

"Olaf asked me, 'Did I do that right?' It was his first formal introduction."

Lars took Brophy down to the pier to inspect his boat while Clarissa and Beth tended the steaks on the grill and sipped white wine.

"How's the wound healing?" Brophy asked.

"No problem," said Lars, reaching under his shirt reflexively. "Nancy does nice work."

Brophy asked him about the boat and they made the tour, Brophy making noises to show he was properly impressed.

"We'll go for a sail after dinner," Lars told him. "There's a full moon tonight."

Brophy thought about the night sails with Duncan under a full moon and felt a little sad.

"Duncan Gordon has a boat a little smaller than this."

"How is he?" asked Lars. Brophy didn't know if Lars was referring to the newspaper article. Lars continued. "I like that guy. He's really enthusiastic about what he's doing."

They had dinner on the porch—steaks and salad and wine. The stars came out and the moon hung low over the water. The night was cool and very clear. Clarissa got goose flesh in the cool breeze off the Bay. She looked wonderful sitting with her shoulder next to Brophy. When they finished the wine, they all put on sweaters and went for a sail. Then they said goodnight and Clarissa drove Brophy home.

"What a lovely night," said Clarissa. "I wouldn't complain if the sun didn't rise for a week."

Brophy leaned back and looked at the sky. It had been a nice party with gracious people. They had said almost nothing about the surgery or the hospital. They just mentioned Nancy and some of the nurses a few times. Mostly they talked about life in Barrington, places they'd been and would like to go, kids and schools and good places to live. No one had mentioned Lynn Ann the entire evening.